BURNING SKIES
THE SWORD OF DRAGONS
BOOK 2

Jon Wasik

For my best friend Nick. You've been there almost every step of the way. Through crazy story ideas, painful first drafts, and the incredible experiences of finally getting published, you've been a steady constant in my life.

I couldn't ask for a better friend.

Also by Jon Wasik

Rise of the Forgotten – The Sword of Dragons Book 1
The Orc War Campaigns – A Sword of Dragons Story
Secrets of the Cronal – The Sword of Dragons Book 3

CONTENTS

ACKNOWLEDGMENTS

Thank you to my parents for their undying support and encouragement. To my sister Tanya and her family, for believing in me even when I didn't believe in myself. To my wonderful Starshine, Beck Wasik, for believing in me every step of the way, and helping me through revision after revision, cover designs, layouts, and everything in between!

Thank you Danielle Lirette for beta-reading the 2nd edition and helping me make everything better! Thank you M. H. Lee, a talented writer and friend, for helping me figure out this whole publishing process. Thank you to Chloe for making such incredible maps!

Thank you to all of my blog and Facebook followers, you all rock! Thank you to Wayne Adams of VtW Productions for always being supportive and helpful, and for hosting me on his podcast, Show X.

And a big shout out to the Welts family, Thomas and Renee, Natalie, and my best friend for over 20 years, Nick. I would not be where I am today without your help.

SWORD OF DRAGONS CHARACTER REFRESHER

Cardin Kataar – Cardin trained to become a Warrior, but refused to join at graduation, claiming the Guild had strayed from its original precepts. After living alone for ten years, he became embroiled in the struggle of the Sword of Dragons, and became the new Keeper of the Sword.

Kailar Adanna – A former Warrior, Kailar sought the Sword of Dragons in order to use its power to unite the kingdoms of Edilas under her iron fist. Though she possessed it for several days, it was taken from her in the Battle of Falind. Later while leading an orc invasion of Archanon, a group of Star Dragons stripped her of her powers.

Sira Reinar – A skilled Warrior and powerful Mage, Sira fought side by side with Cardin during the struggle for the Sword of Dragons. Having proven herself a leader in the Battle for Archanon, she has commanded a small unit throughout the Orc War Campaigns.

Reis Kalind – Although he has no magic, Reis is one of the most skilled Warriors in the Tal Guild. Envious of Mage powers, he has chosen to wield a two-handed sword rather than a shortsword and shield. He fought alongside Cardin during the struggle for the Sword of Dragons, and often manages to make everyone smile even in the direst of situations.

Dalin – A young Wizard of 288, Dalin was the first to see Kailar as a threat. Without the support of his peers, he sought out Cardin and brought him into the struggle for the Sword of Dragons. Since the Battle for Archanon, he has trained Cardin to hone his growing powers.

Elaria – A gifted explorer, Elaria is a Dareann Elf who was tricked into helping Kailar. However, at the last moment, she overcame Kailar's hold over her and helped Cardin win the battle.

King Eirdin Beredis – Ruler of Tal, King Beredis was near-death at the beginning of the struggle for the Sword of Dragons, but was healed by a Master Wizard. He is the most cool-headed monarch of the new Alliance, and is often looked to for leadership in Allied Council meetings. He is one of Cardin's strongest supporters as Keeper of the Sword.

Prince Idrill Beredis – A young and privileged young man, he ruled Tal during his father's illness and quickly eroded the trust of the people through his controversial laws.

Wizard King Sal'fe – Originally disguising himself as a hermit, the outcast Wizard Sal'fe maneuvered Cardin into retrieving the Staff of Aliz for him, which he later used to resurrect Falind Warriors and gain the trust of the Falind people. With no heir to the throne of Falind, Sal'fe was voted into power by the governors, and has become the first Wizard King on Halarite.

King Tristen Lorath – Ruler of the southern kingdom of Saran, Lorath is a staunch supporter of Falind and doubtful of anything that contradicts the Order of the Ages. He only grudgingly agrees to allow Cardin to keep the Sword of Dragons.

Queen Sechel Leian – Ruler of the eastern kingdom of Erien, Queen Leian has supported Cardin and her ally King Beredis throughout most of the Allied Council meetings. She is a compassionate ruler under most circumstances, but will always put the good of her kingdom above all else.

Grand Master Wizard Valkere – The oldest living Wizard, Master Valkere is wise but cautious in dealings with humans. He was present 3,000 years ago when the Sword of Dragons was hidden on Halarite. Although he supports the return of the Wizards to Halarite, he fears a recurrence of the horrible war that Klaralin wrought upon the four Kingdoms.

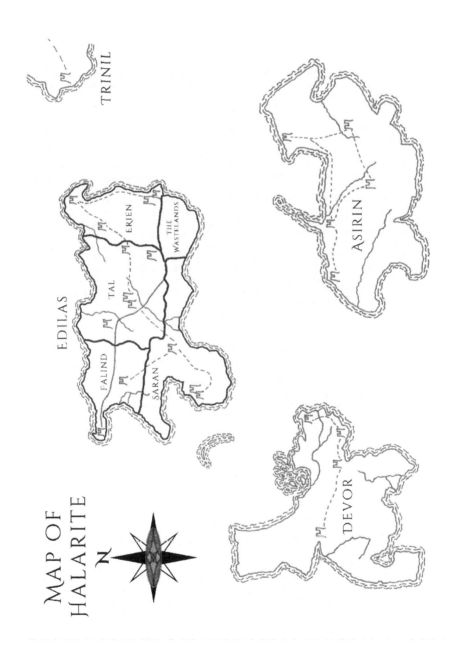

MAP OF
HALARITE

TRINIL

EDILAS

ERIEN

THE
WASTELANDS

TAL

FALIND

SARAN

ASIRIN

DEVOR

EDILAS

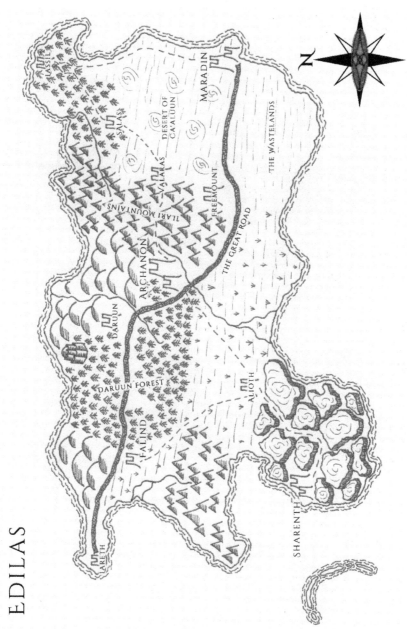

DEVOR

CYRSTAL BAY

CRYSTALLINE PEAKS

CRYSTALLINE FOREST

AGRIAT ISLANDS

TIERAN PORT

BARRIER MOUNTAINS

CORLAS

NEOLAS

EDINGARD

CENTRAL PLAINS

FROZEN PEAKS

PLAINS OF GLASS

N

BURNING SKIES

A shattered world shall return to its people;
Darkness and fire will descend.

For over two thousand years, the most powerful titans in the Universe clashed in a devastating Civil War – dragons, once paragons of peace and morality, had divided into factions of light and darkness, and fought each other with unrivaled ferocity. Their clashes raged across the stars, above hundreds of worlds, and within countless cities.

The first hundred years saw the deadliest battles, bringing about tens of thousands of innocent casualties. Entire cities were wiped from existence, casting civilizations into the shadows of myths and legends.

Above the clouds of one such world, the greatest battle of the war was fought, and brought about the destruction of an empire's world. But not all was lost. When their sun grew dim, and the ground cracked open to swallow their cities whole, the Necromancers of Vestuul fled through portals to an ancient home, long forgotten on another world. They hoped to find refuge in the arms of their kin, but instead they found abandoned ruins, disease, and a dismal future.

When the eldest and wisest fell to his grave, the younger necromancers grew desperate, and turned to the only power they knew. They raised their elder back from the dead. As he rose up, a shell of his former self, the elder gave his kin one ray of hope – a prophecy that foretold of a dark one who would lead their people back to their former glory.

1

But when their world returned to them, it would come at a great cost.

The skies would burn, and darkness would fall.

Chapter 1

THE ORC SHAMAN

Through broken grey clouds, the sun beamed down upon the Wastelands, only to vanish into the black Fortress of Nasara. The towering fortress stood with repairs half-completed, abandoned six months ago when Klaralin never returned. Most of the wooden scaffolding had collapsed, and Cardin Kataar wondered if it looked worse now than it had before the Orc War Campaigns.

From the cover of the sickened forest that bordered the clearing, Cardin shifted uneasily. The fortress appeared abandoned. There was no movement, no evidence of life. The only sign that the fortress might be occupied were fresh tracks near the open portcullis.

He felt overly warm in his leather armor. It was winter in his home city of Daruun, but the Fortress was so far south that the temperature rarely reached freezing. The driest parts of the Wastelands had recovered during the great storm only a few months ago, but already the grass had turned brown, and the leaves on the trees looked sickly.

What he and his companions marveled at was the stench. Whether from the orcs that probably occupied the black fortress or from some other dead, decaying source nearby, he couldn't begin to guess, but it made his stomach twist in protest.

To his right crouched Sira Reinar, and as it always did, her mere presence stirred a gleeful happiness within him. Beyond her physical appearance, he could feel her presence in the flow of magic. Just like he once was, she was a Mage.

Sira wore her typical chainmail and white-dyed plate armor, but she had let her blonde hair grow past her shoulder blades, much to Cardin's delight. Today, in anticipation of combat, her hair was pulled into mirrored braids tight enough that her hair would not flutter in her face.

To his left was his newest friend, the Wizard Dalin. He was young for a Wizard at only 288 years old, but he already had a full head of gray hair, cut short and kept neat. He still bore the same goatee, dark blue robes and oak staff as when Cardin had met him. Sometimes Cardin chuckled to himself and imagined Dalin's wardrobe full of identical blue robes. He had yet to ask Dalin why the Wizards always wore the same colored robes throughout their lives. In fact the only thing Cardin suspected changed for them was that Wizards embroidered more and more runes upon their robes over the course of their lives.

"Still no movement," Sira commented. Though she whispered, her voice echoed in the dead silence of the Wastelands. "I don't get it."

"Neither do I," Cardin replied. They, along with Reis whom Sira had sent to scout the other side of the fortress, investigated the Fortress by order of the Allied Council, suspecting that it had been the hub of all orc activities throughout the war.

Six months prior, Klaralin, a Wizard thought long-dead, attacked the capitol city of Tal kingdom. He had used the same pendant he once used three thousand years before to control the orcs of the Wastelands, and placed them under the command of Kailar. She had led the orcs in the assault on Archanon.

At the height of the battle, the Star Dragons finally appeared and rendered Klaralin's pendant powerless. The surviving orcs fled that night, only to return under their own leadership to attack the four kingdoms. Cardin had spent the past six months side by side with Warriors from every kingdom to not only fend off the orcs, but route them back to the Wastelands, decimating their numbers at every engagement.

Their victories were largely thanks to the fact that the Warriors and Wizards had banded together to overwhelm the orcs. More than that, they had the Keeper of the Sword on their side.

That was what the jade-colored Star Dragon, Endri, had called Cardin. The Keeper of the Sword. A title once held by another Star Dragon, defeated by Kailar when she stole the most dangerous weapon known to them all – the Sword of Dragons. The blood-red blade that was now sheathed upon Cardin's back.

It was oversized for a human, forged thousands of years ago to be wielded by a species called the Vrol, whom Cardin had since learned were considerably taller and overall larger than humans. Yet despite its size, the Sword was cast in a strange material, not even the Wizards knew what, and it was as light as a dagger.

Never-the-less, he felt its weight as if it were an iron claymore, heavy on his shoulders, a burden beyond any he had born before. Regardless, he felt the weight was worth it. The Sword was worth protecting.

Already it had taught him powers that allowed him, in some respects, to equal Dalin. He had become far more powerful than any Mage could hope to be, and as Dalin had pointed out, Cardin's abilities would one day surpass Grand Master Wizard Valkere.

He felt his stomach clench and his jaw tighten every time he thought of that. To posses such power was the most terrifying idea of his life. But it also gave him purpose. Cardin would have the ability to affect the fates of thousands. To save thousands.

Several minutes passed in silence, and he felt himself losing patience. He knew they needed to wait for Reis to return before they were supposed to report back to the Allied encampment several miles away. However, as time passed, he began to come up with a different idea.

"Dalin," he looked to his friend. "Are you still unable to open a portal inside?"

"Correct," the Wizard replied, his watchful gaze upon the fortress unwavering.

Cardin was about to say something else, but the sound of crunching grass startled them. They spun around, and found that Reis Kalind had returned from his scouting mission. Reis stood a little taller than Cardin and wore bronze-dyed armor. Although he had no magical abilities, he wielded a two-handed long sword just like mages usually did. His long, auburn hair was pulled back in a pony tail and he still wore the hint of a grin on his face in spite of the sweat collected on his brow.

"There's no one around," he spoke softly while he crouched beside them. When he looked at Cardin, his brown eyes showed his amusement. "I think we were wrong about this place."

Cardin shook his head. "No, I don't think so." He ran his hand through his cropped, not-quite-black hair. "Everything points to this fortress, and Elaria's description matches this place." Elaria was the elf that had warned them of Klaralin's impending attack. Although she had long ago left their world to return home, her appearance on Halarite, her mere existence rippled throughout the world. She was proof that the humans of Halarite weren't the only intelligent beings in the universe. Her existence directly contradicted the teachings of the Order of the Ages.

"Plus..." he glanced back at the fortress, and once again extended his awareness of the currents of energy out towards the black walls. "There's a presence inside. I can feel a power in there."

Sira shuddered. "You don't think Klaralin could still somehow..."

"No," he shook his head, adamant. "It doesn't feel anywhere near as powerful."

"Then what?" Dalin asked. "I cannot feel the presence you speak of."

"I know," Cardin nodded. "But trust me, what or whomever it is, it isn't my imagination. You're the one who taught me how to extend my awareness out like this."

"Indeed," Dalin looked at him with concern. "The fact that your ability has surpassed mine in this matter amazes and-"

"Concerns you," Cardin interrupted, "I know. I'm starting to hear that from you too often."

"It doesn't matter," Sira placed a hand on his shoulder, which warmed his face. Even after spending so much time with her on the front lines, she still elicited such reactions from him. "We accomplished our mission well enough. Let's report back to the General."

"Or," Cardin raised an eyebrow. "We could do more."

She hesitated. "What do you mean?"

"Obviously there aren't as many orcs here as we thought there would be," he motioned towards the empty fields. There were signs of encampments long abandoned, but nothing recent.

Sira's jaw fell open. "Cardin, no. I know you've grown powerful, but we have no idea how many orcs there are inside."

"Hey, I know I'm not invincible," he shook his head. "But look at what we've got here, two Warriors, one of them a talented Mage," he smiled to Sira, "A Wizard, and the Keeper of the Sword."

"And if there are over one hundred orcs in the fortress?" Dalin asked. "Or more? We cannot contend with such numbers."

"Not in the open, no," he smiled. "But what about in the confines of the corridors?"

Reis smiled, "That would put us on more even footing."

Sira narrowed her eyes. "That's assuming we could reach the entrance before every orc inside emptied out and surrounded us. Or closed the entrance before we got there. Either way, it's too dangerous."

"Then I'll go in alone," he stood up and faced the fortress.

"Cardin, no!"

Before she could say more, he instantly gathered power from the surrounding world into him and used one of the first abilities he had gained from the Sword – he enhanced his own strength, and took off at a dead run for the fortress at a speed greater than any human should have been able to run.

"Cardin!" he heard Dalin shout after him.

In an instant, he was in the field, and he covered the distance lightning quick. Not quick enough, however, as a guard in a turret, previously unseen, sounded an alarm.

In a gruff, barely intelligible voice, he heard the orc shout down, "Close the gate!"

Cardin felt another surge of energy accompany the power he had used, and he felt himself run faster. The wind whipped in his face, and for a moment, he almost felt like he could fly! His spirits soared, and the danger ahead of him barely registered in his mind. He wondered if this was how it felt to be a dragon in flight, the wind screaming by and the ground a nearly-forgotten feature.

The dark-steel doors began to close, but he was faster than they could have anticipated. The guard in the turret must have realized that as well. His senses warned him of danger, more than that he felt a sudden snap of energy.

The orc must have had one of the enchanted bows from their assault on Archanon. An arrow, infused with elemental cold magic, snapped at him. With barely an effort, he raised a magical barrier above him, and the arrow shattered several feet before it reached him.

From behind, another intense source of magic, no doubt Dalin, gathered and released. A bolt of lightning connected with the orc, and it tumbled from the turret with a hole burned through his armor.

With the doors barely open enough for him to slip in, Cardin finally reached his destination and practically flew into the antechamber beyond. Right into a wall of orcs.

He bounced off of one of the armored creatures, and found himself momentarily dazed with his back against the now-closed entrance. He looked up at the orcs, and they likewise looked down at him in shock.

They were larger than humans, hairless, mottled gray monsters with long, powerful arms and muscular legs. Their faces seemed like a nightmare with razor sharp teeth, and their eyes varied between green and orange. They all wore the same dark-steel armor that Klaralin had somehow produced for them, and all held darkened-steel swords and maces at the ready.

Their moment of surprise was all he needed. He reached back and wrapped his hands around the Sword of Dragons, and with a quick mental command, the sheath the Wizards had given him vanished, and the Sword was free.

The orcs attacked, but in the blink of an eye, he had gathered power into himself, extended it into the Sword, and released it as he swung the blood-red blade over his shoulder. A wave of destructive blue-white magic slammed the orcs back against the wall. Moments later, they slumped onto the ground, dead. *This time it worked,* he thought with a smirk.

They were only the first wave. From the corridors on either side, several more stormed into the room. Cardin again enhanced his strength with magic and threw himself at the closest orc.

With precision he had learned over the last six months, his use of his relatively new powers was deliberate and controlled, and the orcs never stood a chance. Each one he came up against, he cut down in quick order, but he also knew that they could get the upper hand sooner or later if he didn't change tactics.

He pushed to the right, cut through one orc, shoved another back into his companions, and rushed past them into the corridor. Another orc stood in his way, but Cardin was too fast for it, and as it raised its sword above its head, he stabbed straight into its heart.

As he pulled the Sword out of the one orc, the others came from the antechamber, so he powered up his weapon again and jabbed the Sword behind him. The energy released in a straight line, and the lead orc was blasted back into his companions, all of whom fell in a pile.

There was a probing touch against his mind, and he realized it was from the same power source he had felt earlier. Whomever it was, it wanted Cardin to find it.

An orc came around the corner ahead, but it suddenly stopped. That same power had reached out and touched that orc's mind, along with every other orc in the fortress. The connection was eerily familiar, and he realized it was the same connection he had felt between Kailar and Elaria moments before Elaria nearly stabbed him in the back. This same being exerted control over the orcs, but to a degree far greater than Kailar's tenuous grasp over Elaria.

The orc ahead of him lowered its weapon and stared forlornly at Cardin. He could tell it was disappointed, and its voice echoed that feeling when it spoke. "My master wishes to speak with you. You are free to pass."

Cardin's heart still raced from battle, so the sudden end to combat stunned him. He wasn't sure what to do next, but the orc sheathed its weapon, stepped aside, and motioned for Cardin to continue forward.

Uncertain if he could trust the monster, Cardin slowly walked forward until he was only a couple of feet from the orc. It pointed ahead insistently. "I will not attack you. My master does not wish it."

With his grip on the Sword tight, Cardin edged past the orc, but it simply bowed its head. He continued to watch the orc as he backed past it, but when he was finally satisfied that the beast would not attack, he turned and continued on around the corner. Ahead was an old wooden door against the back wall, while the corridor turned right. It was guarded by two orcs, both of whom sheathed their weapons and stepped aside.

Cardin had anticipated a long, drawn out battle. Orcs did not surrender, and he had expected to fight every last one of them. The sudden change in behavior unnerved him.

With care, he approached the metal door. It seemed to be much older than the main gate, obviously never actually replaced. He released his left hand from the Sword and pushed on the door. It groaned and creaked in protest, and inside he was surprised that instead of the war room he had expected, he found a library.

All of the walls were covered with stacks of bookshelves, all of them old and dusty. Cobwebs covered most of them, although some of the shelves appeared to have been cleaned months ago and then allowed to collect dust again. In the center of the room was a circular table with a gap in the middle, large enough that someone could have stood there with room to spare. Several chairs were arrayed around the table, their once-fine craftsmanship now worn with considerable age. *What was this place*, he wondered.

Movement to the left caught his attention, and he watched a small figure emerge from between two of the stacks. It appeared to be an orc, but it was much smaller than any he had ever seen before. In fact, if he had to use a single word to describe the orc, scrawny was the one that came to mind. When he realized it was a woman, he felt his jaw drop. Female orcs were closely guarded because of their scarcity, so he was uncertain why he had been allowed to get this close to her.

That was when he realized that the source of power he'd felt before had come from her. She was the one who called off the orcs. She was a Shaman, and if he was right, the first to be seen in over three centuries. Early in the war, the generals were certain a shaman commanded their numbers. However, as the war wore on, they had become increasingly disorganized, and the existence of a shaman was called into doubt.

Suddenly he felt completely unprepared, and he had no idea what to expect, let alone what to do. Orc Shamans were supposed to be extremely intelligent compared to their brutish kin, and their natural talents with magic were legendary.

She was definitely more powerful than any single Mage, but her power felt like a maelstrom, untempered and untrained. That might be an advantage for him in the fight that he knew was coming.

However, much to his surprise, she didn't attack him. "Greetings,

Cardin Kataar," she spoke with surprisingly clear and precise words.

"Hello," he spoke slowly, carefully. "Who are you?"

"My name is Oreag."

There was a moment of silence between them, and he felt wary of the situation. How was one supposed to communicate with an orc?

Finally, he asked what he thought was the obvious question, "Why did you let me get to you without a fight?"

She smiled, a somewhat sickening sight on her rather monstrous face. "I wished to meet you, face to face. If you had found me whilst you fought my servants, you would have attacked me without hesitation, and we would not have had the opportunity to speak."

"Ok," he frowned. "And why did you want to speak with me?"

Her smile vanished. "Despite my powers, I am afraid I am trapped upon your world. I cannot leave, because I no longer have the power to." She looked at him curiously, "Nor do you, I sense. Strange. The other who once wielded the Sword of Dragons could make portals."

Cardin looked at the Sword and felt his face turn red. "Kailar. You met her."

"Indeed," she nodded. The fact that she spoke so eloquently still unnerved him. "I met her shortly after I was brought to this world."

His head snapped up. "Brought to this world?"

"Yes," she nodded. "By Klaralin. He took me from my home quite some time ago and brought me here in an effort to once again assume control of the orcs."

Hesitantly, he said, "You imply that orcs exist elsewhere."

"Oh yes, there are many orcs across many worlds. We did not originate on this world." She frowned and commented, "Curious that you did not know that. Many believe my world to be the origin world of orcs, but there is no proof. Our origin is as mysterious as the origin of the human species."

When she spoke those last words, he felt his stomach drop. "What do you mean 'is as mysterious as the origin of the human species?' There are no other humans."

The Shaman sighed and ambled over to the table, where she leaned heavily against it, her back turned to Cardin. "I sometimes forget that your world has been isolated for so long. The humans of Halarite are not the only humans in existence. In fact," she looked at him over her shoulder, which made her appear sinister to him, "your species is rather common. Some might even call you a plague. You are spread out across countless worlds, you intermingle with countless cultures and have developed countless cultures of your own. Humans," she practically spat the name out, and scoffed at him.

It took several moments for the revelation she had just given him to sink in. When the Sword was first revealed to the world, when he had learned about the Vrol and the Star Dragons, he had accepted it relatively easily. The idea of other sentient beings was not unheard of on Halarite, but it had been an idea rejected by the Order of the Ages, and to suggest they were wrong was considered the greatest blasphemy.

Idly, he wondered how the Order and people in general might respond to this new revelation. Was there anything specific in the Cronal that claimed that humans only existed on Halarite and nowhere else? The answer was obvious when he realized that the Order of the Ages claimed that no other worlds existed.

Then again, he had just learned this from an orc. Could he even trust what she said? He knew that anything she told him should be treated with suspicion, but he also couldn't shake the feeling that she told the truth.

She turned to face him. "In any case, I did not wish to speak with you to teach you about your own species. I feel compelled, for reasons beyond my own understanding, to warn you." He raised a curious eyebrow, but before he could inquire, she continued, "You believe your world has changed considerably, and you are right. Your kingdoms have united, and you have been forced to accept realities that you find uncomfortable and difficult to believe. However, this is only the beginning."

"This doesn't come as a surprise to me," he spoke slowly. "There is a lot we still have to learn about the universe, a fact that you have already made abundantly clear."

"More than that," she added, narrowing her eyes to slits, "You already know that Klaralin visited many other worlds before he returned here. What you do not know is that he gained much of his new power through the aid of something else. Something terrible."

He frowned. "Something. Not someone?"

"Allow me to rephrase. It is not a single entity. It is many." She looked at him with an intensity that sent shivers down his back. "An army large enough and powerful enough to invade entire worlds." Even Cardin had a hard time comprehending those numbers and that kind of power. His people hadn't even fully explored Halarite yet, let alone built a force capable of leaving a military presence in every corner of the world. As it was, the colonies on the southern continents were without adequate military protection from the dangerous animals of their new lands.

"They taught Klaralin what he needed to know to defeat the Wizards," the orc continued after allowing Cardin a moment to digest the new information. "And I fear that they did so with malicious intent for your world. I do not know much beyond that. However, with the defeat of Klaralin and your acquisition of the Sword of Dragons, I have no doubt that Halarite has become their new focus."

Cardin considered the orc's words carefully. She had just told him of a critical threat to his people, but gave little to no detail. More than that, however, another question came to mind. "Why are you telling me all of this?"

She looked at him and scrunched her nose. "Because you are perhaps the only one who can stop them, some day. I know not today, your powers are not nearly great enough."

"Ok," he frowned. "That brings up another question. Why do you care if they are stopped?"

Her face softened into a forlorn look, and for the first time in his life, he felt a pang of sympathy for an orc. He knew, before she even said it, why. "I told you that Klaralin took me from my world. What I did not say was that he rescued me from its burning ashes. The army came to my world to enslave us."

He felt numb inside and uncertain how to react. She was his enemy, but he felt sympathy for losing everything dear to her. Her home was lost to her, now and forever. How would he feel if the same happened on Halarite? What lengths would he go to in order to save everyone he knew?

"I'm sorry," he said, even though he knew it would mean little to her.

"I do not ask for your sympathy, human," she shook her head and her face hardened into a scowl. "I only tell you this so that someday you may stop them. I know you think of orcs as your enemy, and the ones I control on this world would slaughter you if they could." She slowly approached him, and he tensed up in response. He tightened his grip on the Sword, but she did not attack him.

"Not all orcs are your enemies. Not all humans shall be your allies. The universe is a complex place."

Her shoulders slouched and she sighed. "That is all I can tell you."

"Wait, you were there when they attacked your world," he reached a hand out to stop her as she turned away from him, but she batted his hand away. "You can tell me more about them. Their troops, their strengths, maybe a weakness."

"Do not mistake my actions as one of peace," she scowled. "Klaralin rescued me. I owe him my allegiance."

"Klaralin is dead," Cardin stepped back to create additional distance between himself and the orc. He felt her power begin to intensify, and he knew she prepared to attack.

"Never-the-less, you were his enemy, and you have slain countless of my kin. You are my enemy." She paused and let that sink in. With a wicked smile, she raised her fist up and opened it to reveal a small ball of flame in her hand. "Prove yourself by destroying me."

With that, she thrust her hand forward, and the ball of fire leapt at Cardin. On instinct alone he raised a shield in front of him, and the fire erupted into an explosion all around him. He felt the heat and pressure through the shield, but nothing hot enough to hurt him.

The explosion set the stacks ablaze, but that was the least of his worries. As the flames in front of him dissipated, the orc lunged at him, a long, curved dagger in hand. She screamed like a wild animal, her intellect forgotten in her blood rage. As she brought her dagger down upon him, he deflected with the Sword.

He spun to the side and allowed her momentum to carry her out into the corridor. Cardin turned, charged the Sword with as much ethereal energy as he could, and thrust it towards her. Much to his surprise, she absorbed the blast and even turned it back on him. His shield absorbed most of the blast, but he still was thrown back further into the library, where he crashed against a chair and the table. His back screamed in protest where he'd hit the edge of the table, and he collapsed to the ground.

Through tears in his eyes, he noticed that the fire spread fast, and he realized that with all of the cobwebs, old tapestries and dried out rugs, he had only moments to escape the library, perhaps the fortress itself.

She was a creature of intense power, and his own abilities in magic would not be enough to overcome her. That left him one other option. Cardin stood and faced her as she barreled down on him.

The Sword of Dragons was oversized, as long as a claymore, longer even, and she carried with her only a dagger. Once again she leapt into the air at him, but this time he didn't try to deflect her blade. Instead, he jabbed his weapon straight into her torso, where it pierced her clothes, while he used his left hand to generate a quick, small shield that deflected her dagger.

Her weapon clattered to the ground, and she looked at him first with surprise, and then with satisfaction. He felt her power begin to diminish quickly, but she had enough life left in her to say, "Thank you for an honorable death."

As the final thread of life slipped away and her presence vanished, he lowered the Sword and allowed her body to slip off. He stared at her, curious at her last words.

But then one of the bookshelves collapsed, and he realized that the carpet had caught on fire, which spread quickly towards him. He leapt over the fire, felt the flames lick at his feet, and was out in the corridor in a heartbeat.

He left behind the most curious person he had met so far, to be burned in what he hoped would be a cleansing fire upon a blighted land.

Chapter 2

THE NEW WORLD

Kailar wiped sweat off of her brow and stepped up to the gangway on the deck of a small, square-rigged ship. She had travelled aboard the vessel for the past month and a half, and was ready to disembark. It was summer on the southwestern continent of Devor, and the air was hot and humid. The smell of seawater was still strong, and she worried that she would never get the smell of fish out of her clothes or hair.

The dock, though relatively small compared to the one they had set sail from, was busy. Another ship had docked less than an hour ahead of them, and its cargo was still being unloaded by crew and dock workers.

From the deck of the ship, she took in the small port city of Tieran. The ports on Edilas were bustling cities by comparison, but she reveled in it. It was freedom, and a far cry better than what some in the Allied Council had planned for her.

Many on Edilas had demanded her execution. Some in the Allied Council voted for such punishment. But for whatever reason, the dragons had asked King Beredis to spare her, and make her suffer a life without magic. That plea for her life had swayed most of the leaders, and so she was ultimately exiled from Tal.

It seemed to many like a lenient punishment, but it wasn't. She was alone, powerless, and had a price on her head so big that it didn't matter which kingdom she fled to, bounty hunters would follow.

Leaving Edilas had been her best choice.

Despite its small size, Tieran port had grown considerably in the decades since it was founded. Two-story wooden homes, built no doubt from materials gathered from the near-by forests, dominated the town.

The ship rocked a little as a larger wave came in from the sea, and she felt herself still a little unsteady, so as soon as the ship stabilized, she hurried down the gangway until she was on the dock.

The dock was blessedly stable, and she felt herself finally relax. Then her tension returned when someone shoved past her, nearly sending her into the sea. She glared at the offender, a large man that she recognized as a member of the ship's crew. He didn't even give her a second glance as he lugged a large sack towards the city.

Kailar forced her jaw to relax and reminded herself that she hadn't travelled so far just to cause trouble in the port. More important than that, six months ago her connection to magic was severed. Not just the new abilities she had gained from the Sword of Dragons, but all magic. All power.

If she did get into a fight, she would have to rely entirely on her melee skills. With only a long iron dagger hidden under her black cloak, she felt vulnerable.

Slowly she took in a deep breath, and tried to ignore the salt in the air. "Ok," she said to herself with a sigh. "Just brush it off, and move along."

With another deep, salt-filled breath, she headed for shore. The dock was wide, meant to accommodate large cargo and considerable traffic, but she still had to dodge workers and passengers going to and from the docked ships. Finally, she made it onto solid ground.

The dock led straight into the main avenue of Tieran, so the crowd wasn't any better there. It was a busy day as fresh trade supplies were being unloaded and other items were stacked up and ready to be loaded onto the ships for a return voyage to Edilas. The store fronts along the main avenue were busy, and she felt sick to her stomach by the smell of raw fish.

Kailar grumbled and pushed into the crowd. More than once she was nearly knocked over, and her backpack felt unusually cumbersome as she tried to squeeze past people. She also felt paranoid and kept checking her pack to ensure no one tried to steal anything from it.

Finally she pushed out past the worst of the crowd, and took her first real breath of fresh air. Even there she could still smell the fish, but it was at least tolerable.

Which left her with one inescapable fact. She had no idea where to go next.

She had seen older maps of the continent before, but she didn't have one in her possession. While there was supposed to be a well-travelled road that headed westward, she couldn't leave it up to chance. She had to find the fabled Crystalline Peaks, and she didn't want to spend the rest of her life searching for them.

No longer feeling crowded, she carefully regarded the shops around her, and searched for a general vendor who might sell a map, or even a shop dedicated to selling maps. Surely there were enough adventurers as to warrant the dedicated work of cartographers.

Unfortunately, a map was harder to come by than she expected. She checked out several shops, but she felt so insecure about her situation that she never spoke to the shopkeepers and only looked. No one appeared to have any maps for sale, or if they did, they didn't display them.

Her frustration grew deeper, and she realized that there was no way around it. Finally, she asked one of the shopkeepers if he knew where she could find a map.

The shopkeeper, a stocky blacksmith, barely glanced at her. "The last ship that came in had an expedition from the new Alliance. They bought up as many maps as they could find. Still, try Dillarn's shop on the edge of town. He's our best map maker."

The blacksmith gave her barely adequate directions, and she made her way towards the edge of town. As expected, not far off of the main avenue was a tiny one-story building with a rough carving of the southern continent on its sign. She noted what appeared to be a small caravan out in front with a wooden cart drawn by two horses. Around it stood a small group of men and women, one of whom, a particularly large man with cropped black hair, eyed her suspiciously.

Kailar kept her eyes down and stepped inside to find the shop devoid of maps. It wasn't a big building to begin with, and she suspected the front of the building was the shop while the rest served as the owner's residence. Inside stood a single man, but she immediately guessed he wasn't the shop owner. He wore well-worn boots, obviously well travelled in, and clothing that looked as if he had been on the road for weeks. He was fairly tall, and she could tell that he had well-defined muscles even beneath his rough, white tunic. His hair was red and he had a beard that looked to be only a few weeks old.

She was slightly surprised when his stance changed to a defensive posture when she entered, and he quickly looked her up and down. It was something she would expect from an experienced soldier, not a caravan merchant.

Her first instinct was to try to present herself as capable of holding her own, but that faltered quickly. So she instead slackened her stance and averted her eyes from him, to present as little of a threat as possible.

The shop owner was nowhere to be found, so she began to look around. Although there were no maps on display anywhere, he seemed to have several other trinkets and assorted treasures. Clearly he sometimes bartered his maps rather than sold them for coin.

Kailar noted the varying styles of daggers and knives, swords, pieces of armor, and jewelry. Some of it she could tell was relatively normal, but a few pieces seemed to stand out to her as unusual.

When she stopped to look at a curved, exotic looking dagger, she was startled when the red-haired man stepped closer to her and said, "Unusual, isn't it?" His voice was fairly strong and mid-range for a man, and she found it surprisingly pleasant.

She glanced at him, and felt stunned when she noticed the deep blue eyes he had, but she didn't let her eyes linger. "I suppose so."

"It's one of Dillarn's fabled oddities."

Curious, despite her uneasiness, she asked, "What do you mean 'oddities'?"

"Most everyone attributes trinkets and weapons found around the new continents as belonging to previous adventurers," the man explained. "But Dillarn insists that much of it comes from a civilization that he believes once lived here thousands of years ago."

At first she wanted to say that was impossible, since the Order of the Ages taught that all civilization on Halarite originated from the region around Archanon. However, given everything she had learned six months ago, she realized that she couldn't hold anything the

Order claimed as truth. She had met a Vrol, fought a dragon, and encountered an elf, all of which disproved the Order's claims that humans were the only intelligent creatures in existence. What else were they wrong about?

"Do you think he's right?" she asked.

"I don't know," he sounded amused. "Most everyone thinks he's crazy, and he's even received a few threats for his beliefs."

She shrugged easily, but still avoided looking at the man. "That doesn't surprise me. Especially after…" she trailed off, suddenly self-conscious about giving any clue to her identity.

"Especially after what happened in Tal," she saw the man nod out of the corner of her eye. "A lot of people are having trouble believing the stories. Some are scared and getting violent."

It was the same everywhere, as the stories of the Sword of Dragons, the dragons themselves who had helped defeat Klaralin and herself, and especially of the elf, spread to every corner of Halarite. What surprised her was that most people had a hard time accepting the existence of the elf, and the fact that she wasn't a demon, but they had little difficulty accepting the existence of dragons.

"Letan!" a deep voice suddenly called out. Kailar and the red-head spun around to find that a tall, skinny man, obviously older than either of them, had entered through a door near the back. He had graying hair, was very bald, and his eyes were a strange hazel color. He wore a broad smile on his face as he approached the red-head, whom she guessed was named Letan.

"Hiya, Dillarn," Letan shook the shopkeeper's hand.

Dillarn glanced at Kailar and said, "I'll be with ya in just one minute." He turned his attention back to Letan. "Got something for me, do ya?"

Letan pulled out a small pouch and overturned it to let a small pendant fall out into Dillarn's eager hands. The shop keeper flipped it over, and his eyes grew wide. "Oh wow! I've not seen this symbol before."

She was curious, and tried to get a better look, but that caught the attention of the other two. She felt her face turn red, and looked down. "It's ok, lady," Letan said. "You can look too."

Not used to being talked to that way, she felt her face turn even warmer, and she backed away. "No, it's ok."

"Hey," Letan stepped towards her, which she reacted to by pulling even further away. "We're not gonna hurt you, lady."

"I know," she shook her head. She wanted to say that they couldn't even if they wanted to, but she held her tongue. "Look, I know that seems fascinating and all, but I just need a map."

Dillarn shook his head, "I'm sorry, I'm sold out of new maps right now." Her heart sank, but she wasn't entirely surprised.

"I see…"

"I'm working on one now, should be ready in a few days, if you aren't in a hurry."

"I sort of am." Which she was. Not because there was an urgent task that was time critical, but because of her destination, and the rumors that surrounded it. She hoped to regain power, some power, any power. Anything to alleviate her feeling defenseless and useless.

"Well, where are you headed?" Letan asked. She finally looked at his face, and felt her cheeks grow warm again. His eyes were a blazing, sharp blue, and even through the red beard, she could see he had a strong jaw line. He was a simple man, that much she could tell by the way he spoke, but something about him definitely caught her attention.

Paranoia set in at first, and she was about to tell them off for even asking. Then she realized that she couldn't find her way without at least some sort of assistance. Maybe they could point her in the right direction.

"I've always wanted to see the Crystalline Peaks," she lied. "But I can't stay away from home for long, so I need to get there and back again as soon as possible."

"You came here by yourself?" Dillarn asked.

Her temper flared. "I am fully capable of taking care of myself!"

"Easy there, lady," Letan raised his hands disarmingly. "No one suggested you couldn't."

"Never mind," she turned to leave, her frustration and feelings of defeat building.

"Hold on just a second," Letan said. Something about his voice, she wasn't sure what, made her stop just short of opening the door. She slowly turned to face him. "Look, I live in Corlas." When he saw that she had no idea where that was, he continued, "It's right by the Crystalline Peaks. My caravan and I are heading back, and the roads can be dangerous. I know you can take care of yourself, but don't underestimate what's out there. A lot of strange creatures roam the countryside, especially at night."

"I don't need your help," she growled. "I can do it by myself."

Once again she turned to leave, but Letan spoke up again, "Then let me at least get you started. The main road, follow it of town." She didn't turn to face him, but she lingered long enough to let him finish. "It'll take you onto a well-travelled path, take it southwest to a town at the foot of the Barrier Mountains. That's a good waypoint, it's called Edingard. Maybe someone there will have a map for you."

Although she didn't look right at him, she did look over her shoulder and nodded. "Thank you."

With that, she opened the door and stepped outside. She was again assaulted by the sea air, but she took comfort in the fact that she was about to head inland. The members of the caravan glanced at her as she walked by.

She at least had a direction to start in. It was better than nothing. Grudgingly she realized that her journey would be even harder than she originally thought.

Kailar stopped by a couple more vendors to purchase some food, and then found a public well to fill her two flasks. Finally, when she was sure she had what she needed, she set out on the road, into a land she had never seen before.

Chapter 3

THE ALLIED COUNCIL

After six months of travelling back and forth between the front lines and Archanon, Cardin was used to the sudden change in scenery. But as winter had set in on the First City, the change from too warm in the Wastelands to too cold in Archanon was still a shock.

He passed through the portal Dalin had created, another reminder that he still didn't know how to create one himself, and sighed as Sira continued to lecture him, their conversation unbroken.

"There's no other way around it," she glared at him as the valley outside of the western gates appeared before him. "It was reckless and stupid, and you blatantly ignored my orders."

"I didn't hear your orders," he defended himself.

Cardin turned away from her to wait for Reis and Dalin to follow them. Unfortunately that didn't sit well with Sira, who stepped beside him and continued, "That's because you didn't give me time to give the order! All I got out was "no" and you took off on your own."

Reis stepped through and cleared the portal to let Dalin through, who followed right behind him. The portal closed shortly after, and both Dalin and Reis gave him sympathetic cringes as Sira continued. "It was impulsive and stupid, completely irresponsible! You agreed to follow orders, and General Artula placed you under my command with the understanding that there wouldn't be a conflict of interest."

He briefly turned to her and said, "My actions had nothing to do with our friendship." He then turned and preceded the others towards the city gates. "You've seen how I work under other commanders."

Dalin and Reis stayed a few steps behind him, but Sira fell into step beside him and waved her hands in exasperation. "Right, your usual excuse, you're used to working by yourself. You're part of a team now, Cardin! Whether you like it or not!"

"I know…"

"You have to understand that your actions have consequences for others. I thought you learned that lesson six months ago when your mistakes plunged Edilas into war!"

He felt his face turn red, and through a clenched jaw, he said, "I know."

"I don't think you do," she continued, undaunted, her hands waving around erratically. They passed through the open gates into the city. He saw one guard attempt to suppress a chuckle as they passed by. Inside of the city, shops were closing down for the evening. The day was almost over, and the sky was already growing dark. He felt a shiver as the temperature plummeted.

They passed by one of the taverns from which the smell of roast chicken wafted out, and Cardin's stomach grumbled. He wanted to get into the Allied Council session as soon as possible, make his report, and then find a hot meal to help warm him up and push away the cold he was beginning to feel in the pit of his stomach.

That feeling distracted him from Sira's lecture, and he walked mostly unconsciously towards the inner city and the castle. That cold feeling was something he always felt before he had the dream. The same dream he'd had for weeks, the same one that woke him up to a cold sweat.

They began to climb the small hill up towards the center city, and that was when he suddenly realized that Sira's lecture hadn't ended. He caught what she said mid-sentence, "because being alone for so long addled your head? Or do you just not care about anyone except yourself?"

His blood boiled when she said that, and he stopped and turned to her. She seemed to anticipate his actions, but Reis and Dalin nearly plowed into them. "You know better than anyone that I care about what happens to others," he said to her with more venom than he intended. "I have continually placed myself in harm's way despite the fact that I don't have to. I am not a soldier or a Warrior, I don't have to be here or take orders from you or anyone else. I'm here because I want to make a difference, to keep people safe, to prevent the destruction of everyone and everything I know and hold dear."

He slowly shook his head while images from his nightmares flashed through his mind. "I am the only one who can keep us all safe, and you can't understand the burden that has placed on me, you can't possibly imagine what it's like to possess and protect the Sword of Dragons!"

Cardin didn't realize he'd raised his voice to a shout, but the stunned and hurt look on her face suddenly tempered his anger. For a long time, they stared at each other. Neither moved, neither said anything. Out of the corner of his eye, he saw that Dalin and Reis also stood in stunned silence.

His stomach sank, and he felt his chest tingle. After what seemed like an eternity, she turned and walked towards the castle's main entrance. Watching her walk away from him, he realized that he'd gone too far.

Dalin slowly walked past, glancing at him as he did so, and then hurried to catch up to Sira. Reis stepped beside him and clasped his hand on his shoulder. "Well," Reis sighed. "You certainly have a way with people…"

Cardin smirked, "Thanks."

"Come on," Reis pulled him along before he finally released his grip. "Let's get this council session done. Then you can apologize to her."

As they entered the castle, Cardin's guilt didn't abate, but he thought back to when he'd started to feel anger and realized he'd been set off not so much by Sira's words, but by the impending nightmare. It haunted him, and frustrated him, because it felt so real. He feared it was somehow a dream of the future, but the kind of devastation and destruction that he saw was unfathomable.

When they finally reached what was once the castle's war room, Sira and Dalin waited outside. The doors that led in were closed, and he knew that the meeting was already in session. The leaders met frequently, thanks to the convenience of Wizard portals.

He was grateful that they weren't expected to sit through another full meeting. Politics were not his strength, and he found the meetings to be tedious, frustrating, and boring. He understood their importance, otherwise the new Alliance would have collapsed as quickly as it had formed, but that didn't change his impatience with politics.

Sira didn't turn to face him, she simply stared at the doors. The two Archanon soldiers that guarded the door stood stoic and expressionless, their leather armor new, and their black tabards bore the kingdom's symbol, a mountain guarded by two swords crossed before it, in silver rather than white, a sign that they were part of the royal guard. Dalin was quietly humming a tune to himself, something he often did during an awkward silence. Reis exchanged a knowing look with Cardin, and he debated whether or not to say something.

He wanted to apologize to Sira, but he wasn't sure what to say. How could he explain away his frustration without telling her about his dream? He was afraid to tell anyone. As irrational as his fear was, he thought that if he told someone about it, it would somehow make the dream come true.

More than anything, he was afraid that something horrible was coming, and that there was nothing he could do to protect the people he cared about. The people that he loved.

Before he could think further on the matter, the doors opened from within. Governor Maral, an elderly woman with gray hair that was cut to a line just below her ears, slowly came out of the council chambers and nodded to everyone. She wore her usual black, white, and blue court robes and her face was somewhat hard today, a sign that the meeting so far had been difficult.

"They are ready for you," she said in a voice that betrayed her frustration and exhaustion. "Please enter."

Sira continued to avoid looking at Cardin as the four of them entered. After Cardin's actions at Nasara, they had reported back to General Geildein Artula at the Allied base camp several miles from Nasara. Sira's lecture had started the moment he'd escaped the fortress, and it hadn't stopped even in front of the General

During the debriefing, the General had decided they needed to brief the Alliance leadership on what Cardin had learned, so he had sent a messenger by way of Wizard's portal to ensure the evening meeting would make room for their briefing.

As they entered the chambers, Cardin found it to be an all too familiar sight. The six rectangular tables were arrayed in a circle around a central open floor, and the walls were lined with chairs. At four of the tables sat the kings and queen of the four kingdoms. King Beredis sat with Cardin's father, Draegus Kataar, at Tal's table. Beredis was an aging but loved king, dark skinned with a kind face, but his face could easily turn serious and command attention when he needed it to. Cardin's father had aged well and still had mostly black hair, with only some strands of gray lightening its overall appearance. Governor Maral also had a seat next to the King, but at the moment she led them into the center.

To the right of Tal's table was Falind's, where Wizard King Sal'fe sat along with Falind city's governor, Prelin. Sal'fe had been selected as Falind's new king after Kailar had assassinated their former king and usurped the throne. Sal'fe had won their support by using the Staff of Aliz to resurrect fallen Falind Warriors, and later used it to take Klaralin's life in the Battle for Archanon. Sal'fe still wore his Wizard's robes, but now he wore a necklace with a pendant bearing the kingdom's logo, a bronze wolf's head, as well as the kingdom's bronze crown.

To Cardin's left was Saran Kingdom's table, headed by King Tristen Lorath. His graying blonde hair was still very fair, and his strong jaw line made him particularly popular amongst Saran's maidens, or so rumors claimed. Other rumors abounded that he didn't just stop at maidens.

To the left of Saran's table was Erien Kingdom's table, headed by Queen Sechel Leian, a tall, dark haired woman whose skin still bore a tan from the ample sunlight their coastal kingdom received even in the dead of winter.

The other two tables were reserved for special attendants and members of the Alliance. Left of Erien's table was the Covenant's table, head of the Order of the Ages. Although there were still four chairs behind their table, only three members attended. A fourth member, Pevrin, was banished from the Covenant after he orchestrated the abduction of Elaria during the Battle for Archanon. They had yet to appoint a new member to the Covenant. Left of their table was the Wizards' Guild, headed by Grand Master Wizard Valkere, who wore white robes with gold embroidery. Valkere was the oldest and most powerful Wizard.

The chairs against the back walls were occupied by attendants to the leadership present, or by special guests. He didn't immediately recognize anyone, but his attention was distracted by his own feelings of guilt and by the nervousness he always felt when he addressed the assembled leaders.

"My Lords and Ladies," Maral said, "may I present to you a contingent from our deployed Allied troops from the Wastelands. Sira Reinar and Reis Kalind of the Tal Warriors' Guild; Dalin of the Wizards' Guild; and Cardin Kataar, Keeper of the Sword of Dragons."

Cardin and the others bowed to the assembly, and Maral retreated to take her seat next to King Beredis. King Beredis stood up, and as usual was the de facto speaker for the assembled leaders. By his efforts more than any other, the Alliance endured. He drove the meetings forward, kept them from turning into brawls, and somehow commanded the respect of everyone present.

"We understand that you have some matters of importance to report," he spoke in a deep, powerful voice. "You have our undivided attention."

Sira spoke first. "My Lords and Ladies. Today we were ordered to scout out the Fortress of Nasara, which we presumed was the source of the continued orc resistance." Her voice was quieter than usual when she addressed the assembly, and Cardin felt that was probably due to their conversation.

She seemed to hesitate for a moment before she continued, "Cardin was able to infiltrate the fortress and found that an orc Shaman was present." At those words, the entire assembly shifted uncomfortably and there was a low din of conversation. Cardin heard more than a few say, "Impossible! There hasn't been a Shaman in three centuries."

It was a fact of politics Cardin found disconcerting and annoying. Politicians always refused to believe difficult facts at first. In the full sessions he had sat in on, he found that when one politician needed to tell the others a difficult fact, they eased into the topic, and sometimes spent entire sessions hinting more and more at the truth, until the others could finally accept it flat out. However, there was no time for such tactics this late in the evening, and Sira was someone who preferred getting straight to the point over dancing around the truth.

"How do you know it was a Shaman?" King Lorath asked, doubtful.

Sira didn't look at Cardin directly, but she turned her head to indicate she wanted him to answer. He turned to the Saran King and nodded. "She had considerable power. Greater power than I have. In a battle of pure magic, she would have defeated me."

"Then how did you defeat her?" Queen Leian asked.

"For melee, she had only a dagger," he replied. "I had the clear advantage in weaponry and skill. I also observed that she had the ability to exert direct control over the Orcs."

King Lorath shifted uncomfortably in his seat. "Are you saying there may be another artifact capable of controlling the orcs?" He referred to Klaralin's Pendant, which had been destroyed following the ancient enemy's defeat six months ago.

"I don't believe so," he shook his head. "This felt like it came directly from her. And…I can't explain how I know this, but it felt like she could only directly control a few orcs, and only influence the rest."

"Orc Shamans have always been known to be powerful beings," Master Valkere spoke up. "And unusually intelligent. With the death of this one, it is likely the orcs will become even more disorganized and less of a threat."

"Agreed," Sal'fe added, his voice stronger than ever as he gained confidence in his relatively new position of power. "There should be no trouble hunting down and eliminating the remaining clans."

For a moment, silence fell over the assembly. Finally, Beredis looked at them curiously. "The messenger General Artula sent seemed to indicate there was more to your story than just this. That you learned something of great importance."

Cardin hesitated to answer. What he had learned was difficult for him to accept, even though he felt in his heart that it was true. Convincing politicians would be a challenge. He turned to Master Valkere, since he knew that the Wizard had travelled to worlds beyond Halarite and most likely knew the truth. Realizing that fact, Cardin wondered why the Wizard had never told the other members of the Alliance. He wondered if the Grand Master knew of the threat that the Shaman had hinted at.

Finally, he began, "The Shaman was not born on Halarite." He let that set in for a moment, and was surprised that no one immediately objected to his claim. So he continued, "She claimed to have been brought here from another world by Klaralin. A world she said was often attributed as the origin world of orcs."

Valkere narrowed his eyes at Cardin, but he couldn't begin to fathom what the ancient Wizard thought. He hoped Valkere would affirm his claim, but for the moment, the Wizard said nothing.

After several moments of silence, King Lorath spoke up. "This revelation does not surprise me."

Astounded, King Beredis asked, "It does not?"

"It would have surprised me a year ago," Lorath continued. "However, given what we learned six months ago, I began to suspect the orcs were not always present on Halarite. The historical records in Archanon's sanctuary are more extensive than my kingdom's, so I have taken the opportunity lately to study some of those records. It would seem that encounters with horrible creatures in the Wastelands did not originally include orcs. In fact there is no mention of them in historical records beyond three thousand years ago."

"Then it is possible they were brought here by Klaralin," Queen Leian said.

"I believe so," Lorath nodded. He looked at Cardin, "Although you learned this from an untrustworthy source, I believe my own research supports this revelation."

Time and again, Cardin had been surprised by Lorath's intelligence. It had always been a contradiction in his mind, since the Saran King often refused to believe obvious facts. However, he was grateful to have support from the most unlikely source.

He felt more than saw Valkere's piercing stare. When he turned to the Master Wizard, he nodded to Cardin. "There is more."

"Yes…"

"Continue," Beredis insisted.

Cardin exchanged glances with Dalin and Reis, but Sira still refused to look at him. He tried to ignore the void that formed in his stomach, and turned to Beredis. "The Shaman claimed that there were other humans on other worlds."

There was a quiet murmur of dissenting opinions on his statement, but it wasn't the outburst of refusal he expected. He hesitantly turned to the Covenant's table, but they were the only ones in the entire room who weren't conversing amongst themselves.

They simply stared at Cardin. Once again he found himself surprised. They had admitted in recent months that their interpretation of parts of the Cronal may have been mistaken, and that perhaps there *were* other worlds with other intelligent life on them, but they needed to study the Cronal further to confirm.

"You cannot trust the word of an orc," Lorath stood up. "She may have told the truth about her own kind to make anything else she told you seem like truth as well."

"I don't believe that's the case," Cardin shook his head.

"And what evidence do you have to support your opinion," Lorath demanded. "Or is it another 'feeling' that the Shaman told the truth?"

Cardin opened his mouth to speak, but was interrupted by Valkere, "He speaks the truth."

This didn't help the situation, and suddenly the room erupted in shouts and accusations. Cardin specifically heard Lorath state, "Of course Wizards support their pet Keeper!" After the assembly had accepted the truth about the orcs rather calmly, Cardin felt even more surprised that this was the one topic they chose to argue over.

However, the eruption of shouts was cut off by a loud command from Beredis, "Silence!" How he was able to command such attention and respect from the others, Cardin didn't know, but it worked, and the room quickly grew quiet. Beredis looked at Valkere and said, "Please continue, Master Wizard."

As Beredis sat down, Valkere bowed slightly. "Thank you." He then looked around at the general assembly. "As you all know, I have travelled to many worlds, although it has been quite some time since I last did so. In my travels, I have encountered many species of intelligent beings. I realize this will be difficult to accept, especially considering the…misinterpretation of the Cronal by the Covenant prior to now," he nodded respectfully to the Covenant table, "but there are countless species out there. I found that many species are spread across several worlds. What I have not told this assembly before now is that there are many humans as well."

All eyes turned to the Covenant table. They exchanged glances, and then one of the women at the table stood up. Cardin remembered her name was Alaia. Under her hood, he saw that she had deep blue eyes, and she wore no makeup. "There is nothing within the Cronal that explicitly indicates Master Valkere or Cardin are incorrect or correct. However, I believe they may be correct, and the Shaman told the truth."

The stir within the room mirrored Cardin's own shock. More often than not, the Covenant members didn't lightly agree with such shocking revelations.

"This is indeed disturbing to me," Lorath sat down very slowly and deliberately. "However, after everything we have learned in the last six months, I feel I have no choice but to accept it, given how many sources claim it to be true."

"As I am forced to accept it as well," Leian nodded from her seat.

Sal'fe did not speak, but he had never refuted any of Valkere's claims before, so it was assumed he would also agree. Beredis also did not speak, but he did nod once.

"Then there is one other thing the Shaman told me," Cardin continued. His nightmare flashed through his head one more time. Did the nightmare and the Shaman's warning have anything to do with each other?

"Please continue," Beredis said.

He took in a deep breath before he began. "She spoke of a growing threat. An army that she believes helped Klaralin gain much of the power he used to attack us. She also says this army did so with malicious intent for our world."

There was another general stir of the assembly, but for the most part, all remained quiet and listened intently to Cardin. "The Shaman believes that with the defeat of Klaralin, they may begin to focus more on our world. Nothing she said was concrete, but according to her, she has seen them first hand. They invaded her world, successfully, and Klaralin saved her from them."

"If Klaralin worked with them," Lorath frowned, "why would he save her from them?"

It was a question that Cardin had thought of earlier, and he had a theory. However, before Cardin could reply, Sa'lfe said, "Perhaps as a ruse to gain her loyalty. He was very manipulative." Cardin recalled that Sal'fe had personally battled Klaralin three thousand years before and knew, probably better than anyone else alive today, Klaralin's tactics and tendencies.

"Did she give you any more details?" Beredis asked.

"No," Cardin shook his head. "Unfortunately not. She told me this because she feels I may be capable, some day, of stopping them.

It was out of a desire for revenge against them that she warned me of their existence. Beyond that, however, she remained loyal to Klaralin. She attacked me and I defeated her, but not before she started a fire in the fortress. As we speak, it still burns."

"Then there is nothing more for us to do," Beredis said quietly.

"Perhaps not directly," Valkere said. "I can begin to send out some of my pupils to other worlds, to ask if this is true. I do not know which world Cardin spoke of, but we may be able to learn which world the Shaman came from, and therefore we could then send scouts there to determine if there is indeed a threat."

Beredis appeared to consider the proposal, and then nodded. "It sounds like a good plan." Cardin felt a surge of hope within him. As the Keeper of the Sword, he might be an ideal candidate for such a scouting mission. The chance to set foot on another world was an exciting prospect. "Let us consider this for a vote. Master Wizard Valkere proposes gathering information to determine the veracity of the Shaman's claims. All in favor?"

Around the circle, the leaders all nodded and said aye, until it came back to Beredis, who also assented. "Very well. Master Valkere, at your discretion, send your Wizards. When the location of the orc world has been determined, we shall meet again and decide who to send along on a scouting mission." Cardin wanted to step forward and volunteer, but he knew it could be days, weeks, or even months before they found the orc world. He had plenty of time to put his own name forward off the record.

Beredis then looked back towards Cardin and his companions. "Sira, your team has gained valuable, if controversial information, and have destroyed an enemy fortress. You have performed a great service for the Alliance. Well done."

The four of them bowed together, and Sira said, "Thank you, my lord."

"The hour is late," he looked to the rest of the assembly. "Unless there are other urgent matters to discuss, I recommend we call this session closed."

When no one objected, the guards at either side of the room opened the doors, and the crowds began to filter out. Cardin turned to his companions, but Sira had already left the center and quickly headed for the door.

He had been distracted from his guilt throughout the meeting, but now it returned full force. He didn't know how he could apologize to her, he just knew he had to.

But as she disappeared through the crowd, he realized it would not be easy.

Chapter 4

THE WOLVES OF DEVOR

Kailar was ever so thankful to have gotten away from Tieran, and the smell of fish, and the smell of sea water. That was probably the tenth time that thought had crossed her mind. In all of her life before she had found the Sword, she had stayed away from the coastal cities, not because she knew she didn't like the sea or the smell of uncooked fish, but because she'd never had any reason to go there.

However, this also wasn't her first visit to Devor. When she had first learned how to create portals under Klaralin's manipulative guidance, she had visited both of the southern continents. It had been winter on Devor at the time, and she had arrived much further south than she was now, so it had been very cold. Now it was warm, bordering on hot. Summer was in full swing, and she found that once she got away from the coast, she rather liked the new land.

After she had left Tieran, she travelled quickly. She no longer had the enhanced strength and endurance the Sword had helped her achieve, but she was still fit, even after her long shipboard voyage.

Now she walked along a path that weaved in between hills and rock outcroppings. The terrain grew hilly the further away from Tieran she traveled, but that did little to darken her renewed spirit. She could just barely see the Barrier Mountains peaking over the horizon, but knew that she was still at least a few days away from them.

It was an agonizing distance given what she hoped to find.

Hope. What hope was there, really? She felt powerless, vulnerable. Useless. She still had her melee abilities to fall back upon, but she had come to depend so much on magic to help her fight, to help her get where she needed to be.

The world was still broken, she was still convinced of that. Even Cardin Kataar had believed it. She wanted to fix it, she tried to fix it, but they had stopped her, and she'd lost everything she held dear. She'd lost herself.

Then she had heard a rumor. A rumor that the Crystalline Peaks, mysterious mountain-sized crystals on the western quarter of Devor, held great power. The rumor was that any Mages who ventured close to the crystals suddenly gained greater power.

It wasn't permanent, or so the rumor claimed. When the Mages moved away from the crystals, their powers returned to normal. She also heard the rumors that anyone who ventured down the paths into the Peaks never returned. That indicated there was a danger within the peaks somewhere, and was why the miners only stayed in the caves southeast of the peaks, and didn't try to mine the peaks themselves.

It was the only hope she had left, and was tenuous at best. Hope that the crystals might somehow be able to restore her powers. She had to try. She had to do something. She couldn't carry on as she was, powerless and useless, for the rest of her life.

She didn't pay attention to where she walked. Following the well-used path wasn't difficult, and allowed her mind to wander. She should have paid closer attention. She might have heard the growls from the outcropping to her right. She might have noticed the movement out of the corner of her eye. It also didn't help that the sun was in her eyes.

By the time she did notice something, it was almost too late. A sharp, high-pitched howl startled her, and she spun to her right to see a very large wolf-like creature leap out from behind one the boulders in the outcropping. It landed only a dozen feet away from her, and as the moment seemed to freeze, she took in its appearance.

It was gray with a black patch on its back and the top of its head. Its eyes seemed to glimmer a bright blue in the sunlight. It opened its mouth in another growl, which revealed razor sharp teeth. The wolf was larger than any she had ever seen before, almost as tall as she was.

Kailar was terrified, but fear gave way to instinct. When the animal leapt at her, she tucked and rolled to her right, the creature swiping at her as it sailed past.

The moment she was back on her feet, she drew her dagger and faced it as it likewise turned to her. Six months ago, she would have sent out a wave of deadly magic to destroy it. Today she was powerless. She was dead.

The creature leapt at her again. All she could think to do was thrust her dagger straight at it, and she embedded it straight into its open mouth, but its momentum brought it tumbling over her. It still lived, despite the blade lodged in its throat. She screamed in agony when it bit down on her hand. Even louder when its claws tore into her arm.

She felt her dagger shift a little, and suddenly it gurgled blood. She pushed past the pain and managed to pull her hand and the dagger out of its mouth. It would never eat again, and she knew she had wounded it enough that it would soon die, but not soon enough. So she thrust the dagger up through the bottom of its neck. It let out an airy whimper, and then stopped moving.

For a moment, she lay on her back with the creature on top of her, its blood still trickling down on to her. She pushed it aside and yelled in surprise and pain when the wounds on her arm stretched and tore.

With the weight of the creature off of her, she rolled onto her back again and breathed heavily. Her heart pounded in her ears, and the world began to fade into the pain. She'd suffered worse wounds, but nothing so shocking. She didn't want to move, probably couldn't stand if she wanted to. So she lay waiting, willing her heartbeat to slow.

Until she heard another growl. She looked towards the outcropping, and felt her stomach sink when two more wolves came into view. She knew she was dead.

But she wasn't about to go out without a fight. With a fresh surge of energy, she reached over and pulled her dagger out of the first one's throat. She tried to stand, and the pain and agony fought back, but she wouldn't stop. She would never stop.

Before she could contemplate a strategy, a sudden blast of magic tore into one of the wolves and sent it sprawling backwards.

The other one yelped and raced back behind the rock outcropping. It was over.

Kailar turned towards the source of the magic, not knowing what to expect. Her mind raced with possibilities, but what she saw, *who* she saw was wholly unexpected.

It was Letan. He wore a cloak and held a two-handed Sword. Without her connection to magic, she couldn't have known before now that he was a Mage. She realized that his caravan wasn't anywhere in sight, so she realized that he must have followed her from town. That terrified her almost as much as the wolves had.

As the surge of adrenaline within her dwindled, she started to feel lightheaded, and her legs buckled underneath her. She collapsed to her knees, but she kept a steel grip on her dagger. Why did he follow her? Was he a threat? Did he know who she was and wanted to take revenge on her? Did he intend to mug her? Or worse, did he intend to rape her?

Her mind raced with terrifying possibilities. But he rushed nearer to her when she collapsed, so she pointed the dagger at him. It was her only protection, and she knew it really wasn't enough. He was a Mage and could disarm her from where he stood.

Raising his hands disarmingly, he said, "Easy there, I'm not going to hurt you."

She found it difficult to focus on his words, but she forced herself to try. "Then why are you following me?"

Even with her vision blurred, she saw his face turn a shade of pink. "Well, I guess because I was curious." He stared at her for a moment before he quickly added, "And concerned. There are a lot more dangerous animals out here than there are back in…Tal? Is that where you are from?"

She frowned at him. "How do you know that?"

"Your accent."

Her brow furrowed deeper. "What accent?"

He smiled. "Each kingdom has a subtle accent, surely you've noticed that before."

"Yes, but…" Then it occurred to her, and she was surprised she'd never realized it before. If she thought the people of the other three kingdoms had accents different from her own, then surely others would detect an accent in her voice. She also realized he didn't seem to have an accent. That could mean only one thing. "You're from Tal as well."

"My parents were, yes," he nodded. "But we stopped thinking of Tal as home a long time ago."

She wasn't quite sure what he meant by that, but her arm was tired and in a great deal of pain, and she realized she'd started to let the blade lower. She felt a fresh surge of panic and raised it again. He took a step back, and then slowly sheathed his sword.

"Look," he said. "You're hurt. Let me help you."

"I don't know you," she said flatly.

"Yeah, but I just saved your life," he smirked. "Surely that counts for something."

She shook her head. "You were only able to save me because you followed me. That doesn't exactly boost my trust in you."

"I already told you, I was curious. About you. And concerned for your safety. We call those things Duzai Wolves. They're all over out here, but they're afraid of Mages. They usually won't even come by us, but when they do, usually all we have to do is attack one and the rest run."

She considered his words for a moment, and tried to shake the growing fog from her mind. "Why were you curious about me?"

Once again his face flushed. He thought about it for a few moments before he finally replied, "You aren't like the other explorers that pass through here. You seemed completely unprepared."

She clenched her jaw in anger, "I am prepared, I have plenty of supplies to get me to the next town."

"Yet all you carry is a dagger," he replied with a frown. "Unless you're a Mage, travelling these roads without a sword or axe is suicide." She started to feel weaker, and her dagger dropped. "Look, you're hurt, you need help."

"I don't need your help!" She had shouted that without thinking, but a moment later, she realized she really did need his help. She had supplies to tend to wounds, but her hand and both arms were badly hurt. Not to mention if more Duzai attacked her, she would not be able to defend herself.

She didn't trust him, but she also realized if he wanted to hurt her, he could have easily done so already. Although she felt like it was a mistake, she lowered her dagger. "Alright," she nodded. She slowly lowered back to sit down, but as her butt met the ground, she continued to fall back, and the world suddenly started spinning.

A moment before she blacked out, she felt his arms and saw his face. Something in his eyes comforted her.

Chapter 5

REUNION

Moments after Reis followed Sira and Cardin through the portal to Daruun, it closed behind him, leaving the three of them in the dark, snow-covered streets of their hometown. Dalin did not accompany them, and instead was bound for the Wizards' Guild Hall, located in another realm separate from Halarite. He would return in the morning to take them all back to Archanon, where they were to stand before the council for further debriefing and new orders.

It wasn't something that Reis looked forward to. In fact, he would have preferred going back to the allied camp in the Wastelands. Instead, they had been ordered to remain away from the front, and were granted leave to return to their home town for the night.

Cardin and Sira didn't say a word to each other, and Sira made quite a show of turning away and stalking off, her feet crunching in freshly fallen snow. Cardin called after her, but she still ignored him. Reis placed a hand on Cardin's shoulder to stop him from going after her.

"Let her go tonight," he said to Cardin.

His friend looked at him in shock, "I can't, I need to apologize, I need to make things right. You're the one who said I could do so

41

after the council session."

"You won't be able to tonight," Reis nodded after her. "When she gets this way about anything, it's best to just leave her alone and let her calm down."

He looked confused, but stopped resisting Reis's firm hand. "Alright. I suppose you know her better than I do."

"No," Reis smiled wryly, "Not really, you've just forgotten a lot, and have to relearn it all."

Cardin looked to Reis with guilt in his eyes. "I am sorry for what I said. It hurt her, but it applied to all of you, and I shouldn't have said it."

Reis felt his jaw clench, his previous anger and disappointment at Cardin's words coming to the surface again. He hid the anger he'd felt then with a quick joke, but now he couldn't help but say, "We all swore an oath, Cardin. To stand by your side."

"I know that, and..."

He squeezed Cardin's shoulder, harder than he should have, but to his friend's credit, he didn't wince. "To help keep the Sword safe, as well as you. That means whatever you feel you have to do, you don't have to do alone. You are not solely responsible for the protection of our world."

"Maybe not," Cardin shook his head, and then shivered and wrapped his arms around himself. "Listen, I don't have my cloak with me. Can we talk later?"

Reis shivered as well, his own cloak woefully inadequate to keep out the winter cold. He released his death grip on Cardin's shoulder, patted him on the back, and nodded. "Good idea. Good night, my friend."

"Good night," Cardin turned towards his home and walked off.

Reis wrapped his cloak tighter around him and was about to turn towards his small house, but before he even took one step, he decided against it. It was still early, and he felt uneasy about being taken away from the front. So he instead turned north towards the Warriors' Guild complex. He wanted to check in and see if they needed help with anything. He doubted it, but it would at least make him feel useful.

The streets were empty and quiet, no one liked being out in the cold at night. His footsteps crunched in the snow quite loudly and echoed off the walls of the closed up shops and homes. Aside from his footsteps, it was a peaceful night. The clouds were quickly clearing from what had no doubt been a good snowfall, and the stars were very beautiful.

However, he hadn't even walked for a minute when there was a sudden burst of wind in the area. It penetrated his cloak and bit at his skin, even through his armor, and it set his teeth chattering. Snow blew everywhere and occluded the street in a white haze. Then he saw a bright flash of blue-white light all around him. He spun around, and saw what he expected to find – a portal had opened. Had Dalin decided to come to Daruun after all? Or was it another Wizard?

Neither. Although it was difficult to see in the unnatural blizzard, the person that walked through the portal was decidedly not a Wizard. They wore a grey cloak with the hood up, although that hood threatened to blow back in the wind. The person was tall, taller than Reis, and seemed quite slender. When he stepped away from the portal, Reis noted that his gait was casual and light, which most likely meant he was not a trained soldier.

Not a Wizard, and able to create a portal? Reis immediately thought of the worst possible scenario, especially after Cardin had told them of an army that could threaten their entire world. He opened his cloak, the cold momentarily forgotten, and drew his bronze-dyed sword. Whoever the person was, they were an intruder.

"Who are you?" Reis challenged in his most commanding tone of voice.

The newcomer raised his hands up disarmingly, although Reis saw that he shivered as a result. And that was when Reis saw the clothing underneath. The man didn't wear armor, he wore actual clothes, quite regal looking, almost as if they were council robes, but they were earthen colors of brown, green, and dark blue. The man also wore a pendant upon his chest that Reis recognized, but he couldn't place why it seemed familiar.

The newcomer didn't respond, and Reis suddenly felt vulnerable and alone. He had proven six months ago that he could keep up with Mages in a fight, but if this person was capable of creating portals, he was more powerful than any Mage.

And that was when Reis realized the portal hadn't closed. The wind had died down, but the blue-white shaft of light persisted, with small tendrils of lightning bolts occasionally shooting out to harmlessly connect with a nearby building. He'd become accustomed to those stray bolts of energy and no longer flinched.

A moment later, another figure emerged from the shaft of light, which finally closed afterwards. Reis immediately took several steps to his left to get a better view of the second arrival. They were shorter than the first, and wore a dark-blue cloak that almost seemed black in the sudden absence of the light from the portal. The street lamps were surprisingly still lit, but they did little to help illuminate the new arrivals.

With the wind now gone, the snow settled, but he still couldn't see faces. The two stood side by side, and exchanged glances. And then a soft, distinctly female voice spoke from the second arrival.

"Do you mean to attack us, Reis?"

He felt the color drain from his face, and his stomach turned in a mixture of surprise, fear, and guilt. He recognized the woman's voice. "Elaria?"

The second arrival reached up and pulled her hood back, which revealed the same deceptively beautiful face he'd seen six months ago just before the Battle of Archanon. She had several striking features, including eyes the color of sunset orange and red-orange hair pulled back in mirrored braids, similar to how Sira often styled her hair lately. Reis only now made the connection and realized Sira had copied that hair style from Elaria.

More striking than anything, however, were Elaria's ears. They were long, pointed ears, the point almost twice as high as human ears. Elaria was an elf, the first and only one Reis had ever met. Until now.

The first arrival reached up and pulled his own hood back, revealing the telltale pointed elf ears. His eyes were a bright violet color, and his long hair, pulled back into a loose pony tail, was silver. Based on the deep wrinkles in his skin, he was much, much older than Elaria.

Slowly, Reis lowered his sword. "No." He felt his face flush. "Um, not this time."

She smiled and nodded. "Good. I'd like to think that despite everything, we parted on peaceful terms last time."

Reis, at the behest of Pevrin and Prince Idrill Beredis, had helped abduct Elaria on the eve of the Battle of Archanon. Based on everything he'd ever been taught by the Order of the Ages, he believed then that Elaria was a demon, come to destroy or corrupt them all. He'd helped torture her, hurt her...he had done things that he now regretted. He still wasn't fully convinced she wasn't dangerous, but Cardin had convinced him that she was not a demon. Later, the Covenant had conceded that they had misinterpreted the Cronal, and perhaps there were indeed other intelligent species.

It wasn't easy for him to accept. It hadn't been then, and even now he felt a sort of sickness at seeing them. It just didn't sit right with him.

For a long moment, there was an awkward silence between them. The silence didn't last long. All around him, doors had opened up, and curious onlookers were coming out to see what had happened. They no doubt had looked out their windows when Dalin's portal had brought them there, but by now the citizens of Daruun were used to seeing Warriors and Wizards using portals to come and go. What they weren't used to seeing was a tense standoff in the middle of the street.

Reis felt his face turn even redder, and he quickly put away his sword. The cold suddenly became persistent again, so he wrapped his cloak around himself. He nodded to the first arrival, "Who is he?"

"Oh, yes, I apologize. This is Ventelis."

The older elf bowed gracefully. "Greetings."

"Ventelis, this is one of the humans I told you about," she looked at Reis, and he could tell she wasn't sure if she was happy to see him or not. "Reis Kalind."

Reis also bowed, though not as deeply.

"I think," Elaria glanced around at the onlookers, "that it is fortunate we ran into you. I did not think to return to Halarite so soon, and I am not certain our presence is welcome yet."

Reis agreed, and asked, "Why are you here?"

Ventelis replied, "I seek the Keeper of the Sword. Elaria has told me much of what kind of man he is, and I would like to speak to him directly. You are more than welcome to be present during this meeting. I prefer not having to explain the same matters twice."

Reis was suddenly reminded of some of his former instructors from his youth, as well as some of the Wizards he'd met in the past six months. Ventelis was well educated, and knew it. He was also old and didn't hold back his thoughts and opinions. Reis wasn't sure if he liked or hated those traits.

He knew he should have taken them to Warriors' Guild complex first. However, there hadn't actually been any sort of official protocol established for the arrival of non-humans on Halarite. So he wasn't obligated to.

Plus, and he hated to admit it to himself, he still felt remorse for what he'd done to Elaria. He felt as if he owed her.

So, he decided they would first see Cardin, and then he could take them to the Guild complex. "Very well. Come with me."

Elaria fell into step next to him, and Ventelis did so on his other side. He noticed Ventelis was shivering, his teeth chattering, and that made Reis feel a little bit better. They weren't human, but at least they were still vulnerable to the elements. However, Elaria seemed unfazed by the cold.

Beneath her cloak, he caught sight of the same leather-scale armor she'd worn before, although it was now almost white, helping her blend into the snowy environment. He remembered that it changed colors at her command. Then he realized that while Elaria was a seasoned explorer, Ventelis, who wore plain clothes beneath his cloak, was not, and therefore was unprepared and unused to extreme weather.

"How has your world progressed since I left," Elaria asked.

Reis wasn't sure he should reply, but when they locked eyes for a moment, he saw the same thing he had seen in her eyes six months ago, when Cardin had asked them all to look into her eyes. A kind soul, a good person, hardened by years of exploring but still pure.

In that moment, he felt like he could trust her. He also felt warmth in his cheeks, and he realized he did, in fact, find her to be quite beautiful. So he did the only thing he could think to do and answered her question.

"The idea of other intelligent races was not easily accepted, and still isn't," he shook his head and averted his eyes from hers. "However, the Covenant has since come forward with the revelation that they may have misinterpreted the Cronal, our central religious document. They continue to review it now, but this admission by them has…shaken many."

There was a moment of silence before Elaria said, "Including you."

Once again his cheeks reddened. "A little."

They spent the rest of the walk in silence, until they came upon Cardin's home. It was in better repair now, since he'd been able to hire someone to keep it in relatively good condition while he was at the front. Through the windows, Reis could see a lamp burning on the table and a glow from the fireplace. He walked up to the door and banged twice on it.

He heard the latch release, and the door creaked open. Blessed warmth from inside washed across Reis's face. Cardin's face went from a frown when he saw Reis, to a look of surprise when he saw Ventelis and Elaria, to a broad smile.

"Elaria!" She rushed forward and embraced in him a tight hug, which he returned heartily. "I didn't think I'd see you again so soon!"

"Nor did I," she pulled back, but kept her arms wrapped around his neck. "I'm so happy to see you!"

Cardin seemed to hesitate at her actions, and even in the low light Reis noticed his friend's cheeks turn a shade of red. Reis also felt a twinge of jealousy, but immediately pushed it aside. It was an elf. He couldn't feel jealousy over her.

His friend untangled himself from Elaria's arms, and looked curiously to the other elf. Now it was Elaria's turn to blush. "This is Ventelis. Ventelis, may I present Cardin Kataar. The Keeper of the Sword."

Reis noticed that the Sword was not actually in Cardin's possession, and was probably inside somewhere. However, when Cardin's title was mentioned, he glanced nervously into the house. "Hello," he reached forward to shake the elder elf's hand, but the elf didn't seem to know what to do with the gesture.

"A pleasure to meet you," Ventelis bowed. "Elaria has told me much of you, and I have come specifically to see you."

"I see," Cardin hesitated. "Well, please, come in." He gave a knowing look to Reis, and Reis recognized it as a look that said he was unsure if this was a threat or not.

As Cardin retreated into his home, no doubt to secure the Sword, Reis ushered the other two in and closed the door. He stood back by the door while the elves walked into the center of the room. Cardin was by his kitchen table, the Sword, still in its sheath, was on the table. Cardin turned and leaned back against the table, the Sword easily within reach.

Although he tried to hide his worry, Elaria noticed it. "Do not worry, Cardin," she smiled. "He is a friend."

"I mean you no harm," Ventelis added. He pushed his cloak off of his shoulders so that Cardin could easily see his frame, and the distinct lack of weapons. Despite that disarming act, Reis recalled hearing how Elaria had pulled daggers from seemingly nowhere at the height of the battle, moments before Kailar tried to force her to assassinate Cardin.

"Alright," Cardin nodded, but didn't seem to relax at all. "What can I do for you, then?"

"I am a historian in the College of Serelik," Ventelis said. "In fact I am head of the historical sect. I have come here because there may be another elf on your world."

Reis exchanged a shocked glance with Cardin. "Who," Reis asked.

"One of my most gifted students, Baenil. He has been particularly interested in studying human history."

Cardin seemed to consider that statement for a moment, before he asked, "So why would he come here?"

"He has been searching for the origin world of all humans," Ventelis walked closer to the fireplace and put his hands closer to the warmth. "He found reference to this world and he thought this might be where all humans came from."

The revelation that other humans existed in the universe was still new to Reis, and he found it disconcerting that they spoke of an origin world of all humans so casually. He wanted to say something to make them understand that this wasn't a topic of casual conversation, but he decided against saying anything. Instead, he let Cardin drive the conversation forward.

"I don't understand," Cardin shook his head. "Why did he think that?"

"It has to do with historical records recovered on other human worlds," Ventelis looked at Cardin but stayed close to the fire. "Baenil found an artifact in our archives that was labeled as having been found here, however no one had identified the language on the artifact before Baenil looked at it. He became quite excited, and said it was the earliest variant of your language he had yet found."

"Wait," Cardin shook his head, "I've spoken to the Wizards about our history. They say that only the dragons and Vrol knew about Halarite until this year. The only reason Elaria found it was because she was drawn to the power she sensed from Kailar."

Ventelis shook his head, "I am afraid your Wizards are mistaken. Your world was documented a long time ago, well beyond your own written historical records." Reis felt a void grow within his chest. The Order of the Ages clearly stated that human history began ten thousand years ago on Halarite. He had come to accept much, but to believe that there was a history beyond humanity's dominion over Halarite was impossible.

Or was it? Could there have been others on Halarite before humans? He still had trouble believing what the orc shaman had told Cardin, but so much had changed in their understanding of the Universe. Given everything that had happened, maybe it wasn't so hard to believe after all.

"Many references to Halarite are incomplete," Ventelis continued, "however there was enough for Baenil to determine how to create a portal to here. He did so more than ten years ago."

Yet again, Reis and Cardin exchanged surprised and worried looks. "Wait," Reis stepped away from the door. "You mean there's been an elf living on Halarite for over ten years?"

Once again, Ventelis did not look at him, and Reis began to wonder if he didn't like him for some reason. If Elaria had told him everything, perhaps he had good reason not to like Reis.

"I do not know," Ventelis sighed and looked back at the fire. "I attempted to convince him not to come here. We knew nothing of your culture, and we needed to send a scout first. However, no one in the college was willing to send anyone at the time. So Baenil left me a letter stating his intention to come here. He hasn't been seen or heard from since."

Ventelis turned around, presenting his back to the fire, and nodded to Elaria. "When word reached the college of Elaria's experiences here, I realized there was an opportunity. I could perhaps finally find out what happened to my student. I approached her and asked her to tell me everything she could about this world. After that, I asked her to bring me here."

Elaria looked apologetically at Cardin. "I know that now might not have been the right time to bring another Dareann Elf to your world." She stepped closer to Cardin, "But that's also why we came here, to this city. Just like when I tracked you before, just like when I tracked Kailar, I arrived as close to where I felt the power of the

Sword as I could. Fortunately Reis," she glanced back at him, "was there to greet us. Your world may still be in turmoil, however if Baenil was discovered now, without explanation...I was worried his presence might be misconstrued as hostile."

Grudgingly, Cardin admitted, "Unfortunately there are plenty who would. You did the right thing. But I don't even know where we could begin looking."

Ventelis again nodded to Elaria. "She has told me all that she learned while she was here, and I understand your capitol city, Archanon, is also known as The First City. It is the oldest city, and has a more complete historical record than any other city. I believe Baenil would have started his search there."

Cardin nodded. "Then we should start there as well, see if we can figure out where he might have gone after that."

"I have become quite familiar with his work," Ventelis said. "I will hopefully be able to determine that."

"We'll need to first make sure your presence is known to the council," Reis said, his sense of duty overriding any other feelings.

"Do you think that's wise," Cardin asked.

Reis looked at Cardin in surprise. "It's the right thing to do. Two elves have arrived, and a third may have been here for the last decade. We can't keep this from them, Cardin. Their unannounced arrival may not be well-received, but it is necessary. Let's do this the right way."

His friend sighed, but moments later nodded in acceptance. "Very well. We'll need to..."

Cardin stopped mid-sentence as his head snapped to the front windows. Reis spun around and saw moving lamps outside. Before there was a bang at the door, he already knew what was coming.

Reis recalled that several people had noticed the arrival of the elves. No doubt word had travelled to the Warriors' Guild, and that meant only one thing.

As he stepped aside, Cardin approached his door with sheathed-Sword in hand, and opened it. As expected, Idann Kale, the Daruun Warriors' Guild commander, stood at the door. He was tall and had a wide face with blonde hair, still cropped, and he did not look happy. Beside him stood his aide, Verin Ashall, always attached to his side like a tick.

"Cardin Kataar," Idann sneered. "I am not at all surprised."

"Good evening, Idann," Cardin gave him a false smile. "How may I assist you?"

"By handing over the elves," he glanced over Cardin's shoulder at the two newcomers. "Now."

Behind Idann and Verin stood six more Warriors, all of whom Reis recognized. Idann had no doubt brought them to add weight to his demands.

"I'm sorry, but I can't do that."

Idann obviously expected Cardin's response and quickly replied, "That is an order!"

"I don't take orders from you, or the Guild at large," Cardin made sure his frame blocked anyone from entering his home. "I take orders from the Allied army and King Beredis. As do you."

The Commander glared at Cardin, then looked to Reis. "I heard about their arrival, and that you," he said with considerable venom in his voice, "brought them here."

Reis felt a lump form in his throat, and he looked down. "They asked to see the Keeper of the Sword. I…"

"Silence!" Idann commanded. He turned his attention back to Cardin. "You are not above the law, *Keeper*. They are intruders and a threat to our people."

"They," Cardin motioned to Elaria and Ventelis, "are guests in *my* home. *I* will vouch for them. I will keep an eye on them, and ensure their safety and the safety of the city. If you have a problem with that, you can take it up with King Beredis in the morning. We will be appearing before the council anyway, you're more than welcome to come with us tomorrow."

Idann's anger and frustration was apparent, but Cardin had played a smart card by mentioning King Beredis. Idann knew that Cardin had the King's favor, and technically Cardin did not fall under Guild command. He was not in the wrong.

Idann knew he had no choice. As long as the elves were in Cardin's house, they were safe from him. "Very well. I shall accompany you in the morning. Kalind!"

Reis felt his stomach leap into his throat, and then moments later sink when he realized what was coming. Cardin didn't fall under Guild rule, but Reis did. "Yes, sir?"

"You're on wall detail tonight. Report to the watch commander at the Guild complex for assignment at once."

Reis sighed and nodded. "As you command."

Cardin slowly moved aside to allow him to pass. Reis looked to his friend, and then glanced one more time at Elaria. She seemed to be focused entirely on Cardin.

"I guess I won't be going with in the morning," he said to Cardin. "Good luck, my friend."

"Stay safe tonight," Cardin nodded.

With that, Reis walked out into the cold darkness. Tonight was going to be a very, very long night.

Chapter 6

LIES AND HALF-TRUTHS

When Kailar awoke, she felt disoriented and uncertain of where she was. She smelled smoke from a near-by fire, and heard the crackling a moment later. It was either sunset or sunrise, there was a hint of orange to the sky and she could see only a handful of stars. She lay on her back, covered by a light blanket that made her feel a little too warm.

The fire was to her right, and she could see what appeared to be several figures sitting around it. She didn't dare move, afraid that whoever they were, they had ill intentions for her.

Then she remembered what had happened, the wolves that attacked her, and Letan saving her. She flexed her right fingers and found that it caused her a fair amount of pain. She tried to be silent, but a small whimper escaped.

Someone to her left, whom she hadn't noticed before, stirred. "You're awake," Letan's voice spoke softly.

Slowly she turned her head to look at him and found that he sat beside her with a tin cup in his hand. Steam rose from it, but she could not smell what was in it. "What happened?" She glanced towards the fire, and noticed those who sat around it had turned to look at her. Even in the low light she recognized them as the same people who stood outside of the map maker's shop earlier that day.

"You collapsed," he said. "I'd gone ahead of my companions to…" He hesitated. "To follow you." Her pulse quickened, but she felt like she couldn't move beyond swiveling her head, so she just turned back towards him. She was completely helpless.

"Anyway, I knew I couldn't move you by myself, so I tended to your wounds and waited for them to catch up. We hoisted you into the wagon and kept going. We don't travel at night, so now we've stopped to make camp."

Again, she flexed her wounded hand, but this time she was able to manage her response to the pain. "I see." She paused for a moment and stared into his eyes. "I don't know what to say. Except thank you for saving me."

"You're welcome," he beamed. His smile charmed her, and she felt her face flush a little. "I'm sorry I followed you, but you were just too interesting to leave alone. Plus I knew you wouldn't be able to defend yourself against the creatures in this land. There are far more dangers here than there are back on Edilas."

"So it would seem," she nodded. She wasn't sure what to say, what to do, but she knew she needed to keep calm and determine if she was safe. Unfortunately, she realized that meant sticking with him for now.

She tried to sit up, but putting pressure on either arm caused excruciating pain, and she collapsed back onto the makeshift bedding. She realized it was just some cloth laid down on the ground, but that was more than she was used to.

"Hey now, no need to push yourself," Letan said in a soothing voice. "You were hurt pretty bad, and you bumped your head pretty good too."

Having experienced a concussion before, she frowned. "Why don't I have a headache, then?"

He nodded towards the fire and said, "Adira knows the local plants, she's lived here a long time. She used some local herbs to help you. In fact, your arms would hurt a lot more too if it weren't for her."

Kailar glanced over by the fire, and the only other woman in the troupe nodded. Kailar hated being indebted to anyone, but she was grateful, so she said, "Thank you."

"You're welcome," the woman replied in a sweet, quiet voice.

Letan continued introductions, and as he said a name, another member of the group nodded, smiled, or waved. "Tanneth, Borlin, Geris, and Benton. We all live in Corlas." She remembered Letan had mentioned that town earlier. It was the mining town near the Crystalline Peaks.

"What were you doing in Tieran?" she asked and turned her head back towards him.

"We are taking our turn on a quarterly run to the port with materials we've mined. Mostly crystals, but some metals as well. We also pick up supplies from Tieran that we can't make or get in Corlas."

"Hence the wagon," she said when she noticed it parked off to the side. The two horses were also tethered down and were enjoying some feed.

"Yep," he nodded.

It seemed all so mundane and unusual. She'd lived a rather extraordinary life since she'd left the Warriors' Guild, so to hear of ordinary people, going about an ordinary life, made her realize that no matter what, the world still moved along. She wasn't sure why, but all things considered, that somehow comforted her.

"So you know my name," he ventured after a few minutes of silence. "What is yours?"

She glanced at the others, but they had resumed staring at the fire and chatting quietly amongst themselves. At first, she wasn't sure how to reply. Her first instinct was to lie. After all, if they recognized who she was, they might turn on her. She still believed that what she'd tried to do six months ago was right, but it had spiraled out of control. She had been banished from Tal, and there was a bounty on her head in Falind. In fact she knew her name was cursed everywhere on Edilas.

She didn't like the idea of flat out lying to him, but she was afraid of what he'd think of her if he knew who she really was. He'd shown her such kindness, and that was something she wasn't accustomed to. Although she hated relying on anyone, she wanted that kindness to continue, at least for now, so she decided to lie. "My name is Fiera." It was the first name she could think of, and had been her mother's name.

"A fine pleasure to meet you, Fiera," Letan nodded his head. "So why are you really looking for the Crystalline Peaks?"

Once again, she felt the need to lie, but she worried that if she told only lies, she would eventually slip up and Letan would figure her out. She needed to ensure she was as truthful as possible for as long as possible. "I heard a rumor," she said. She wished she could sit up to speak to him on equal setting, but even moving her arms caused incredible pain. "Something about Mages gaining greater power when they approached the crystals."

Letan furrowed his brow and shook his head. "I've heard that before, but to be honest, I've stayed away from the Peaks. Even from Corlas, I can feel something is off about those mountains. They're beautiful to behold, but they just feel wrong."

He was a potential source of valuable information, she realized, so she asked, "Have you ever known anyone who's gone near them?"

"No," he shook his head. "I mean I've heard of people in Corlas who have, we're a growing community and all. But everything I hear is rumor. I do know that there have been people who have actually gone into the mountains. We've never heard from them since. I also heard that if you touch the crystals with your bare skin, they hurt you."

"How?" she asked.

"I don't know, it's just general knowledge. The town's been around for a long time, a lot longer than I've lived in it. Anyway, it's just generally accepted knowledge. Something about the first settlers going there and getting killed when they touched the crystals, but I don't even know if it's true. Honestly, no one is even willing to test it. No one wants to die."

"I see." She looked up at the sky. It was almost pitch black, the sun was long gone. The stars were burning bright, and she found some comfort in them.

After a few more minutes, he asked, "So why are you interested in all of that?"

Once again, she knew she couldn't tell him the truth. If she told him she hoped they might restore her powers, he might figure out who she was.

"To be honest," she tried to force her face to turn red, but realized it didn't matter in the dark, "I've always envied Mages. I've always wanted to be able to use magic. Maybe I can get that ability from the Crystalline Peaks."

In the flickering fire light, she saw Letan's brow furrow once again. Somehow she found that scrunched look on his face cute. "But the rumors say it enhances existing power. Nothing says they can grant non-existent power."

"I don't care," she replied faster than she meant to. She sighed and forced herself to calm down. "I don't care. I have to try."

"Why?"

She shook her head. "I'm sorry. There are some things I'd rather just keep to myself." She looked at him and tried to give him what she hoped was a convincing smile. "I'm allowed some secrets, even from my rescuer, am I not?"

He didn't respond at first, but then his face warmed into a smile. "Yeah, you are. Everyone is. Myself included."

She felt a moment of suspicion when he said that. He was hiding something from her. But what? And after what she'd just said, did she have the right to pry? She also worried that if she didn't let well enough alone, and pried deeper and deeper into him, he might do the same to her.

So she let it rest, and gazed up into the night sky. A shooting star burned across the darkness, and that made her smile. She'd spent so much of her life in the wilderness, and the stars had become old friends.

For a moment, she allowed herself to be lost in those stars, and she forgot where she was and what her situation was. She forgot about the pain in her arms, or the dull ache that had crept into her head. All she knew was that as long as she could see stars, she was alright.

For how long? How long could she be safe? She looked at Letan and asked, "What happens now?"

"Now," he stood up and walked around her towards the fire, "You eat." He bent over the fire and pulled something off. The wind had shifted earlier and she was now upwind of the fire, but he pulled off what looked like a piece of cooked steak. Her stomach suddenly growled, and she realized she hadn't eaten since morning.

He placed the strip on a tin plate, picked up some utensils, and brought it over to her. "The wolves around here are dangerous, but believe me," he smiled. "They taste great!"

She returned the warm smile, and tried to sit up again, but her arms still refused to work without screaming in pain. "Let me help you," he said as he set the plate down beside her. He gently placed his hands behind her back and helped push her up. She didn't have to use her arms as much, but she still felt sore, and her head swam a little at the change in orientation. Finally she was upright, and her stomach growled again.

Slowly she picked up the plate, every movement aching, and realized that despite being in company, cutting up her steak to eat it properly wasn't an option, so she simply tore into it with her teeth. It tasted as amazing as it smelled, and she didn't care that it came from the same carnivores that had tried to devour her hours ago. She just wanted to eat, and somehow it felt like poetic justice.

She ate very well that night, and Letan sat quietly by her side, fetching her water and more food when she asked. At first she felt satisfied that he was at her beck and call. However, as the night wore on, she began to feel guilty over that satisfaction. He'd risked his life to save her. He deserved better than to be ordered around.

Although she'd been unconscious for half of the day, fatigue set in early. Adira gave her an herbal tea, which eased the throbbing that had started in her head, and after some time, Letan helped her lay back down.

She had more questions for him, but within moments, she fell asleep.

Chapter 7

HIDDEN AMONG US

The next morning, Cardin found himself before the Allied Council again, and just like his last visit, he was there to present news to them that many would no doubt overreact to. He wore clean clothes, not his armor this time, a simple white tunic and black pants, as well as a thick brown cloak for warmth. The only battle ornament he wore was the sheathed Sword of Dragons on his back.

Beside him stood Ventelis, still clad in his earthen-colored robes and gray cloak. Cardin learned last night that the pendant around the elf's neck was enchanted to allow him to understand other languages and be understood by those who spoke other languages. It also created an illusion so that Ventelis's lips appeared to move correctly with the words heard by a listener. In actuality, when Ventelis spoke, it was in his form of Elvish. Elaria also wore such a pendant, and had worn it when they first met six months ago, but she always kept hers tucked beneath her armor.

Elaria entered behind them, escorted by Idann, and behind them another pair of Warriors from Daruun followed. Idann was still paranoid and believed the elves were a threat to Tal. It didn't help that Elaria hadn't forgiven him for his part in her abduction during the Battle of Archanon. She was short-tempered with him and never missed a chance to glare at him or insult him.

The rear of the entourage was taken up by Dalin, who had appeared in the main square of Daruun on schedule that morning. Cardin had quickly filled his friend in, and they wasted no time travelling to Archanon. Dalin had then found Master Valkere and explained the situation to him, and Valkere promised to speak to the other leaders to make Cardin and Ventelis's appearance before the Council the first order of business that day.

Reis had stayed in Daruun to sleep after his long night, and Idann, no doubt out of spite, ordered Sira on a morning patrol so that she could not accompany them.

The Warriors that accompanied them remained by the entrance door, but Idann joined Cardin, Ventelis, Elaria, and Dalin in the center of the room. All of the seats lined up against the walls were filled with people who wanted to see an elf in person. For once Cardin felt glad that he was not the center of attention in one of these meetings, but he sympathized with the elves. With that many people in the room, it felt stuffy and overcrowded.

Just as Cardin expected, Elaria immediately showed her discomfort. Ventelis, on the other hand, appeared to take it in stride, either due to his age or because of his experiences in the elven College.

King Beredis stood up, and after a few moments, the room grew silent. When he was satisfied that he had everyone's attention, he looked directly at Cardin, and Cardin felt his cheeks flush. "Cardin Kataar," he spoke in his powerful voice. "You seem to enjoy stirring the pot, as it were."

Cardin's cheeks felt even warmer, and he bowed to his King. "Yes, Sire."

Beredis then looked to Elaria. "I confess I am not entirely pleased to see you again, Elaria. As we discussed last time you were here, the people of Halarite are not yet ready for the presence of an elf, let alone two."

"My apologies, King Beredis," Elaria bowed low. "However, my companion here felt it was necessary, and I agree. May I present Ventelis of the College of Serelik, our most honored institute."

"Master Valkere briefed us," Beredis nodded to the Grand Master Wizard, "But he did not know precisely why you have come. Please, Ventelis, feel free to speak."

Ventelis took a step forward to separate himself from the rest of the group and took his time to turn and nod to each member of the Council. He obviously was accustomed to politics. He finally settled on King Beredis and began, "Thank you, King Beredis. I am grateful for the opportunity to speak before your Allied Council." Cardin suppressed a chuckle. Ventelis really *was* used to speaking to royalty, or whatever the elven equivalent was.

"I regret to inform you that I believe another member of my College, a student of mine named Baenil, has previously visited your kingdom, unannounced and without your permission, some ten years ago."

As Cardin expected, the entire Council stirred. The din of quiet conversation filled the room, and he watched as Beredis lowered his head to consider the startling news.

"I assure you, it was without my consent," Ventelis spoke over the din. "I urged him not to go. We knew nothing of this world, and it is among our strictest rules that members of the College do not visit such unknown locations."

King Lorath spoke out in response, "Then how do you explain Elaria's presence?"

"I am not a member of the College," Elaria spoke for herself. "I am bound by no such rules, although I never would have travelled here had I not sensed the unusual power in Kailar when she possessed the Sword of Dragons."

The glare she gave Lorath reminded Cardin about what he'd heard of her last appearance before the leaders of Halarite, before the four kingdoms and the Wizards' Guild had officially formed the Alliance. Lorath had grilled her vehemently. He was, at least publicly, a devout follower of the Order of the Ages, and he had tried to trick her into revealing that she was actually a demon.

That, in and of itself, had probably played a large role in the Council asking her to leave and not return for a long time. Cardin sympathized with her, but he also tried to catch her eye so that he could warn her to be careful.

Thankfully, Beredis, ever vigilant, headed Lorath off before he could reply. "Let us not stray from the immediate topic at hand." Lorath didn't take his eyes, narrowed in suspicion, off of Elaria, but he did not speak further. Beredis nodded and said, "Ventelis, please tell us more."

Ventelis hesitated, no doubt only now realizing the difficult situation he had placed himself in by revealing the truth to the Council. "As Cardin Kataar informed me last night, it was only yesterday that you learned about the fact that there are other humans beyond Halarite. Baenil's focus in the College was humanity and its history, and he believed this world could be the origin world for all humans. His research had uncovered this world's existence and that many humans had once lived here before they left tens of thousands of years ago."

That information was news even to Cardin. Ventelis had spoken of Halarite as a possible origin world, but now he implied that the history of Halarite was well beyond the ten thousand years of written history. He knew that the Order spoke of events that occurred prior to ten thousand years ago, but Ventelis had just said tens of thousands of years.

Movement from the Covenant's table caught his attention, and he looked to find that they talked, rather animatedly, amongst themselves. They were quietly whispering, but their arms moved as if they tried to convince one another of something rather passionately.

Unaware of their conversation, Ventelis continued. "He came to me with a plan to explore your world, to try to find evidence that this was, indeed, the origin world for all humans. I reminded him why he could not. The next morning, he did not show up for his classes. I found his quarters empty, except for a note in which he apologized to me, and that he would soon return with his proof."

"So you imply that an elf has lived amongst us for ten years," Queen Leian asked, obviously put off by the possibility.

The elf turned to her and nodded. "I am only implying that he has…" Ventelis's voice trailed off when the conversation from the Covenant table grew more intense. Everyone else followed his gaze to them. Several moments passed before they fell silent and looked around, suddenly aware that they were the center of attention.

"Alaia," Beredis spoke to the leader amongst them, suspicion in his voice. "Is there something you wish to discuss with the Council?"

She looked again to the other members of the Covenant, both of whom glared at her in warning. She sighed slowly and shook her head. "I apologize for our disruption, King Beredis. We do not have anything to add at this time. Please, Ventelis, continue."

Cardin found their behavior suspicious, and wondered if they knew something of Baenil's presence on Halarite before now.

After a few moments, Ventelis again looked to Leian. "I do not know if he has been here for the last ten years. I do believe that if he had left Halarite, he would have come back to the college first before going anywhere else."

"How could he live among us for ten years," Lorath asked, "and not be discovered? Do not take offense, but your kind stands out amongst us, and not just because of your ears."

Ventelis nodded. "That is true, we are not familiar with your culture, not entirely. He is a quick learner and I believe he could have learned to blend in effectively. However, his curiosity could have brought him into danger."

"Not to mention," Lorath sneered, "that if he had been discovered ten years ago, or any time between then and now, he would have been mistaken for a demon. He may have been killed."

Once again, all eyes fell upon the Covenant. If Baenil had been discovered and mistaken for a demon, they would have most likely been informed. However, Alaia shook her head, and seemed to speak very carefully and deliberately. "There has not been any such report to the Covenant that I am aware of."

After another long pause in the room, Beredis spoke next. "Perhaps we can yet locate him. Where would Baenil have begun his investigation?"

Ventelis turned to the King. "Without a deeper understanding of this world, he would have first needed to learn more about it. As I have learned from Elaria as well as from Cardin Kataar last night, this city is considered the First City, the oldest. He would have sought the oldest historical site known to your people to begin his investigation."

Silence fell upon the room. Cardin hadn't mentioned it last night, but he knew where that was. It was right there, in Archanon, but not in the castle. Beredis realized this as well, and slowly sat down in his chair. "The Tomb of the Ascended," the King spoke softly.

Everyone in the room stirred uncomfortably. Ventelis glanced around, and then pressed the King, "Please, tell me of this Tomb."

Beredis hesitated, but then said, "As you no doubt noticed, part of this city's wall connects with the cliff side. Within and beneath that cliff are catacombs, including the Tomb of the Ascended."

"In other words," Alaia spoke, "The tombs where the two most important figures in the Order of the Ages are laid to rest."

"Important to this Kingdom as well," Beredis nodded. "The first kings. Archos and Talus."

Cardin ventured forward, no longer content to be a bystander in the meeting. "I think it's important to say that the catacombs have never been fully explored."

"Indeed," Beredis agreed. "The Covenant has barred any exploration into it, citing it to be a holy site."

"Which it is," Alaia stood up. "I know where this line of thought is taking us, but I cannot agree to it. We cannot allow outsiders into our most sacred ground. Especially since they still could very well be demons."

"I thought you said you misinterpreted the Cronal," Sal'fe spoke up for the first time. "That you now believe it possible that there are other intelligent species outside of humanity."

"That does not mean that the elves aren't demons," she countered. "We do not know, one way or another."

"We are not demons!" Elaria glared at Alaia. "We are intelligent, self-aware people, with culture, and…"

Ventelis placed a hand on her shoulder to stop her. "Elaria, please calm yourself."

Cardin understood that Ventelis was not, strictly speaking, her superior, but she seemed to respect him none-the-less, and she backed down.

"The determination was made six months ago that they are not demons," Beredis said. "My son made that determination and I back his belief."

"It is for us to decide, not the Prince," Alaia stated defiantly.

Cardin snapped his head back to Beredis, ready for a very harsh retort and a threat from the King. But it never came. And that's when Cardin realized Alaia was a citizen of Falind, not Tal. Pevrin had been the member of the Covenant who had been a citizen of Tal. Beredis could have commanded him, but he technically had no authority over Alaia.

It seemed as if Beredis realized that at the same time that Cardin did. "Perhaps, but the catacombs are on Tal soil. And no one is above my rule in this kingdom, not even the Order." It was a bold statement, but it was not the first one he'd made. Beredis had become quite bold ordering actions that countered the Covenant in the last six months, as if he had grown tired of their half-truths.

Alaia didn't back down either. "You, along with everyone else here, have agreed to fall under the decisions of this council."

Even as Beredis gave his response, Cardin knew Alaia had just made a mistake. "I agree. The cultural and historical significance of the catacombs and the Tomb means the decision of whether or not to allow a search party must be put to a vote. Unless anyone objects to such a vote?" No one spoke, but Alaia's shocked face almost made Cardin laugh. "Very well. All in favor of this action?"

King Lorath shook his head, a definitive no. Cardin was not surprised, given his loyalty to the Order of the Ages. However, everyone knew that the swing vote would come from Queen Leian, who was next in the circle. Everyone hinged on her next move or statement. If it came to a tie amongst the six representatives, there would be an endless debate, and Cardin didn't look forward to that.

To his relief, she nodded. "Aye."

The vote was essentially already decided, unless Sal'fe voted opposite of what everyone expected. Alaia looked defeated as she shook her head. Valkere nodded and said, "Aye," followed by Sal'fe, until it came back to Beredis, who also nodded.

"Very well," Beredis nodded. "Cardin, you will be responsible for escorting Ventelis and Elaria into the catacombs."

Before Cardin's surprise could fully register, Idann objected. "My Lord!"

"Be silent, Commander!" Beredis gave no room for interpretation. "You may accompany them, but you will be there to ensure the safety of the visitors. You *will* set aside your personal feelings in this matter or you will go back to Daruun immediately, do I make myself clear?"

Cardin did his absolute best to suppress a smile. Idann had appeared more than once before the Council objecting to Cardin's involvement in the war, or to the decision to allow him to keep the Sword, or to allow him to work with Sira and Reis. However, Beredis had always shown patience with the Commander. It seemed as if that patience had run out.

Idann bowed, "I shall accompany them, my Lord. My apologies for my outburst."

Cardin knew Idann only agreed to come so that he could keep an eye on them, and if need be intervene if they crossed the line. Never the less, he was pleased, perhaps more than he should have been, that Idann had been dressed down in public.

Once that feeling died, however, Cardin realized what Beredis had said before. Cardin would be in charge of the group, not Idann, nor anyone else. It was the first time he'd been given any sort of leadership role. "Cardin?" Beredis looked at him.

He bowed low, "As you command."

Chapter 8

THE TOMB OF THE ASCENDED

It was midmorning in Archanon and still very cold. Although the sun rose ever higher behind them, Cardin felt like he couldn't keep himself warm and pulled his cloak tighter. Cardin, Dalin, Ventelis, Elaria, and Idann stood before the ancient stone entrance to the catacombs set into the cliff face, which made up the northwest corner of the city's outer wall.

The area around the entrance was considered as holy as the catacombs themselves and was an open field, covered in a mostly undisturbed layer of snow that gave it a majestic and surreal feeling. During Klaralin's occupation of the city three thousand years ago, the area had been left untended, and all of the ancient structures had been torn down to make room for his orc army.

Once the city had been recaptured and Klaralin defeated, there had been a desire to simply leave the ground open, without artifacts or structures, and to leave it up to nature what to do with it. It would have been prime farming ground, but the Order still held great influence, and even King Beredis wouldn't allow farmers to till the ground in front of the entrance.

Two of the Covenant's own guardians stood in front of the stone entrance to protect it from unauthorized visitors. They wore cloaks over their leather and chainmail armor, and looked decidedly uncomfortable. Cardin felt soft, small points of power within them and knew that they were Mages.

Alaia had also accompanied them, a last minute decision due to her desire to ensure nothing was damaged within the catacombs by the unwelcome visitors, and to ensure the guards let them pass. She was not pleased about the decision to let them explore the catacombs, but just as the four kingdoms and the Wizards' Guild had agreed to abide by the Council's decisions, so did the Covenant. Doing so was the only way they hoped to influence the council, but today that hadn't served them so well.

She moved to the front of the group and looked at the two guardians. "Let us pass."

They recognized her and stepped aside immediately. The stone entrance appeared to be nothing more than a cave entrance into the wall, but it was adorned by an ancient stone archway. Each stone had the symbol of the Order, six expanding lines from a central circle, engraved in it. He noticed that there were everlasting torches visible beyond the entrance, enchanted to burn forever just like the city's street lights.

"Do not touch anything," she glared back at them, and then led the way in. Cardin followed directly behind her, and Ventelis behind him. The entrance was wide enough for two at a time, but Cardin didn't want to be berated by Alaia if he accidentally touched the walls, so he stayed two steps behind.

The torches emanated very little heat, but as they passed further into the cave, Cardin noticed a slight increase in temperature, especially after the passageway turned to the right and began to descend. The ceiling of the tunnel varied but generally gave them enough clearance that Cardin didn't have to hunch over. Ventelis, on the other hand, was taller than the rest of them and occasionally bent lower. The torches provided ample illumination, but when the entrance was no longer visible, and Cardin could only see descending tunnel ahead of him, he began to feel trapped, and he had to force himself to remain calm.

It's going to be okay, he thought to himself. He'd been in caves before, including the dragon's cave in the Ilari mountains and the long-abandoned mine that Kailar and her orcs had used as a hideout in Daruun forest. In fact, it was that mine that had been on his mind ever since he'd heard Ventelis's implication that Halarite's history was well beyond ten thousand years.

In that man-made cave beneath the forest, stalactites and stalagmites had grown massive. No one quite understood how the process worked, but it was believed that such formations took many thousands of years to form. That meant that Kailar's mine had been carved beneath the forest well over ten thousand years ago.

He moved aside a little and allowed the Professor to catch up to him. They continued along, silently, but Cardin found himself glancing at the elf now and again. Finally Ventelis said, "Is something on your mind, Keeper?"

"I find that this past year, I've learned so many things that just...are hard to believe," he shook his head. "I mean I seem to take it better than most people, you saw how the Council reacted to your news, but you've implied our world's history, my people's history is much older than anyone thought possible."

"That is what I do at the College," Ventelis nodded. "I have been alive for well over one thousand years, and in that time, I have made discoveries about my own people that likewise have disturbed many. For someone like me, however, it is exciting to discover new facts, new ideas, no matter how much they challenge even my own beliefs about our existence."

Cardin felt himself smile, and a sense of excitement began to build up within. "That I can understand. Six months ago, I saw and experienced things I never dreamt of." Referring to dreams suddenly made his stomach flip. He had, as he expected, experienced his recurring nightmare last night, and he had woken up in a cold sweat.

He realized that perhaps that was why the revelations of the past two days had disturbed him rather than excited him. The dream made him fear for the future, and the unknown, in a way he never had before.

All of his life, he loved learning new things, he loved exploring, especially Daruun Forest, but in general he simply wanted to know and see more.

No matter what he learned today, he was now somewhere he had never been before. He would, for the first time in his life, get to see the Tomb of the Ascended.

"It is exciting," he nodded. "You're right."

Behind him, Elaria had walked closer to them so she could hear.

He couldn't hear her quiet footsteps, which he realized wasn't unusual for her, but he could feel her presence.

"It's why I do what I do," she said. He glanced over his shoulder at her and saw her give him a warm, enchanting smile. "You wouldn't believe some of the places I've seen, some of the people and creatures I've met."

Cardin returned her smile. "Someday you'll have to tell me about some of those."

She shrugged, "I can do better than that. I can take you to some of those places. We can see them together!"

The idea had never occurred to him before. Leave Halarite? He already had, the few times he'd been to the Grand Wizard Hall, but to go to another world altogether was something he hadn't considered. Valkere had been one of the few people from Halarite to do so, but so had Klaralin. The idea made him nervous, but was also enticing.

"That might be a possibility," he smiled back at her. "Someday, when everything here has stabilized more, I'd love to explore other worlds."

She blushed, which made him uncomfortable. It was very apparent that she had a crush on him, but he could never return those feelings for her, and he didn't know how to tell her that without crushing her soul.

Alaia came to a stop at a fork ahead of them. Cardin realized he'd lost his orientation through the twisting and turning tunnels, but he simply used his connection to magic to determine that they faced southeast now, but exactly where they were underground he couldn't guess.

Alaia seemed to hesitate for a moment before she looked up at him. "The catacombs are quite maze-like, in many ways. I know how to get us to the Tomb, and can take us straight there, or we can explore other areas." She looked at Ventelis. "Where do you think your student would have gone?"

Ventelis considered the question for a moment, before he said, "The tomb is a good place to begin."

"Very well," she nodded, and led them down the left tunnel. As they walked along, several other branches led off, and Alaia took them through several forks. Cardin decided he needed to pay closer attention, so that if he needed to leave in a hurry, he wouldn't get lost. He didn't expect trouble, but he was always cautious.

After a long descent, they finally found their way to a spot where the tunnel leveled off. They came to what appeared to be a T-intersection, but it was actually the entrance to a room. That was when Cardin realized where they were.

No one knew exactly why the Tomb of the Ascended had been placed so deep in the catacombs, but down there, it was actually much warmer than the surface, and quite damp. Cardin had already thrown the cloak off of his shoulders so that it only covered his back and adjusted the strap on the Sword's sheath so that it held the cloak in place, and he felt a little bit of sweat on his brow.

Alaia turned to them and blocked them from entering. "I will say this again, do not touch anything, do not disturb the tombs." She looked directly at Ventelis. "This is the most holy ground on our world."

"I understand your caution," he bowed to her. "I hold history in the highest regard. Religious significance notwithstanding, this is a historical site. I would never do anything to damage it."

She sighed, and then stepped aside. "Very well. You may enter."

Cardin stepped ahead first, still cautious. He began to feel something strange, but he couldn't tell if it was just his own apprehension about being so deep underground in man-made tunnels, or because there was actually a danger ahead.

So he slowly stepped through the entrance and into a surprisingly small room. It wasn't much larger than his house, except that dozens of holes had been dug into the walls to his left and right in columns that were four tall, and inside each of them was a wooden or stone casket. He expected there to only be the two Kings, but apparently there were many more buried in the Tomb of the Ascended.

In the center of the room were two stone tombs, each with ornate carvings inscribed along the edges of their lids and with writing in the ancient language of the first kingdom. Behind them stood two stone statues that reached all the way up to the ten foot tall ceiling. Statues of the Kings, wearing their ancient leather armor, bearing the crown of Tal. Both held long swords in front of them, their tips resting on the cave floor.

He felt his breath leave him when he realized what he now saw. The tombs of the first kings of Tal, the first known kings of Halarite. A part of him was almost disappointed to realize that they may not actually be the first leaders of Halarite, but he put that aside for a moment, and just marveled at the significance.

Ventelis stepped up to his left, Elaria to his right. They also admired the statues and the tombs, and Ventelis in particular stared in wide-eyed wonder. "Amazing," he breathed.

The moment didn't last. Cardin caught a flash of movement from behind one of the statues, the blur of a person, skilled in hiding in the shadows. He couldn't sense a presence in the energy around him, so he didn't know what to expect, but if whomever it was made a point to hide from them, he didn't think the person was friendly.

He reacted on instinct, reaching back to take hold of the Sword and willing the sheath into nothingness. The unknown person also reacted quickly and came flying out from the shadows at him. He pulled the Sword over his shoulder as quickly as he could, just in time to intercept and deflect another sword.

Elaria reacted quickly as well, and managed to pull Ventelis back out of danger while Cardin pushed forward. The unknown person was a woman with very short black hair and striking blue eyes, and she wore full-body leather armor. Her sword was of a type he had never seen before, long and narrow, two-handed, with a slight curve to it. It looked very light and very deadly.

With all of his strength, he pushed with the Sword and shoved her back, but she didn't lose her balance, and immediately went into another attack posture. He sized her up and realized she was an extremely skilled combatant. But before he could regard her further, she attacked again, this time with a thrust.

Cardin side-stepped and deflected her blow, and then tried to counter, but she was as fast as he was and countered his move. She swung her blade from overhead. His blade met hers, and she seemed surprised about something, but she continued her attack unfazed.

He knew he had to end the fight quickly, but he was hesitant to use any of his powers in the tomb, fearful that he could damage the statues or the tombs or, worse yet, bring the entire ceiling down upon them.

"Anila, stop!"

The attacker suddenly ceased mid-swing. Cardin almost took advantage of her hesitancy, but realized that the voice that commanded the attacker was Alaia's. For what felt like a long time, Cardin stood in his defensive stance and faced his assailant. She stepped back into her own defensive posture, ready to resume their duel at the slightest provocation.

Alaia stepped in between them and looked directly at the woman. "They are here with my consent. Do not attack."

The attacker's eyes darted between Alaia and Cardin before she finally nodded and stood up straight. "As you wish." Her voice was quiet but determined.

Alaia then looked at Cardin. "Please. No fighting in here."

"Who is she?" he asked, not ready to trust the stranger.

"This is Anila Kovin, our most trusted guardian. She is under the Covenant's direct orders, and will follow my commands. She will not attack you again." Alaia looked around her and then pleaded with him. "Please. No more fighting in here."

He felt a lump form in his throat. For a moment he continued to stare defensively at Anila, but finally he sighed and stood up straight. Reaching overhead, he placed the Sword against his back and willed the scabbard back into existence.

That was also when he realized that their duel had lasted only a matter of seconds, not even enough time for Idann or Dalin to get into the room to help, nor enough time for Elaria to do anything other than pull Ventelis out of the way. Anila may not have been a Mage, but she was very well trained and experienced, and faster than he thought possible.

Idann, who had apparently drawn his own longsword when he heard the battle, stepped to the left side to get a clear view of both fighters. He looked at Alaia and asked, "You have a habit of keeping your most elite guardians down here at all times?"

Alaia shook her head, "No not normally. Anila, why are you here?"

Although Anila looked at Alaia, Cardin could tell she made sure to keep Cardin within peripheral vision. She believed him to be the greatest threat, but he knew that was only because she probably wasn't aware of how powerful Wizards were.

"Delkin ordered me down here this morning," she said. "To see if I could find any other clues about..." Anila trailed off and glanced at Cardin and the others.

Cardin felt more than a little annoyed. They still hid something down there, and given the hushed conversation the Covenant members had held during the Council meeting, he began to wonder if it had something to do with the elves and Baenil. So he turned to Alaia and looked at her expectantly.

Alaia met his gaze unwavering, but did not speak at first. He realized that she had a strong will and wasn't likely to back down through intimidation, but he also decided a long time ago that she was a good person. He suddenly got the impression that she had wanted to tell the Council something, but the others had forced her not to.

She shook her head. "This has gone on long enough. Anila, lead the way to the map chamber. I will explain along the way."

The guardian seemed displeased with the turn of events, but she did not question her master's orders. Without a word, she slid her sword into a sheath strapped to her left hip, turned around and headed towards the back of the chamber. Cardin hesitated, but at Alaia's insistent motion, he followed Anila. Alaia stayed with him. Idann hesitantly sheathed his sword and stepped up behind them along side Ventelis, and the rest of their group followed behind.

"The others said not to reveal this, but something has happened and I believe we can no longer keep it a secret. Especially not with your arrival," she looked back at Ventelis. "Ten years ago, almost exactly, Anila was down here on a pilgrimage to the Tomb. She heard a noise down another corridor that led her to find what she assumed was a demon."

Cardin looked ahead at the leather-armored woman. Behind the statues there had been a pillar that blocked the view of the far back wall, but as they rounded it, he noted there was a narrow passageway centered in the back wall. The entrance was bracketed by two torches. Anila took up one and continued into the chamber.

"Has this always been here?" he asked as he preceded Alaia into the passageway.

"Yes," she replied. "It wasn't exactly hidden, but most people who make a pilgrimage here do not venture behind the statues. We've known about this tunnel for quite some time. We actually have explored much of the catacombs, they are more extensive than you might imagine."

"That does not surprise me," Ventelis spoke up from behind Alaia. "Humans tend to make their catacombs extensive, for a variety of reasons, but especially when they wish to keep something hidden. These definitely would have excited Baenil, they are clearly quite ancient. Some of the markings on the walls indicate as much."

Cardin looked at the passageway walls and frowned. "I don't see any markings."

"They are there, if you know how to look for them," Ventelis replied with an amused tone.

"Which apparently your student was able to do," Alaia continued. "Anila followed him, and he eventually led her to the chamber we are going to now. All of our explorations, and we hadn't found it before. It really is easy to get lost down here."

The passageway branched off several times as they continued on, and Cardin found that even with his ability to sense their direction, he was already lost. He worried for a moment that Anila and Alaia led them towards a trap, or meant to leave them lost below, destined to wander aimlessly for years. As long as they were still within the boundaries of the city, even this far underground Dalin would not be able to open a portal to get them out.

Suddenly Anila disappeared, or at least that was what it looked like. It appeared as if she'd turned to the right and walked *through* the wall, except that the light of her torch still illuminated the corridor.

He stopped, hesitant and worried that he had been right to fear a trap, but Alaia gently pushed him on. "It's ok, this is why we never found the chamber before."

Cardin stepped closer to where the torchlight came from. He expected that it was an illusion and the wall wasn't real, but it was actually much simpler than that. The passageway was intersected at an extreme angle by another corridor, such an angle and such a narrow corridor that if Anila hadn't turned down it, he would have walked right by and never known it was there, not unless he came back the same way.

Anila waited patiently in the corridor until Cardin saw her, and then she continued down it. The corridor quickly curved left and she was out of sight a moment later. He looked back the way they came to see that Idann had taken the other torch at the entrance, and Dalin took up the rear and used his staff to also light the way.

Again Alaia lightly urged him forward, so he followed Anila in. He could see the glow of her torch as it illuminated the walls, and when he came around the bend, he found that it was a very short corridor, and that it immediately opened into a large chamber, larger than the Tomb of the Ascended.

Several torches lit up the room, and he was glad they were the magical, everlasting type. Smoke would have otherwise built up and probably would have suffocated them all. The chamber ceiling reached up much higher than anything else he'd seen in the catacombs, but that wasn't saying much, less than fifteen feet, but the chamber itself had at least twice the floor space than the Tomb had.

Cardin stepped into the center of the room and took in the view. On either side of the entrance were large, flat surfaces carved into massive underground boulders. Their flat surface was probably not natural and had been carved that way.

Painted on one wall was something he quickly recognized as a map representing the continents. It showed all of the continents, including Edilas, the two southern continents, and the newly discovered fourth continent, Trinil, far to the east of Edilas. However, the representation of Trinil was complete. No one had yet to explore the entire extent of the new land, which in fact appeared to be composed of four landmasses separated by wide channels of water.

"Amazing," he breathed. The others had entered the chamber while he stared at it, and Idann and even Dalin stared in awe.

"This appears to be an accurate representation of the landmasses of Halarite," Dalin said quietly.

Cardin looked at him in surprise. "You knew of the extent of the fourth continent?"

"Of course," Dalin nodded. "The Wizards have known of it for quite some time."

"We have only known about its existence for less than ten years…" Idann's voice trailed off, and Cardin immediately realized what that most likely meant.

He turned to Alaia and said, "This was how we discovered the new continent."

"Yes," she nodded.

Anila stepped closer to them, "When the demon led me to this chamber, I subdued him and brought him before my masters." Her speech was the precise talk he expected from a well trained soldier, clear and concise. "I led Master Pevrin here to show him."

Alaia nodded, "And not long after, Delkin convinced Queen Leian to commission an exploratory mission from Maradin. Delkin accompanied the mission and was able to direct the ship's Captain to where we needed to go."

Cardin turned to look at the other flat wall to find that it was inscribed with text, but it was in a language he didn't recognize. The others turned to follow his gaze, and Ventelis rushed towards it. "I've seen this language before," he exclaimed in excitement, and began to read from the top, his fingers tracing along just above the stone, careful not to touch it.

"We hadn't," Alaia said. "We had no frame of reference, no way to translate it. However, Baenil did. After we determined that he was not, in fact, a demon, we brought him back down here to translate."

"All of this under the nose of the King?!" Idann did not sound happy, and Cardin found himself in agreement. The Covenant had kept a lot from the people. For the first time in a long, long time, he felt himself sympathetic to Idann's anger.

"We had to," she said. "We made Baenil endure several of our tests, we figured we finally had proof of demons, and we wanted to be able to show what it was. However..."

Ventelis stopped reading and turned to her slowly. "What sort of tests?"

"Among others," she gulped, "demons are said to not bleed. He bled." Anger flashed on Ventelis's face, and Cardin noticed out of the corner of his eye that Anila placed her hand on her weapon. He felt anger in his own heart, and felt tempted to support any aggressive move Ventelis was inclined to make, but he knew that would be counterproductive.

"Demons also are resistant to magical attacks and can only be injured physically," Alaia added, her eyes turned down. "Baenil was wounded by magic. There were several other tests, and every single one proved that he wasn't a demon."

"Because he isn't," Elaria glowered at Alaia. "We are not demons."

"You must understand," Alaia shook her head, "we did not believe that he could be anything else but a demon. We had never encountered another species that was intelligent, our beliefs state there could not be any."

"What of the orcs?" Elaria asked, incensed. Anila pulled her sword just enough to allow an easier draw if it became necessary. He looked directly at her to make sure she knew he had seen her move.

She acknowledged his stare, but she didn't take her hand off of her weapon.

Alaia snorted in amusement, "The orcs we have encountered are hardly intelligent."

"Where is Baenil now?" Cardin cut off further argument on the subject.

All eyes fell back on Alaia, and she shifted uncomfortably on the spot. "Once he finished the translation for us," she sighed, "We shipped him to the new continent to help with some of the ruins we had found there."

"Ruins?" Dalin asked. Cardin was surprised at the existence of the ruins and considered what it meant for a moment, but then he realized the significance of the fact that Dalin hadn't known there would be ruins. According to history, civilization began on Edilas. The existence of ruins on Trinil seemed to prove otherwise.

"Ruined structures, older than anything we've ever seen before," Alaia nodded. "If any of the structures had writing on them, they were long ago worn off, but we hoped Baenil would be able to help us learn more."

"How long ago was that," Ventelis's hands were clenched in fists. Cardin knew he wasn't a fighter, but Elaria was, and if Ventelis attacked, Elaria would support him. He gave a warning look to Ventelis, but the elf didn't seem to notice.

"Almost a year ago," Alaia said. "He is still there. However…"

A realization occurred to Cardin. "Something has happened." He recalled she had stated that fact when she decided to confess everything.

"We have not heard from the colony in many months," she said morbidly. "At least three ships were supposed to have returned by now and haven't. We don't know why."

Cardin looked at Ventelis, who appeared to have to force his fists to unclench. "Then we must travel there immediately. We must leave the city at once so that we can create a portal to that colony. We will retrieve Baenil, you have held him against his will for long enough."

Alaia cringed hesitantly, "The others in the Covenant may not agree to that."

"That is no longer their decision," Cardin stated before Ventelis could reply. "The Council will need to make a determination."

She nodded hesitantly, and Cardin understood her hesitance. That meant bringing the subject up before the Council, in front of her peers. Soon enough they would find out that she had gone against the group consensus and revealed their crimes. Even the Order of the Ages was not above the law.

Chapter 9

CROSSROADS

Kailar wasn't sure if she felt happy or apprehensive about the fact that the town of Edingard lay within sight ahead of them, framed by the massive Barrier Mountains. Those mountains stretched seemingly forever from north to south and reached impossibly high into the sky.

Only a few days had passed since she had been attacked by the wolves. The morning following the attack, she was capable of standing on her own, although with considerable pain, and so she walked behind the caravan. Letan had insisted she could ride on their cart full of supplies purchased in Tieran, but she refused.

She didn't feel like she could walk with them, she was too afraid one of them might recognize her. If one of Letan's group recognized her, they might try to collect the bounty on her head. More than that, she worried that Letan would no longer treat her the way he did, would no longer look at her the way he did.

That bothered her more than anything else. The idea that Letan's opinion of her was so important to her was unexpected. Although he seemed to trust her, she knew not all of his companions agreed with his decision

Tanneth, a particularly large man with distrustful eyes and cropped black hair, seemed to be especially suspicious of her. It wasn't that he said as much, it was simply the way he kept looking at her. Everyone else in the group showed her a modicum of sympathy and kindness, even if they weren't comfortable sharing their supplies with a stranger and leaving her unguarded. Tanneth, however, never seemed to lower his guard around her, and never showed her courtesy.

She wondered if he knew who she was, but if so, why hadn't he told anyone? Perhaps he wasn't sure and was simply waiting for her to slip up. She always made sure to listen for the name she had told them, Fiera, because if he was suspicious of her, the moment she didn't respond to that name, he would likely become certain she had lied to them.

Letan hung back from the group and allowed her to catch up to him as they approached the town. He smiled warmly at her, which made her cheeks feel just as warm. However, his smile faded when he said, "I guess this is where we'll say goodbye."

A part of her wanted to shout out 'no, not yet.' Over the last couple of days, he had occasionally walked back to talk to her like he did now, and she enjoyed his company. Every chance she could get, she stole a look into his eyes. He would always meet her gaze, but that frightened her, and she would quickly look away.

Once again she followed that routine and looked at him, where he met her gaze. She tried to make herself hold it, but her cheeks burned hotter and she couldn't help but turn away. Her stomach flipped a little with a fluttering sensation, another feeling she wasn't used to. It was as frightening as it was exciting!

"It would probably be best," she said as she looked down at her feet. "You've been a big help, but I can't be your responsibility anymore. You have your companions to look out for."

Letan laughed a little, "Fiera, you haven't been a burden at all on us. Aside from using some supplies to clean your wounds and keep your headache down that first night, you've insisted on doing things yourself, scavenging your own food, making your own fire away from us. You don't have to do that, you know, you could have joined us every night. You still can."

"No," she shook her head and looked back up towards the town. It was a larger town than she expected, although it was considerably smaller than the port city had been. She knew it had most likely started as a mining town, but it had grown to accommodate more functions, including plenty of lodging for the countless explorers who passed through to cross the Barrier Mountains.

Those mountains loomed behind the town, stretching high above and no doubt casting Edingard in shadows very early in the afternoon. At the moment, the sun was still behind their party, and she could easily see the towering peaks in all of their beautiful detail.

"I have to go alone," she nodded in determination.

For a moment, Letan did not speak. She could already begin to hear banging and pounding from blacksmiths. While much of the metals mined from the mountains were shipped to Tieran to be sent to the four kingdoms, the growing population and economy on Devor meant business was only getting better for blacksmiths.

"Why?"

The question caught her off guard, and she realized Letan hadn't actually asked it before. She stole another glance at him, but purposely avoided his eyes. She clarified his question, "Why do I have to go alone?" He nodded.

She didn't know how to answer. She knew why, but how could she tell him without revealing too much? How could she tell him she didn't want him to find out who she really was? Or that she felt useless around them, like she couldn't truly contribute to their group or repay them for the kindness they had shown her? How could she tell him that losing her connection to magic made her feel like a burden, and a failure?

Kailar wasn't entirely sure how much time had passed in silence, but Letan broke that silence. "Listen, there are still dangers out there, in the mountains and on the other side of the mountains. A lot of creatures around here seem to know when someone has magic and when someone doesn't." She felt her cheeks burn again, but this time in embarrassment. "They'll hone in on you by yourself, like the wolves did, but as long as you're around a Mage, they'll usually stay away."

"I can take care of myself," she spat back. Ahead, Tanneth's head snapped around to look at her with suspicion. She realized she'd raised her voice more than she meant to.

Quietly, Letan replied, "I didn't mean to imply you couldn't. I'm sorry."

His apology made her feel guilty over her reaction. She sighed and absently clutched her stomach, a reaction to the strange sensation she felt inside. At first she wanted to apologize, but that just made her feel worse.

So instead, she asked, "Why do you care what happens to me?"

Although she hadn't looked at him, she saw in her peripheral that he looked at her and held his gaze. "Because I do." She almost visibly smirked at his response and wanted to ask if it was really that simple. He continued, "You're a good person, and I see a pain in your eyes and in your every action that makes me think you've been terribly hurt."

Another uncomfortable sense began to build within her at the memory of losing her abilities, so she deflected, "I'm not a good person."

"Now why do you say that?"

Once again she felt embarrassed and mentally chastised herself. She looked away to her left and saw a farmer tending to a field outside of the town. She focused on that farmer for a moment, as he moved through the field inspecting the growth, though what was growing she couldn't tell.

It was an attempt to avoid answering his question, and he knew it. He lightly touched her arm, an act that startled her. She snapped her head over and looked at the offending hand, and he retracted it quickly. "Look," he said a moment later, "I don't know what is going through your head, why you think you have to punish yourself, but I stand by what I said. I stand by what I see in your eyes." She looked ahead again and intentionally avoided looking into his eyes. "And we're going the same way anyway. Corlas is right by the Crystalline Peaks."

She shook her head, but she felt the pull of his plea, and was compelled to assent to his request.

"You don't have to join us at night," he finally said, defeat in his voice. "Just walk with us like you have, that'll help keep anything from attacking you. You don't have to talk to us, don't have to do anything with us, just…stay in proximity."

It was a compromise. She wanted to reject it out of hand, but part of her realized the wisdom in staying near a group. If, as Letan said, the dangerous beasts of Devor avoided Mages and attacked anyone who didn't possess a connection to magic, she would be a prime target. He offered to let her stay near them without actually joining them.

Tanneth still kept glancing back at her, and she thought about also staying with them simply to annoy him and keep him on edge.

It would also mean that she didn't have to say goodbye to Letan. She loathed admitting it to herself, but she wanted to stay near him. There was still the fear of being discovered, but her desire to be near him overrode that.

Now she felt confused, and she despised that feeling. All of her life, she had been decisive, in control, always knew what to do and when to do it. Now she felt more uncertain than ever. Not just about staying near Letan, but about her course in life. More than that, for the first time since she could remember, she felt lonely.

She sighed and glanced at him. "Alright," she nodded. "I'll stay with you. I still want to find a map, though, in case we get separated."

"Good idea," he beamed a smile at her. "I hope you won't mind, then, but we'll stay here overnight."

Kailar began to object, but then she realized it might not be a bad idea. The horses that drew the cart had been pushed hard on the way to the port, let alone since they left the port, and they could use a rest. His team also looked worn out, and she wondered for a moment why they had rushed their supply run to Tieran.

In any case, she still felt sore, and a day's rest didn't sound like a bad plan.

They had finally entered the edge of town. The main street was heavily trafficked on the sides but relatively clear down the middle. Another cart headed in the opposite direction passed by them, led by two women who were dressed in peasant clothing.

As busy as the town was, she realized there were plenty of places to stay the night, and her fears and paranoia took hold of her again. "I won't stay with your group tonight," she said defiantly.

Letan glanced at her in surprise, but then slowly nodded. "I understand. I think."

As they passed further in, she stopped, as did Letan. He looked directly at her, and she allowed herself another look into his eyes. "We usually stay at Orin's Inn on the west end of town, it's the largest inn here. If you need anything…"

"I won't," she looked away. She thought about it for a moment, and then looked at him again and smiled, "but thank you."

He returned the smile, and then rushed to catch up with his friends. She watched after him, felt that feeling of butterflies in her stomach again, and sighed and shook her head.

"What are you doing?" she chastised herself. "Stupid…"

With that thought, she looked around the main avenue. She located the nearest supply shop and was pleased to find they had a couple of maps in stock. The shop's proprietor claimed they were accurate, and she compared what she knew of her short time on Devor to the eastern part of the map and confirmed that it was at least accurate in that quarter.

Once she completed the purchase, she left the shop. On her way out of the door, she bumped into a small, skinny man with ragged blonde hair. He very nearly ran her over, obviously not paying attention to where he was going. His clothes were a mess, a dirty white tunic, stained black from working in the mines, and he smelled like he had just come back from a shift.

The man glanced at her and apologized, but then he did a double-take on her. He didn't say more, but she felt very self conscious. She pushed past him out into the street and walked away, but she glanced back at him a couple of times. He stood at the entrance to the shop for some time and stared after her, and she feared the worst.

Had he somehow recognized her? Was he a threat to her?

She turned down a cross street and rushed out of sight of the ragged miner. If he had recognized her, he could report her to the nearest Warriors' Guild hall. She had to get out of sight and stay that way.

As such, she knew she couldn't stay anywhere near the main street. She had to find a more out of the way inn, so she headed for the north end of town. It was a small town, so she didn't have far to go until she reached the edge. There was another road, less travelled than the east-to-west road, that led out of town and seemed to stretch on forever along the range.

Only one street over from that road was a small inn that looked like it wasn't very well kept up or popular. It was most likely much cheaper than other inns, and had few patrons, so she decided to check it out.

The name on the sign out front said "Black Horse Inn," but she was amused to find a white horse munching lazily on hay behind a fence next to the inn.

She looked around to make sure she hadn't been followed before she opened the door, whose hinges screeched and were in dire need of oiling. Once inside and the noisy door secure, she took a look around. It was almost as she expected, a small room with only a few wooden tables, not even a bar. From a back room came a short, stout woman with graying hair.

The woman looked Kailar up and down and seemed to make a split second decision about her. "You look like you've been through rough times, deary," she said, surprisingly friendly. "Well have a seat and I'll bring you some lunch. You're my first customer of the day."

Kailar nodded, took her backpack off, and sat at the nearest table. She set the backpack on another chair and took a moment to stow the recently purchased map inside of it. The old woman quickly stepped out of sight into the back.

The sweet scent of stew cooking in the back reached her nose and she suddenly realized just how hungry she was. She looked around the inn and saw three open doors that led into unoccupied bedrooms. The door immediately to her right was closed, but the window next to it made her realize it led out to where the horse still munched on its own lunch.

When the woman came back several minutes later with a bowl of stew and a hunk of bread, Kailar arranged to stay in one of the rooms for the night. After she finished lunch, the old woman, named Ira, gave her a key to the room closest to the entrance door.

As paranoid as ever, Kailar immediately lit the candle on the night stand next to the bed and closed the curtains. She didn't want the miner, or anyone else, to be able to look in and see her. She closed and locked the door and then lay on the bed. Within minutes, she fell asleep.

Chapter 10

THE WHITE CITY

Over the course of the past six months, Cardin had visited the Daruun Warriors' Guild often. The memories from when he had trained to become a Warrior were no longer as prevalent as they used to be, and his memories of imprisonment within the dungeon back when he'd helped Dalin also had begun to fade, until now.

As he stood within the courtyard, a new mission before him, he recalled his first meeting with Dalin and the events that led to him become the Keeper of the Sword. So much had changed for him since then, and today they would begin an expedition to a new land!

That had been the result of their discovery in the catacombs. They had reported back to the Allied Council, along with the guardian, Anila. Many in the Council were furious that the Covenant had never reported Baenil's presence, and it wasn't long before the Council session erupted into heated arguments.

After King Beredis finally got the meeting under control, Cardin was able to complete their briefing. Valkere had ordered one of his Wizards to scout out the newest colony, called the Port of Hope, to determine why three ships had failed to return on schedule.

The Wizard came back several minutes later and said that he was unable to create a portal to the colony, or to anywhere else on Trinil.

That news greatly disturbed the Wizards, and even Cardin felt concern. To their knowledge, the only place on Halarite that the Wizards were unable to create portals in was within the walls of Archanon. Who could possibly create such a barrier around an entire continent?

After some discussion, the Council decided to send a new expedition via ship. They all agreed that Cardin would go, since he fell under the Council's direct orders and was supposed to represent the interest of all of the members. He asked if he could select his own team, but they insisted he was not yet ready to lead. He agreed, and indicated that Sira had led him and his other companions very well during the war. He neglected to mention their recent spat or remind them of his actions at the Fortress of Nasara.

The Council, or most of them any way, agreed that their effectiveness as a team was well documented. King Lorath wasn't entirely happy, but then the Covenant requested that a member of their delegation should accompany them, and Lorath agreed.

Cardin wasn't happy to have a member of the Covenant along, given their history with the elves, but he also realized that it was probably members of the Order of the Ages that held Baenil now. Cardin's team would need a representative of the Covenant to secure the wayward elf's release. He requested Anila be that representative. He certainly didn't trust her, but she would be a valuable companion if they encountered any threats. Thankfully all parties agreed to his request.

In the end, the expedition consisted of Cardin, Sira, Reis, Dalin, Anila, Ventelis, and Elaria, along with a small contingent of Marines from Erien to back them up. They were to set sail from Erien's capitol city, Maradin.

Idann had insisted he be allowed to accompany them, but Beredis wanted him to remain in Daruun, and Cardin was outwardly jubilant about their decision. It seemed as if Beredis had become bolder over the last several months in his willingness to give orders that went against the wishes of key figures. Cardin respected him for that, but also worried that the King would lose too much support if he wasn't careful.

He still hadn't seen Sira since then, and it had taken a couple of days for arrangements to be made in Maradin for their expedition. A ship was being prepared in a rush for the three to four week journey to Trinil. He'd tried to find Sira in Daruun over the last couple of days so that he could finally apologize to her, but he hadn't been able to locate her, and he believed that she intentionally avoided him.

That morning, however, that would no longer be possible. Soon Dalin would create a portal and they would journey to Maradin with only a day to spare before they would leave the shores of Edilas.

They had begun to gather in the courtyard of the Warriors' Guild. It was essentially a fortress, and it had to be, given the fact that Daruun had often been a contested city in the Lesser Wars. The compound's outer wall was shared with the city wall, but it was separated from the rest of the city by its own inner wall.

Cardin accompanied Reis to the complex. Both carried small backpacks with some gear, including at least one change of clothes, while they wore light leather armor for the journey. Toting around their chain mail and plate armor wasn't feasible. Cardin also wore his favorite black cloak, while Reis wore a light brown cloak.

Dalin, Ventelis, and Elaria were already inside the courtyard, but Sira was still not present. Cardin scowled as he saw Idann lurking nearby with his aide, Verin, at his side. They both eyed him with distaste as he and Reis walked in.

They met up with the others in the center. As expected, Dalin wore his usual blue robes, but he also had a backpack, which surprised Cardin. In all of their time on the front lines, he'd never seen Dalin carry anything other than his staff. Ventelis and Elaria had briefly returned to their own world to gather their own supplies and prepare for the journey. Elaria wore the same scale-leather armor and cloak she always had, but Ventelis had changed into a warmer looking set of travelling clothes and cloak.

"Anyone seen Sira?" Reis asked. Everyone shook their head no, but at that moment, Cardin looked over near the barracks and saw Sira had walked out and was adding a few final items to her backpack.

He looked at the others and excused himself before he walked over to her. If they were to work together, he needed to talk to her now. He needed to make up for his harsh words, for the way he had treated her. No matter what, he needed to make things right with her.

She glanced up at him as he approached, and he felt a slight stir of power around her, no doubt unintentional.

"Cardin," she said curtly to him.

"Hi," he tried to manage a smile, but it felt weak, and he was unsure of himself.

"Are the others ready to go?"

He glanced back at them, and they all stared at him and Sira. When he looked at them, they suddenly looked away and began nervously chatting with each other. "Yeah," he nodded to her. "Are you?"

She sighed, closed up her backpack, and stood up straight. Finally, she looked him squarely in the eye. "If this is going to work," she stated, "I need you to follow my orders."

"I know," he met her gaze. "That's why I came over here. I…I'm sorry, Sira."

She crossed her arms and waited patiently for him to go on. He felt his cheeks redden. "Not just for going off on my own, but for what I said afterwards."

Again she said nothing and simply stared at him. He wanted her to say something, anything, but he also knew she was still mad at him, and disappointed.

"I am, really. I shouldn't have said it. I remember what you and the others did and said after the Battle of Archanon. You swore an oath to help me bear this burden," he almost absently reached for the Sword, strapped to his back underneath his backpack. "And I insulted that oath."

"No," she shook her head. "You insulted me. And Reis and Dalin. We're your friends, we've been here for you through all of this, and then you go off and try to pretend you're alone in this fight?"

"I was wrong, I know…"

"Yes you were," she raised her voice and threw her arms out for emphasis. "You fell back on your old ways again!" Then she seemed to catch herself and stopped her lecture. She let her arms fall to her sides and sighed. "And once again, I'm not helping things."

He couldn't help but grin. "It's ok. I deserve it."

She rolled her eyes. "No doubt. But I've already given you this lecture."

There was a long moment of silence between them, and they didn't look directly at each other. Finally, however, she looked him eye to eye. "What has you so damn scared?"

It was a frank question, and the nightmare flashed through his mind again. They'd spent many nights sleeping side by side in the field, and she was aware of the fact that he'd been having nightmares recently, but beyond that, he told her nothing. He still felt afraid to. Still worried that if he told anyone about it, it would make it real somehow. It was nonsense, he knew that, but he didn't feel ready to say anything just yet.

However, he wasn't about to lie to her either. So he gave her some of the truth. "I'm afraid, Sira. You heard what that dragon, Endri, said. Something about a prophecy being at hand and he needed to gather the other dragons. I feel it, Sira. Something is coming, something dark. And I'm going to be in the middle of it all. I don't think we've yet realized how much of a burden this Sword is going to be…"

She came forward and took hold of both of his hands. They both wore gloves due to the cold of the winter, but even still, the gesture made him feel warm. "I know that, Cardin. I knew that when I swore that oath." He felt surprised, but knew he shouldn't have. "Look at how much our world has already changed. Much of it for the better, but how many lives had to be lost, how much suffering was there involved in those changes? And we were lucky. It should have been worse, a lot worse."

Cardin nodded. If Sal'fe hadn't used the Staff of Aliz to revive as many fallen Warriors, soldiers, and Wizards as he possibly could, their casualties would have ranged in hundreds, perhaps thousands. Never the less, those who had been resurrected by Sal'fe after the battle of the Great Road still remembered how they had died. It disturbed many of them, and there was still a lot of bad blood between Falind and Tal Warriors because of it.

She raised their hands up and clutched his tightly. "We're here for you, Cardin. I am here for you. Stop fighting that."

He smiled, and felt the warmth grow within him. They stared into each other's eyes for what felt like a long time, before he finally moved forward and clutched her in a tight hug. Neither spoke.

She tightened her hug for a moment before they separated. She smiled, and he smiled back. Raising an eyebrow, she said, "Let's go have an adventure together, eh?"

With that, Sira picked up her backpack and swung it over her shoulders. They walked over to the rest of the group, who stared at them, no longer trying to be inconspicuous. He noticed Elaria wore a long face, but Reis and Dalin both had broad smiles.

"About time you two made up," Reis chuckled.

"Indeed," Dalin nodded. "Otherwise this would have been an extraordinarily awkward trip."

Reis looked at Dalin, "I told you Cardin would buckle first."

"Hey!" he frowned at his friend. "I didn't buckle."

Dalin looked at Sira, "Who made the first move?"

She smiled at him, "He was smart enough to come to me and apologize."

"Exactly as I knew he would," Reis said. "You buckled!"

"Reis," he warned through red cheeks.

"Everyone ready?" Sira asked. They all nodded, but then she frowned and looked around. "Where's Anila?"

"I've been here for some time," her voice came from behind Cardin. They all turned and saw her approach. She hadn't made a single noise, and somehow they hadn't seen her. Cardin wondered how she did that, and wondered at how she still had no presence that he could feel. The Covenant confirmed that she had no powers, she was not a Mage, but he still should have felt *something*.

Anila said nothing else and simply stood by them, silent and patient. Sira nodded. "Alright. Dalin, if you would, please."

The young Wizard nodded and separated from the group. As he did so, Cardin felt an intense surge of power gather within Dalin, and then it channeled into his staff. A moment later, he planted his staff firmly in the ground, and there was a loud bang.

The energy leapt out of Dalin's staff and gathered in an intense storm of magic. Cardin paid extra careful attention to the formation of the portal, hoping someday soon he could learn to create his own. A wind stirred up around them as opposing powers created a maelstrom, and the point of energy suddenly expanded into a shaft of blue-white light.

The portal stabilized, although tendrils of tiny lightning bolts occasionally lashed out harmlessly. Everyone looked at each other, and then Sira led the way, with Cardin behind her. She disappeared through the shaft of light, and a moment later he followed.

It was considerably warmer on the coast of Maradin, but not hot like the Wastelands. To Cardin, it felt like a breath of fresh air.

Their arrival had been pre-arranged, and they'd been asked to appear outside of the north-western gate to the city. As Cardin stepped through to the other side and moved out of the way to allow the others to follow him, he noted that there was a large honor guard present, with Queen Leian in front.

As the others emerged through the portal, Cardin took in the sights. The sun was barely rising above the city wall before them, and although not as tall as Archanon's wall, it was still an impressive sight to behold. Beyond its obvious size, it wasn't made out of stone or the kind of gray brick used in Tal, but instead was made of pale, sand-colored bricks. It still had turrets, but none of its architecture appeared rounded, and instead everything appeared squared off.

They stood upon a stone road, but the stone was more like sandstone or flagstone, and it was a very wide avenue. He'd heard of that road, and knew that it split off in two directions not far outside of the city. One path led north along the coast until it passed the northern reaches of the desert, where it turned west and led to the city of Salas. The other direction led to the Great Road, the ancient passage between the Desert of Ca'aluun and the Wastelands, leading all the way to the western coast of Falind.

Dalin was the last to step through and the portal closed behind him. Once that happened, the Queen stepped closer to them with a broad but fake smile and opened her arms. "Welcome to Maradin."

The city gate behind her was already open, and through it came a slight breeze and a scent he had never smelled before - sea water. Ocean. He had never seen an ocean before, never been to any of the port cities. The sight itself was said to be impressive, but he was already intrigued by the smell of the sea. All of this was new to him, and he loved every second of it!

Sira, as leader of the expedition, stepped forward and bowed before the Queen. Cardin and the others followed suit. "Thank you, Queen Leian."

Leian looked at Cardin specifically and smiled. "It is truly an honor to welcome the Keeper of the Sword to my kingdom and our great city."

At this, Cardin felt uncomfortable, and he shifted on his feet nervously. "The honor is mine." Although Leian had started with a fake smile, when he said that, her smile became genuine.

The Queen turned to her left and motioned to another woman who wore courtly robes. "This is the governor of our great city, Onaia Fendis." The woman was elderly, her hair silver and her skin wrinkled, but she had sharp blue eyes and there was intelligence and strength behind those eyes. Onaia half-bowed to them in greeting.

Leian then turned to her right and nodded to a man Cardin recognized as the General of the Erien Warriors. "I believe many of you have met General Zilan." Although General Artula was in command of the Allied Forces that continued to fight the orcs in the Wastelands, General Zilan had often participated in those efforts as part of the joint task force. His impression was that Zilan was intelligent, but he seemed to be too politically motivated for a military man, and Cardin found that trait to be potentially dangerous, not to mention annoying.

The Queen then nodded to Dalin, "I am afraid my Court Wizard is away on other business and will be unable to join us tonight." Dalin nodded, but didn't seem particularly disappointed.

With introductions made, Leian once again opened her arms wide, "Please join me, I would be pleased to accompany you on a tour of our city."

Sira and Cardin exchanged excited glances, and she nodded to the Queen eagerly, "That would be fantastic!"

The Queen nodded, and motioned to some of her guard, "Please take their packs for them." To Sira she said, "They will be taken to your quarters within the palace."

Cardin felt a little uncomfortable letting his belongings out of sight, but there was nothing in his pack that was irreplaceable. They most likely wouldn't need any of the supplies they had brought with them, but as Warriors they had always been taught to prepare for the unexpected, and they didn't know what they would find once they reached Port Hope.

If Sira had any similar reservations, she did not show it, and willingly took her pack off and offered it to one of the guards. Cardin did likewise, as did the others. The only one who didn't was Elaria, who insisted she was fine. His first instinct was that she had something hidden in her pack, but then he dismissed the notion and realized that she simply didn't trust humans in general, and perhaps with good reason.

With that, they were led into city, and Cardin was once again astonished by how different it was from any other city he had visited. It was an old city, not as old as Archanon but it had been untouched by most wars, so some of the buildings were ancient. There was a mixture of architecture. Some of it matched that of the wall, made of the same sand-colored brick and of the same squared architecture. However, there were several buildings made of other materials, predominantly white colored, with rounded spires that towered into the sky. He now understood why it had become known as the White City.

That wasn't even what impressed him most. At the north-west corner of the city, they were at the highest point of the hill that the city was built upon, and as they came to where the road, and indeed the entire city sloped downward, he had his first view of the ocean.

It was one of the most impressive sights he had ever seen. He could see the docks, which spread through much of the city's coastline, and several ships of varying sizes moored to the docks. Further out into the ocean was a larger ship, one which he knew to be the flagship of the Erien fleet. It had several masts and even from this distance looked impressive.

Beyond the ship, the dark blue ocean stretched on forever. The sunlight seemed to sparkle off of it, dancing like the fall leaves danced in the wind. It was absolutely beautiful, and he felt his breath catch for a moment. Even in winter, the heat of the Maradin sun made him sweat, but the breeze from the ocean was a welcome relief.

Cardin noted that the city's walls did not end at the edge of the water and stretched far out into the ocean. Where the walls did finally end, breakers formed a partial fourth wall to help keep larger waves from entering the city's bay, but the flagship was well beyond those breakers, much too large to enter into that bay. Personnel and supplies were probably ferried by dinghies.

The city itself was larger than he expected, extremely impressive and even daunting. His view of it from this, the highest point of land, was amazing. He looked to the south and saw that the Palace stood higher than the walls, an impressive sight and clearly a newer structure, made of the white rather than yellowish brick. One of the former Kings centuries ago had ordered the old Palace dismantled and the new structure built in its place.

Cardin looked to Sira and Reis, both of whom held their eyes wide open in wonder, and he suspected they looked very much like he did at that moment. They noticed his gaze and returned it. Both smiled, and he realized how glad he was to share a new adventure with them.

When he looked at Dalin, however, he found the Wizard to be

less than impressed by the sight. Dalin looked at Cardin quizzically, but then he looked bemused. "I have visited Maradin once before."

"Have you now?" Queen Leian asked.

"Indeed," he nodded to her. "Although it was not an official visit. It was shortly after my apprenticeship ended in the Guild. I began to explore many places on Halarite. I was always curious about that which had been our home long before I was born." Dalin took in a big breath of air, and his face softened into a smile. "I loved the smell of the sea then, as I do now."

After they had all taken in the view, the Queen led them down one of the main avenues towards the docks. It was an easy walk, the slope relatively gentle. The street was extremely busy with merchants and customers, but there was plenty of room, and everyone parted in respect as the Queen passed.

As they drew close to the ocean, a new scent reached him, not nearly as pleasant. "What is that smell?" Reis asked.

"That is fresh fish," the Queen smiled. "It may not be the most pleasing scent, but it smells considerably better when cooked and tastes magnificent when prepared properly. Not to mention shrimp, muscles, and so many other kinds of sea food. You shall all enjoy everything we have to offer."

Cardin knew that fish was a plentiful food source on the coast, and he'd eaten plenty of fresh river fish before, but never had he seen, or smelled, so much before. He also was in awe at just how large some of the ocean-caught fish were, some looked bigger than humans!

"Fish is our most common food source," Ventelis told them. As they began to pass by some of the vendors who sold fresh fish, he frowned. "Although our fish definitely looks different from yours, it is much more colorful."

"What about your land-locked cities?" Sira asked.

"We have no land-locked cities," Elaria replied. "In fact, none of our cities are on land."

Everyone, including the Queen, looked at Elaria with surprise. "What do you mean?" Reis asked her.

"We are a people of the water," she said. "In fact that is the meaning behind our name, Dareann Elves. All of our cities float upon lakes, and a few out in the calmer seas of our world."

"You must tell us more," the Queen said in awe, "But perhaps not now. Many of my court would greatly enjoy hearing about you and your floating cities." She stopped them as they came upon the docks and smiled back at them. "In fact I would like you all to attend a royal banquet and ball tonight! Our banquet hall is quite impressive, our cooks the finest, our musicians the most skilled. This event shall be in honor of hosting the Keeper of the Sword!"

Cardin felt his cheeks turn red, or redder than they felt in the warm sunlight. "Um, thank you, Queen Leian."

"We would be honored," Sira said, but hesitated. "However, we did not bring appropriate attire for such a formal event."

"Oh do not worry about that," the Queen beamed. "Once our tour is complete, you shall all be fitted by our finest tailors for tonight's festivities."

Cardin grimaced. He didn't know what they had in mind, but he felt certain he wasn't going to like whatever they wanted to dress him up in. He noticed that Sira tried to hide a grimace as well, but she put on a brave face. "Thank you…"

The tour continued along for about half of the length of the docks. At one point, the Queen pointed to a smaller ship, with several workers busy loading cargo onto it and crew members making hasty preparations. "That will be the ship that will take you to Port Hope," she stated. "It is the fastest ship we have, the Sea Wisp."

The tour reached another major artery in the city, which they turned up. After several miles of touring crowded streets, they eventually arrived at the palace. As he expected, it was surrounded by its own, smaller wall, made of the same white brick as the complex itself. Up close, it was even more impressive, and the spires towered high above them.

As they passed through the golden doors into the courtyard, he noted that the main building was obviously built in a time of peace for Erien. Defense had not been strongly considered. Archanon's castle had no direct path from the main entrance to the throne room to ensure that if anyone ever breached the castle's main entrance, there was plenty of opportunity for them to be stopped en route to the throne.

In Maradin's Palace, however, the main entrance led directly into the throne room itself, which was absolutely grand and opulent. Its walls stretched high to a domed ceiling with several skylights in it. At the far back was the Queen's throne with another, smaller throne next to it, where her long-dead husband once sat beside her.

They came to a halt within the throne room, and the Queen took her leave of them. Several servants rushed forward, and they were all taken to their own quarters. When Cardin entered his, several floors up, he was certain there had been a mistake, for his quarters were almost as large as Archanon's throne room, ridiculously large, wasteful even.

Inside, a tailor waited for him next to a mirror and a stool. Several ready-made coats, shirts, and pants hung in a large, moveable wardrobe. The tailor, a well-fed man with short brown hair and clothes that made Archanon's governor look like a peasant, smiled at Cardin.

"Ah yes," he said, his voice soft and cool. "This will be an interesting challenge."

Cardin grimaced at first, but then he took some comfort in the knowledge that the rest of his friends were about to go through the exact same thing.

Chapter 11

LOST

A cool breeze passed across Kailar's face and raised bumps on her skin. She closed her eyes and allowed herself to enjoy the moment. It was the dead of winter in Tal, so she found Edingard's warmth this time of year unexpected and quite enjoyable. At a time when she was normally cold and had to seek any source of heat that she could, she found the cool breeze a welcome reprieve in the hot afternoon air.

She'd only slept for a couple of hours at the inn, but it had been enough to rejuvenate her. When she had walked out into the rest of the inn, the windows had been left open to allow the mountain breeze in, which served to draw her out into the open air. She always loved hiking through the Ilari Mountains, so being this close to the Barrier Mountains brought back many pleasant memories, a respite at a time in her life when she needed it the most.

After only an hour of loafing around in the shadows of the inn, she couldn't stand it anymore and decided to go for a walk. She knew it was a risk, knew that someone might recognize her in town, but she couldn't stand sitting indoors any longer.

So she had spent the entire afternoon exploring the town. She thought of it as a sort of game to entertain herself, she stuck to the shadows or the crowds, made sure she slipped in between notice, avoided anything more than a cursory glance from anyone, and even tried to avoid that.

It was something she was quite skilled in doing, she had practiced a lot over the years. However, she used to rely heavily on magic to give her a greater awareness of her surroundings. Now that she no longer had that connection, she had lost an edge, lost the ability to follow an otherwise unrivaled instinct.

As far as she could tell, she succeeded in avoiding garnering any significant attention. No one gave her double-takes like the miner had earlier that day, no one recognized her, no one met her eyes. It wasn't a large town by any means, but the people present were so accustomed to strangers passing through that she probably seemed like just another explorer, no one worth paying attention to.

That gave her the ability to observe the town, to get a sense of it and its people. It was a relatively new town, only a few decades old, but it had grown very quickly in that time. There was a definite schism between those who had been there for decades and the newcomers who had moved in to make a better life for themselves. The oldest part of town wasn't in the center, but was closest to the mountain, and the town had spread out away from the mountains. A river passed through it, and it seemed like the single bridge, a stone and mortared construct, was brand new.

She began to wonder if Letan chose to stay at Orin's Inn because he had deep roots in the community that had formed on Devor. She found the large inn at the western part of town, so that suggested it was owned and operated by someone who had lived in town for a long time.

The town's Warriors' Guild complex was, well, not a complex. It was a two-story building near Orin's Inn, but there were no banners that hung from it to indicate to which kingdom it held loyalty to. She first suspected it was the Guild's building when she noticed who entered and left it. Warriors were well trained soldiers, and they often had a way about them, how they walked, how they regarded others. She could tell that those in and around the building, even though most of them wore plain clothes, were definitely Warriors.

They would regard anyone, newcomers or not, with a keen eye, so she made especially sure to avoid being seen by them. They didn't seem to have a particularly strong presence in the town, so that helped her relax some.

Orin's Inn aside, most of the buildings nearest the mountains were smaller, a sign that they had been built when the town was new and gathering building resources was a chore that could not be shared by many. As the town had grown eastward, the buildings had grown in size. Newer inns seemed more popular with people she realized were the explorers she had heard about, and she was surprised at how many there seemed to be. There were several inns near the center of town, as well as general goods shops, trinkets, hunters' supplies shops, everything an explorer would need to survive in the wilderness was available in the center and eastern half of town.

Very early in the afternoon, the sun dipped behind the towering Barrier Mountains, and the temperature began to drop quicker than she expected in summer time, but it was a welcome break from the heat. She realized it was probably less than pleasant in the winter time.

By the time she had thoroughly explored Edingard, it was evening, and her stomach growled at her. The various inns had already been hard at work cooking the evening meals, and the various smells of food assaulted her and made her mouth water. She knew she should have returned to the Black Horse Inn, but she didn't want to wait that long, so she selected one of the larger inns near the center and entered.

As she had hoped, it was crowded and noisy, the perfect place to enjoy a meal in relative anonymity. Kailar worked her way to a table near the back and sat down. She took a moment to look around and get a sense of the place. Most of the visitors were groups of explorers who took up a handful of tables each, and each of the groups stuck to their own and didn't interact much with the other groups, but amongst themselves they were boisterous and obviously enjoyed the local ale.

It was quite different from the inns and taverns she had visited in Tal, where most of their patrons were regulars, so no one was shy about sitting down at just about any table and striking up conversations with anyone. They were often even noisier, with more activity, but harder to hide in for someone who wasn't a regular patron.

Eventually a bar maiden came by and told Kailar what was available for dinner that night. She decided to take advantage of the nearby farmland and asked for a selection of vegetables and fruits, along with a small bowl of stew.

He didn't show up until she was more than halfway through with her meal. Another group of people entered, but they were not explorers, or so she surmised when the bar maiden recognized them and greeted some of them by name. They were regulars, and amongst them was the miner she had bumped into that morning.

Kailar tensed when she spotted him, but she immediately averted her eyes and merely watched him out of the corner of her eye. His focus was on his friends, and they made their way over to the only unoccupied table in the room.

However, as they sat down, he looked her way. He didn't seem to react to her, nor did his gaze linger, but even in her peripheral she saw that he had looked directly at her.

She wasn't the only person alone in the inn, but there were few enough others that it was no wonder he looked her way.

It was possible he didn't recognized her, and his reaction that morning could have been for any number of reasons. She had merely assumed that he'd recognized her as Kailar, wanted by Falind, responsible for the deaths of hundreds in Falind and Tal.

What frustrated her even more was that she couldn't feel anything, she had no instinct beyond natural senses. Was he a Mage? Had he honed in on her, focused on her without her knowing it? Was he a threat to her in any way?

After several minutes, she decided she couldn't risk it. So she placed some of her precious few coins on the table to pay for her meal and quietly slipped out of the inn. Once outside, she headed for the nearest south-bound road. No doubt her quick pace caught the attention of some, but she needed to get away from there as quickly as possible.

She hadn't even completely crossed the road when she heard the inn's door open and close behind her. Part of her was tempted to look back and see if it was as she feared, but she dared not make herself look too suspicious, so she kept her quick pace.

Even without magic, she knew she was being followed. She could hear the noise of a quickened pace behind her, someone walking along the streets in the same hurry she was in. Her heart raced and she wanted to start running, but she had already drawn far too much attention to herself. If a curious Warrior noticed her walking at that speed with someone behind her, they might grow curious and investigate.

If the miner did indeed follow her, if he had recognized her, she realized she couldn't lead him back to the Black Horse Inn. Furthermore, she needed to find out if he really was a threat. So she turned west suddenly and began to look for somewhere she could confront him unobserved. It was growing darker, and the streets were fairly empty since everyone was inside somewhere, enjoying their dinner.

The only thing she could think of was to duck in between buildings, and hope that no one walked by while she confronted him. She found a narrow gap between two single-story buildings, walked about halfway towards the back, and then turned to face him.

He came careening around the corner, but then stopped when he saw her. A small grin crossed his face, and she could tell he thought he had her trapped. "Decided to stop running," he said as he entered the gap. "Good. I have a proposal for you."

"Who are you?" she asked.

He shrugged. "It doesn't really matter, now, does it? What matters is who *you* are."

She tensed. He knew. "Who do you think I am?"

A short, confident laugh escaped him. "I've only just started working here," he replied. "I came from Falind, and I was there when you assassinated our King. You are Kailar."

She shook her head. "You're mistaken. My name is Fiera."

"You're Kailar Adanna," his face hardened into a frown. She realized it had been a long time since she'd heard her last name spoken, and it sounded strange to her. "And there are a lot of bounties for you. With good reason."

Her hand automatically moved towards where she kept her dagger, and he noticed that. "Easy, now," he cautioned, his hands went up defensively. "I'm not armed."

She rested her hand on the dagger, but didn't draw. She realized that if he wanted to turn her in, he would have done so by now. "Then what do you want?"

"It's real simple," he looked down, almost ashamed to say what he was about to say. "I'm a poor man, working off the debt from my passage here. Give me what I need to pay off my debt," he shrugged, "and I won't tell the Guild you're here."

At that, she frowned. "That's it? Passage here doesn't cost that much." She knew that from her own sea voyage. There were so many ships going between Devor and Edilas, all of them full of valuable trade cargo or needed supplies, that shipping people for cheap simply made sense. Their payment was for the food and water they would consume during the trips as well as extra to give the ships' crews a little more income. Relatively speaking, it was inexpensive.

"For you, maybe," he frowned. "Not for someone like me."

Someone like him. She realized he was desperate, he wanted out from under whatever debt he was in. He wanted freedom. But something didn't track right with his story.

"If you're so poor, how do you afford eating at the inn?"

"I don't," he shook his head. "The innkeeper is the one I am indentured to. Everyone you saw walk in with me, my friends, we all are under his thumb."

So that was it, servitude. They were out of luck, poor farmers or miners from Edilas. Somehow the innkeeper had contacts in the four kingdoms, others who would send people his way. He would pay for their passage and more, and probably told them they owed him more than they actually did, which effectively made them his slaves. They lived off of what he gave them, which meant he probably took almost all of the money they earned from working the mines or doing any other job, no doubt claiming it was payment for what he continued to give them. That meant it would take them years to work off their 'debt.'

It was illegal in Tal and Erien, but there were no laws one way or the other governing it in the other kingdoms, let alone the colonies on the new continents.

Rumors had abounded in the kingdoms that there were a lot of under-the-table deals and a general immoral attitude amongst many on the new continents, including crime rings unchecked by the Warriors' Guild.

This poor soul was one of probably hundreds in such situations. He was desperate, he wanted out from under his master, so that he could truly start a new life. She felt for him, but only so much. He was also a threat.

Furthermore, she had no way of knowing if he would turn her in after she paid him, if only to collect more money from the bounty. She didn't know how much would be rewarded for turning her in, but it was probably more money than he had ever seen.

She couldn't take that risk. But she didn't want to chase him down in the streets, either. So she felt she had only one real option. "Very well," she nodded. "How much?"

"I still owe four gold and three silver."

That was almost as much as she'd paid for her own passage. She wondered just how long he had been on Devor. It was also far more than she had remaining.

"I don't keep that much money on me," she said. "I have it stashed in my room at the Black Horse Inn," she pointed over his shoulder. "Edge of town."

He looked over his shoulder, and then looked at her, clearly hesitant. He didn't trust her, and she thought to herself that it was an admirable trait. However, his own desperation was his undoing, and he nodded. "Right. We'll go back there, you give me the money, and you never see or hear from me again."

"Deal," she nodded, and took her hand off of her dagger. She stepped towards him and motioned for him to precede her out.

The miner turned and began to walk towards the street, and that was when she made her move. Quickly and as silently as she could, she stepped up behind him, drew her dagger, reached around in front of him, and sliced his throat.

He tried to call out in surprise, but all he could manage was a gargling sound. Blood poured from his mouth, his hands clenched around his neck to try to stem off the flow. He turned to face her, only to fall to his knees, his arms falling limply at his side. A moment later, he fell over, and she knew he was moments from death.

She looked out towards the street and was thankful that no one walked by. Looking towards the backyard, she was equally relieved that no one had snuck up behind her. No one had witnessed her actions.

Wiping the blood from her dagger on an unstained sleeve of his shirt, she then sheathed it and began to drag him away from the street. There was no telling what was behind the buildings, but she hoped there would be somewhere she could hide him.

For once, she got what she wished for, and there was a stable with a couple of horses and a large pile of hay. It wouldn't conceal his body for long, but it would be long enough, she hoped, for her to get out of town.

When his heart stopped, the blood stopped flowing from his neck, but there was still a lot of it, and it wouldn't do her any good to have blood-stained hay visible, so she pulled him next to it, found the nearest pitchfork and used it to essentially move the pile over on top of the body. She worked as fast as she could, but her arms screamed in pain from her previous wounds, and when she was finished, she was ready to scream in agony.

She put the pitchfork back where she'd found it, looked around to make sure no one had seen her, and then ducked back in between the buildings, where she took a moment to catch her breath and let the pain in her arms fade.

Several minutes passed, and she noted that it was growing darker. It wouldn't be long before people would start to come out of the inns and taverns, and she needed to be far away from the body when that happened.

However, when she started towards the street, she looked down and saw the pool of blood, and she stopped cold. For the first time, she realized just how horrifying her actions were.

There had been plenty of times when she had killed men and women in battle. She had sent orcs to kill even more. Six months ago, she had used her powers to force the Falind King's trusted guards to murder him. Taking a life was nothing new to her.

This time it felt different. And she wasn't exactly sure why. It scared her, and she thought of Letan, and what he would think if he found out.

The turning in her stomach made her feel sick, and the horror within her grew stronger. She didn't know what was wrong, so she hopped over the blood and quickly walked out into the open street. The area was still relatively empty, so she set a brisk pace and headed south towards the inn and the safety of her room.

Her anxiety grew rapidly, and she felt a panic set in. Before she knew it, she was running. She passed by a few people who stared at her, but she didn't care, she had to get out of the open, she had to get somewhere safe, somewhere that she could be alone.

Finally she reached the inn, and she burst inside. There were two patrons finishing their meals, and they gawked at her in bewilderment. Ira came from the back in a rush.

"What's wrong, deary?" she asked, genuine concern in her voice. Kailar could only imagine what her own face looked like.

She ignored the old woman and rushed to her room's door. She fumbled with the key, and it took several tries before she finally got it to unlock. She rushed in, slammed the door shut, locked it, and suddenly felt very much alone in the dark, which was what she had wanted until that very moment.

She dropped the key on the floor and took several steps inside. The panic settled a little, but the anxiety grew.

What would Letan think if he found out? She had just committed a murder, out of fear of being discovered. Letan wouldn't understand. She wasn't sure she understood. Everything she had done before she'd lost her powers was towards one goal, the goal of some day making a better future for the four kingdoms, for everyone. She had done everything for a greater purpose.

Today, she had taken a life for a completely selfish reason. She had killed a man out of pure and simple fear. Out of a desire to ensure someone she barely knew didn't find out who she really was or what she had done.

It didn't make sense. What had she accomplished? *Nothing,* she thought to herself. *I've taken a life for nothing. What have I become? Oh gods, what have I become?*

She collapsed to her knees, shaking. "What have I become," she said aloud.

Letan had said she was a good person, that he could see it in her eyes. She wasn't. She had gone too far. Tears welled in her eyes, blurred her vision. She rolled onto her side, and the feeling of guilt, of fear, of uselessness, everything she'd felt over the last six months suddenly came streaming out, she couldn't control it anymore.

Tears came faster and harder, and she began to sob. She tried to keep quiet, but that was impossible. She wanted to scream, she wanted to burst open, she wanted to punch something, anything, as hard as she could, over and over and over again until her hands bled.

But all she could do was lie on the floor, crying, and she kept thinking to herself, whispering to herself, sobbing to herself, "What have I become? What have I become?"

She had lost her way, she had lost herself.

She was lost.

Chapter 12

BANQUET OF THE SEA

When Cardin was still just a trainee, he had attended a couple of formal functions in uniform for the Warriors' Guild, including once hosting the General of the Tal Warriors. Mostly Warriors wore ceremonial armor during such times, but for trainees, they were forced to wear cloth uniforms, not having yet earned the right to wear ceremonial armor.

He felt as ridiculous now as he had then. When he wasn't in leather or metal armor, he wore simple tunics and trousers, perhaps a cloak, but that was it. Now he wore what was considered formal wear amongst the four kingdoms – a long sleeve silk white shirt underneath a burgundy tunic with black trim, the trim having been sewn on by a fast and skilled seamstress at the request of the tailor. The burgundy was meant to match the Sword, which he still wore over his clothes. The materials of the tunic and shirt were the finest he had ever worn, and from the moment he had put them on, he'd been afraid he was going to tear or stain them somehow.

Likewise the pants he wore were black silk, and the boots were of the finest black leather he had ever worn. All of these clothes fit rather close to his skin with little extra room, as was the current trend in Erien. The tailor had told him it was to show off his physical form. He had noticed that the nobles of Erien were, in general, very fit, and they liked to show that off. He was surprised he wore a tunic over his shirt, as that partly concealed his physique.

He hadn't seen any of his friends since they were separated that morning, and he hadn't been allowed to eat either, as the tailor was on a mission to ensure that Cardin was ready on time. As he walked through the corridors up on the fourth floor in the East Wing of the palace, his stomach growled. Whatever uncomfortable situations he would find himself in tonight, he was looking forward to the banquet.

The ball, however, not so much. Dancing. It was his bane when he was a trainee, and it had taken considerable effort for him to learn formal dancing. More than ten years had passed since he last used those skills. He hoped he could remember enough.

The king that had commissioned the construction of the new palace had not been shy about making it opulent and impressive, meant no doubt to impress any who walked its impressive corridors, including, or perhaps especially, other royalty. The corridor he walked through had white marble floors with white stone and gold inlaid patterns, truly a sight he had never imagined. The walls were high, the ceiling arched, and he felt like a giant could walk through it.

Nothing, however, prepared him for the banquet hall. The ceilings in the corridor were short compared to how high the ceiling stretched in the hall. In a way it reminded him of the throne room he had seen earlier, and perhaps that had been intentional when it was built, except for one thing. The entrance he came through was on one side, and he could see on the other side several more entrances, but to his right was a massive open balcony that looked east, towards the ocean.

From his vantage he couldn't see the endless sea, but even from within the well-lit banquet hall, he could see stars.

Tables were set up on the opposite end from the grand balcony. The head table was the only one that was parallel to the back wall, and it was exceptionally large with opulent chairs on one side only, so that the royalty and their guests had an unobstructed view of the dance floor. The other tables bracketed the dance floor and were parallel to the side walls, six total, three on either side, with less comfortable, but still cushioned chairs on all sides. In keeping with the white or sand-colored architecture, the tables were made of a pale stone, and the chairs a tan wood with fine-material cushions of blue, to help keep the theme of the country's colors.

In fact, there were Erien banners hanging from every pillar or wall in the hall. Cardin assumed this was normal for any functions in the banquet hall, but he couldn't help but wonder if it was intentional tonight, as a way of impressing upon the Tal natives that they were in foreign territory.

The Queen already sat at the middle of the royal table. Directly to her left sat Governor Fendis, and further left from her sat General Zilan. The General wore Guild ceremonial leather armor, adorned with a sash that bore several medals. The Governor wore a simple emerald gown with long sleeves. The Queen, as Cardin had expected, wore an extravagant navy blue dress with white trim. Her dress had sleeves, but they were detached from the rest of the dress; they started below the shoulder and ended at her wrists. If there was an actual term for such sleeves, he didn't know it.

He had seen the Queen many times during Council sessions, but never before had he considered her pretty until now. Her hair was up in a complex hair style, which he was sure had a name but he didn't know what, and that allowed her to show off her long neck, her small pearl-studded earrings, and her smooth, tanned bust.

In a way, seeing her in such an attractive fashion made him uncomfortable. She was royalty and a politician at heart, and he didn't want to see her as anything other than that. So he looked away across the hall to one of the other entrances, where he saw Reis enter.

At the sight of his friend, Cardin couldn't help but grin. Reis also wore a silk white shirt, but his copper tunic was left open rather than buttoned up, a move his tailor probably had objected to, but one which made Reis look much more comfortable than Cardin felt. He wore brown trousers and leather boots, but what truly made Cardin smile was the copper-colored velvet flat cap Reis wore. The cap was titled to Reis's left, no doubt on purpose, and it gave him a somewhat comical and barely formal appearance. Cardin also noted that a shield with the colors and logo of Tal had been embroidered onto the vest's left breast. Given all of the Erien banners, he was glad someone represented their home kingdom, and Cardin wished he had likewise asked his tailor put something like that on his tunic.

He also noted that Reis wore his sheathed sword on his hip, but instead of his left hip, as was usual for a right-handed person, he wore it on his right hip. Cardin recalled that such an act was symbolic and ceremonial, but he didn't remember why.

Reis saw Cardin's face, and shot a wry smirk back across at him. Then Reis's face slackened into one of awe as he looked behind Cardin. He turned to see what had shocked his friend and discovered that Elaria had come up behind him.

He had always found the elf to be attractive, but now even the word beautiful scarcely described her. She'd kept her sunset-red hair pulled back in mirrored braids, as she often did, but she had allowed locks of hair on either side of her temples to hang down, which accented her ears.

Elaria's dress was stunning, and his respect for tailors suddenly grew ten-fold. She wore a mostly violet silk dress with satin, lilac-colored highlights and full sleeves. While the sleeves ended at her wrists, from there they hung down and tapered to points at her knees.

When the sight of her was taken in whole, the dress, her eyes, her hair, it gave the illusion that he saw a living sunset, and for a moment it stole his breath. She smiled at him, which brightened her face even more, until she stepped up next to him.

Cardin hadn't even noticed that Ventelis accompanied her, and he startled Cardin when he spoke, "I must confess, your society's sense of style is intriguing."

When he did finally look at Ventelis, he noted that the silver-haired elf wore a dark-gray tunic with silver trim and like-colored pants. He also wore a medium-brimmed gray hat with a white feather on its right side. He looked rather bold in his clothes, and Cardin once again was surprised and impressed by the tailors of Erien.

"Yes," Elaria agreed with Ventelis as she looked Cardin up and down. "You look rather handsome."

He felt his face grow warm at her compliment, and all he could think to do was give a half-bow and thank her. He then turned away from her, to hide his embarrassment, and noticed Dalin had joined Reis across the hall. Dalin, much to Cardin's amusement, still wore his Wizard's robe and still held his Wizard's staff. He'd have loved to have been a fly on the wall when Dalin flatly refused the help of the tailor.

Several servants had joined them, one for each of the new arrivals, and began to usher them to their seats. A steward made the announcements as they were led down the middle of the empty dance floor towards the head table. "Cardin Kataar, Keeper of the Sword. Reis Kalind, honored Warrior of Tal. Elaria of the Dareann Elves." Several of the nobles and other guests at the side tables started to whisper to each other when Elaria was announced, and the whispers continued when the steward finished, "Ventelis of the Dareann Elves."

It was an aspect of society Cardin found troubling. Even after six months people still had trouble accepting the existence of elves and other intelligent species. No doubt Ventelis and Elaria would garner stares throughout the entire night. Hopefully everyone would behave themselves and no one would attack them.

They came before the head table and stood before the Queen. She stood up, curtsied to them, and motioned for them to join her. The servant that had ushered Cardin took him ahead of the others, and apparently had been ordered to ensure that he sat next to the Queen.

"Rather dashing, Keeper," she smiled to him while he was being seated. Reis sat to his right, followed by Elaria. An empty chair was left next to Elaria, he guessed for Sira. To the left of the General sat Dalin and then Ventelis. Cardin wondered if the elves had been intentionally split up.

"Thank you, my Lady," Cardin smiled to her, and forced himself not to look down at her bust. He also overheard Reis compliment Elaria.

When he looked back to where Reis had entered from, he once more felt his breath stolen from him. For the first time that night, he saw Sira in her gown, and he couldn't take his eyes off of her. She had let her blonde hair down, the first time he'd seen her do that in forever. Her hair somehow had what looked like natural waves to it, and even from here he saw her sharp blue eyes find him.

Her dress was beyond beautiful. It was a sleeveless white and red dress, the white clearly silk, much like his shirt, but he guessed the red was a velvet material. The red formed the core of her dress, from just under her bust down to her waist, where it continued down but tapered to ends in quarters, which allowed the white gown underneath to flow out between the red, while the top of her dress was also white silk. Her gown was complimented by a red stole draped over her shoulders.

When he met her eyes again, she smiled at him, and his heart lit up. She had smiled *at him*. And somehow that made him feel like the most important person in the room, greater than the Queen, than anyone. A boyish grin crossed his face, and he couldn't take his eyes off of her.

The Steward announced, "Sira Reinar, honored Warrior of Tal." As Sira was seated, Cardin suddenly felt annoyed that a seat hadn't been saved next to him for her, and he was half-tempted to tell Reis to get up and let her sit there, but he decided against it a moment later. There would be time later in the night to spend with her, and perhaps dance with her.

When Sira sat, he finally turned his attention back to the situation as a whole. The Queen motioned to her Steward, who stepped out of sight down another corridor. Moments later, several servants streamed out with covered tray after covered tray. That was also the first time Cardin noticed in front of him a large glass plate with several forks, a spoon, and a couple of knives of varying shapes and sizes on either side of the plate. He had absolutely no idea what possible purpose there could be for more than one of each utensil, and for a moment he felt embarrassed about his ignorance.

The embarrassment vanished when trays were laid out on the tables before them and their lids taken off. The sight and scent reached him almost simultaneously, that of seafood the likes of which he never thought to see! Fish he could recognize, but much of the rest he had only read about or heard about before now; shrimp, clams, lobsters. Still more seafood was laid out throughout the tables, much of which he had never heard of, and that in a way made his stomach turn.

"What is *that*," he asked as he pointed to a particularly odd looking, steamed creature.

"Ah," the Queen smiled, "That is an octopus."

"I've heard of it," Reis smiled. "I've heard it tastes better than it looks."

"Considerably." She smiled to one of the servants. "That shall be his first taste of seafood."

The servant nodded, used a knife to cut off a tentacle, and served it to Cardin. He looked at it curiously, glanced at the Queen, who smiled at him, glanced at Reis, who smirked, before he picked up one of his many forks and knives and moved to cut a small piece off.

"That is the wrong fork," the Queen said. He looked at her, raised an eyebrow, and proceeded to use it any way. Gingerly he stabbed into the tentacle, cut a piece off, and brought it up to his nose, where he took a whiff. He wasn't sure how to describe the smell, but it was surprisingly appetizing. So he slowly tried a bite, and found the taste to be striking and, as Reis had suggested, much better than expected.

"Fantastic," he smiled. "I never would have imagined."

"Our cooks are the best the kingdom has to offer," she smiled. "Although we stand on ceremony here, we aren't the type of royalty and nobles who eat something just because it is popular. It had better taste exquisite, or we will not consume it."

Cardin smiled as the servants began to place portions of other seafood on everyone's plates. He began to try every single thing as it was placed before him, an assault of new and amazing flavors and aromas, each bite he enjoyed more than the previous, until he had tried everything and found he couldn't decide what he liked more. Anything that was shelled, the servants opened for them before placing just the meat on their plates.

The Queen seemed much more selective of the forks and knives she used, but he didn't care, nor did he pay close attention to it. He looked over to Reis, who likewise seemed to be enjoying himself. He leaned forward to look further down the table, and caught a glance of Sira as she tasted a piece of clam meat.

As the banquet wore on, the Queen began to chat with him in between bites. He wasn't surprised by her first question. "Tell me, Keeper, how has your training with the Wizard progressed?"

He glanced past the Queen down the table, where he saw Dalin enjoying an engrossing conversation with Ventelis. He realized that those two likely had much to talk about.

"As I briefed the Council," he looked at her eyes, and once again had to force himself to not look down, "Initial progress was fast, but it has since slowed."

"Why do you suppose that is?" she asked. "You became so powerful so quickly in the beginning."

He nodded, took a bite of a sweet and flavorful fish, and continued after he swallowed, "In some ways I've already surpassed Dalin, but those are mostly in powers that he himself does not possess. He told me this is expected."

Dalin had apparently overheard some of his conversation and piped in, "Amongst the Wizards, we go through periods of intense, fast growth in our powers, with periods of slow or even no growth in between."

The hall had quieted down to listen to their conversation, but Cardin scarcely noticed. "As it is, I'm stronger than anyone, faster than anyone, and I have a greater sensitivity to magic than even Dalin." He noticed a raised eyebrow from his mentor, and quickly added, "However, I have not yet learned how to cast elemental magic, despite Dalin's best efforts to teach me. Furthermore," he hesitated, realizing that he was about to admit to something he hadn't told many people. "Well," he blushed, "I still haven't figured out how to create portals."

"Curious," General Zilan said. "By your own account, that was one of the first powers that Kailar learned."

Cardin nodded. "Yeah, that fact hasn't escaped me."

"The Sword," Dalin stated, "was not created with humans in mind, it was meant for another species."

"The Vrol," Leian nodded. "I recall your statement to that fact."

"Indeed," Dalin said. "Cardin has learned the powers he was meant to learn for the time being, and I believe his body and mind are adjusting and growing accustomed to his new abilities. When he is ready, he will learn more from the Sword."

The room remained quiet after that, and Cardin felt a little embarrassed by it. The Queen rescued him, "Well as far as I am concerned, Keeper, you have performed admirably and gained the respect of many. General Zilan tells me that Erien Warriors who have fought alongside of you were greatly impressed not just by your skill, but your willingness to ensure the safety of those around you."

He smiled, not sure what to say in response.

A general din of conversation once again fell over the banquet hall for a while, and Cardin continued to enjoy his meal, until he felt like he could eat no more. He wanted to try more, to eat more, but he could not clear his plate, for as he continued to eat, servants added new items, most recently dessert items.

Recalling the conversation during their tour, Cardin asked the Queen, "Didn't you want to hear more about the elves and their homes?"

"Yes!" she replied, apparently having forgotten. She stood up, which was a silent cue for everyone else in the room to stop talking. "Before we begin with that, however," she looked around the room, "I want to make something very clear. Elaria and Ventelis are guests under my roof. They are not demons, and I expect everyone here to treat them with the same respect and kindness you would the Keeper or any other guest of mine."

As Cardin looked around the hall, he noted some disgruntled looks on some nobles' faces. Never the less, it had been a command from the Queen, and they all seemed ready to listen to what the elves had to say.

"Please," she looked first to Ventelis, and then over to Elaria, "you spoke of your homes earlier today. Tell us of these floating cities of yours."

Even from where he sat, Cardin saw Elaria blush. She leaned forward to look pleadingly at Ventelis. She, like Anila, was used to keeping to the shadows.

In fact, that was when Cardin realized he had not seen Anila enter the hall. He looked for her, but didn't see her amongst any of the guests or at their table. She hadn't spoken more than a handful of words to him, or anyone else, since they had first encountered her in the catacombs, and he was quite curious to see how she would handle such a situation.

Ventelis stood up, dabbed at the corners of his mouth with a silk napkin, and then smiled to everyone. "As we have already said to the Queen, Dareann Elves are people of the water. We were not born on the water, quite the contrary our people come from the land. However, some four thousand years ago we left the land to find our way on the seas and lakes."

While Ventelis spoke, Cardin decided to try something. Before, in the catacombs, he had not felt the presence of Anila. In fact, she had been a distinct void in the magical energies that surrounded them. That made her stand out from others who had no powers, as they at least had a presence.

So he closed his eyes and began an exercise he had learned from Dalin. He took in a deep breath for four counts, held it for seven counts, and then slowly exhaled for eight counts. When he exhaled, he imagined his own essence expanding out from his body.

Dalin had taught him to have at least a general sense of the ebb and flow of magic around him, but without focusing on that ability, it was a very general sense at best. Now that he focused on it, he could begin to detect individual points of energy in the room, some strong, others not so much.

"It started," Ventelis continued, Cardin scarcely aware of his speech, "by linking boats together and building platforms on top of them. However, this did not prove stable during severe weather, and we realized it was not a good long term solution. We knew magic was the solution."

To his right, Reis was a small wink of light. Beyond him, he felt the warmth he had come to associate with Elaria, her power strong, refined, and definitely unique and even out of place on Halarite. It was magic, but it felt like a different kind of magic, like she drew her power from a source different from what Mages and Wizards drew their power from.

He lightly touched Sira's core of power. Part of his growing abilities was that what had once been a vague but strong sense from her now was a small, weak power, definitely not as powerful as Elaria, nor as refined. He had begun to understand why Wizards did not consider Mages to be true powers in magic, as it also felt untempered. However, he refused to ever think of himself as above Mages.

To his left, the Queen, an untrained Mage, also had a presence of her own, stronger than Reis's but weaker than Sira's. Her lack of training was apparent, however, in that the power that flowed in and out of her was in spurts, uncontrolled, uncalled for, just simply there, as if a natural part of the world around her.

"So we constructed, in small parcels of land, a part of the first city," Ventelis continued, "made of stone, of metal, of wood, of any material we wanted. And with the combined power of hundreds of elves, we *moved* that part of the city from the land to the lake. This was the beginning of our first city, Qeyaras."

Dalin's presence was a strong, steady pulse, completely under control, but still a pulse and not a constant flow. He also felt that the energy the Wizard apparently 'exhaled' was slightly altered from that which he took in, and was how he had come to associate the Wizard's presence, that subtle feeling of a change in the surrounding magic.

Ventelis surprised him. The elder elf was much stronger than Dalin, and he did not take in any power, but only radiated it. It was the same warmth he felt from Elaria, but stronger, and it almost overshadowed those around him. Cardin had to force himself to tune that feeling out, and expanded his search further into the room. Person after person, he felt the presence of each individual at every table.

"Our cities float," Ventelis said, "but not because of buoyancy. The magic imbued into their structures ensures that they will not sink. Without that magic, our cities could never stay afloat, and would have broken apart at the first minor storm. You can feel the magic within our cities; the floors, the walls, every bit of our structures, every bolt, every screw, and every pillar."

When he hadn't found Anila amongst the seated guests, he expanded even further, stretched out. He could sense power in general from great distance, but to look for something specific, to look for an *absence* of power, he needed to keep his sensitivity high. It was like searching a large field with a fine-toothed comb, and it stretched his abilities to their limit.

Reis commented, "I remember Elaria told us when we first met her that everyone in your species has some ability in magic."

"Indeed," Ventelis replied. "We understand that this is not so for humans, and many other species, but elves are, by our very nature, magical."

"Amazing," he heard the Queen breathe. "Such a society must be very different from ours."

Finally Cardin found the strange absence of power, in fact he had almost completely missed it. She was to his left, and he glanced over. She stood inside of one of the corridors, and simply watched the assembly from the shadows. He could just barely tell that she still wore her leather armor. She had apparently decided not to participate in the night's festivities, which would explain why a seat was not kept empty for her at the head table.

She didn't seem to be looking at anyone specifically, and slowly moved her head around to keep an eye on the entire hall.

He turned his head forward, closed his eyes, and again focused in on where she was. The absence of power was almost unsettling. It nearly made him turn away, made him never want to touch that void again, but his curiosity got the better of him. So he dug deeper, increased his sensitivity, and allowed the absence to occupy his every thought.

Who was she? How could she have no presence within magic? It was not normal, and in fact he had only once felt something similar before, when Kailar's power had been stripped from her by the dragons.

No, he thought, *that's' not true. I couldn't feel Sal'fe's power in the forest.* So he dug deeper.

Suddenly what felt like a shock struck him, and he instinctually retracted his essence. He'd dug too deep, and beneath the absence was a presence. She wasn't powerless. Her powers had been cloaked. But how?

The ability to hide one's presence in magic was not unheard of, but it seemed uncommon.

Cardin's powers, and his sensitivity to magic, was greater now. Is this how Sal'fe would have felt if Cardin had obtained the Sword before he met the old Wizard? Or was this different?

He once again looked at Anila, and she stared right back at him. Clearly she wasn't who she pretended to be, and she knew she had just been found out.

Chapter 13

THE ROYAL BALL

Cardin scarcely paid any attention to Ventelis as his mind swam with what he'd just discovered. Anila Kovin, trusted servant of the Covenant of the Order of the Ages, was not powerless. In fact, as far as Cardin knew, Mages did not have the ability to hide their power or their presence in magic like Anila did.

That meant one of two things. Either she was a Wizard or she wasn't human. Both possibilities were unsettling. However, he also realized that he shouldn't make a scene of it by confronting her in front of everyone. He had briefly felt her power, and if she was a Wizard who didn't want to be known, there was no telling what she might do if he publicly revealed her secret.

She looked physically younger than Dalin, so if she was a Wizard, she was probably not as powerful as Dalin, but that was an assumption. There was no way to know how old she was, or how powerful.

After some time had passed, time which Cardin hadn't even noticed had passed, Ventelis finished telling everyone about the Dareann Elves, and Cardin wished he had paid attention.

That was when the Queen decided it was time for the Royal Ball to commence. Musicians came in and set up to perform at one corner of the hall. Once they tuned their instruments, it was time.

One of the servers pulled the Queen's chair out for her as she stood and turned to Cardin. "Keeper, please join me for a dance."

His mind had been so focused on Anila that the Queen's request completely caught him off guard. He stared at her offered hand, looked up at her in shock, and she gave him a fake smile, one which said to him 'take my hand and dance with me or I'll destroy you.'

Not knowing what else he could do, he smiled back, took her hand, and stood up. Hand in hand, they walked around the table, and he noticed that Sira raised her eyebrow at him as they passed. They walked, alone, onto the dance floor. The entire assembly waited and watched, and he felt panic begin to set in. He tried to remember the dances he had learned in his youth, but his mind was completely blank.

She stopped them and turned to face him. Once again, he had to consciously keep his eyes up. She turned her head to the musicians and nodded.

They began to play, and as the music started, he recognized the tune, and a long-forgotten memory surfaced. It was a waltz, and he knew how to waltz! The Queen curtsied, he bowed. He raised his hands into the proper frame, and she slid into that frame with practiced ease, ensuring that she placed her left hand beneath his scabbard.

Within moments, he had the rhythm down, and with a gentle nudge, he led them into the waltz. Queen Leian looked as surprised as he felt.

Quietly, she said, "To be honest, I expected to have to lead."

He smiled and felt his face grow a little warm. "This is one dance I actually remember."

"Excellent," she smiled. "I did not want this to be too uncomfortable for you."

At her comment, he tilted his head to one side. A part of him knew he shouldn't say what he had just thought. She was the Queen, after all, and he was in her kingdom. Yet he couldn't help himself, and he commented, "But you wanted me to be a little uncomfortable?"

With her fake smile, she replied, "Perhaps, but only a little."

After a few measures of the song, other dancers joined them on the floor. Cardin only paid enough attention to them to ensure he didn't lead the Queen into another couple, or hit someone with the Sword, but then he also realized that everyone else would ensure that didn't happen. It wouldn't do to cause the Queen any sort of embarrassment.

"We aren't your enemies," he frowned at her. "Even before the Alliance, our two countries were allies more often than not."

"Indeed," she replied. "I have not done any of this to alienate you. Rather I wanted to test you, to see how you acted under a different type of pressure."

"And?" he asked, curious.

"I am not surprised to find that how you act, what you say, none has changed even under such unique circumstances. You still speak your mind, even when it is not appropriate. You still care about your companions. However," she frowned, "I watched you become quite distant towards the end of dinner."

He averted his eyes from hers and tried not to show his concern. "I was distracted."

"By what?"

At first he didn't reply. He didn't want to, something in his gut told him it would not be a good idea to make a scene with Anila.

"It doesn't matter," he replied at length.

"I would think I am the one who would be the judge of that," she said, her eyes narrowed. "It would not do to keep secrets from me."

He looked her in the eyes and shook his head. "With respect, my Lady," he tried not to say that last part with disdain, "I am a citizen of Tal, not Erien."

She didn't reply at first, and looked ready to kill him on the spot. Then her face softened, and she threw her head back to let out a laugh that filled the hall. "You are correct," she smiled, this time genuinely. "No one here would ever dare challenge me in such a manner. It is refreshing."

After she said that, she grew silent, and simply stared into his eyes. The longer she did so, the more uncomfortable he felt. He had the growing impression that she saw him as a challenging prey.

He didn't know what to say or do, except to keep dancing. He averted his eyes from her, and simply looked over her right shoulder. That was when he noticed something he didn't expect. Reis and Elaria danced together, and even more surprising, Reis seemed to be enjoying himself. He said something, and it made Elaria giggle, but as they turned and moved about, Elaria looked towards Cardin and smiled.

Once again he felt uncertain and uncomfortable about the kind of looks she gave him, and he looked again to the Queen. She looked at him with curiosity. "You truly are distracted tonight."

He nodded and said, "This is all very different for me. I've never been to a banquet and ball like this." All of which was true. "I'm out of my element here."

"You feel you belong on the battlefield," she said.

It was an honest point, and he realized she was right, to a degree. "Not so much the battlefield," he corrected, "but just out. After I declined Guild membership, I spent more time out exploring Daruun Forest than I did in Daruun itself. At least, that's how it felt sometimes. And since I took up the Sword, I've spent time in the field, hunting orcs." He shook his head, "No, it's more than being outside. At least, now it is. Now it is a matter of being useful."

He looked at her, realized who he was talking to, and snapped himself out of his introspection. When she saw him do this, she smiled. "It is ok, Keeper. I am glad you felt comfortable enough to tell me this."

At that moment, the song ended, and the dance was over.

Cardin broke their frame and stepped back. "Thank you, my Lady," he bowed to her. She seemed shocked by his sudden departure, and as a force of habit, she curtsied in return. Movement in the background caught Cardin's attention, and he noticed Anila had stepped out of the shadows long enough to head towards the balcony. The musicians began to play another song, one he didn't know how to dance to.

He gave the Queen his best fake smile, and stepped towards the balcony. The other dancers began to move to the new song, and he found he only vaguely recognized their movements, but couldn't put a name to the dance.

Some of the attendees stared at him as he weaved his way across the dance floor, and he felt more than a little relieved as he stepped out of the crowd. He looked back to find that the Queen watched him, but a moment later she was distracted when Dalin approached her and asked her to dance. Cardin smiled at his friend, and then continued to make his way out to the balcony.

The only thing that separated the hall from the balcony was a line of columns, but somehow the banquet hall remained warm. Now a cool breeze from the ocean gave him chills. When Cardin stepped past one of the pillars, he caught the sense moments before he saw the movement. Anila waited for him, and remained in the shadow of the column.

She looked intently at him, and he stared right back at her. He didn't know what to do or say at first, nor did she, but she looked as tense as he felt.

Finally, he asked the obvious question, "Who are you?"

"Not your enemy," she replied evenly.

Cardin shook his head. "How do I know that? You're clearly not who you claim to be. You have power, and you've hidden it."

"I am not an exiled Wizard, if that's what you are thinking," she narrowed her eyes.

"I know," he nodded, "all of the exiles were accounted for six months ago. That just makes me even more suspicious. They found all exiles except Sal'Fe, and assumed he was the one who helped Kailar. Turns out they hadn't thought about Klaralin."

She frowned. "They didn't think about Klaralin because they didn't know he was still alive."

He considered her statement for a moment, and tried to figure out what it was she had just implied. "So who or whatever you are, they failed to consider that you could even exist? That implies you are at least somehow connected to exiled Wizards…"

"I am," she nodded. "The exiles lived on Halarite for over three thousand years." When she said that, a thought occurred to him, and he suddenly realized what she probably was. She nodded and continued, "I am the daughter of an exile and a Mage."

His surprise soon turned to confusion. "I didn't think Wizards would ever intermingle with Mages." He frowned, "Then again, I didn't think they would intermingle with any humans, since they consider themselves a separate species."

"Not all Wizards thought of themselves that way," she corrected. "Some knew the truth and didn't let arrogance blind them. That is why most of the exiles remained on Halarite. They knew that this world was their home, and humanity their kin. They wouldn't leave that behind. And when Klaralin attacked…" She broke off her sentence and looked down. "Forgive me. I have never spoken of this subject with anyone…"

Cardin frowned. "I don't understand, why would you hide this?"

She shook her head. "That is a discussion for another time. I do not wish to reveal too much about myself at this time."

It didn't surprise him. A woman who had clearly lived in secret for so long would naturally want to keep as much of her life to herself as she could. "I have only told you what I have so that you would not tell others that I am a threat."

Cardin shook his head. "You are still an unknown. You have hidden who you are from us. How do I know you're not a threat?"

"I am devoted to the Covenant," she frowned at him, "and I will follow their orders. That you can be certain of."

"Do they even know who you really are?" he asked.

"Yes," she didn't even pause in her response, and he realized, as she stared into his eyes, that she did, indeed, tell the truth. "They know."

For a while, he simply stared at her, and she stared right back at him, unafraid. Finally, he sighed and nodded. "Alright."

"Please do not tell the others," she insisted. "I do not wish my parentage to be widely known. I do not wish others to know that I have power."

He was about to ask why, but knew that she wouldn't tell him. So he sighed and nodded. "Very well. But I'm going to keep a very close eye on you."

"I would question your competence if you did not," she stated in a very matter-of-fact way. "As I will keep a close eye on you."

Cardin looked to his left and saw Sira walking towards him. When he looked back to where Anila was, she was gone. He looked around for her, but she had somehow slipped away quietly. He wondered if she had a power that allowed her to do that, or if it was a natural skill.

As Sira came out onto the balcony, she looked around as well. "Who were you talking to?"

He smiled and shook his head. "Anila. She was just here."

When he looked at Sira, he once again felt breathless. She raised an eyebrow, "Looked like quite a serious conversation." It was almost a question more than a statement.

For a moment, he didn't reply as he instead considered what he should tell her. As the leader of their expedition, Sira had a right to know anything that could potentially compromise the mission. Furthermore, he felt like he already kept too much from her.

However he then realized that, in a way, Anila had confided in him.

Would her parentage truly be a threat to them? *No,* he thought to himself. *It shouldn't be.* So he shook his head and said, "We just had to clear up a personal matter."

Sira frowned, "I can't imagine she's too forthcoming about personal matters."

Cardin laughed a little, "No, she really isn't." Then he stared into her eyes, and he felt a sort of tingle in his stomach as she stared back. "You are so gorgeous."

Even in the low light on the balcony he could see her face turn pink and she looked breathless. "Thank you," she said through a full smile. "I don't think you, or anyone else for that matter, has ever said I'm gorgeous. Pretty, beautiful even…but never gorgeous."

He wanted to be charming, wanted to flatter her without being too obvious or without making a fool of himself, but he couldn't think of what to say, and in and of itself that embarrassed him. He stumbled with his words, tried to find something, but before he could make a fool of himself, she stepped forward and lightly touched her hands to his arms. "It's okay," she smiled, "I know what you're trying to say. Cardin Kataar, able to give moving speeches to the Allied Council, able to sway the opinions of royalty with words alone, but never able to compliment a lady without tripping over his tongue."

He laughed easily. "Yeah. I guess some things never change." Her warm smile took the bite of the chilly breeze away. Then something caught her eye over his shoulder.

Cardin turned, and saw that one of the moons had started to rise over the sea. From where they stood on the balcony, up on a hill overlooking the city, they could see the moon reflected by the sea, almost like a glowing eye that slowly opened.

She wrapped her arm around his and together they walked to the balcony's edge. He rested his hands on the railing while she drew tighter to him, and he felt her shiver. At first he was about to suggest they go back inside, but then he felt something inside of himself, a new kind of warmth, the likes of which he'd never felt before.

Sira seemed startled and looked at him with a frown. "How…did you do that?"

Without even knowing he'd done it until after the fact, Cardin had somehow begun to generate a field of warmth around himself. It was new, he realized, a power he'd never known could exist.

"I don't know. I just thought that I wished I could keep you warm, and it happened."

She smiled and leaned her head on his shoulder. "Well don't stop. I like it here."

He wasn't quite sure how he had done it or how he could control it, but he continued to channel a bit of energy into himself and formed it into that core of heat. Sira stopped shivering.

Above the rising moon, there was a spark, and a streak of light flew overhead, across half of the sky until it winked out almost directly overhead. "Did you see that?" Sira asked, excited.

He smiled as memories from their childhood and teen years came back to him. "I did."

"Cardin, we haven't seen a shooting star together since we were sixteen!"

They looked into each other's eyes, and he felt like time had reversed, and they'd gone back to when they loved one another and openly admitted it to each other. He loved her still, he had never stopped.

But how could he say that to her now? It should have been easy, but for some reason it scared him. Especially when he thought of the conversation they'd had on the eve of the Battle of Archanon. She'd said that she was proud of the person he was becoming then, but she also had said 'not yet.' When would it be the right time? Would there ever be a right time?

It seemed like there was always something going on, something changing, some shattering revelation about their world, their species. The foundations of every belief on Halarite had been shaken in the past six months, and they continued to be shaken again and again. He had said their world was practically turned upside down when they had watched that sunset together. Would it ever stop? Should they really let the world dictate whether or not they could be together?

He wanted to be with her again, wanted to hold her like he did now every day. He never wanted to let go again. And as he stared into her eyes, as he allowed his own energy to reach out and connect with hers, he wanted nothing more than to declare his love for her again.

And then their moment of privacy ended when he heard someone else step out onto the balcony. She broke eye contact with him, or he did, he wasn't sure who looked towards the newcomers first. Reis and Elaria had joined them, and he noted a sullen look on Elaria's face. A pang of guilt rang in his stomach. How could he tell Elaria that his heart belonged only to Sira without breaking the elf's heart?

"Thought you two could sneak away, huh?" Reis asked with a smirk on his face.

"No," Sira turned away and looked at the rising moon. It was almost completely above the horizon now, more than half-full, and so it created an unusual reflection on the ocean's surface.

It had been a moment where he and Sira had connected again, just like they used to do all the time. A moment where he felt complete, no longer alone, no longer isolated.

Now that moment was gone, and his spirits sank.

Then he realized that she still held on to his arm. Even if it was just for warmth, he took comfort in that. He also took comfort in the realization that it was more than just the physical warmth he provided.

He had no way of knowing if she still loved him or not, and he was afraid to ask. However, tonight she had shown him that she still cared for him and felt comfortable with him. Perhaps, for the time being, that was enough. It would have to be.

Reis and Elaria joined them at the balcony's edge and stared at the rising moon with them. There were no clouds in the sky, so as Cardin looked up, he had a perfect view of the stars. There, amongst those pinpoints of light, he drew greater strength and comfort. Ever since he was a child, he felt comforted by them, and it seemed like he found an even greater strength and comfort from them since he'd taken up the Sword of Dragons.

Out there, under the sea of stars, he felt at home.

"You have such a beautiful world," Elaria commented. "I'm glad I was able to come back to see more of it."

Cardin was about to say he was glad too, but Reis beat him to it, "I am too."

He wondered at that. Six months ago, Reis thought she was a demon and had helped capture and torture her. Reis had also not been shy about showing his continued distrust of her when she'd first returned. Now he seemed completely smitten with her.

At first he wanted to pull his friend aside and caution him, but then he thought better of it. Their world was being forced to deal with so many changes so fast, and even tonight there was an obvious level of distrust and discomfort with the elves amongst the nobles, let alone the general population.

Could Reis fall for Elaria? And could she forget her infatuation with Cardin long enough to see that Reis was a good man underneath his mistrust? If those two could reconcile and fall for each other, maybe there was hope for the humans of Halarite.

He looked at Sira again, and she returned his gaze just long enough to give him a smile. Maybe there was hope for them all.

Chapter 14

THE DAGGER'S EDGE

Mid-morning had passed, and it grew closer and closer to midday. Letan grumbled to himself, and he could hear whispers of discontent from his companions. They had packed up and were ready to leave town, and had been for quite some time, but he insisted that they wait for Fiera. She still hadn't shown.

They were still outside of the Inn, their cart ready to go, the horses impatiently stomping their hooves. He sympathized. Fiera didn't seem like the type to be late.

Adira finally seemed to be the one 'elected' by the others to talk to him, and she cautiously approached him. "Letan," she sang in her sweet, quiet voice, "she's not coming."

His mind raced for an excuse to stay longer. "She's a smart girl. She knows she'll need help to keep the predators away. She wouldn't just…"

"What, go off on her own?" Adira shook her head. "You saw how stubborn she is. She's a loner, Letan. And we don't actually know anything about her beyond that."

"I know enough," he defended, glancing around, hopeful that she'd be rushing towards them, simply late.

"We can't delay, we have to get these supplies back to Corlas."

That much was true. Like most of the other towns on Devor, Corlas relied on regular supplies and trade. They had purchased much-needed equipment for mining and farming.

"I know," he sighed and felt defeated. He couldn't help but think that a decision to leave now was tantamount to abandoning Fiera. Perhaps that wasn't actually true, but he saw within her deep emotional scarring. She wasn't likely of rational mind and he didn't want her to think he would abandon her.

So he resolved not to. "Look, I'm faster when travelling alone." He gave Adira what he hoped was a determined look. "So you all go on ahead without me. I'll see if I can find out what happened to her and then catch up. Even if you get to Neolas without me, keep going."

Adira gave him a bewildered look. "What is it with you? I've never seen you so smitten with someone before, never seen you even *suggest* something so reckless before!"

"Adira!" His voice had changed to one of command, a voice he was accustomed to using. She knew he'd just made that an order, and that he didn't appreciate her questioning him.

With a reluctant sigh, she turned and walked back to the others to tell them. He walked up to the left side of their cart and unlashed his backpack from the side. He took a quick inventory to ensure he had everything he'd need to survive on the road by himself, and then swung it onto his back.

The others all stared at him for a moment, so he gave them a reassuring, resolved nod. No one returned the nod. Tanneth shook his head, one final, silent attempt to make Letan change his mind, but he ignored the plea. Finally they headed out, with Adira leading the horses.

He stared after them for a short time. Adira was right, he was being reckless and it was completely unlike him. But he couldn't give up on Fiera.

Was he really 'smitten' with her? He had lived in Corlas for a long time, and had always been a very serious person, even in his teen years. He had never 'chased girls', and never really considered any of the local women his age to be potential companions. They were friends or subordinates, most felt like family to him. So he'd never fallen in love, never even felt more than a passing attraction for someone.

So was this what it felt like to fall for someone? Had he finally found a potential companion?

As he turned towards the center of town and began walking, he thought about that. Why was he attracted to her? He saw in her eyes a genuine good, but he also conceded that his own infatuation with her might have influenced his ability to judge character.

He continued to feel completely fascinated by her. He'd never encountered anyone he couldn't feel some sort of presence from, especially in close proximity, especially when he'd physically touched her. How could she be a void in magic?

The first place he went to was the Warriors' Guild, where he described her as best as he could and asked if they'd seen or heard about her. None had.

There were a lot of inns in Edingard, but he wouldn't give up until he'd searched each and every one of them. So he began in the center of town, where most of the inns were. He described her to each innkeeper, each barmaid, every single person he could. It seemed fruitless, until finally he came across one where the innkeeper remembered seeing her. He told Letan that she had come in yesterday for supper, but had rushed out before she could finish it, and looked terrified.

That didn't give him much to go on, but it did worry him. She seemed like a very strong woman, and he wondered what, or who, could have frightened her. The innkeeper then mentioned that one of his own miners, a man from Falind named Devlin, had chased after her. And Devlin hadn't reported to his mining shift that morning.

"If he's run off with her or something, I'm going to find her and make her pay dearly," the innkeeper threatened.

"Hey, easy, Brask," Letan raised a hand up. "I'm sure that's not the case. She's not the kind of woman to give her feelings away easily. Trust me on that. Did they speak to each other at all?"

"No," he replied gruffly. "If you find him, you make him come back, you hear?"

Letan felt his jaw tighten at Brask's demand, but as he always did with those he knew were part of the criminal underground, he bit his tongue and said nothing. He turned and walked outside, where he took a moment to calm himself down.

With his wits intact, he began to think more carefully. Brask hadn't said she had purchased a room there. So why had she eaten supper there, and not at whatever inn she had decided to stay the night in?

He realized that the only reason she would have done so is if the inn she'd chosen to stay in was much further away from the center of town. Given her paranoid mentality, that suddenly made sense to him, and he felt stupid for looking in the center of town. She would stay at the edge of town, in an area with less traffic. A place she could easily slip away from and leave town unseen if she needed to.

On instinct alone, he found the main cross road that intersected the east-to-west road, and headed south. He came to the edge of town, and began to investigate the handful of smaller inns.

Eventually he came upon the Black Horse Inn, a place he'd never been to before, when his search finally ended. The innkeeper, a sweet old woman named Ira, was busy preparing for the lunchtime meal when he entered. Ira had heard the door open and came from the back.

She took one look at him, focused on his backpack, and smiled, "Ah another weary traveler. Can I offer you a room and a bite to eat, young man?"

"No," he smiled, "But thank you. Perhaps you can help me, I'm searching for a woman named Fiera. She has…"

"Black hair, unusually pale skin for a traveler," Ira finished for him.

He stopped short, and felt his heart leap. "Yes!"

Ira eyed him suspiciously. "Why are you looking for her?"

"She's my friend, and a travelling companion," he took an excited step closer. He glanced around the inn and noticed only one of the rooms had a closed door. Was she in there? "She didn't show up this morning when we were supposed to leave town, and I'm worried about her."

"Are you now?" Ira narrowed her eyes. "Tell me, if you're her friend, why didn't she stay in the same place as you?"

He laughed a little. "If you've met her, you'd know. She's not the most sociable or trusting person in the world."

Ira chuckled a little. "No, indeed."

"Please," he pleaded with the old woman. "Please, if you know where she is, tell me. I think someone might be after her for some reason."

The innkeeper sighed and looked at her feet for a moment, and then looked at the closed door. "I hope this isn't a mistake. She came back last night, pale as a ghost. Well," Ira smirked, "paler than she normally is. She went to her room, slammed the door closed. Hasn't come out since, not even for breakfast. And..." Ira hesitated. "I heard her crying throughout the night. The other customers complained about it a couple of times, but she refused to answer the door when I knocked."

Letan fixed on the closed door, and without asking permission, he crossed the distance in a matter of seconds and tried to open the door. It was locked, so he began pounding on the door in a near-panic. "Fiera!"

When there was no answer, he continued to pound on the door. "Fiera open up! Please open the door!" He began to fear the worst. What could make her cry? She seemed like the toughest woman he'd ever met, and he couldn't ever imagine her in tears.

The panic grew when no answer came, not a sound from inside. Why would that miner, Devlin, chase after her? Letan knew Brask was an unsavory character, and he wasn't sure he trusted anyone under his employ, whether they worked for him by choice or not. Had Devlin followed her here, broken into her room, and done something to her?

He almost demanded Ira for a key to the room, and he considered going around outside to see if the window was intact, assuming it even had a window. However, a moment later, he heard the lock click from inside.

His breath caught and he stared at the latch for the door, waiting for it to open. But it never did. So he cautiously tried it, and it opened without protest. Letan eased the door open, but could see little inside. The curtains were drawn and let only the slightest glow in. That and the light from the rest of the inn was all that lit the room. She stood in the center with her back to him, but slowly she turned her head to look over her shoulder, probably to make sure it was Letan and not someone else.

He took two steps in, but then paused when he saw her shoulders tense. "Fiera..."

"Don't," she began, but stopped.

"Don't what?" She didn't reply. "Fiera, what's wrong?" Again she didn't reply. He noticed another shadow cross into the room, and he looked behind him to see Ira, the deepest concern on her face. He gave her a look that conveyed his belief that they should be alone. Ira seemed skeptical, but nodded and disappeared into the back room in a busy haste.

"Fiera," he turned to her again.

"Nothing is wrong," she said quietly. "Leave me alone. Go, leave town with your team."

He frowned. "I'm not going to abandon you."

Her right hand was in front of her and he couldn't see it, but he saw her left hand clench into a fist. "I'm not going with you."

"I thought we'd come to an agreement yesterday," he insisted. He was worried, but he felt a pang of anger and frustration too. "We're going to get you as far as Corlas. You know you can't make it on your own."

Her left fist seemed to shake a little when he said that. "I told you to leave." Her voice began to shake. "I don't need you."

"Fiera…"

"Stop calling me that!" She spun around to face him. He noticed her dagger was clenched tightly in her other hand. That made him tense up. He felt bewildered at her reaction, and she seemed taken aback by herself. The anger seemed to fade from her face, but only partly. "You don't know who I am. You don't know what kind of a person I am."

He wanted to step closer to her, but he could tell that she was scared, and anything he did that could be considered a threat to her could make her instincts kick in. She might do something she didn't mean to.

"You said you think I'm a good woman," she said quietly. "But how do you know? What if…" She took a step back, as if stunned. "What if I've done horrible things?"

His stomach sank when an incident from his past played through his head. A time when he'd made a horrible mistake, and people died because of it. He pushed the memory away and tried to look her in the eye. She avoided his gaze. "Sometimes people make mistakes. It's part of being human."

She laughed. "Human. Am I human?"

That seemed to be an odd sort of question. "What else could you be?"

"Am I still human even after I've committed inhuman acts?"

135

Deep inside of him, a part of him began to suspect what she meant. What could be so horrible that she could call it inhuman?

"Humans are capable of some pretty atrocious acts, it doesn't make you any less human."

"Then it just makes me a horrible human." She took another step back, and bumped into the small end table next to the bed. "It makes me a horrible person."

He was about to say something by starting with her name, but realized that she seemed to hate her name. So instead he said, "I see in your eyes an inner good, a genuine desire to do good." She scoffed. "Whatever you've done," he continued undaunted, "I can only imagine that you're feeling overly guilty over something small." Then he made a mistake by taking a step forward and said, "Fiera, I…"

Her eyes lit up again. "You don't know me! You don't know who I am, what I'm capable of, what I've done, what I want to do!" She came towards him suddenly, fast enough that it took him completely off guard. She grabbed him by his shoulder and pressed the dagger's point up against his throat.

"Stop saying that name," she shouted at him. "Stop acting like you know me. Stop acting like you have any idea what I've done. I am not a good woman! Would a good woman do this? Would a good woman threaten your life?"

Letan opened his mouth to reply, but realized he had no idea what to say, especially not with a dagger at his throat. He resisted his instincts, because if he followed them, he would respond violently, and she wouldn't stand a chance. She would already be dead if he had let his instincts control him.

So he took that moment to look her in the eyes, and for the first time she looked right back at him. He saw in her a killer instinct. If she took his life now, it wouldn't be the first life she'd taken, that was clear. However, he also couldn't judge her by that. He had taken human life as well.

Behind the killer instinct, he saw what he'd always seen in her. Behind the anger, hatred, fear, and paranoia, he still saw the good in her. Buried as it was under scars and still-open wounds, it was still there.

"I know you won't do it," he stated resolutely. He never broke his gaze, but she seemed to falter at his words. "I know you're scared, confused. But you won't hurt me."

She shook her head. "You've known me three days." She no longer shouted, but she was still scared and angry, and her voice still shook. "How can you possibly say that about me, especially now?"

He waited a moment, stared into her eyes long enough to let her know he wasn't about to budge. "My father taught me to believe in the good in everyone, despite living on this forsaken continent. I've seen so much darkness here, encountered so many criminals and other unsavory types. Despite what my father taught me, despite how much I want to, I can't see good in everyone. Yet I can see it in you." As he said it, he realized it was true. He didn't trust many people. How could he, after growing up in a place where criminals went unchecked? "I believe in the good in you."

For what seemed like ages, she didn't respond. He searched her eyes to try to anticipate her reply, but it seemed like a thousand emotions passed through them. Finally, she laughed a little, a nervous, fearful laugh. "Then you're an idiot."

Slowly she pulled the dagger away from him, and she let her iron grip on his shoulder and neck relax. He sighed in relief, and rolled his right shoulder to help the muscles relax.

"Maybe so," he said, trying to put on a charming smile, but realized he had no idea what a charming smile actually looked or felt like. "But I said I knew you wouldn't kill me, and I'm still alive."

She managed a tiny smile when he said that. She looked down at the dagger in her hand, stared at it as if it were something offensive. However, she also didn't throw it away. "Letan," she started and stopped. She clenched the dagger hard, and then slid it into the sheath on her belt. "I don't know what to do. I don't know who I am anymore. I'm holding onto hope for something that is hopeless."

When she looked up at him and met his eyes, he noticed that tears had started to form in her eyes again. "I don't know what to do with my life anymore."

At first he didn't reply. He waited for her to tell him more, but she offered no more explanation. So he smiled and said, "Whatever is in your past, it has hurt you gravely. If the Crystalline Peaks can give you hope, no matter how small that hope is, then you're doing the right thing."

"And if I get there and it turns out they can't help me?" As she said it, her voice quivered.

He stepped closer to her, and slowly, as unthreateningly as he could, reached his hands out. He took her free hand in his, and squeezed it reassuringly. However, she backed away and broke their handhold. Whatever he was about to say, his mind suddenly went blank. He thought his actions had been appropriate, but clearly not.

Never the less, he smiled. "Then you'll find something else to keep you going. Something else to give you hope." He wanted to try to tell her that he was there for her, but somehow he knew that wasn't the right thing to say at that moment. "You'll find a reason to keep going."

She nodded, but obviously didn't look satisfied by that. "I understand if you don't want me to go along with your group any more. Especially after this."

He smiled wryly. "You don't give up, do you?" She didn't look at him, and seemed to go out of her way not to look at him. He sighed. "It's going to take a lot more than all of this to scare me off. So come on," he glanced back at the door. "Let's get some lunch and head out."

She hesitated, and for a moment he thought she might tell him to leave without her anyway. Their eyes met again, and he hoped she could see his genuine desire for her to keep going with them. Finally, she nodded. "Alright."

Chapter 15

WIZARD'S FLAME

It couldn't have been a better day to start their journey on the open sea, Dalin decided. He stood upon the private balcony for his room in the palace and stared into the open blue sky. It was a beautiful day, and there was a breeze out of the west that would help their ship leave port. It was almost time to go.

His assignment to train Cardin had been one of the highlights of his life so far, and a welcome distraction in the aftermath of the Battle of Archanon. For years, he had often travelled to Halarite, despite constant warnings from his elders. Those journeys had been only for a few days at a time, and always he returned to the Guild Hall, where he had naught but an artificial sky to watch and a closed air cycle to breathe. Now for the past six months, he'd spent most of his time on Halarite.

For the first time in his life, he felt at home.

Today he looked forward to an exciting new experience, time on a ship on the open sea! That meant several things, not the least of which was ample time to enjoy the open skies. However, it also gave him the chance to do something he hadn't yet been able to do, and wasn't sure he wanted to.

Ever since the Battle of Archanon, he hadn't had much time to his thoughts. Always busy, always working with Cardin to train, to battle orcs, to help keep the allied forces working together. There hadn't been time to truly grieve for the losses they had suffered six months ago, to contemplate the events that had transpired.

He was 288 years old, and in all of his life, until now, he'd always had ample time to take in everything that happened in his life, to give it thought, to understand it. Those days had ended when the Sword of Dragons surfaced.

During their journey, he would still need to train Cardin, but Cardin hadn't gained any new abilities in quite some time, so there was little more to do except work towards being prepared for the next set of abilities he unlocked. That would leave Dalin with enough time to reflect on the events, to reflect on the losses they had endured.

Time to reflect on the death of his mentor, Aenar.

From his vantage, he could see activity had picked up at the ship the Queen had pointed out yesterday, the Sea Wisp. Somehow during the night the ship had been turned around and faced the open sea. Final supplies were being loaded, and soon the passengers would board.

Dalin turned and walked into his quarters and was not at all surprised to find his pack was nowhere to be seen. Most likely it was already down on the docks, carried down by a palace servant. So he moved for the entrance, but moments before he opened the door, there came four knocks. He paused and reached out his awareness, but immediately felt mixed feelings about the power he felt on the other side.

It was another Wizard, not a Master but still more experienced than he was, older. He deduced who it was, and his instincts proved right when he opened the door and found a woman in emerald Wizard's robes on the other side.

"Teira," he faked a smile.

"Hello Dalin," her smile was not fake, but he could see a hint in her eyes that she understood his was. "I am sorry I was not at the Royal Ball last night, I hear it was quite a feast."

"Indeed it was," he replied, resisting the urge to shift his weight. "And an enjoyable dance."

She smirked. "The Queen tells me that you are quite an impressive dancer, and not shy about demanding she dance with you."

He tried to make a fake chuckle, but ended up sounding ridiculous. Dalin's cheeks reddened, so he cleared his throat to cover. "How may I assist you?"

Teira's smile faded, and pretense ended. "May I at least come in?"

He wanted to say no, and almost did. It wouldn't have been the first time he didn't stand on ceremony. This wasn't a part of his past he wanted to mull over at the moment. Never the less, he stepped aside and motioned her in.

As she passed into his quarters, he told her, "We are departing shortly."

"Yes, I know. The Queen sent me to escort you to the courtyard." Teira was one of the Wizards who had been assigned as a 'Court Wizard.' After the Alliance had formed, to facilitate the numerous meetings of the Council, a Wizard would always stay with the leader of each respective Kingdom so that no destination was more than a quick portal away for them. Furthermore, they acted as advisors regarding the rapidly-changing reality that Halarite faced.

"Did she indeed," he raised an eyebrow. "Hardly a job for the Court Wizard."

She turned, her smile fading. "Very well. I asked to be the one sent to your quarters. We have not spoken since…"

"Since we both agreed not to speak to each other," he nodded. "That was a long time ago."

"Not so long," she shrugged. "Not to a Wizard."

"Exactly." Dalin stared evenly at her. He wanted her to go away, to not talk to him. She stared right back, and her gaze never wavered. As happened frequently when they did so, a charge began to build up in the room, energizing the surrounding magic. It wasn't the kind of charge that built up between rivals, but rather it was an indication of the chemistry they had always shared. Any Mages in the vicinity would feel it, and he worried that they would panic and think something was wrong, so he turned his gaze away and broke their connection.

"What do you want?"

Without skipping a beat, she began, "I have heard that you have visited the Council of Masters several times since the Battle of Archanon."

"What of it?" He still avoided her gaze.

"My friend," she began, but then paused. "Dalin," she started again, "you must take care. You have always been impulsive and impatient. They have not been fond of your visits and you are beginning to lose whatever favor you held with the Council."

He felt anger flare up within him, and he glared at her. "They are slow and obstinate, they do not seem to fully grasp the changes that have occurred, nor the changes that are coming. We cannot afford to hide in our private universe anymore. We must return to Halarite."

"We have!" She waved her free hand in exasperation, her other hand grasping her staff tighter. "Why do you think I am here? Master Valkere spends more time at the Allied Council than he does the Council of Masters."

"Yet those who survived the Battle of Archanon continue to stay away from Halarite." He began pacing, a habit he realized he'd begun to pick up in the past six months. "I am not speaking of a few Wizards, I mean we must completely return to our *home,* where we belong. Here, on Halarite."

"Neither of us were alive when our kind lived on this world," she reminded him. "So why is it so important to you?"

"It is important because we are human," he leveled his gaze at her. She gave only the slightest hint of surprise, but there was more disgust than shock on her face. "We came from Halarite, we share ancestors with these humans."

She walked up to him and physically stopped his pacing with a firm hand. "Not everyone shares that belief within the Wizards' Guild," she chided. "In fact hardly anyone does. We are not human, Dalin. Even if we came from humans, we have evolved beyond them."

"Yet we continue to make the same mistakes that humans do," he frowned. "We have the same faults. Including arrogance," he said the last word in frustration. She looked ready to object, but he interrupted her, "The only difference is that when we make mistakes, when we let our arrogance blind us, thousands suffer or die."

She let go of him. "That is one of the reasons we have always been isolated from the rest of civilization. Why our first Guild Hall was far in the North, nowhere near civilization, and why our new Guild Hall is in another universe."

"Isolating ourselves did not protect the humans from Klaralin, did it?" She had no response to that, except to glower. That anger, he guessed, was because she didn't want to accept the reality he presented. "It also did not protect them from the Sword of Dragons. It was our responsibility to keep it safe. We did not believe Kailar, a Mage, was a threat, and we were proven gravely mistaken."

"It was Klaralin who helped her find the Sword," she defended quickly. "She would not have been able to find it otherwise."

"Perhaps not, however that is precisely my point. We had no presence on Halarite, we could not foresee his return."

"Could we have, even if we were here?"

Dalin bit his tongue for a moment, because what he was about to say, he didn't want to admit. "Sal'fe saw the signs." He swallowed hard and felt acid rise from his stomach. "Whether or not he knew it was Klaralin, we may never learn. However, he knew Kailar was a threat, he told Cardin as much. Furthermore, he asked Cardin to retrieve the Staff of Aliz from her, the staff that was eventually used to destroy Klaralin and bring back many fallen Warriors, soldiers, and Wizards."

Most of the Wizards Klaralin had killed were completely destroyed, and without a body to resurrect, the Staff of Aliz was useless. Sal'fe was only able to resurrect about a dozen of their fallen ranks. The Wizards' numbers were staggeringly low. For the first time ever, their entire guild had felt the ravages of war. Many still felt the shock. Not a single Wizard that still lived hadn't lost a friend or loved one.

Including Teira. Including Dalin. They were both favored apprentices of Aenar. For many years, they trained together under his tutelage. That was why Dalin was able to predict her response.

"The humans have always resented us," she stated coldly. "They wanted us to leave. When we returned, our thank you was the death of hundreds of us."

"Indeed," he nodded, trying to push back the sting in his eyes. "However, think of how much worse it could have been. If we had not come back when we did, Kailar would still have the Sword and likely have conquered the four kingdoms. Her powers would have grown, and eventually she could have found our sanctuary and helped Klaralin destroy us all. Master Valkere understands at least that much, why can you not?"

She looked away with a scowl, but then visibly hesitated. He had struck a nerve with her. She believed in rank, and therefore revered the Grand Master. What Valkere thought, she thought. That more than anything was what had driven a wedge between them over fifty years ago, when she had graduated from apprenticeship and subsequently shunned him.

After a moment of silent contemplation, she looked at him. "So what would you have us do?"

"I have tried to convince the Council of Masters that we must rebuild our Guild Hall in the North, and to return to Halarite." She shook her head and laughed, but then once again hesitated. She narrowed her eyes, and he got the impression she had just thought of something. "Teira?"

"Is it because of your suggestion that they have barred all unnecessary travel to Halarite?"

He felt his face slacken and he absently brought his free hand up to rub the back of his neck. "What do you mean?"

"I mean exactly what I said," she replied, tilting her head to one side. "I learned of it last night. Only Wizards assigned to the courts as well as the Allied Council are allowed to return to Halarite, all others have been ordered to not leave the Hall."

Dalin frowned and slowly shook his head, "No I do not believe that would have been ordered as a result of my suggestion. I do not see how they could be connected."

"Then why?" She placed her free hand on her hip. "What could make Master Valkere believe Halarite is too dangerous for us?"

He considered her question, and once again found himself pacing. He could not come up with an answer.

"Would you stop that?!"

Dalin's cheeks grew warm and he stopped. "I apologize. Teira, I have no answer for you, but I also do not believe in coincidence."

"I know you do not," she rolled her eyes.

"Neither should you, given what you have learned as a Wizard." She didn't seem particularly happy about a younger Wizard lecturing her. "If you want answers to your questions, I suggest you begin digging for further information."

"Dalin I am not like you," she shook her head. "I trust the will of the Masters."

"I am not saying you do not. Yet you clearly are perplexed by this new order." He walked up to her and placed a firm hand on her shoulder. "I am leaving soon and cannot investigate this myself.

Please, Teira. I fear more is happening here than any of us knows. Look into this matter, find the connection. You once had a keen mind for piecing together puzzles."

She smiled a little and said, "I still do."

"Then use that intellect. If I am wrong and there is nothing more to this matter, then you will have peace of mind. However," he squeezed her shoulder a little tighter, "if there is more to this, then your experience on Halarite these past six months may give you the insight you need to do something positive about it."

She looked at his hand, and then with her own free hand, she reached up and took hold of his. After a moment of holding it, she squeezed, an unsaid assent to his insistence, before she pulled his hand off of her shoulder and let go. "I will see what I can learn. However, there will be no way I can tell you any of what I learn until you either return or restore our ability to portal to Trinil."

"I know. However," he smiled, but wasn't sure he truly believed what he was about to say, "I trust you to do what is best with whatever you learn."

She smiled at his white lie. There came another knock at the still-open door to his quarters, and they both turned to find a servant at the door. "My apologies for interrupting. The party has assembled in the courtyard and the Queen wishes to know why you have been delayed."

"Right," Teira looked embarrassed. "I was supposed to escort you down. Please, follow me."

She led the way, and together they descended to the ground level, passed through the throne room, and came out into the courtyard. There Sira, Cardin and the others waited impatiently along with Queen Leian and General Zilan. The Queen looked at Dalin and Teira curiously.

"My apologies, Queen Leian," Teira bowed to her. "Dalin is an old friend and we were caught up in conversation."

Dalin noted how the Queen smiled warmly towards Teira, and did not rebuke her as he would have expected. Instead, the Queen nodded. "Apology accepted."

Queen Leian then smiled to Sira. "Well then. I am sorry, but I will not be able to escort you to the port. Teira and I must travel to Archanon for another Council session. General Zilan will escort you to the docks."

Sira raised her hand to her stomach and bowed, "Thank you, your Majesty, for your hospitality. It has been a pleasure and an honor."

"As it has been for me," she smiled and looked pointedly at Cardin. "Keeper, the task before you may be a daunting one. I trust you to keep my ship and its crew safe."

Cardin visibly blushed. "I will certainly do everything in my power to keep everyone safe," he said with a bow.

"Safe journey to you all, and may the winds carry you to safe haven."

The Queen and Teira left, but as they headed into the throne room, Dalin saw Teira turn to look at Dalin one more time. He gave her an encouraging smile before she disappeared through the entrance.

General Zilan wore the same ceremonial armor he had worn at the dance the night before, and his posture was a precise military stance. He was obviously very concerned with tradition and image.

The General addressed Sira specifically, "Please follow me."

As the General led the way, Cardin fell into step beside Sira while everyone else followed behind. Dalin tried to take up the rear, but Anila made sure she stayed behind everyone. He knew she didn't trust any of them, but Dalin also didn't trust her. She was hiding something, he knew that much, and the fact that he could not sense any sort of presence from her unnerved him.

Ventelis fell into step beside Dalin and smiled. He and Dalin had struck up conversation many times since the elf had arrived on Halarite, and he found the elder elf's intellect and wit enjoyable. "Did I sense some tension between you and the other Wizard," Ventelis asked.

He wanted to say no, but he knew that Ventelis would probably see through that lie. "We do indeed have a difficult history," he sighed. They passed under the portcullis out of the courtyard and turned onto a road bound for the docks.

"Fascinating," Ventelis smiled. "I would be most interested to learn more about the social interactions of Wizards."

Dalin raised an eyebrow at the elf. "Is that so?"

Ventelis didn't seem to get the social cue Dalin had tried to give him. "Yes, please tell me more! There seems to always be considerable similarities in social norms between cultures, but the details, the minor differences, those are of great interest to me."

146

Dalin couldn't help but smile at the Professor's curiosity, and it was a trait he usually valued in others, but today he found it to be annoying. "I would rather we not discuss the matter," he said pointedly. "Not now, at least. We have at least a three week journey ahead of us to explore such topics."

At first Ventelis seemed ready to insist, but finally seemed to understand. So instead, he nodded. "Very well."

The rest of the walk was spent in silence for Dalin, but he could see that Cardin and Sira tried to get General Zilan to be more talkative. The General was polite, but seemed disinclined to socialize with them, and in fact seemed uncomfortable at their attempts. Cardin seemed to understand this, and so pushed harder for socialization. Normally Reis was the mischievous one, but Cardin didn't let up, and Dalin had to suppress a chuckle at the increased discomfort this caused the General.

He was also pleased to see that Cardin and Sira continued to grow closer. In his training sessions with Cardin, he had learned much of their past, and a part of him wanted to cheer them on. It had not always been easy, and there were times when they argued, but somehow they always reconciled. It would be interesting to watch them during the voyage. He smiled when he also realized that Ventelis probably thought the same thing.

Finally they reached the pier that the Sea Wisp was docked at and marched down towards the end.

The pier was made of a pale, thick wood, and he knew it could bear considerable weight. To their right were two small fishing ships, but to the left was the Sea Wisp. As they approached the gangway, a man with clear confidence and pride descended it to greet them. He wore a shirt that Dalin swore was made from sail canvas, and very loose-fitting pants held up by a leather belt, while his black leather boots and hat were highly distinctive. Dalin surmised that the man was the ship's captain, especially as two crew members who started up the gangway suddenly stopped and got back off to allow the man to come down unobstructed.

The General brought them to a stop as the man stepped onto the pier in front of them. He had blonde hair and very green eyes, and his face looked solid enough to take a beating without a bruise. "May I introduce Captain Etil Noric of the Sea Wisp," General Zilan stepped aside. "Captain, this is Sira Reinar."

Captain Noric and Sira exchanged slight bows. "A pleasure to finally meet you," Noric said. "It is my honor to receive you and your party."

The men who had made way for the Captain, their hands full of cargo, slipped behind their commanding officer and made their way up the gangway. Sira glanced at them as they went, and then looked the Captain up and down. "Please take no offense, Captain, but…except for your boots and hat, you don't seem to wear anything to distinguish your rank from your crew."

"Yes," Zilan snuffed at the Captain. "You knew you would be meeting them today, the least you could have done was put on your shore uniform."

In a voice that dripped with sarcasm, the Captain looked at Zilan and said, "Yes, because taking the time just before we set sail to look pretty is the most important thing in all of Edilas." Zilan scoffed, but Noric ignored him and addressed Sira. "While we do have uniforms we wear while on shore, aboard ship we care more about function than we do about our looks. Our job is to keep the ship going and in one piece."

Sira looked down at her own clothes, which consisted of a simple tunic and trousers with a comfortable pair of leather boots, and nodded. "I can certainly understand that, we dressed comfortably for the long voyage ahead."

Two more sailors carrying a barrel between them walked past Dalin and the others and said, "Excuse us, Captain." Norric had already begun to move out of their way as they passed him by. Dalin marveled at the man, he was by no means like the politically minded General or anyone else he had met since they arrived in Maradin yesterday. It was a breath of fresh sea air.

"I want to establish something up front," Norric looked at Sira and then took a moment to look at each and every person. "My crew is used to occasional passengers, though usually not in this many numbers. However, we are not a passenger ship. If you wish to reach Port Hope within three weeks, you'll need to make sure you stay out of the way. If I or one of my crew tells you to move, do so without hesitation or question. You are welcome on the deck during normal operations, but there may be times when I order all hands on deck or we call for general quarters. If this happens, it also means non-essential personnel must go below decks unless I say otherwise."

Dalin found the Captain's change to a commanding stance abrupt, but he knew that once they stepped aboard the ship, they were in Noric's own little kingdom and he was the king. It made sense that he established that fact up front before he let a single passenger aboard. "Understood, Captain," Sira nodded. "We do not wish to interfere in any way. While aboard your ship, we fall under your command."

"Excellent. Please," he motioned his hand towards the gangway, "follow me." The Captain led the way up, and everyone followed. Sira, Cardin and Reis had some trouble as the ship, and therefore the gangway, shifted from incoming waves. Elaria and Ventelis didn't seem bothered at all, but given what he had learned about the elf cities, Dalin was not surprised.

He glanced at Anila, who stared at him stoically and waited for him to precede her. He looked uneasily at the gangway, uncertain how his balance would be. With a big breath, he took the gangway at a brisk pace and quickly went on deck before he could lose his balance. Once there, he stopped for a moment and got a sense for the shifting ship.

It was a strange sensation he had never felt before, and he could tell that Sira, Cardin and Reis were also unused to it due to the way they held their hands out a little at their sides, as if to gain a greater balance. Dalin was surprised that it didn't feel like the ship moved from side to side, but more like it moved up and down. Once he realized that, he found it easier to keep his balance. He moved aside to allow Anila to board.

The deck of the ship was somewhat larger than he expected, but it and the various ropes and masts, rigging if he recalled his terminology correctly, were full of sailors preparing the ship.

The Captain made a point to turn to them all and say, "Welcome aboard the Sea Wisp." A woman, barefoot like most of the rest of the crew and without a hat, but otherwise dressed similarly to the captain, came down from the raised deck at the back of the ship and stood beside Noric. She had jet black hair pulled back in a very tight bun, tight enough that Dalin wondered if it made her head hurt. Her jaw line gave the impression of something sharp, but her sea-blue eyes were in sharp contrast to her hair. "This is my first mate, Commander Elia Devral."

"Hello," she nodded curtly. "Captain, that barrel of water was the last of the cargo to be loaded. We'll be secure in a moment and ready to cast off."

"Thank you Devral," Noric nodded. "Please show them to their bunks. If you'll excuse me, we'll be departing shortly. I'll need you to stay clear of the deck until we are under way."

Beneath what Dalin thought was called the command deck was a simple wooden hatch that led below, and the Commander led the way. Dalin glanced back down at the pier and saw that the General had already left. He took one last look at the city behind the ship before he ducked under the entrance and into the darkness.

Chapter 16

THE PRICE FOR PEACE

Ever since Kailar had left the Tal Warriors' Guild, she had grown accustomed to travelling alone. Even when the orcs had followed her, she never talked with them, she never considered them anything more than mindless monsters bent to her will. Her thoughts had been her own, and she spoke to no one.

It was therefore difficult for her to get used to travelling with a group of people. Even at a brisk pace, she and Letan hadn't caught up with the rest of his group until late the following morning. It took more than four days to traverse the passes through the Barrier Mountains, until they finally came to another 'gateway' town on the other side. This time, she walked with the group rather than behind, mostly at Letan's insistence. And this time, there was considerable conversation.

Initially the others had tried to ask her questions to get to know her better, but once they realized they weren't going to get anything out of her, they started talking about themselves, telling her stories about their lives. All of them, that is, except for Tanneth. He still clearly didn't trust her, and he more than once made snide remarks about delaying their departure from Edingard because of her.

Initially she rather liked that he didn't talk to her much, though she grew tired of his suspicious glances. She did acknowledge to herself that his suspicions were probably close to the mark, but the stress she felt over it was unwelcome.

As the others spoke to her, she felt annoyed in the beginning. They were obviously as physically fit as she was and the climb through the mountains did not leave them breathless, so all they did was talk. However, as time went on, she began to enjoy their company and conversation, especially that of Adira, the herb specialist.

Adira was a peaceful woman, not at all violent. She was very young when her family came to Devor, and since then, she had learned much about herbs and various floras on Edilas. From the moment her family came ashore, she began to learn about the plants of Devor, initially from books written by explorers who had already experimented, and then later by finding new plants and experimenting herself. She had become something of an authority on medicinal and harmful effects of plants, especially near Corlas where her family had settled.

That was why Adira travelled to Tieran Port, to sell healing poultices and salves for export to Edilas and the other southern continent of Asirin. She made good money from her wares, and lived relatively well in Corlas. Kailar had asked her why she didn't pay someone to take her wares to Tieran or why she never brought a horse to ride upon, but she said she liked hiking at least once a year across the continent, especially through the mountains.

Borlin and Geris both worked in the Corlas mines, and Borlin was also an apprentice blacksmith. Kailar learned that they were brothers, which she found surprising since they looked nothing alike. Borlin had blonde hair with blue eyes and was a little taller than Kailar was, while Geris was shorter than she was, had dark brown hair and brown eyes. Both were born and raised in Corlas, and Borlin was betrothed to a woman named Mira, whom he couldn't stop talking about. They'd met when she had followed her parents to Corlas from the city of Freemount in Tal. Her father was also a blacksmith, while Mira had learned leatherworking from her mother.

Kailar found it amusing that Borlin was learning the blacksmith trade from Mira's father. It made sense, especially to have a blacksmith and a leatherworker working together, but to have to train under the father of the woman you were going to marry? She didn't envy him.

Benton was a farmer, and had specifically come to seek out and buy the much needed farm equipment for Corlas. He was the oldest of the group and claimed to be among the first generation of children born in a Devor colony, but she doubted he was actually that old. He had wild tales of his time there, and she felt he often embellished his tales or made some of them up. After a time, however, she enjoyed his fables, and began to pay closer attention to them, especially when they would sit around a fire at night to wind down and prepare to go to bed.

Neolas was the town on the west side of the Barrier Mountains, and when they did finally arrive, it was already sunset, so they spent the night and left early in the morning. Since then, they had hiked for an additional four days, and were deep in the Central Plains of Devor.

She'd seen some flat lands in her travels in and around Tal, but never had she seen a land so absolutely level and boring. There were no real trees, or at least not the kind she was used to, but instead there were what she called miniature trees, most no taller than the average person, in clusters all along the path. Their trunks were very short and never grew straight and their branches were never very thick, but they burned hot enough, and the nuts they bore were quite tasty. She also found the smell they produced when burned to be quite pleasant, but couldn't identify what it smelled like, certainly unlike anything found in Tal.

It was mid-afternoon and the sun was in their eyes. Kailar kept her cloak off of her shoulders, but used the hood to help shield her eyes from the sun. In a couple more hours, it would be directly in her face and the hood would do nothing to help her with that.

She strode along side of Letan just ahead and to the right of the horses and cart, while Tanneth and Benton strode behind the cart and behind them. Borlin and Geris were on the opposite side of the cart chatting amongst themselves, and Adira sat upon the seat on the cart to take her turn driving the horses.

Letan was in the middle of telling Kailar about one of his childhood memories. Her appreciation for him and her attraction towards him had only grown since he had rescued her from her tears at the Black Horse Inn. The entire afternoon and evening after they left Edingard, he had left her in peace, left her to her thoughts and her embarrassment.

She respected him for that freedom. He allowed her to decide when they would start talking again, and the next morning she had begun to ask him more about himself. He was, much to her surprise, somewhat evasive about his more recent history, but he told her all about his childhood. And not once had he asked her about what had set her off in Edingard, or why she told him to stop calling her Fiera.

Letan had grown up in Archanon, but had moved to Corlas when he was still just a teen. She hadn't learned a whole lot about who he was now or what had brought him to Devor, but she enjoyed his childhood stories.

When he finished his latest tale, a silence fell upon them, which was not uncommon on their journey. Although there had been considerable conversation amongst the entire group, there had been plenty of times when they just hiked silently.

Kailar stared silently at the ground ahead of her and tried to decide whether or not to ask him why he was on Devor, when he had left Edilas, or what exactly he did in Corlas for work. However, before she could, he spoke, "So you realize this works better when it goes both ways."

She frowned and looked at him, puzzled. "What does?"

"Conversation. Getting to know one another. You know so much about us, but you haven't said a word about yourself." He looked back at the others, and then quietly added, "If you don't want them all to hear we can speak quietly."

She also glanced back and noticed the suspicious look on Tanneth's face. She smirked in his direction, which made him clench his jaw, before she looked Letan in the eyes again. A part of her wanted to tell him more, but she also couldn't help but feel afraid. If she revealed too much about herself, Letan or Tanneth or one of the others might figure out who she was.

However, part of what she'd wrestled with the last few days was that her fear was no longer focused on being discovered and arrested or killed. Now she feared that Letan would find out what she had done in Edingard, or the atrocities she had committed in Tal and Falind. She was worried she'd lose his approval and respect. Somehow he continued to see good in her, even after she had threatened to kill him.

How could that be? How could he trust her, or believe in her?

She wanted to believe it was because he was using her, because he wanted something from her. Yet the longer she walked with the group, the more she realized how unlikely that was. Letan seemed to be a truly good man, and that made his faith in her all the more surreal and difficult.

She looked ahead and continued to consider what she might or could tell him, but her thoughts were interrupted when she realized that there was a group of people on the trail ahead of them, at least a dozen individuals, plus horses for each of them.

When she realized they'd come that close to the group without her realizing, she cursed herself for another lapse in her awareness. "Letan..."

He also looked ahead, and then sighed. "It's okay. They are bandits."

She snapped her head over to look at him in puzzlement. "How is that okay?"

Letan did not answer, and instead looked up at Adira and signaled to her. She reached back into the cart and pulled out a pouch that jingled with coin. She hefted it a moment, looked ahead in disgust, and then tossed the coins down to Letan.

Kailar repeated her question, "How is that ok?"

"Look," he finally looked at her, "this is how it works on Devor. They'll require a toll from us, we pay, we go on free."

She felt her blood boil, and she glared ahead at the interlopers. They seemed to be patient while they waited for Letan's group. No weapons were drawn, and no one looked worried or prepared to attack. "How can that be the way it is here?" She looked to him for answers. "How can criminals be given free reign?"

"It isn't free reign," he hushed his voice and waved his hand to tell her to keep her voice down. They drew closer and he obviously didn't want them to overhear their conversation. "I'll explain once we're past."

She shook her head. "We can't let them go free. Do you have a spare sword?" She felt for her dagger, and knew that with the help of the others they could defeat the bandits, but she would feel much more comfortable with a sword.

"No!" He gripped her shoulder tightly and looked at her with a deep insistence and a stern look. At that moment, she realized that he wasn't just a natural leader, but he had actually been trained to be a leader, and she began to suspect who or what he was. "No," he repeated quieter. "Do not attack them."

Kailar had never seen him act in such a manner, and the grip on her shoulder actually hurt. She looked at his hand, which immediately made him soften his grip, before she looked in his eyes. "Very well. I will follow your lead."

A few moments later, Letan brought them to a stop a hundred feet from the bandits. Tanneth came up to stand beside Kailar, but the rest stayed where they were relative to the cart. One of the bandits, a stocky looking man with black, long hair that fell loose around him, stepped forward.

"Hello Letan," the bandit smiled, and revealed his surprisingly straight and clean teeth. He wore black trousers and a clean white shirt under a tan leather vest. He had obviously been on the road for some time, but he still seemed to take pride in his appearance.

"Egil," Letan nodded to the head bandit. "I didn't expect to see you this far east. I thought we had at least a week before we ran into your lot."

Egil shrugged easily. "I can't just stay in one place, now, can I? Even on the plains, some folk might find a way around us without being seen." He placed his hands on his hips, most likely to emphasize the longsword he wore. "Not that I'm saying you would ever try such a thing. That takes guts. Guts what you don't have."

The last sentence he'd spoken had a hint of an accent to it, and she thought it was one she had heard only from commoners on Edilas. She suspected he had humble origins, and perhaps had even come over from Edilas under similar circumstances to the miner in Edingard that she had killed. In either case, the other bandits surrounded him in what was both a protective and respectful half-circle – he had become a respected or feared leader amongst them.

She wanted nothing more than to pull her dagger and cut the grin from his face for insulting Letan, but she kept herself in check for the moment.

Letan hefted the pouch in his hand once before he tossed it to Egil, apparently unaffected by the bandit's jibe. Egil deftly caught it and opened it to inspect its contents. He smirked, pulled the draw string on the pouch closed, and tossed it back to one of his subordinates. "As usual, not even so much as a fuss from you," he laughed, which elicited snickers from the other bandits. "I like you,

Letan. Cowards like you are always easy prey." Kailar clenched her jaw and very nearly drew her weapon.

Egil waved his hand, and without another word, the bandits parted to allow them to pass. She looked at Letan to see his jaw was also tight, but he gave no other indication that he was perturbed. "Come on," Letan started forward. Everyone else followed suit, including Kailar, but she glared at Egil as they passed by him.

"What you lookin' at, girl?" He narrowed his eyes at her. She returned his stare evenly, but said nothing. "Hey, your tongue broken or something?"

They passed by and she looked ahead, but still said nothing, afraid to start an incident, but getting ever closer to not caring. She could see out of the corner of her eye that Letan glanced at her nervously.

"That's not surprising, is it boys," Egil jibed. "She looks tough but has no backbone, does she? I suppose only cowards would follow a coward…"

They had passed the bandits, but her temper flared and she spun around. "And I wonder just who is truly the coward here?" The cart continued past, but Benton stopped beside her and gave her a warning look, one which she ignored.

Egil glared at her. "Careful now, lady. You don't want your temper to get you into something you don't have the guts to see through."

Her right hand grasped her dagger. "Watch who you're calling a coward." She felt another firm grip clench her shoulder, but she shrugged off Letan's hand and moved towards the bandits. "You have no idea who I am or what I am capable of. You're the cowards, you who take coin from those who actually worked for it."

Egil pointed at her, and that was apparently an unsaid command for the bandits to surround her as she approached him. "Fiera, no," Letan called to her.

"Keep back, Letan!" Egil kept his glare on Kailar. "She wants trouble, she's got it."

"The kind of trouble that means you have to work for your bounty," she sneered.

She faced east, which meant even surrounded, she could anticipate attacks from behind thanks to shadows, and that was precisely what happened. She saw a shadow coming towards her, so she drew her dagger, and as a bandit's arms came around her to try to put her in a bear-hug, she thrust her left elbow back and firmly planted it in the gut of her assailant. He tried to cry out in surprise, but it came out as nothing but an airy gasp. When the others moved in to attack, she spun enough to jab her dagger into the first assailant's side, effectively ending his role in the battle.

Kailar didn't have armor, but she was fast, nimble, and precise, and she knew it, so instead of facing her opponents, she continued her spin and moved fast. The others had pulled weapons of varying types and tried to attack her, but they were not an effective combat unit, and when they tried to attack her all at once, they ended up meeting their own weapons as she ducked and weaved out of the way. She swung her down-turned dagger and sliced the arm of one bandit, the leg of another, and she kept going, knowing full well that if she stopped moving, she was dead. A moment later, the bandit leader was before her with his sword raised. As it came down on her, she side-stepped and brought her dagger down to cut his left wrist, and then she brought it back up and cut his arm. He screamed in pain and surprise and stumbled backwards.

Suddenly a blast of magic threw three of the bandits to the ground at once. Another blast took down two more. This continued until all of the uninjured bandits were off their feet.

Kailar spun around and saw Letan had drawn his own sword to use his powers. "Enough," he shouted as some of the bandits tried to stand and attack him. He used another blast to knock them down, and he repeated, "I said enough! This battle is over, now!"

Egil clutched his wounded arm and glowered at Letan. "She challenged me! Blood must be spilled."

"Blood has been spilled," Letan spoke with the kind of authority she would expect from a trained and experienced Warrior. "Your blood. Do you want to lose more?" Letan brought his sword back and held it with two hands. "You have wounded to attend to. Let it go at this, Egil."

The bandit leader clenched his teeth and looked ready to pick up his weapon again, but he looked once more at Letan and thought better of it. "Very well. Get out of here, Letan. And expect your next toll to cost you triple!"

She reeled on him and prepared to attack. "Fiera," Letan shouted. "I said this battle is over!"

She was surprised at the forcefulness of his voice, the anger, and she felt a strange tingling sensation in her stomach. She lowered her hands, and Egil looked at her with a combination of fear and hatred.

"We must leave," Letan insisted. "Now!"

She continued to glare at Egil for a moment longer, but she already felt a sinking sensation in her gut, so she turned and headed towards Letan. He still held his sword, but was no longer in a combat stance. He didn't look at her, his eyes drating around at the others, ready to defend if they changed their mind.

When she came within ten feet of Letan, she spun around, not willing to leave things the way they were. "If you should ever threaten Letan or his people again," she clenched her dagger. "I will hunt every single one of you down!"

Egil looked ready to say or do something in response, but Letan once again shouted, "That is enough! Fiera, leave now before they change their mind."

She swallowed an instinctive response down, spun around, and stormed past Letan, now unwilling to look at him, both out of fear of the disappointment that he no doubt had on his face, and fear that she would say something to him that she would regret.

Tanneth stood with his own weapon drawn, and the others also looked prepared to draw weapons, but she quickly passed them and continued on the path towards the setting sun. She wasn't sure how long or how far she walked before Letan finally caught up to her, but the sun was now directly in her face.

"Fiera, wait," he pleaded. She ignored him, her emotions tumultuous at best. She wasn't sure if she wanted to shout at him or apologize, but the burst of energy she felt from the heat of battle was starting to wear off, and her temper had begun to wane.

Once again she felt his vice grip on her shoulder, but she had had enough of that. She dropped her dagger, reached back, ripped his hand from her shoulder, and shoved him away. "Do not touch me again!"

He looked with shock and hurt at her, but then his face hardened. "Do you realize what you've just done?"

Behind him she saw the cart and the others approaching, but she had marched on a long distance ahead them. The bandits were far away, but still visible as small dots in the distance. "I've placed fear back in the bandits, as it should be," she retorted.

"You've disrupted the balance that exists on this continent

between the lawful and unlawful," he replied. "You've threatened everything!"

"Threatened the balance? Are you kidding me?!" she waved her hands around in bewilderment. "They're bandits! Why haven't the Warriors wiped them out or arrested them?"

"There are too many of them," he replied, anger still evident in his voice. "This land is rife with criminals, much of it organized. If we stood up to them, they would destroy us, or at the very least plunge the land into complete chaos." He waved his hand to the northeast, "The four kingdoms have never sent us the help we need to stop them. We are on our own here, and we have to do whatever it takes to keep some semblance of peace and security!"

She wasn't sure what to say to that, but she still felt incensed, so she changed topics, "And why didn't you ever tell me you're a Warrior?"

Letan clenched his hands into fists, but then lowered them to his sides and forced them open. He clearly was attempting to calm himself. "Because you seemed like you were running from something," he looked evenly at her. "I didn't want to scare you off."

"Scare me off? Why would it matter if I ran off? Why do you care so much?"

He replied tersely, "Because I find..." He trailed off, clenched his fists again, and then seemed to sigh in defeat. "Because I find you enchanting."

"Oh," she unconsciously replied, and then felt a lump in her throat. Her stomach turned in butterflies, and she felt her fingertips tingle. "I...enchanting?"

"Yeah," he looked down and his face turned red. "I'm, um, sorry."

She wasn't sure how to reply, she couldn't think of any words, and for a moment, they stood in awkward silence. A part of her wanted to tell him it was ok, and she was flattered, but in reality she was scared. Scared that he would find out who she was, scared that he would hate her for it. Worse still, she was scared that he would still find her 'enchanting' even after learning all of that, and she had no idea why that frightened her so much.

It hadn't been her intent to go down the path that she now faced. She would have been perfectly content to have travelled alone, to find the Crystalline Peaks on her own. She didn't want anyone else in her life. She didn't deserve to have anyone else in her life.

"Letan..." she started to say, but couldn't find the words to continue.

"I know you don't approve of the situation," he changed topics, obviously embarrassed by his own admission. "But the deal the leaders of our cities struck with the criminal element has saved so many lives, and kept order for us all. Egil will report this incident to the leaders of the criminal underground, and they will retaliate, if not against us directly, then against innocents." She started to say something, but he interrupted her, "And there is nothing anyone can do, not without inviting further bloodshed."

She almost told him that she would be willing to lead the charge against them, that it was better to die fighting than to live in fear. But then she remembered what that usually cost others, and she knew that Letan would never willingly risk the lives of innocents to fight a possibly hopeless cause. He cared more about protecting lives than sticking up for himself.

Maybe Egil was right, maybe he was a coward for that. *Or,* she thought to herself, *it makes him the bravest man I've ever known.*

In either case, she realized she couldn't do anything without risking his life and the lives of those he cared about. "I'm sorry," she looked down at his feet. "I didn't realize the cost of my actions. You tried to warn me, and I didn't listen."

He reached forward and gently touched her chin to make her look him in the eyes, but then his face turned red again and he pulled away. "I understand, Fiera. I really do. You have no idea how hard it is for me not to fight them."

She attempted to give him an encouraging smile, but couldn't find it within herself to give a convincing one. "Thank you for saving me back there."

The cart had caught up to them, so she picked up her dagger and sheathed it.

"You're very welcome," he gave her a rather charming smile. Together they fell into step where they had been before, just ahead and to the right of the cart. "Let's get at least some distance between us and the bandits before we stop for the night."

She looked apologetically at the others in the group, but they all just looked scared. All of them except Tanneth. He looked at her

with even greater suspicion. So she simply smiled at him.
That really seemed to aggravate him.

Chapter 17

DERELICT

Cardin awoke in a cold, panicked sweat. The same panicked sweat he'd woken up to many times in the past months. It was dark, except for a small lamp lit somewhere nearby. He looked around to get his bearings, and found some comfort in the now-familiar sight below decks on the Sea Wisp. The ship creaked and groaned as it glided through the waves.

He slept in a hammock near the back of the ship, which swayed back and forth hypnotically. He found it a comforting motion that actually helped him sleep at night. *If only it could do something about the nightmares,* he thought.

The same nightmare. Except ever since they had left Maradin, a new element had been added to it, a new horror. He shuddered at the memory, and rolled out of the hammock onto the deck as quietly as he could. At night, he couldn't sleep in the hammock with the Sword strapped onto his back. So he always pulled the scabbard off and kept it at his side. He picked it up and swung it around onto his back.

The lamp light came from near the entrance to the sea deck, as was usual during the night watch. If anyone needed more light, they would light their own lamp and move silently amongst the sleeping crew and guests.

Without looking at any of his other companions, he began to make his way forward. He still had trouble walking on the swaying ship when he first woke up, but soon enough he found his 'sea legs' as the crew called it. He stepped over Reis's errant arm that lay in the middle of the walkway. Reis couldn't sleep in the hammocks, the constant rocking of the ship by itself had made him sick many times during the voyage, and the hammocks only seemed to make it worse for him.

Cardin gripped the wooden railing to the steep steps and ascended up on deck. It was still night, but he couldn't tell how late, or rather how early it was. The watch bell sounded to indicate the passage of another hour.

He looked back towards where the wheel was, and saw the watch commander, a young officer who'd taken night watch many times named Parlich Evrin, standing next to the wheelman. Parlich saluted Cardin, as did the wheelman, and he nodded back to them. It felt odd to be saluted by the crew, but Captain Norric had ordered his crew to treat them like officers of the Royal Navy.

The sea was fairly calm. Cardin made his way to the left side of the ship, or rather it was called the port side, as he'd learned early in their journey. It had been two weeks since they had left Maradin Port, and in that time he'd learned much about the workings of the ship, but still found there was a lot he didn't know. He was a long ways away from ever being able to serve as a member of the crew, but that was fine by him. He had enjoyed the new experience and the adventure of sailing, but now he felt ready for dry land again.

The sky was clear and he saw the stars as bright as day. They had sailed east by northeast the entire journey, so he had a perfect view of the northern sky. He located a few constellations idly, and used them to identify exactly where north was, and smiled. The stars had always enchanted him, and he found comfort in him. The nightmare did not fade from his memory, but he felt a little less shaken.

A bright streak of light flashed across the sky, another shooting star. They had seen many during their voyage, more than he was used to seeing. A glow had started to appear to the east, and he realized that it was near dawn.

He felt more than heard another person approach, and soon realized that it was the warm presence of Sira. She came up beside him and leaned against the side of the ship. She must have heard him get up and followed him up on deck.

She smiled at him, and he tried to give her his best fake smile, but he knew he'd failed. "The nightmare again?"

At first he hesitated, but then he nodded. "Yes."

"They're coming more frequently," she said. It wasn't a question. "Almost every night now."

He looked back out towards the horizon, not sure he wanted to face her probing eyes. "I know. I'm almost afraid to go to sleep every night."

The familiar, comfortable sensation of her hand on his shoulder warmed him further. "Cardin...are you ever going to tell me what the dream is about?"

A lump formed in his throat, and he found that he had no answer for her. It had become like a giant wall that separated them, and he worried that the rekindling of their relationship would never happen so long as he kept things hidden from her. Yet the nightmare terrified him so much that he still felt afraid to tell her, or anyone else, about it.

The fact that Maradin was now a part of it made him think it really was just a dream, but he also couldn't discount how real everything felt, even when he jumped from location to location, seeing equal devastation everywhere.

Staring out to sea as he was, he felt alone. Very alone. Then he remembered how alone he felt when he faced Kailar in the Battle for Archanon, when he had told Sira and the others to leave because he was afraid they would get hurt by a stray blast of magic. At the time, he had considered the probability that he would need to get used to being alone, that no one could help him, that the burden of protecting the Sword would isolate him more than ever.

And then Sira came back, along with Elaria and a contingent of Warriors. They came back and helped him defeat Kailar. His heart had swelled then, and a couple of days later, Sira, Reis, and Dalin had sworn an oath to help him protect the Sword and face his future together.

So he told her. "It always starts the same," he looked into her eyes, at least as best as he could in the low light. "Remember when we were young, I used to dream about a black and white dragon?"

She frowned, but nodded. "Of course, you always loved those

dreams."

"I did," he smiled weakly. "I found the dragon to be amazing. Those dreams started out as terrifying reproductions of the myths we'd heard, but eventually the dreams turned to that dragon becoming my ally, and fighting alongside of me. These new nightmares start out the same, with the dragon as my companion. But he always disappears, and I start to see…" He trailed off, unsure if he really wanted to tell her, but knowing full well that he needed to.

The hand she'd placed on his shoulder now reached down and took hold of his hand. He realized he had started to shake as the memories filled his mind, and she helped steady him.

"I see fire," his voice shook as he said it. "The skies burn. I see Archanon in flames, Daruun forest completely ablaze. Falind castle is utterly destroyed. And…" He clenched his eyes shut, but it was a mistake, and the image flashed in front of him again. When he opened them again, Sira looked at him with deep concern. "Ever since we left Maradin, I've dreamt of a giant wave washing over the city."

She squeezed his hand reassuringly, but that wasn't the end of the dream, and he continued. "When it ends, the world is surrounded by darkness. I am consumed by it. Everyone is." He looked intently at her. "*Everyone* is."

Her eyes showed the fear she felt at his last words, but they quickly turned to sympathy and concern. Without a word, she grabbed his arm, turned him towards her, and clutched him in a tight hug. He wrapped his arms around her and held on, afraid that if he let go, the nightmare would become reality, and she would disappear into the darkness.

Except that the darkness was quickly retreating. The predawn glow grew brighter, and he knew within minutes the disc of the sun would peak over the horizon. He did not let go of Sira, nor did she let go of him, but he turned his head towards the east to watch.

For a long time, they embraced each other, neither willing to let go. Moments before he knew the first rays of the sun would peak over the far horizon, they pulled apart, and Sira grabbed hold of both of his hands.

"Sira," his voice still shook. "I am so scared."

"It's just a dream," she tried to smile encouragingly.

"I don't think it is," he grimaced. "It feels too real, too vivid.

More than that, I can feel it in my heart. Something is coming, something terrible. And I am so afraid that no matter how powerful I become, even if I learn new powers before it happens, I will be powerless to stop it."

She looked down and considered his words for a moment. He wanted to know what she was thinking, but was also afraid of what she might say next. He hated that feeling, hated being afraid.

"If what you saw is meant to be," she looked into his eyes, "then we must face it together. If destruction comes to our world, and we cannot stop it from happening, then we must do the next best thing."

He frowned. "What's that?"

She gave him a smile that warmed his heart. "Save as much as we can, save as many people as we can. Protect those we can protect. And fight one battle at a time." She squeezed his hands. "One battle, Cardin. Because no matter how powerful you are destined to become, you can't fight the universe."

He realized just how much truth there was in her words. The weight in his heart seemed to lift, if only a little, and he found himself smiling. "You're right," he laughed a little. "You're absolutely right."

"Of course I am," she smirked. "I'm the commander of this mission, remember? I'm always right."

He raised an eyebrow at her, smirked, and then embraced her in another tight hug.

"Mast-ho!" a shout came down from the crow's nest.

Cardin and Sira pulled apart and looked up at the crow's nest. The sailors on duty in the nest both pointed towards the rising sun. They looked out where they pointed, but neither could see anything.

It was possible it was still beyond the horizon from their perspective, so Cardin and Sira both made their way up the steps to where the wheel was and where Parlich stood. He was at the starboard side and stared out at the rising sun, a telescope in his hands but unused. Cardin and Sira both looked out in that direction, and against the rising sun, they saw a sliver of a line near the middle of it.

Parlich couldn't use the telescope to look at the mast, not with the sun directly behind it, it would blind him. So they simply stared at it, their eyes squinting as the sun rose higher and grew brighter.

"What should we do, sir," the wheelman asked.

"Steady as she goes," Parlich replied. "We don't know what it is yet."

"No one else should be out this far," Sira commented with a frown. "Except maybe for the ships that never returned."

"It could be pirates," Cardin suggested, even though he knew that wasn't likely the case. "Maybe that's why we haven't heard from the other ships."

Parlich shook his head. "They usually stay closer to land."

Sira looked at Parlich pointedly. "Usually."

In the distance, the sliver of the mast continued to rise over the horizon, and though still in front of the sun, they saw a hazy form take shape beneath it that Cardin surmised was the ship that the mast belonged to.

Parlich sighed. "Either way, you're right. Whoever they are, they shouldn't be out here."

Cardin noted that the rest of the night crew was also on the starboard side of the ship and stared out at the rising sun and the errant mast. Another few minutes and they would sail far enough to be able to use a telescope.

After another moment of hesitation, Parlich looked to his left, where another crew member stood. "Sound quarters."

With that order, the crew member stepped back, picked up a drum, and wrapped the strap around the back of his neck. He took hold of a pair of drumsticks and began to beat a rapid call to general quarters.

Parlich stepped away from the rail and shouted, "All hands to stations! Mages to the starboard side. Crow's nest, keep an eye out for any other sails."

The tired night shift suddenly surged into action. The few Mages on shift immediately pulled out their swords, not for possible melee combat, but to use them to focus their powers should they need to fire upon another ship. Bows and arrows, or even crossbows, were not very effective from long range, and space on the deck of a ship was considered prime real estate, so smaller ships never carried catapults or other siege-type weapons. Even on larger ships, long range ship-to-ship combat was best accomplished through the use of Mage powers.

At long range, a Mage could never strike a target like a human, but a ship was a much larger object. It was how naval warfare was fought, and the skill and power of the Mages was as important as the ability of a ship's crew and its Captain to command them.

The sleeping day shift below decks woke quickly and climbed up, and within minutes, the deck and all of the rigging was filled to the brim with active crewmembers.

Captain Norric and Commander Devral climbed up to the command deck and stood beside them all. Reis, Dalin, Elaria, Anila, and Ventelis followed shortly after. "Sira," the Captain looked at her curiously, but did not yet order her or the others off of the deck. After another moment, he looked at Parlich and ordered, "Report."

"Mast spotted off the starboard bow, sir, towards the rising sun. Another moment and we'll be clear to use telescopes."

Norric and Devral both moved to starboard and looked out towards the rising sun. It was almost too bright to look directly at it now, but the hazy, distant visage of the ship was already clear of the disk and, as the Sea Wisp sailed at top speed, was quickly growing distant from the disk.

"And you sounded quarters?" Devral looked at Parlich with a frown.

Parlich looked uneasily towards Sira before he answered, "Well, there shouldn't be anyone else out here. Except maybe the lost ships. We...I didn't know what to expect, we don't know why those ships never reported back."

"You did the right thing," Norric grabbed the telescope from him. "Take your station, Lieutenant."

"Aye, sir," he replied, and moved back towards the wheelman.

After another moment, Norric brought the telescope up and looked out towards the other ship. Devral secured another telescope and likewise took a look. Cardin wished he had one as well, but was forced to be content to stare out at the small, hazy shape on the horizon.

"I don't see colors flying," Devral commented.

"And it looks like its sails are up, but torn to shreds," Norric added. "But it's a three-mast square rigger. Probably the Avendal."

"I don't see any movement on deck," Devral said. "No crew?"

Norric looked back at Parlich, "Come to starboard, ten points south of the rising sun."

"Aye, sir," Parlich replied, and passed the order on to the wheelman.

"We won't have the weather gauge with us," Devral pointed out, a term Cardin still didn't understand.

"I know," Norric replied. "But somehow I get the feeling there is no threat on that ship."

Time seemed to pass slowly, and it took them ages to catch up to the other ship. While their previous northeastern course had them travelling at over sixteen knots, they were down to ten knots on their intercept course.

The Captain's ability to turn the ship as needed was uncanny, and as they drew closer to the other ship, it always stayed away from the sun from their perspective, and they were able to keep an eye on it during the entire approach. More Mages were on deck and were at stations on the starboard side, ready to attack if needed. The crew worked hard to coax more speed from the sails, and it paid off with an extra knot of speed.

As the ship grew closer, the Captain ordered Devral to let Sira borrow her telescope, so that Sira could get a look at it. "We're coming at them from their broadside," Norric told her. "No way of knowing what her course was before she became a derelict."

"How do you know what ship it is?" she asked him and passed the telescope to Cardin. He took a look through it and was surprised at how much it magnified his vision. He could see most details of the ship, and it looked like they were practically on top of it, not several miles out.

"I don't exactly, her name will be on the stern," Norric replied. After Cardin was satisfied to have seen what he needed, he passed the telescope on to Reis, who took one look through it, looked a little ill, and tried to pass it to Elaria. She smile, glanced through it only in amusement, and then gave it back to the first officer. "But of the ships missing, the Avendal is the only three-mast ship that should be out here."

"If it is indeed one of the known missing ships," Dalin said, "Then at least we will shortly have a clue as to what has happened out here."

"Yeah," Sira nodded, her eyes fixed on the derelict.

Cardin wasn't sure how much time had passed before they were within shouting distance of the ship. They still saw no crew on deck, and the shredded sails fluttered in the wind. Cardin saw where the ship's flag should have been, but there was nothing. If it was the Avendal, it should have been flying Erien colors.

The first officer shouted orders and several sails were let out to allow the Sea Wisp to slow their approach. Norric looked back at Parlich, "Keep her on our starboard, away from the sun. We'll swing around aft and come up on her port."

"Ready the grappling hooks," Devral ordered. "Marines stand by to board."

Sira ducked below deck to grab her own sword and came back up as quickly as she could, but Reis had come up on deck ready to fight and his sword was already secured in its sheath on his belt. Dalin was never found without his staff, while Elaria, seemingly weaponless, probably had her daggers somehow hidden on her. Ventelis still had no weapons, and would likely not immediately board with the marines or with Cardin and the others. Anila was also, as always, prepared.

As they came around the derelict's stern, they had their first clear view of the registry below the windows to the Captain's quarters, and sure enough, it was the Avendal. The Sea Wisp was moving faster than Cardin expected, but Cardin knew it was because as soon as they turned to match the ship's course, they would pass through the area where the wind would be ahead of them, and that meant they would need to 'douse canvas,' as they called it, and let their momentum pass them through the turn and come up along side of the ship.

That was when he felt it. A brief touch against his mind, a strange sensation as if someone had gently pushed against his thoughts with magic. It was an altogether unfamiliar sensation, and he knew it couldn't have come from anyone aboard the Sea Wisp. "Something else is aboard that ship," he said quietly.

Sira was the first to reply, "What do you mean?"

He looked at her, not having realized he'd said that out loud. "There is a presence aboard, something with magic, but…"

"I sense no such presence," Dalin stated matter-of-factly. "Are you certain?"

He hesitated, looked to his friend, and shook his head. "No, not exactly. But something, or someone, just touched my thoughts."

"Hard to starboard, douse canvas!" Devral shouted.

Cardin realized that the Sea Wisp had just started to pass the aft end of the Avendal. The wheelman turned hard over, and the ship quickly turned as the crew let the wind spill out of the last sail still up.

"Is what you feel something of concern," Captain Norric asked.

Cardin looked intently at the derelict. "I doubt it is hiding its presence for fun."

"Just because someone hides doesn't mean they necessarily have malicious intent," Anila stated idly. The night of the Royal Ball flashed through his mind, and he remembered that she had, indeed, posed no threat. So far.

As the ship's momentum carried them to starboard and they came along side the Avendal, they got their first unobstructed view of the Avendal's deck. There was visible damage to the deck and to parts of the rigging, and it indicated that there had been Mages involved in a battle.

"Look at that," Devral frowned. "No damage to the hull, but obvious Mage combat on deck. If they had been attacked by another ship, there should be hull damage."

Cardin felt a chill crawl down his spine. There was something there, on the very edge of his perception. He was certain of it, now more than ever.

Without having to be ordered to, crew members on the starboard side threw grappling hooks across the short divide to the Avendal. The hooks caught and the crew secured the lines before they became taught, and the Sea Wisp lurched beneath their feet as their momentum slowed dramatically to match the Avendal's. Once there was slack on the lines again, the crew took hold and began to pull their ship closer to the derelict.

"I still do not sense anything," Dalin stepped closer to the edge of the Sea Wisp's deck and frowned at the Avendal. Cardin felt the Wizard's power flare as he used every sense he had to find what Cardin felt.

"And with each passing moment, I feel more certain there is something aboard," Cardin looked intently at his friend. "We must be cautious."

"Marines will board first," Norric ordered loud enough for all to hear. Then he looked at Sira, who was ready to protest. "Then your team can follow. My Marines are trained to board ships under combat conditions, and we don't know what to expect."

Sira hesitated, and then assented. "Fair enough."

Cardin wanted to be the first to board, he felt the chill run down his spine again, but the Captain was in command.

As soon as the Sea Wisp was close enough, several boarding

planks were dropped across the shrinking divide, and with a shouted order from the lead Marine, several sailors holding one-handed swords rushed across. Cardin felt a rush just watching them, and waited anxiously for something horrible to go wrong.

Nothing happened. The Marines boarded, and a few moments later, the Sea Wisp bumped gently against the Avendal. The deckhands secured the lines, effectively mooring the two ships together. The Marines immediately spread out across the deck of the Avendal. Sira looked intently at Cardin, and then led them down the stairs to the main sea deck.

Cardin and Sira took different planks each, climbed up onto them, drew swords, and quickly ran across to the Avendal. When Cardin took his first step on the derelict, another chill ran down his back and made his hairs stand on end.

The damage seemed even worse up-close, and there were literally holes in the deck. Splinters in many of the holes pointed outward, indicating that there had been battle below decks as well and Mages had blown holes in the ship from the inside out. He realized they were lucky holes hadn't been blown through the hull below the water line, or the ship would have sunk long before they found it.

Elaria had followed Cardin easily, the elf's experience on the sea obvious, but Dalin struggled a little to cross over. Cardin looked back at the Sea Wisp and saw the first officer was ready to cross, but Reis was struggling to keep his legs beneath him.

Devral clasped his shoulder. "Maybe you should stay here," Cardin overheard her say.

"I can do this," Reis insisted, and then finally clambered, on all fours, across the plank. When he came off the plank onto the deck, he nearly fell over as the ship lurched a little from an errant wave, but then got his footing and drew his sword. Devral effortlessly crossed behind him.

"Sea deck clear," a Marine reported to the first officer.

Devral drew her own one-handed sword, Cardin couldn't quite remember what their swords were actually called. "Start below decks, now," she ordered.

Cardin moved to try to get ahead of the Marines before they could go below, but Devral quickly reached out and stopped him with a firm hand. "Your weapons, especially your Sword, will be useless in the tight confines below decks."

He looked at her, looked at the Sword, and then imagined trying to wield the Sword of Dragons below decks on the Sea Wisp. "You're right," he realized. "Worse still, I could easily cut through parts of the ship without much effort."

"And this ship would probably break apart if it suffered much more damage," she nodded. "Stow your weapons, and follow me down."

For Cardin and Sira, that was an easy suggestion to follow, they still had magic to fall back on. For Reis, it wasn't quite so simple. As Cardin placed the Sword in its enchanted sheath, Reis came up next to him and whispered, "I'll be defenseless."

Sira had been close enough to hear him, so while she likewise sheathed her sword, she ordered, "Stay on deck, then. Whatever did this, if it gets past us, you must not let it get aboard the Sea Wisp."

Her reasoning for the order was somewhat patronizing, given that there were still plenty of Mages aboard the Sea Wisp, but Reis seemed to be ok with that. "I understand," he smiled wryly. "You two need some alone time..."

Sira rolled her eyes, but Cardin chuckled at the remark. He was glad that, even under these highly unusual circumstances, Reis still had his sense of humor.

The Marines had already disappeared below decks, except for two who had been ordered to secure the sea deck, so Cardin, Sira, Dalin, Anila and Elaria followed Devral as she descended into the bowels of the ship.

As they came to the first deck, Cardin noted the Marines had lit enchanted lanterns. He felt the tiny, pin-prick points of energy in the lanterns, and was curious what they had used to light the fires. There were still plenty of enchanted items of various makes that could light everlasting flames or turn a torch into an enchanted, everlasting torch, but their numbers weren't nearly as many as they used to be, and they were considered highly valuable.

Between the lamp lights and the holes in the ship that allowed beams of sunlight through, Cardin was able to get a clear view of the hold, and he felt his stomach sink. "It's a good thing Reis didn't come down here," Sira remarked.

Dried blood was everywhere, and in some cases, more than just blood. The smell was sickening, and Cardin felt ill himself, despite having been around plenty of bodies in the past year. Flies buzzed everywhere, and on more than one occasion he had to swat one off of himself, their bites surprisingly painful.

He coughed a little, and then managed to ask, "Why didn't we see anything like this up top?"

Devral held her hand over her nose for a moment, her eyes watered. "Most likely this ship's been adrift for a while. One good rain storm would have washed the blood away."

"Even still," one of the Marines commented, "blood stains in wood aren't easy to get out. This ship has been adrift for a long, long time."

As they started to look around, Cardin's sense that something else was aboard the ship returned. The fact that no one had sounded a sighting of anything made him wonder where the person or creature was hiding. He saw a few Marines descend to another deck below, but he didn't want to stray far from Sira. A Mage relied on their weapons to focus their magical attacks. They still could use their powers without weapons, but they were unfocused and therefore less effective. He wanted to be able to protect her should something attack.

Dalin held his staff out ahead of him and lit his focusing crystal to produce another light. Cardin also noted wryly that, as suspected, Elaria had produced her two daggers from seemingly nowhere and held them at the ready. He realized that in these tight confines, her daggers were very appropriate. He also realized that shouldn't have surprised him, now that he knew what kind of environment the Dareann Elves lived in.

Elaria was also the first to notice and point out what should have been obvious to them all, "Where are the bodies?"

As soon as she said that, Cardin looked around more intently. He saw dried blood and innards that had no doubt been splayed out from slain crewmembers, but there were no bodies

"That doesn't make any sense," Devral sounded almost panicked at the realization. "Even if this ship had been out here for months, the bodies would still be here."

"Unless whoever or whatever attacked took the bodies with them," Dalin stated.

"But why would anyone do that?" Sira asked. "What possible value is there to taking the bodies of the slain?"

"Even more puzzling," a Marine came from a hold in the aft,

"there doesn't seem to be anything missing."

"What?" everyone asked almost at once.

"The supply room is still well stocked," the Marine stated. "The silverware was laid out in the Captain's quarters, with a meal still set. Nothing of value has been taken from this ship."

"Commander!" a panicked shout came from below deck. There came an ear-splitting screech, followed by the screams of the Marines Cardin had watched descend further below.

Devral was somehow faster than he was in reaching the stairs, but Cardin was right behind her, and they both descended as quickly as possible. Sira came right behind him, but he didn't pay attention to who followed behind her. The sight they came upon was entirely unexpected.

Just as it was on the first deck, there was dried blood everywhere, and the smell was somewhat worse, but it was the creature they found that surprised him. It was a serpent, but not a serpent. It had a somewhat humanoid torso, had two pairs of arms, and a roughly humanoid head. Taking in the image all at once was almost impossible due to the very unique nature of the creature that was before him. Where the torso ended, a more serpentine nature began, a long, thick body of a giant snake that held the creature up from the deck, and slithered as she moved around.

She. Cardin realized the creature had very obvious feminine features, visible even beneath her armor. The armor appeared to be made out of some sort of colorful coral, but looked as if it could endure blows as easily as steel. It also looked as if the armor had seen combat, with several nicks, chinks and scratches visible.

Despite having four arms, the creature held no weapons of any kind, but the claws at the ends of her fingers were several inches long, and looked capable of piercing steel. Her fingers were webbed, but the webbing, he noted, retracted as she flexed her fingers.

Even in the low light from torches, he saw her face quite clearly. To call it humanoid was a rough estimate, but what surprised him still was that despite her green and sea-blue scales, and despite the fins where ears and hair should have been, she was surprisingly attractive.

Once he had taken the visage in, he noticed the situation itself. The two Marines that he'd watched descend to the lower deck were sprawled out on the floor, and one had three deep gashes in his chest where the creature had attacked him. The other one was scrambling to his feet. He held the hilt of his sword, but the weapon had been cleaved, and the blade was nowhere to be seen.

When the creature saw Devral coming at her, she raised her hands up, and let out a terrifying, ear-splitting screech that stopped everyone cold. If Cardin had held his Sword, he would have dropped it to cover his ears. Devral did just that.

In fact, he noted the only one who didn't drop her weapon was Elaria, though she visibly cringed at the sound. When the screeching stopped, Devral quickly moved to pick up her sword again, but Elaria shouted, "Stop!"

Devral's hand hovered over the hilt of her sword and she looked intently at Elaria, then with fear at the creature. The creature, surprisingly, kept her four hands raised up disarmingly, or as disarmingly as she could with her claws.

Devral finally grasped her sword, but Elaria stepped closer to her, "She said stop!"

Cardin felt puzzled at that statement. "She said?"

When he spoke, he noted that the creature's expressions changed, and he had the distinct impression it was an expression of anger and disgust.

"Yes, she said," Elaria stated. "What you heard as a screech," Elaria's voice softened as she looked at the serpent, "was a cry to stop."

"How do you know that," Devral asked, anger in her voice. "It was just an animal cry."

"No, it was speech," Elaria gently rested her hand on Devral's back. Devral, the sword in her hand, cautiously stood up straight. "She spoke."

"And you understood her?" Devral looked at Elaria suspiciously.

That was when Cardin remembered the pendants that the elves wore. "Just like Elaria can understand us, and we understand her. Elaria has an enchanted pendant that allows her to communicate with anyone, that translates language back and forth."

"I'm not actually speaking your language," Elaria said to Devral. "It is an illusion created by the magic of my pendant. To you my mouth moves as if I am speaking your language, but I am actually speaking the language of my kin. When you speak to me, I hear my language, and see your mouth move as if you speak my language."

Devral raised her sword between herself and the creature, and the creature hissed at this. "She means us no harm," Elaria insisted.

"Tell that to my Marines," she glared at the creature. Elaria repeated the statement, as if to be an interpreter.

A series of hisses and short screeches emanated from the creature. Elaria translated, "Your slaves attacked me, despite my warnings. What do you mean slaves?" The creature again hissed and screeched. "She says the men, your male slaves." More hisses and screeches. "She did not realize that they could not understand her warnings. She is prepared to compensate you for the loss of one of your slaves."

"They aren't slaves," Devral shouted. She looked at the dead Marine, and then sneered at the creature. "They are good men. He was a good man! His name was Worten Menil, he had a wife and a daughter. He served aboard the Sea Wisp for almost as long as I have."

Elaria translated, although with less emotion than Devral had used. The creature seemed confused by what Elaria stated, and replied.

"She says she does not understand. He is a man, and you clearly own all of the men here." Elaria raised a hand to forestall Devral's response. "I think this is a case of differing cultures. I have met many different people from many different cultures, and in most of the cultures I've encountered, one gender is dominant over the other." Elaria nodded to the creature, "In your culture, women are the masters, men are your subordinates." The creature hissed. "Slaves. They are your slaves."

For a moment, everyone remained silent while that fact sunk in. Cardin realized that what they most likely had before them was a new sentient species, like the elves or the dragons. This brought forth a question, "Where did she come from?"

The creature hissed angrily at him, her arms lowered somewhat menacingly. "Please, remain calm," Elaria said as soothingly as she could. "The humans of Halarite are different, one gender does not hold dominance over the other. Men and women are considered equal." The creature hissed and gave a disgusted look. "It is merely different," Elaria replied. She looked at Cardin and suggested, "Perhaps you shouldn't speak right now…"

Cardin was about to protest, but one look from Sira was enough to shut him up. He felt like it wasn't right, and wanted to say as much. Never the less, he wasn't about to go against Sira's unspoken order. Not this time.

"May I ask, what is your name," Elaria asked the creature. She replied with a short screech. "Ligeia. I am Elaria. This is Commander Elia Devral, and this is Sira Reinar." Ligeia hissed, and then to everyone's surprise, folded her arms and bowed, or that was what it looked like to Cardin. She couldn't actually bow, since she had no legs, but she curled her body near where her torso met the serpent part seamlessly.

Devral wasn't impressed. "Why did you attack this ship? Where is the crew?"

Elaria repeated Devral's words. When the creature spoke, Elaria translated, "She did not. She found the ship this way."

"You lie," Devral shouted, and looked ready to attack. Ligeia backed up defensively, but looked ready to strike Devral down in self-defense.

"Commander!" Sira stepped in front of her, placing herself between Ligeia and the first officer. "Please, be calm." Cardin felt a small amount of panic set in. He was fearful that Ligeia would go through Sira to strike at Devral, but the attack never came.

"Do not give me orders," Devral snapped at Sira. "You are under my command during this voyage, not the other way around!"

"And if we attack Ligeia, more blood will be shed." She waved around at the dried blood that painted much of the lower hold. "Let's keep calm and find out what really happened."

Ligeia screeched and hissed, and Elaria translated, "This ship strayed close to her home, and she was sent to scout the ship and determine what it was, whether or not it was a threat. She boarded shortly before sunrise, and found it like this." Elaria frowned, and asked, "What do you mean?" Ligeia explained and Elaria continued, "She says she smells death. But so do we, this is not surprising."

The serpent shook her head, a surprisingly human-like gesture, and continued. "She says it isn't that. A different kind of death. Animated death. What does that mean?"

"Living death," Dalin breathed. Ligeia hissed angrily. "Forgive me," Dalin bowed very low to her. "May I speak?"

Elaria translated to Ligeia. She regarded Dalin for a moment, and Cardin was surprised by the Wizard's humbleness. After a moment, Ligeia nodded silently.

Dalin continued, "I believe she speaks of the undead." While he spoke, Elaria repeated what he said to Ligeia. Cardin felt a new chill race up and down his back at Dalin's words. "And it would explain why there are no bodies. They were killed, and brought back as the undead, or living dead."

Elaria spoke for Ligeia, "She says that is correct."

"Necromancy," Devral said, finally lowering her sword, slowly, as if in shock. "But that's not possible."

"Perhaps it is possible," Dalin said quietly. "However, it is surprising. Necromancy is an entirely different kind of magic that the humans and Wizards of Halarite have never been able to master. We only know of it because the few Wizards who have travelled to other worlds have encountered it before."

Cardin was about to ask for more information, but realized he hadn't been given permission to speak, as Dalin had. He was about to ask for that permission, but Sira asked the very question he wanted to ask, "How does it work?"

"I do not know exactly," Dalin shook his head. "I have read only passing references to it. There seems to be varying levels of power involved in Necromancy. The older a corpse is, the more power it takes to raise it. It is possible to raise a body when all that is left are bones. Furthermore, the undead are notoriously difficult to slay."

Ligeia screeched, "She says she can smell that a 'leader of the dead' was aboard this ship, just one."

Cardin frowned, and before he realized he shouldn't have, he spoke, "How does she know what it 'smells' like?"

The creature looked ready to strike him down, but Sira covered for him, "It's a fair question. Have you encountered them before?"

"Yes," Elaria translated. "She has."

"On your world?" Sira asked.

Ligeia looked at her in puzzlement. "This is her world," Elaria replied, visibly surprised by Ligeia's response. "Her people have lived upon this world for tens of thousands of years."

Cardin and Sira exchanged glances. Even Dalin appeared surprised. Sira asked, "Then why have we never seen your people before? Humans have been around for at least ten thousand years, according to our history books."

Elaria translated, "She says they live beneath the sea. Their cities float with the ocean currents, and they only surface their cities under rare circumstances. They do not usually interact with humans, they only observe." Elaria frowned at Ligeia, "Then how do you know what Necromancers smell like?" Ligeia replied, and Elaria looked at them in shock. "The Necromancers have also lived on this world for a long time, but not as long as your people have."

Even though he knew the answer, Cardin asked, "Where?"

Ligeia glared at him, but answered, "On the landmass to the east."

Chapter 18

SHADOWS OF THE PAST

At the mid-day meal break of yet another Allied Council meeting, Teira watched intently as all of the attendees stood up within the council chambers. She likewise slowly stood up from one of the guest chairs behind Erien's table. Although she was still and always a member of the Wizards' Guild, it had been Master Valkere's idea that Wizards assigned to each court should sit with the monarchy they were assigned to.

Naturally for Falind there was no assigned Wizard, as Sal'fe neither wanted nor needed assistance from the Guild. He could create portals himself to travel between the kingdoms, and he still was not entirely welcomed by the Guild, especially after his actions leading up to and following the Battle for Archanon.

For Tal, the Wizard that had been assigned was a man older than Teira, named Gerrin. She had known of him most of her life, but did not personally know him. Saran's assigned Wizard was even younger than she was, barely out of apprenticeship, a man named Wilick.

As the room began to clear, Teira eyed Master Valkere, who conversed with some of the other Wizards that accompanied him. The attending royalty would be taken to their own quarters for mid-day meals, but the Wizards who sat at the Guild's table always returned to the Grand Wizard Hall to eat. She wanted to catch Master Valkere before he left.

So she quickly made her way to the Erien Queen and said, "Your Majesty, with your permission I would like to be excused from your service for the next hour."

It was no small favor that she asked for. The Queen always valued Teira's input about what she had observed in the meeting and what her thoughts were on the subjects that had been discussed. However, she would not be very useful today since she had not paid close attention to the Council session.

The Queen obviously had recognized as much. "I am not surprised," she looked at Teira disapprovingly. "You have been distracted of late, my friend."

Teira felt herself blush a little. The first time Leian had called her 'my friend,' she had assumed the Queen used the term as a way to try to gain favor with Teira, so that she could gain better insight into at least one of her political adversaries, Master Valkere. However, since then she had come to realize that the Queen truly respected her, as she did all strong-willed women.

In a way, she had begun to consider the Queen a friend as well, which in and of itself was an unexpected shift in her reality. Teira had grown up in the Grand Wizard Hall and never thought she could feel any respect or feelings of friendship towards a human. She had come to feel the same animosity towards humans that most other Wizards had. Yet the Queen was nothing like what she had expected. She was always honest and forthright with Teira and treated her with more respect than she expected from human royalty. In public attendance, she did not hesitate to give Teira orders, in an effort to ensure she kept up her 'royal image,' but they were never given harshly nor were they ever unfair. In private, she was highly informal and quite kind to Teira.

"I apologize, Your Majesty," she bowed a little, in an effort to keep up the public appearance. "I have something I wish to discuss with Master Valkere."

Leian eyed her suspiciously. "Ever since you met with Dalin, you have had to leave on personal errands almost every single night. Where do you go? What do you do?"

She glanced at Master Valkere as he passed through one of the doorways, and she felt a little panic. She didn't want to lose track of him. If she had to wait another day to do what she intended to do, she feared she would lose her nerve and not follow through. "I am sorry that I cannot tell you what I have been doing. It is a matter that is, for the moment, internal to the Wizards' Guild." That statement affected the Queen more than she expected, and she gave Teira a hurt look. "I apologize, Your Majesty, but I must speak to Master Valkere before he leaves."

The Queen looked down for a moment, indecision clear in her eyes. "Very well. You have my leave."

"Thank you," she half-bowed again, and then rushed out after the Master Wizard. Teira knew he would be headed for one of the gates of the city, and most likely would make for the Western Gate, but she wanted to talk to him alone, and on Halarite.

She pushed past everyone in the crowded hall, which elicited a few grunts, and she even accidentally hit a servant in the shins with her staff. He cursed at her, but that got him a smack on the back of his head by whomever his master was.

Finally she caught up and called out, "Master Valkere!"

He and the other Masters with him paused long enough for her to catch up, and then they resumed their intent march out of the castle.

"What is it, young one," he asked, his voice as comforting as ever to her.

"Master," she looked nervously at the other Masters present, "may I please take a moment of your time? In private?" He looked at her curiously, and she knew that her approach was, in the strictest sense, a violation of propriety. Rank was important in the Guild, and if she wished to speak with the Grand Master, she needed to do so by speaking to a Master Wizard, who would then pass her request along to the Council of Masters.

When he did not respond and continued to walk with a thoughtful look in his eyes, she added, "Please, Master, it is important." Being a Court Wizard, she anticipated that he most likely thought she had vital information regarding Erien to discuss with him. If that misconception allowed her a private audience, she was willing to let him believe that for the moment.

The castle was not altogether large, and by the time he made a decision, they had reached the main entrance. Guards on duty had opened the doors for the outbound crowd, and a cold winter wind blew in and chilled her. He looked at the other Masters, and they exchanged meaningful glances. Finally he sighed and nodded. "As you wish, young one." To the others, he said, "I shall follow shortly, there is no need to wait on my account."

In unison, the other Masters bowed deeply to him and then made their way across the stone courtyard, their staves clicking as they used them like walking sticks. Vanity was not a trait most Wizards felt, but she did not look forward to the day when she would feel age begin to catch up to her and force her to lean so heavily on her own staff.

The guards who held the massive wooden doors looked at Valkere and Teira with an unsaid question, and Valkere shook his head in response. Without another word, the guards closed the doors after the other Wizards had departed. A large fire burned in the hearth at the back of the foyer, so the winter cold faded quickly.

Knowing that sound traveled within the corridors, he turned and led the way to where she knew quarters were set aside for the Wizards, even though they rarely used them. It took them a few minutes to travel through the castle, and more than once they had to wave off servants who asked if they needed anything.

Finally, they opened the door to the guest quarters and walked in. It was empty and quiet, the windows provided some light, but the fire in the hearth had not been lit and the room was frigid. She closed the door while Valkere made his way to the hearth. A quick rush of highly focused energy emanated from his staff, and an instant later, a fire roared in the fireplace.

He stayed close to the hearth, so she joined him there. He turned to face her, but did not say anything, and instead waited patiently for her to begin.

She took a moment to gather her wits, and felt her stomach turn a little. To outsiders, what she was about to do was not entirely uncommon, but to her, she was about to directly question the actions and intent of the Grand Master Wizard, and that was almost criminal.

"Master, I have done considerable research recently," she began. "Much of it in the library at the Grand Wizard Hall."

"Yes, I know," he interrupted, and stared at her evenly. She searched his face to try to figure out what he meant by that.

"You do?"

He nodded, his face still emotionless. "Of course. As you know, the Council has restricted any Wizard from leaving the Grand Hall unless absolutely necessary, the exception of course being Court

Wizards and myself. Therefore I am aware of every single Wizard that leaves or arrives at the Grand Hall."

She nodded and realized she should have expected that. However, before she could continue, he said, "I also know that you have spoken to several Master Wizards lately, and have investigated much that you perhaps should not have."

Her cheeks warmed considerably and she felt a small amount of panic set in. She stuttered and tried to defend herself, but he held up a hand to forestall her attempts to excuse herself. "Do not be frightened, child. I am surprised that it is you, of all of the younger Wizards, who has taken up this responsibility. However I am not surprised that someone has investigated. Tell me, do you no longer trust the wisdom of the Council of Masters?"

Again her cheeks burned and her stomach turned. "It is not that, Master. However…"

"Something Dalin said to you incensed your curiosity." She nodded, and for the first time his stolid facial expression turned into a smile. "Curiosity is not a crime. What have you learned?"

Once again she took a moment to collect her thoughts. Now that she didn't have to hide what she had done or her intent, she felt she could be more direct. "That all Wizards gifted with foresight, or rather almost all Wizards," she nodded at the Grand Master, "have been isolated from the general population of the Grand Hall. Even members of the Council of Masters. I also learned that when this was done, the order restricting travel to Halarite was given. I can only assume that this was not coincidence." She paused a moment to see if he wanted to stop her, but he continued to show patience with her, and he still wore a grin on his face.

"Much of the archives are still restricted to me, so I could not find specific references. However, I began to notice a pattern in many of our historical records dating back to when we first left Halarite. I am concerned with what I have noticed." She hesitated once more, and finally said, "Master, did we foresee Klaralin's conquering of Halarite?"

The grin on the Grand Master's face turned into a full smile. "You are very close to the mark, young one. Well done, indeed." The grin faded to a look of seriousness. "It has been taught to all Wizards that we left Halarite three thousand years ago because we no longer wished to interact with humans, or because we considered ourselves above them. We also wished to ensure our practicing of magic did not one day cause harm to the humans. Tell me, do you see a flaw in that logic?"

She considered his words for a moment, then frowned and nodded. "It has always puzzled me that we would show concern for humans if we felt such animosity towards them."

"Indeed," he nodded, "and I am aware that all Wizards are conscious of this contradiction, but still do not question it. They, like you, trust their elders."

She considered his implication for a moment. "Dalin does not."

"Not implicitly, no," he shook his head. "He has questioned this logic for quite some time."

Upon further thought, she frowned and asked, "Why has he been so insistent that we return to Halarite, then? Did he discover something in the archives?"

Valkere nodded. "As you no doubt know, he has access to many restricted archives, which was necessary to facilitate his new role when we allowed him to learn about the Sword of Dragons. Mostly he has used that access to learn about the Sword, however lately he has read books he should not have. I expected as much from him."

Inwardly she smirked and realized it wasn't surprising at all. He was always nosey, always getting into business that wasn't his, always getting into trouble. For a long time no one knew that he had been given any special access, knowledge of the Sword of Dragons was generally a secret until Kailar obtained it. Only after the Wizards agreed to help fight Kailar did they all learn about the Sword and what it was, including that Dalin had been allowed to learn about it. That increased responsibility changed nothing in him, however, and he continued to be the same man she had known for much of her life.

"He learned the true reason we left Halarite," she said. It was not a question.

"Indeed," Master Valkere nodded, "and he has since begged the Council of Masters to reverse that decision."

She rolled her eyes and looked to the fire, its light warmed her on the inside as much as its heat warmed her body. "He never learns, does he?"

"To be frank, his actions and words are refreshing." She looked at the Grand Master in shock. "He reminds me of another young

Wizard so many thousands of years ago, who likewise questioned everything." Somehow she knew he referred to himself, and he chuckled mischievously.

"So may I ask why we left Halarite?"

He closed his eyes for a moment, and she could tell that he inwardly debated whether or not to tell her. She was very curious as to why, especially since he had said she was almost right in her deductions. However, if it had been kept secret from almost all Wizards, it was more likely that he would deny her.

"It was for the same reason I have restricted all visits to Halarite now," he sighed. "Those with the ability to foresee the future, few as they are, can no longer see anything past a certain point in time." At first she frowned, but then she realized what he meant. Most Wizards who were called 'seers' could see only the present. To see the future was a very rare gift, and it was always very difficult to interpret. It was also considered a dangerous ability. It had been discovered a long, long time ago that knowledge of what was to come allowed a person to change what was to come. To change destiny came with consequences, and not always the consequences that one expected.

"So it was not that the Wizards foresaw Klaralin's war, it was that we could not see it, and..." She looked at him in shock and disgust. "We ran out of fear?" She tried to hide how appalled that realization made her feel, but knew that was impossible.

"No," he shook his head. "As it was then, there was one person alone who was able to catch only a glimpse of the future that the others could not see. Back then, the Grand Master saw disaster coming to Halarite. Disaster that heavily involved the Wizards. This may be difficult to imagine, but the events that transpired when we left were nothing compared to what Grand Master Herrick saw."

The manner in which he said it made her heart skip a beat. The tremble in his voice, the haunted look in his eyes, all of it told her more than she wanted to know. She recalled having read that Valkere had been a member of the Council of Masters when the decision had been made to abandon Halarite. "He told the Council of Masters what he saw."

"Indeed," he nodded. "And so began a long debate amongst all of the Masters as to what to do. What most Wizards do not understand is that we saved Halarite from a horrible fate when we left. For many of us who were on the Council when those events transpired, we eventually realized that what happened to Klaralin could happen to any number of us. Klaralin was a charismatic man, and we did not realize just how corrupting his influence could be. I strongly believe that if we had stayed on Halarite, and had not prompted Klaralin's decision to leave the Guild, he would have won other Wizards over to his side. A civil war would have erupted between Wizards, and this world would have suffered gravely because of that war."

As she considered his words, and thought about what such a war would have been like, she felt another chill and moved a little closer to the fire. The powers Wizards wielded could be intensely destructive, especially when wielded by Master Wizards, but ever more so if they used their powers cooperatively, as was proven when the Wizards helped breach the city wall at Falind.

Then another chilling thought occurred to her. She felt a lump form in her throat, and barely was able to ask, "What have you seen?"

The haunted look in his eyes grew ever darker, and his expression grew distant and cold. "I saw the world burn. I saw it covered in darkness. I saw all life wither away and die."

She physically shivered, and looked again to the fire for comfort. "You believe this might happen because the Wizards have begun to return to Halarite?"

He sighed, placed a hand on the fire mantle, and leaned heavily against it. He became lost for a moment in the hypnotic flames, and she felt sympathy for the weight she only now realized he carried.

"At first, yes. However, I have seen the vision more than once." He shook his head slowly. "Nothing in what I have seen points to the involvement of Wizards."

Once again, she felt shocked, and for the first time, her fear escalated to absolute terror. He was the Grand Master Wizard, the oldest living Wizard, the wisest, the strongest, the most powerful. Everyone looked to him for guidance.

She didn't know what to do or say, but now she understood better than ever why these facts hadn't been revealed to the rest of the Wizards. If they all came to feel the terror she now felt, it could induce a panic. Hundreds of panicked Wizards was a recipe for disaster.

Then another thought occurred to her. Having attended every single Allied Council session, she realized, "You haven't told the humans." He looked at her with guilt in his eyes. "Master, how can we not tell them what is coming?"

"You question my wisdom in this matter?" He glared at her, and the momentary breakdown in rank had ended. "The situation is dire, but for the same reason I should not have told you what I have seen, I must not tell the humans."

Her fear of being insubordinate was occluded by her terror at what she had learned, and she emphatically pleaded with him, "They have a right to know!"

Suddenly all patience was lost, and the Grand Master drew himself up to his full height. "Do not question me!" An intense surge of power stirred around him, and she felt almost physically pushed back by his anger. "I am the Grand Master of our Guild!"

On any other day, she would have backed down, would have been intimidated by his power, his strength, his words. Today, however, she had learned that the world was about to end. In that moment, she realized it didn't really matter.

Valkere seemed to realize he had let his temper flare, and the power he had unconsciously gathered subsided and spread back out harmlessly into the world around them. Quietly, he said, "We did not tell them last time. We acted, and we saved them."

"Only this time we are not acting, we are hiding!" Again she felt his anger flare, but she continued on undaunted. "Master, you said it yourself. Your visions do not show any Wizard involvement. Last time, the Grand Master saw that the destruction of the world would be caused by Wizard intervention. This time it appears that a lack of intervention may destroy it."

"You know not what you speak of," he looked away from her, his eyes betraying an exhaustion that he otherwise hid from everyone.

"Perhaps not." She swallowed her pride and looked intently at him. "Perhaps Dalin does."

As she had hoped, those words were enough to make him pause in thought. She realized that he liked Dalin more than most realized, if only because Dalin reminded Valkere of himself in his younger days.

"I think I understand now why he has tried to convince us to return to Halarite," she said. "You say this world will burn and turn to darkness." He looked at her with softer eyes. "You have lived for thousands of years, Master. You were born here, you lived on Halarite. Many of us do not feel the connection to Halarite that you do. Maybe it is time we all learned to respect this world again. Perhaps we can do nothing to save Halarite, but should we not try? Could you or the others who were born here forgive yourselves for not trying to save it?"

For what felt like a long, long time, he stared at her. She saw on his face sadness, and a longing that she had never seen in him before. Somehow, she didn't know how, he had let her in today, let her see past his façade, past his armor. Emotions he never showed in public were laid bare across his face.

"Perhaps you are both right," he said quietly. "Perhaps it is time for the Wizards to truly return to Halarite." He smiled, and she could see a sense of pride brighten his eyes. "I would be proud to call Halarite my home once more."

She also smiled, even though she realized that every single Wizard could perish in the coming calamity. However, she also felt a sense of pride and accomplishment knowing that she had taken the hopelessness she had seen in the Grand Master and turned it into determination and hope.

"We shall stand together with the humans once again, as we did against Klaralin and Kailar." He nodded resolutely. "Together, we shall face the coming apocalypse."

Chapter 19

FIERA'S SECRET

Kailar sat by herself, as she had ever since their encounter with the bandits, and stared absently into the small fire she had made for herself. She marveled at it, even after close to four weeks of being on the road on Devor. When she would travel alone in and around Tal, she only occasionally made small fires during the day, to cook food or boil water. She never dared create a fire at night, for fear of attracting the attention of creatures or, worse yet, people. Now she had become accustomed to having a fire every night.

Most of Letan's companions still tried to make her feel like a part of the group every day, and every single night they invited her to join them around their camp fire, but most nights she refused.

She wasn't one of them, and no amount of pretending could have ever made her believe otherwise. Their company on the road had become something she enjoyed, but she knew it would eventually come to an end, and that was coming sooner rather than later.

The Crystalline Peaks had been in view for a couple of days, first as distant flashes on the horizon when the sun reflected off of the facets of crystals, then as hazy forms in the distance, until they stood as light-blue, sometimes almost-white shimmering monoliths. The sunset they had just witnessed that night had been one of the most spectacular and memorable she had ever seen, the sunlight reflecting and refracting off of and through the crystals, casting rainbow colors everywhere and bathing them in beautiful light.

To think, she thought to herself, *that anyone who grows up in Corlas sees that almost every evening.* It was a magical place to live in. To some, she was sure, it seemed like a place where dreams became reality.

She hoped for that much. Despite everything that had happened to her, one thing remained the same. She wanted to regain her connection to magic, to regain her place in the world as a power to be reckoned with, to be able to once again change the world.

However, some things *had* changed. Her time spent with Letan, getting to know him, growing close to him had awakened feelings within her that she had never felt before. Grudgingly she had learned to admit to herself that it scared her. He scared her. The fact that he still believed in her, even after she had threatened him, scared her.

She dreaded the coming of the morning, because she knew what was coming. Their time together was about to end.

As such, it came as no surprise to her when Letan walked over to her small, lonely spot and asked to join her. She warmly accepted his company on the outside, but a knot twisted in her stomach.

They sat together for a long time in silence, both staring into her fire. She used a sturdy stick to move some of the logs around and stir the ashes a little bit, sending sparks into the air like a flurry of tiny shooting stars.

Finally, Letan spoke. "We'll reach Corlas by mid-day tomorrow."

She did not look at him, but saw in the corner of her eye that he looked at her. The knot twisted some more, and she felt her fingers tingle. After a moment, she sighed and looked down at her hands. "Then that is when we will part ways."

Anxiously she awaited his response, but it did not come quickly. She wondered how he felt about her reply, and suspected it did not sit well with him. For him to believe in her like he did, she had to guess that he had also grown to like her, as more than just a friend.

"You know, after we drop off the supplies, I could walk with you the rest of the way to the peaks." He looked at her with hopeful eyes. "They're less than a day's walk from Corlas. I can afford to spend a few more days away, or however long it takes."

He'd spoken faster and faster, but then suddenly stopped. She felt the knot twist even further, and a lump formed in her throat. She didn't know how to reply to him, didn't know what to say.

She knew what she wanted to say. She wanted to tell him yes, to embrace him, to feel like she would never have to be alone again. But she also knew that it wasn't that simple. She knew that there was no way they could ever be together. He was a good man, and a Warrior. She was a criminal, an outcast with a bounty on her head, and a woman without power. She wasn't worthy of his feelings.

At that moment, a flash caught her eye, and she looked up into the sky. A shooting star streaked across the darkness. A moment later, it was followed by another. Before she could comprehend what was happening, the sky seemed alight with blue-white streaks, never simultaneous, but seemingly one after another with only a few moments in between each streak.

The others in the camp noticed too, and she heard them voice their awe. Letan also stared up, and she felt the strongest desire to reach out and take his hand. All she wanted, more than anything, was to be held by him. To feel a comfort and sense of belonging she had never felt before, and hadn't really desired before now. To continue to be accepted for who she was.

Who she was. He didn't know who she was. She wasn't even sure who she was anymore. She looked down again, and felt a burning in her eyes. She managed to keep back tears of fear and sadness, but only just barely. "Letan, I can't let you come with me. If you knew who I really was, if you knew everything, you wouldn't want to come." She shuddered a little, but accepted what she said as she said it. "I don't deserve the kindness or affection you've shown me."

Out of the corner of her eye, she noticed his hands clenched into fists. She expected him to stand up in frustration and walk away, but instead he remained. "Then get it over with." Completely taken by surprise, she looked at him for the first time that night, looked into his eyes. "Tell me everything. Tell me who you really are, because I'm getting tired of being in the shadows."

Fear and anxiety surged through her. She knew she shouldn't have been surprised by his demand, by how he felt frustrated about her month-long deception, yet it surprised her and scared her. In a way, she had hoped never to have to tell him. It had been her desire to part ways in Corlas, never revealing her true name, where she came from, what she had done, or what she had lost.

Now he demanded she tell him everything, lay bare all of her secrets. Could she do that? The fear twisted inside into terror, and before she could stop herself, she shook her head and said, "No. I can't, Letan."

"Why not?!" He spoke his question in an elevated voice, loud enough that Tanneth gave his normal suspicious look. A part of her would have loved to stab those suspicious, probing eyes, but that part also scared her. She felt so much anger, so much fear, and she wondered if those two emotions weren't built upon each other.

"It's just best if you don't know who I am," was all she could say.

"Don't you think I deserve at least *some* truth from you?" He glared at her. "We've spent the last month together, I've told you so much about me, we all have. Why can't you open up?" He reached out to take her hand, but she pulled back away from him. "Why won't you let me in?"

She didn't answer him, she simply folded her arms to keep her hands from being open to his and stared at the fire. After a few moments of silence, he asked, "What are you so scared of?"

Her eyes began to burn, and there was an urge in her to let out everything. That urge began to grow stronger and stronger, and she felt a single tear roll down her cheek.

"I can't," she choked out, meeting his gaze and staring longingly into his eyes. "I want my last memory of you to be how you look at me now. How you see me, how you believe in me. I don't want to destroy that."

He gave her an incredulous look and said, probably angrier than he intended, "After everything we've been through together, do you really think I would stop believing in you? What could possibly be so bad that you'd think I wouldn't stick by you?"

"You're a good man," she tried to push back the feelings that boiled up in her, tried to keep control. "The things I've done, who I am, what I've lost, all of it! I am not worth your affection."

"Don't you think that's for me to decide, not you?" He stared evenly at her. "I am more than capable of deciding on my own who is worth my time and who isn't."

She felt herself growing more frustrated, and she wanted to shout at him to leave her alone, to drop the subject, to just go away. Yet even as she thought that, she realized it was actually the last thing in the world she wanted. She never wanted him to go away, she never wanted to have to say goodbye.

Could he fall in love with her for who she really was? Could he still believe in her when she didn't believe in herself?

There was only one way to find out for sure. Fear was something she had allowed to control her ever since she'd lost her connection to magic, and it was what had motivated her to do everything wrong. Fear had motivated her to kill an innocent man. Fear made her push Letan away, when what she really wanted was the opposite.

It's time to stop letting fear control me, she thought.

Letan began to stand up, but she grabbed his wrist. "Wait."

He looked at her with pained eyes, but a glimmer of hope appeared in them. After a moment of hesitation, he settled back down. She released his wrist, but did not give in to her desire to hold his hand. She glanced up at the sky to see that shooting stars still streaked across the sky, though they did so less frequently now.

She felt a fluttering inside of her, another unusual sensation for her. Fear had an icy grip on her, but she wouldn't allow it to control her anymore. So she looked into his eyes, and she told him.

"My name is Kailar Adanna. I was once a Warrior of Tal, and a Mage of considerable skill and power. Several years ago, I left the Guild, and did so in a less than honorable manner." She searched his eyes for recognition, and she saw that he did recognize her name, but couldn't quite remember why.

The next part would no doubt remind him, and would probably change their relationship forever. "I did so because I felt the Guild no longer honored its original precepts, and I believed that our civilization had lost its way. I knew I couldn't change anything from within the Guild, and ever since I left the Guild, I searched for a way to change the world. Over seven months ago, I learned of a powerful weapon that was hidden on Edilas. It is called the Sword of Dragons."

That name sparked recognition in his eyes, and his jaw slowly dropped. She knew he realized who she really was now, and she let it sink in. A tumult of emotions played across his face, within his eyes, and she watched him carefully. News of her actions had most definitely travelled even as far as Corlas by now, so she knew he had heard of her, heard what she had done.

Even she felt her own stomach turn as she thought about it. The worst part was when she had found out she was being manipulated by the greatest enemy of the four kingdoms, Klaralin. A part of her felt sick when she realized she had used the death and mayhem he had caused to try to take back the Sword. How many people died because she let him break into Archanon? He had given her a chance, two days to consider her options. In that time, she had manipulated the elf Elaria and plotted to steal back the Sword. But if she had simply gone to Tal and told them all what she had done…

Letan finally snapped out of his thoughts and looked at her in shock. "You were the one. The one responsible for so many deaths. You worked with Klaralin!"

She felt her face turn red, and she felt a dark void form in the pit of her stomach. "Yes," she said quietly.

"How many people died in Falind?" His voice was decidedly no longer friendly or understanding. "How many died in Archanon, because of your actions?" Then a new realization came over his face. "That's why you're here. I heard that the dragons took your powers from you. You used to be a Mage, but now…"

"Now I am powerless," she nodded. "I am useless."

"And that's why you're here," he frowned. "You came to the Crystalline Peaks to try to regain your powers." Then horror overcame his face. "To what end? What would you do if you gained power again?"

Even as she looked to him in hope, she knew she had lost him. "It doesn't matter," she said, "as long as I have power again, I can choose where to go from there. I am in control of my life again."

"It matters," there was a hint of anger in his voice. "Your powers were taken to make sure you never used them to hurt people again." He looked over at the others, and she wondered why. Had one of them lost someone because of her?

"Letan…" She reached for his hand, completely unaware that she had done so. He recoiled as if bitten by a snake, and he bolted up and backed away.

"No, stay away from me," he looked at her in horror. "I can't…" He didn't finish, and he quickly walked away, not towards the others, but simply away from the camp.

She wanted to chase after him, but her fears had come true, and she had lost him. She knew that he no longer believed in her, and that created a terrible pit within her chest that she knew could never be filled. It had been seven months since she'd believed in herself, and now she had lost the only other person to believe in her.

She drew her knees up to her chest and wrapped her arms around them, and she fought as hard as she could to keep back what she felt. But she couldn't stop the tears, and they flowed freely. It embarrassed her, so she made sure she didn't sob aloud, she couldn't bear the thought of some of the others hearing her cry.

For that matter, she couldn't stand to hear herself cry. She felt weak, and alone, emotions that had become common to her, and she hated that, hated her condition, hated her weaknesses, hated her emotions. Most of all, she hated herself.

She looked to the sky for comfort, but the shooting stars had almost stopped. Every few minutes another would streak across the sky, but the spectacular show was over. The beauty was gone.

Her fire started to die, so she placed another couple of logs on it, stirred the ashes beneath them, and then she lay down on the bedding she had put out and wrapped her cloak around her. Her view of the fire was blurred by tears, and those came even faster.

Kailar cried for hours before she finally fell asleep. That night she did not dream, as was common ever since she had lost her connection to magic.

The next morning, the sun had already risen well above the horizon by the time she awoke. She felt exhausted and wondered just how much sleep she had gotten. She stirred in her bedding, and slowly pushed herself up. The ashes of her fire smoldered but she didn't need its warmth, the day already grew warm.

When she looked over to where the others had camped, she felt another wave of despair grip her. Their camp was empty, the horses and cart gone. They had left without her. She didn't blame them. No doubt Letan had told them who she was. Part of her was surprised Tanneth hadn't killed her in her sleep, or that they didn't bind her to turn her in for the bounty on her head.

She stood and began to pack up, but dreaded having to go to Corlas for supplies. She didn't want to see any of them again, she didn't want to see their accusatory glares. Furthermore, she realized Letan was a Warrior. If she set foot in Corlas, she could still be arrested, and she couldn't allow that, not when she was this close to the Peaks.

She looked west at the sharp-angled peaks. She didn't know how high they reached, but if she made directly for them and didn't go to

Corlas, she could reach them before long, definitely sometime that same day.

As she swung her nearly-empty backpack on, she looked again at their camp, and noticed a small bag had been left behind. She frowned and walked over to investigate. It bulged and was stuffed full of something. Tentatively she reached down and opened it, and found it was full of fruits, vegetables, some nuts, and two flasks of water. Enough supplies for her to at least make it to the peaks.

Whether it was because they didn't want her to ever go to Corlas, or because they felt sympathy for her and showed her one last act of kindness, she didn't know. Either way, she was glad for it, and she placed the supplies in her pack and started the final leg of her journey to the Crystalline Peaks.

Chapter 20

DESOLATE HOPE

A feeling of anticipation began to grow within Cardin. After almost a month at sea, longer than they had expected due to uncooperative winds, they had finally reached the Port of Hope. Now he and Sira sat in one of the dinghies dispatched from the Sea Wisp to shore, while Reis and Dalin sat in the one behind them, and Elaria, Ventelis, and Anila followed in a third. The remaining free space on the dinghies were filled with Marines, rowing with military precision.

At the head of the boat that Cardin and Sira occupied sat the Sea Wisp's first officer. She insisted on coming along, even though Sira would assume command as soon as they stepped ashore. Cardin wondered if Elia Devral could actually take orders from Sira after having given them to her for a month.

They almost hadn't completed their journey to Port Hope. After Ligeia had told them about the undead, they had parted ways, despite Commander Devral's insistence that she be shackled and imprisoned for killing one of the Sea Wisp's crewmembers. The situation had almost escalated again, but Elaria and Sira both managed to talk them down. In the interest of avoiding sparking a war between the Alliance and Ligeia's civilization, the Commander had agreed to stand down and let Ligeia go.

When they returned to the Sea Wisp to report everything to Captain Norric, he had insisted that they should turn around immediately and return to Maradin. He had tried to make his case by stating that they were not equipped to fight off an army of undead, but Cardin reminded him that they hadn't known what they would find from the start, and that was why both the Marines and the Keeper of the Sword had come on the journey.

After hours of arguing, Sira had somehow convinced the Captain that they should continue their voyage. Now it was late afternoon, the sun was behind them, and they were moments from making it to shore. Cardin looked to Sira with concern, but also with excitement, and she returned his look. The view before them was breathtaking! The waves crashed against the shore as the tide rose and helped bring them in, and at the edge of the white sandy beach stood the wooden buildings of the Port of Hope. All around it was an environment he had been told was called a jungle.

There was nothing like it on Edilas, or for that matter on Devor or Asirin. Trinil was the only continent to have such an environment, and he had read about some of the challenges faced within the jungle. It teemed with life, some of it deadly, but all of it exotic. Birds, snakes, monkeys, lizards, all manner of creatures. The winter of Edilas was now long-forgotten, and the heat and moisture was almost oppressive. He and Sira both wore light leather armor, but it still felt heavy. Sweat already covered his face, and he wasn't even exerting himself yet.

The foliage and trees were also very dense, and even with the sun at their backs, they could not see far past the shoreline. It was amazing and beautiful, but at the same time it terrified him, especially since he knew that there were more dangerous things than animals in the jungle.

Undead were considered a fable, a legendary nightmare that had no basis in reality. Ancient tales spoke about how the dead had risen from the graves of Saran, the southern-most kingdom, and attacked the capitol. No official historical record existed of those events, and the Order of the Ages insisted that necromancy could not be real.

The waves made the boat rock and Cardin held on to the sides for dear life. This was the first time he'd been in a small boat headed for shore, and he was afraid a giant wave would come in and engulf them, but the Marines knew what they were doing, and after only a short time later, they landed on the sandy beach when a wave pushed them in. The waters receded to clear the beach, and as he had been told to do before, he and everyone else jumped out of the boat and helped pull it further up shore. They did not stop until they reached the small village, past where the tide would bring the water up to, and then they finally set the dinghy down.

The other boats had made it to shore shortly after they had, and their teams brought their dinghies alongside Cardin's. A fourth boat was still at the Sea Wisp on standby, in case the shore party, as the Captain had called it, needed other supplies or reinforcements.

The moment they dropped the boat, everyone drew weapons and quickly made their way into the village, ready to face anything.

Instead, they found nothing. The buildings still stood, huts built from the indigenous trees and covered by roofs thatched together from some indigenous plant. But there was no movement within the village. South of where they stood on the beach, the villagers had begun construction of a pier that would reach out to sea, which would eventually allow ships to dock without having to anchor off-shore and send dinghies to land. No one worked on the pier now.

From within the jungle, Cardin could hear the noises he had read about, of animals screeching and crying and cawing, and a breeze sent the trees creaking and moaning as they swayed back and forth. Within the village, however, was absolute stillness and silence.

"Cardin!" Sira called to him as silently as she could. She made her way to one of the huts and prepared to enter, the door was wide open. Cardin joined her, noticing the sign above the door identifying it as the local blacksmith's shop, and after a moment, she rushed in with Cardin right behind her.

They burst in to find that it was as empty as the exterior, no one in sight. Scattered about the shop's counters and workbenches were various pieces of crafted items, including a few swords and daggers, but mostly they were more utilitarian pieces such as heads to hammers, woodcutting axes, and even equipment that would probably be used to turn part of the surrounding jungle into farmland, if that was even possible in such an environment.

The forge stood cold, empty but for the ashes left from the fire that had once burned within. Cardin moved to the basin that was used to cool the metal, and found all manner of dead insects floating in the disgusting looking water. The floor and equipment were all covered in dust and grime. "Whatever happened here happened a long time ago," he commented.

"Agreed," Sira called from across the room. She made her way out the back door and he followed to find another forge out back. More equipment lay outside, including raw iron and refined steel, and what appeared to be a half-finished sword in the basin.

From around the corner of the building came two marines who seemed startled to see them at first, but then recognized them and continued to move around, weapons ready.

Together, Sira and Cardin inspected two more buildings within the village, before they heard a call from Commander Devral. Everyone gathered in what was clearly the village square, a large open area surrounded by all of the buildings that contained a sapling from Edilas, meant to serve as a reminder of the home the explorers and colonists had come from. As Cardin looked around, he found no unfamiliar faces. They hadn't found any of the village residents, nor, for that matter, had they found the missing elven archeologist.

"This place is completely abandoned," Devral stated the obvious.

"Indeed," Dalin replied. "The most disturbing, if not unexpected fact, is that there are no bodies, either."

Cardin shuddered. "Does that mean Ligeia was right?"

"Probably," Reis replied. Cardin noticed his friend looked very happy to be on solid land. For his friend's sake, he hoped they could find a way to create a portal back to Edilas.

"So now what?" a Marine asked.

"I've noticed tracks leading to and from the jungle," Elaria stated. She had drawn her two daggers and looked ready for a fight.

"Where?" Sira asked.

Elaria pointed, "Northeast."

"I'll follow them in," Cardin volunteered. "Elaria, show me the way."

"No," Sira stopped him from moving with a firm hand. "I won't let you two go alone, it's too dangerous."

Briefly Cardin wondered if her quick reaction had been due to some form of jealousy towards Elaria. The elven scout hadn't been shy during the journey about showing her attraction to Cardin, or her own jealousy towards Sira. Cardin had meant to talk to her about it, but every time he tried, he felt guilty in knowing that it would break her heart, and he didn't want to do that. He also still secretly hoped that, somehow, she and Reis would grow closer. They partly had.

Most surprising of all, however, was that Reis had somehow managed to befriend the mysterious Anila. The Guardian of the Covenant had made a point to avoid most everyone during the entire voyage. However, shortly after they had left the derelict Avendal, Anila had approached Reis and started to chat with him regularly, often quietly so that no one else could overhear their conversations.

Cardin had asked Reis what they talked about, but he said he respected her privacy too much, and if she wanted others to know about her, she would talk to them. Cardin was a little annoyed at his friend's unwillingness to come forward, but he couldn't judge too harshly since he too kept a secret for Anila.

In any case, it didn't surprise Cardin when Reis stepped forward and said, "Anila and I will go with."

"And what of the rest of us," Commander Devral asked. "My Marines could accompany you."

"We don't want to lead the whole company into a trap," Cardin pointed out. "And scouting becomes a lot harder when there are more people. Reis has always been a skilled scout, and Anila clearly can keep to the shadows with ease," he looked at her, but made a point not to probe her presence again. She wanted to keep her powers a secret, so he would let her.

Devral looked doubtful, but Sira nodded. "Alright, that's good enough for me. If you find the enemy, do not engage. Report back immediately."

Cardin nodded, "Understood."

She tightened her grip on his shoulder. "I mean it, Cardin. Don't go pulling any stunts like you did at Nasara."

He smirked, "Yes, ma'am."

She gave him an icy glare. "Get to it, soldier," she released her grip. She looked at the others who were to join him and said, "make sure he follows orders."

Reis gave a mock salute and Elaria grinned, but Anila remained emotionless. Cardin was curious about how Anila had allowed Reis to volunteer her without a word of protest. How close had they grown? Had she given him a subtle cue to let him know she would accompany them, a cue that only Reis recognized?

Cardin motioned for Elaria to show the way and walked beside her. Reis and Anila quickly joined them to Cardin's left, and together the four set out for the jungle. They reached the edge quickly and paused as Elaria put away both of her daggers. She wore her usual color-changing leather-scale armor and cloak, but did not seem particularly uncomfortable in the jungle heat.

Tentatively, she pressed down on a part of the ground where dead foliage covered it, and then looked ahead. "It's like whomever left these tracks didn't care that anyone could follow them."

"Of course not," Reis knelt beside her and also pressed on the ground with one hand. "They took down the entire village and probably every ship that anchored here, what could possibly threaten them?" He shrugged, "Plus if they really are undead, I doubt they feel anything at all, let alone fear."

"True," she nodded. "From what I've seen, undead don't feel any emotion or retain any personality from who they were before. They fall completely under their necromancer's control."

Cardin wondered why they both kept prodding the ground, but before he could ask any questions, they both stood up and Elaria headed into the jungle. The rest followed, and they moved slowly. Elaria was right, it was not a hard trail to follow.

As they continued on into the jungle, he looked over at Anila, who looked ahead intently, her curved, narrow sword at the ready. He still didn't know what kind of sword it was. It was very light but clearly still strong, and it hadn't broken even when it came blow to blow with the Sword of Dragons four weeks ago.

She noticed that he stared at her, and glared at him. He smiled, hoping his reaction would annoy her. She promptly looked ahead and proceeded to ignore him.

They moved quietly, or as quietly as they could in the jungle. The ground was damp, and he heard the thunder of a coming storm in the distance. That combined with the considerable noise most of the creatures of the jungle around them made helped cover any sounds they made.

He wasn't sure how long they walked, but he was sweating profusely. He wished he'd left his armor behind at the village, especially since he knew he could easily use his powers to protect himself from any attack, but he still felt safer in some form of physical protection.

They had trekked on for a long while before he stopped them all and whispered for everyone to be quiet. Everyone followed his order without question and looked around. Something was wrong, and then he realized what.

"What happened to all of the noise?" he asked. Except for the occasional thunder in the distance and the sound of the wind in the trees, all jungle life had gone silent. When he thought about it, he realized it hadn't been sudden, it had been gradual.

Suddenly Anila ducked, and so did everyone else in response. He felt his heart race, and a surge of energy coursed through his body. She had seen something, something that no one else had. "What is it," he asked. He opened himself as much as he could to the flow of magic around him, and that was when he felt it.

"There's someone ahead of us," she said. "Not moving, just standing there, I can barely see them." That was where he felt the strange sensation too, but it was a presence that he had never felt before. It was cold, ice cold, and gave him an intense feeling of dread.

He moved to his left to crouch behind Anila, and from there he could also see the lone figure, barely visible in the dense jungle foliage.

For a moment he stared at the unmoving person. It was alive, as it swayed a little, but it otherwise did not move. Whatever he felt, it came from that person.

"Spread out," he whispered.

"Sira said not to fight," Reis reminded him.

"I know," he said. "But what if it's someone from the village or a crewmember from one of the ships? We have to at least see if whoever that is actually is still alive."

Reis narrowed his eyes at him, then rolled his eyes. "Alright, it's your hide on the line."

Without another word, everyone spread out from his point, Anila to his left, Reis and Elaria to his right. Slowly, he edged forward, having to push through some of the foliage. For a moment he lost sight of the lone figure while he moved around trees and other brush, but finally he got to where he had a clear line of sight on the lone figure.

The feeling of cold dread took a firmer grip on him now, but the person faced away from him. Was it an undead? He noticed that the person wore chainmail armor and held in their left hand a long sword. The right hand was not visible from Cardin's vantage. He looked to his left, but could not see Anila, nor could he see Reis or Elaria to his right. The jungle foliage was too dense.

There was only one way to find out who the person was. He could try to sneak around and see what the person looked like from the front, but in the eerie stillness of the jungle, his footsteps in the foliage would be too easy to hear.

So he stood up straight. "Hello," he called out. He heard the others stir on either side, and then they popped up too. He looked over, and saw that Reis, who had gone further away from him than Elaria, suddenly had a pale face.

The lone person did not react at first, so he called again. "Identify yourself!"

This time the person moved, and began to turn around. Cardin was not prepared for what he saw. It had been a man. Had been, but was no longer. His face had taken on a hue that Cardin had only ever seen on long-dead bodies, a brownish color of decay, and his skin had dried and become irregular. There was a hole in his left cheek, and he could see through to the man's rotted teeth.

When he turned completely to face Cardin, there was something else that twisted Cardin's stomach. The man's right arm was missing! It had been severed just above the elbow.

Cardin's jaw dropped, but he had very little time to feel sick. The undead man raised his sword and pointed it at Cardin, and then let out a gargled, inhuman noise that he guessed was an attempt at a battle cry, before he charged at Cardin.

That was unexpected. He had somehow believed the undead would be slow and ineffective combatants. He was wrong, very wrong. The undead man crossed the distance in seconds, but Cardin was prepared, and when the man swung his blade from his left shoulder, Cardin met the blade with the Sword. The blow was stronger than he expected, so instinctively Cardin used his powers to give himself extra strength.

He parried the blow away, and then jabbed the Sword at the undead's chest. The blood red blade easily cut through the chainmail armor and through the man's torso, and the battle was won. Or so Cardin thought.

Before he could pull the Sword out, the undead man swung his sword again. Cardin ducked and withdrew the Sword from the man's torso, then stepped back. The undead pressed the advantage and came at him again, and Cardin parried. It made two more attempts to wound Cardin, until he finally deflected a blow and severed the left arm. It fell to the ground, but still seemed to wiggle around to try to swing its weapon at Cardin's ankles.

The undead was not finished, and still came at Cardin with his mouth open, intent on biting him, fighting him with the only weapon it had left.

Elaria got there first, and swung one of her daggers with all of her strength. The head came cleanly off of the undead's shoulders and landed in the jungle beside his feet. The body fell to its knees, stayed there for a moment, and then collapsed. It did not move again.

"Sorry," Elaria breathed. "I forgot to tell everyone, the only way to kill someone raised by a necromancer is by beheading them." She grimaced and added, "or destroying their head."

Cardin raised his eyebrows at her. "That was kind of an important omission."

Her cheeks flushed more than they already were in the jungle heat, "Sorry…"

Anila had reached his position at the same time as Elaria, but she hadn't been able to attack before the elf. Moments later, Reis joined them.

"So," Reis stared at the body. "Definitely not a myth."

Cardin shook his head. "Nope. Not a myth."

Chapter 21

INTO THE CYRSTALLINE PEAKS

Kailar made better time than she had anticipated, and she reached the Crystalline Peaks quickly. She had become completely lost in her thoughts and feelings, and so she had walked at a rapid pace, so much so that she even felt a little fatigued when she finally reached her destination.

On one hand, the Peaks appeared almost unnatural. They jutted out from the ground in angled towering crystals abruptly, there was no gradual build up to them. They were tiered, so that the ones on the edge were lower than the ones much deeper in, giving the illusion from a distance of mountains. Although the sun was high above her now, very soon it would dip below the top of the Peaks.

On the other hand, it was one of the most beautiful and mesmerizing sights she had ever seen. The sunlight reflected off of and refracted through the crystals, and they shimmered and shined before her in such a way that hurt her eyes, but she also couldn't tear her eyes away. Rainbow colors played through the facets as if the crystals were alive and thrummed with energy, a pulse made of light.

Never in her life could she have imagined such a sight. Standing only fifty feet away, she strained her neck to look up towards the top. She had made it! After such a long journey, she finally stood before her goal, her last hope for a return to her old life. She didn't know how she knew, but when she looked at the crystals, she knew that somewhere in there, she would find answers.

Kailar adjusted the backpack on her shoulders, stood up straight, and prepared to take the last steps to the peaks. Until she heard the thundering of hooves upon the ground. She turned southeast, and saw a lone figure upon a horse come over a rise.

She tensed, and briefly wondered if there were more to follow, just below the rise of the hill. Had Letan or one of his companions turned her into the local Guild, and were they now coming to arrest her? She panicked and prepared to make a run for the peaks, knowing that the locals feared them, probably with good reason.

A moment later, the rider drew close enough that she thought she recognized who it was. *No…it can't be!* She waited in intense anticipation and squinted her eyes, but kept her hand on her dagger, ready to draw if necessary.

Finally, she became certain. It was Letan!

Her heart soared when she realized that, and her hand fell away from her weapon. She wanted to shout out his name and run to him, but then she stopped and remembered how they had parted company. The elation within dwindled, and she questioned why he had come.

She would not run. She was done letting fear control her, so she waited for him, and would face him with courage.

When he finally came close enough, he slowed his horse to a trot, and then down to a walk, until he stopped twenty feet away. For what felt like ages, he stared down at her, while she looked up to him, their faces stoic. Finally he dismounted and took two steps towards her. She tensed a little, and he must have noticed because he stopped and his face slackened.

The horse brayed impatiently, ready to continue its run. Letan absently reached back and rubbed between its eyes.

After several more moments passed, he finally spoke. "I'm sorry I left like that."

She didn't know what to say. She never expected him to say he was sorry. She had expected him to come arrest her, or tell her to leave the area before he reported her presence.

He looked down for a moment, clearly searching for words, and then looked at her and said, "I knew you hadn't been honest with who you were, but I didn't expect anything like what you told me, and I didn't know how to react, what to say." She felt guilt stir within her, for what she had kept from him, and what she had done to keep it from him.

She took a step closer to him and asked, "Why did you come here?"

"Before we even made it to Corlas, I started to regret my actions, my response. I shouldn't have left you like that. I told the others to finish without me, took a horse, and started searching for you. Kailar...I see the regret in your eyes, I saw it last night when you told me who you were. I've seen it every day since I met you."

That same guilt and regret continued to stir in her, and she looked away from him. "I don't need a reminder of how I feel."

"I know," he quickly said, "that's not why I'm saying all of this, I'm sorry. But it's that look in your eyes, the one I see right now, that has made me believe in you ever since I met you. Your regret means that you have it within you to feel compassion and kindness."

She shook her head and looked at him with a hard stare. "There are things I regret, but my biggest regret is that I failed seven months ago. The actions I took, if I had succeeded..."

When she didn't continue, he asked, "What? If you had succeeded, what? Why did you do all of that?"

It hadn't been an accusatory question, rather there was something else in his voice, something that said he knew the answer and knew it would prove his point. So she considered it for a long moment before she replied, "The world is broken, Letan. The Warriors' Guild is broken. Warriors fight and kill Warriors, kingdoms are constantly at each other's throats, and there is so much death, so much suffering. I wanted to unite the kingdoms under one banner, and force them to cooperate, force the Warriors to stop fighting each other. I knew they would not do so willingly, so I knew I had to do it by force."

She hesitated, and considered her words carefully. "I recognize today that how I went about doing it is what paved the way for Klaralin to return. I let my ambition blind me. He knew what I wanted and gave me exactly what I thought I needed to achieve my goals. That's why next time..."

Her voice trailed off when she realized what she was just about to say. She still wanted to achieve her goals, no matter what it took. However when she thought of that, she thought of the miner in

Edingard. That had led to her feeling even more frightened and more alone, and it drove her away from Letan. She remembered that night, when she lay in her room at the inn and felt so lost and alone, exactly as she felt now.

And then Letan opened her door, and helped her through it, and made her feel like she wasn't alone anymore. Now, weeks later, he was back. "Letan, why are you here?"

He closed the gap between them a little more and looked affectionately at her. "You've been alone for too long. Now you don't have to be. I still see the same look in your eyes, and just now you hesitated when you wanted to say what you would do next time. Kailar, I believe in you, in the good that is within you. You don't have to do everything alone anymore. I am so sorry I left last night, but I am here to tell you that I won't again. Maybe together we can find what you're looking for, help you get what you want. Let me help you, please."

Her heart soared! She wanted to trust him, she wanted to believe him, and he had been there for her so much already. No one had ever believed in her like he did now, and it scared and excited her.

The heartache she had felt last night was horrible, and a part of her wanted to run away from him, so that she didn't risk ever feeling that way again. Then she remembered their journey together. When he saved her from the wolves, and then when he held her in his arms at the inn. He protected her.

She detested that feeling, she didn't want to rely on anyone to protect her. However, she also understood that while her weakness came from her lack of magic, who she was inside was the same, and someone protecting her didn't mean she still couldn't rely on herself.

She also remembered all of the times he'd made her laugh. That was a feeling she wasn't accustomed to. He had gone out of his way to make her feel welcome, like she was a part of the group, no matter how much she resisted that feeling. He had done everything he could to make sure she didn't feel like she was alone, and she had pushed him away almost every time.

Yet here he was, once again. He knew who she was, but he came back anyway. He knew a lot about what she had done, but he stood before her, ready to walk by her side and face whatever lay ahead. He always kept coming back.

"Letan, I can't promise you that the good you see in me will always win out over the darkness I know exists within my heart." She spoke tentatively, fearfully, afraid that he might finally realize she wasn't worth it and would walk away.

The smile he gave her generated warmth throughout her body. "I know. But as long as I am here with you, you will never have to face that darkness alone."

For a moment, she felt breathless, and for the first time in her life, she understood why people said shows of affection could take their breath away. A feeling she had never known before began to well up within her.

She felt happy.

Without even realizing what she was doing, she finally crossed the few feet left between them and embraced him. He wrapped his arms around her, and they held one another for a long time. "I am so glad you came back," she whispered.

When they pulled apart, she felt embarrassed by her outburst, so she stepped away and felt her cheeks grow warm. He gave her a delighted smile, which only made her cheeks turn even redder.

Letan led the horse to turn it towards the southeast. Unstrapping a pack from the saddle, he swung it around onto his back, and then gave the horse a good slap, which sent it running for Corlas. He was ready to journey with her now. When he turned to her, she felt ready to hug him again, but resisted the urge. He stepped up next to her, and she turned to face the Peaks. Together, they stared at the faceted monoliths.

"Touching the crystals is dangerous," he said. "It's been said that a non-magical person who touches them receives a sort of shock, like a miniature bolt of lightning that hurts and causes their hand to go numb. If a Mage touches the crystals," he paused in hesitation and looked at her. "From what I've been told, most Mages are sent flying across the ground. Most have been killed."

She looked at him with the deepest concern, and suddenly felt regret about his presence. "You don't have to go in there with me."

Slowly he shook his head, "No. I'm not abandoning you now. We go in together or not at all."

A broad smile crossed her face, and she nodded. "Alright."

Together, they walked across the remaining distance to where the first crystal jutted out of the ground. Although the ground they stood on now was grassy, there were several barren, dirt paths that led under the crisscrossing crystalline structures. When they reached the closest crystal, she took in a huge breath, and felt more than a little afraid. What would happen? She had not only been a Mage, but had possessed the Sword of Dragons and had become more powerful than any Mage ever could have dreamed of. Would it affect her as if she still had that power, or would it affect her like she was powerless?

Letan reached out and took a hold of her hand for a moment, and she felt reassured when he squeezed. She squeezed back, and then released his hand, afraid that any shock to her might transfer through to him as well. She stepped a little closer, and slowly reached out her hand, inch by inch, hopeful, afraid, uncertain.

When she touched the crystal, nothing happened. No shock, no force propelled her back, absolutely nothing. She might as well have been a corpse touching the crystal. Her heart sank.

After a moment, she pulled her hand away and let it drop to her side. She stared at her reflection in the blue-white crystal's facets. She had hoped for something, some indication that there was hope for her. That hadn't happened.

However, she hadn't come this far for nothing. She may not have been connected to magic anymore, but something within her had compelled her to seek out the Crystalline Peaks, and she still felt that her answers lay within somewhere.

So she looked at Letan, and said, "I have to go in there."

"I know," he nodded. "There are a lot of paths leading into the interior. But you should know that no one who has ventured in has ever come back out."

"You can still turn back," she said, fearful he would do so.

"I'm with you all the way," he nodded stubbornly.

With a smile, she looked into the latticework of the Crystalline Peaks and found a path in. Together, they entered.

Chapter 22

SURROUNDED

Following the defeat of the stray undead soldier, Cardin and the others carried its corpse back to the village. Cardin and Reis carried the body while Elaria carried the head, a rather disgusting action for all of them. Sira was annoyed that they had fought the creature, but also understood that they had to find out if it was a survivor or not.

They brought the corpse to the village square and placed it, and its head, for all to see. A wave of uneasiness swept over the Marines, and Commander Devral cursed. "I've met this man before," she said, dismayed. "He was the village's master blacksmith."

"So, necromancy is real," one of the Marines said with a shudder. "The dead may rise to become our enemies."

"Which means," Reis commented quietly to Cardin and Sira, "that for every one of our allies that falls in battle, the enemy will have another soldier to add to their ranks."

Tactically it made for a very frightening situation, and Cardin was glad Reis hadn't spoken loud enough for everyone to hear. Fear was already beginning to spread amongst the Marines. The sun had fallen close to the horizon, night would soon be upon them, and that prospect wasn't very appealing when walking corpses roamed the land.

"We should get back to the ship for the night," Devral said, as if she had read Cardin's thoughts.

"I agree," Sira said. "We're vulnerable on land at night." What she hadn't said but Cardin knew she thought was that the necromancers had no doubt converted every villager and ever crew member of the lost ships into undead soldiers. They would easily be outnumbered, and who knew just how much skill the corpses retained or how much power the Mages would have as undead.

"Everyone back to the boats," Devral ordered.

No sooner had she said that, than did they all hear the most unnerving sound. It was almost like a groan, but a scratchy groan, like someone tried to scream but their throat was as dry as the desert. It came from the north, where they had fought the first undead. Another such noise came from the south a moment later, as if they had called to each other. Cardin felt a sudden rush, and his hair stood up on end.

Reis drew his sword. "What in the name of the Six was that?" Everyone else likewise readied weapons, even Cardin, and all stood prepared to fight.

Cardin and Sira pushed out from the middle of the crowd of Marines and made their way to the outer edge, to get a better look at the darkening forest. The light of the sun was fading fast, its disk had already reached the horizon. Cardin looked out at the Sea Wisp, a silhouette against the setting sun. Could they make it to the boats, and then to the Sea Wisp, in time? Or were they too late?

Another scratchy call came from the east, and then another from the north again, and then again from the north east. Within seconds, it came from all directions except the sea, and he knew what it meant. They were surrounded, and by the increasing volume, the numbers of the enemy were greater than he had feared.

He began to feel it too, and he was surprised it had taken him that long to sense their presence. Just as it had been with the first one, he felt cold, but this time the cold began to overtake him. It felt as if ice had begun to form in the pit of his stomach, and his head swam. He started to feel dizzy, and he lowered the Sword while he brought his left hand up to his temple and tried to clear his thoughts.

When he dropped to one knee, he barely heard Sira call his name. It wasn't that he couldn't hear her over the enemy, but he couldn't hear her above the overwhelming sensations in his head and heart.

The enemy was strong, stronger than he ever thought possible.

Suddenly, the fog in his mind cleared, and the noise in his head disappeared. A firm hand was on his shoulder, and he looked up and saw that Dalin stood over him, his eyes closed, his brow furrowed in concentration.

Somehow, the Wizard had connected with him and helped him erect a mental defense against the power of the undead. He slowly stood up, and Dalin opened his eyes when he did so. Cardin understood, in that moment, how to keep the defenses that Dalin had just provided him in place. "Are you ok," the Wizard asked.

Cardin nodded. "I am now. What was that?"

"It is a power unlike anything either of us has encountered," Dalin looked to the tree line. Cardin noticed that they could see dots, like glowing eyes. Strangely they were of three distinct colors, lots of orange, lots of blue, and a handful of green. The Wizard continued to explain, "Mages are not as sensitive to the magic around us as you and I are, fortunately. We could feel the twisted magic in each and every undead, and there are a great many. It overwhelmed you more than it did me because I already know how to protect myself from such outside influences."

He accepted the Wizard's explanation, but then remembered that the elves were very sensitive to magic. He turned to Elaria and Ventelis, but both seemed fine. Elaria looked at him and smiled. "I appreciate your concern, but we both have had ample training in filtering out overwhelming power."

Suddenly, the hundreds of glowing pairs of dots began to move, and from the tree line emerged an army of undead from every direction. Amongst the mass of living corpses were those who clearly had been converted very recently after death, compared to those who had been dead for a long time. The recently deceased still had all of their skin, and aside from battle wounds, looked unblemished. The older ones, however, their skin hung from their bones, rotted and cracked, even missing in some places. He even thought he caught sight of a few skeletons wielding swords and shields. There were so many, hundreds, if not thousands, all crowded around the clearing for the village. There wasn't a single gap in their ranks, but for the shoreline.

"Back to the boats," Devral ordered, but not loud enough above the scratching war cries of the risen. When no one reacted, she shouted the order, "Back to the boats, now!"

The Marines acted faster than Cardin could, but within moments the entire company ran as fast as they could towards shore, racing between buildings at a pace that matched everyone's fear.

Cardin came barreling around one of the buildings, surrounded by Marines, Sira right beside him, and the boats were in sight. However, as the ocean receded from a recent wave, another horrifying sight appeared. The heads of more undead rose above the waterline, followed by their shoulders. It was another contingent of corpse soldiers marching up from the sea. Right by the boats.

The company came to a quick halt, half in the sand, the other half in the grass on which the village had been built. "Uh, bit of a hiccup on that order," Reis shouted.

"Yeah, great, I can see that," Devral replied.

"What do we do," one of the Marines cried.

The undead that rose from the ocean began to add to the scratchy wailing, and now they truly were surrounded. There was only one thing left. "Out of the way," Cardin barked as he pushed through the Marines ahead of him. "Move!" They all seemed too frightened to hear him, and he had to be careful not to hit any of them with the Sword as he moved, but finally he pushed through the line the company had formed and took two steps out onto the beach.

In an instant, he gathered a charge of energy, but knew he had to be careful not to destroy the boats, so he kept the charge relatively weak, and swung the Sword in an arch parallel to the ground. A wave of magic leapt out and slammed into the front line of the undead, but it only took out the first couple rows of them, while more followed behind them. He also noted that the boats had rocked from his wave of energy, so he didn't dare use a more powerful blast.

He took that moment to look inland, and found that the horde of undead had advanced quickly. The sound they made was maddening, and some of them who carried shields and swords began to bash them together. It was meant to demoralize them, and he could see in the eyes of the Marines that it was working. Even Commander Devral looked thoroughly terrified, and he realized that most, if not all of the Marines and crew of the Sea Wisp had never seen combat beyond fighting pirate ships. They had never faced an army.

Then again, he thought, *I've never faced an army of the dead.* He looked out to sea, hopeful that the Sea Wisp could see their peril and send reinforcements, but that was also when he saw the smoke rising from the ship, a column of black against the red-orange disk of the sun. Was the ship under attack as well?

Suddenly, the undead stopped walking. A gap of at least thirty feet was left between the undead and their company, and all fell silent. After the deafening cries of the enemy army, the silence was even more unnerving. Even the jungle beyond the shores was deathly quiet.

For several tense moments, the two armies faced off against each other. The Allied forces had formed a circle, and all were ready to fight to the death, but they seemed absolutely miniscule in comparison to the ranks of the enemy.

Then something he did not expect happened. A single undead, a woman with skin that looked ready to fall from her face, and armor that looked beyond ancient, stepped forward. She spoke directly to Cardin, and not to the rest of the company, "Surrender."

He frowned and looked at Sira, who had also pushed to the front. She stepped out from the circle and stood beside him. She looked at the undead woman and asked, "Who am I speaking to?"

"We do not speak to you," the decaying woman said. "We speak to the one with the greatest power."

"I am in charge of this company," Sira stated defiantly. "And we will never surrender!"

"If you surrender, we will spare your lives." The woman spoke with a scratchy, emotionless voice, and Cardin found it as unnerving as any other part of their encounter so far. No emotion, no passion, just existing.

"Only so you can kill us later and turn us into more soldiers for your army," Cardin asked. "I don't think so."

There was no order given, no command, just a sudden flurry of movement as the undead readied their weapons and began to march upon them once again. They had no choice but to fight. "Cardin," Sira said, her voice somehow strong and steady, despite the fear she likely felt, "Go full power."

"The boats..." he warned.

"We can't fight from all directions, we need at least one flank clear, so just do it!"

Without further thought, he charged the Sword up with as much magic as he possibly could, which was far stronger than anything he had ever done, even in training, and once again he swung. He did so in a careful, controlled arch, so that the leading edges would not hurt his companions, and the blast swept out in a violent, deadly wave that destroyed everything, the bodies of the undead, the boats, and it generated an outward wave in the ocean.

He wondered if the shockwave translated into the water and destroyed those still submerged, but he didn't have time to think about it. The rest of the army was already on top of their company, and with a battle cry, Commander Devral led the attack, and the Marines met the undead blade for blade.

Since Cardin had blown away the enemy on the western edge, he and Sira were now several feet away from the closest enemy, so they closed that distance as quickly as possible, and Cardin leapt into the battle and sliced down an enemy.

He didn't dare use another massive wave again, not with the enemy now mixing in with his companions, but he did use magic to increase his strength, his speed, his awareness of his surroundings, and he moved from enemy to enemy, and took them down one by one in rapid succession. He knew that the ones he didn't behead would still be capable of fighting, so he tried to focus on cutting their necks, but even disarming an enemy would make them less dangerous, and easier for the marines to defeat.

Yet for each one he struck down, more came in their place. There was no end in sight, and he saw that wave after wave of undead emerged from the jungle. The sun was about to set, and soon the only light would be from one of the moons that had already risen. The battle would become more difficult for them once that happened.

Only a few minutes into the battle, and he already knew there had been casualties. He felt a strange flurry of energy, cold and deep, stir from several locations outside of the battle, and then the energy focused in on several points within their ranks. He didn't know how he knew, but he knew that was because necromancers had just revived dead Marines.

Terror overcame him when he realized that one of the undead might now be a friend, or even Sira. He realized that the battle was unwinnable, and if they kept fighting, he would lose Sira.

"No!"

Feeling his control slip, he surged forward and killed three undead in a single blow. He turned back towards the heart of the battle, and saw Sira take down another of the undead ranks. He fought his way towards her, not caring about anything else. He struck down every undead that got in his way, unwilling to let anything happen to her.

Finally when he was close enough, Sira saw him and shouted, "Cardin, we can't keep this up!"

"I know," he swung the Sword high and beheaded a particularly tall undead.

"You know what I have to do, and you know what you need to do!"

He felt terror strike his heart, and he looked at her in bewilderment. "No!"

Another undead tried to attack her, but she parried its blow, and then shoved it towards Cardin. He jabbed the Sword through it, which caught it long enough for Sira to swing her sword and take its head off.

"Cardin, they can't get a hold of the Sword, you have to run!"

"I won't leave you!" He pulled the Sword out from the enemy, and then swung around, sensing the faint cold of another undead behind him. He sliced it clean through the torso, and it dropped to the ground. The torso still lived, and it tried to swing its weapon at his ankle. He hopped back, charged the Sword, thrust it at the creature, and destroyed its head with a single blast of magic.

"If they get the Sword, it's all over," she insisted. "You'll lose me anyway."

Another undead tried to swing at him, but he disarmed it, literally. "But…"

"Just go!"

He looked at her, and they stared into one another's eyes for a split second. In that second, he realized how much he loved her, and how losing her would be the worst thing imaginable. He'd pushed her away over ten years ago, and now had spent the last seven months trying to rekindle what he had destroyed so long ago. They had grown so close, and now…

She was right. He knew she was. Their only chance was for the Allies to surrender, and be taken prisoner. However, they couldn't afford for him to be taken prisoner, for the Sword to be taken up by a necromancer. She was right, he would lose her anyway if that happened.

His only option was to run, run as fast as he could, and come back to rescue her and the others later, before they were turned.

The moment was over. He broke eye contact, turned towards the north, and swung the Sword, releasing a less potent wave of energy that knocked several of the undead down. Then he did something that he had only done in training. He got a running start, and then when he reached the edge of the gap he had created, he channeled as much energy as he could into his legs, and he leapt, high and fast, over the heads of the undead. He charged up the Sword again, and as he came down near the edge of the jungle, he swung the blade and released a deadly blast that tore apart the undead and left a divot in the ground.

Without a second thought, he rushed into the tree line. From behind him, he heard Sira shout, "We surrender!"

And a moment later, he ran headlong into the darkness.

Chapter 23

THE NAVITAS

In the glittering chasms of the Crystalline Peaks, Kailar and Letan continued their journey. The crystal peaks towered above them, as if they scraped the very sky. Under other circumstances, she would have been mesmerized by the rainbow beams of light, the shimmering and dazzling reflections, but instead she felt only frustration.

They had walked for several hours, and she was beginning to grow suspicious. Something was wrong. She had the impression that they were being pushed in a specific direction.

It was hard to keep her bearings, the sun was no longer overhead and the refracted and reflected light deep inside of the Peaks disoriented her. The crystals formed imperfect paths that required them to turn every few steps, but she had the distinct impression they had started to move more northeast now, close to the eastern border of the peaks. She didn't know how or why, but she believed it was by design.

So, as they continued on, and ducked under one crystal that jutted out of the ground, she intentionally took a path that branched in the opposite direction. She stopped them, and looked at Letan, ready to ask which cardinal direction they were headed. However, she stopped short when she saw that his face was pale and clammy. "Are you okay?"

He looked at her and sighed. "For now, yes, but this place..." He wiped sweat from his brow, and then massaged his temple. "I felt it when I first drew close to the peaks. It's just like the stories always said, I could feel my powers increase. It became an intense pressure in my head, and my heart. It felt incredible at first, but now, it just feels overwhelming."

She placed a hand on his shoulder, and then reached down for his other hand and took hold of it. "We can turn back."

He laughed and looked behind them. "I doubt we'll be able to find our way back. We're in now, there is no going back. We have to keep going, and hope that we find something soon."

She nodded, and then took out her water flask. She took a quick drink of it, and then offered it to Letan, but he shook his head and used his own water pouch.

When they were both ready to continue, she led them on. As she had almost expected, the path twisted and turned, until she knew they had been turned around again. "Letan, what direction are we facing?"

All Mages could sense what direction they faced, and it was an ability she had taken for granted before the dragons had taken away her powers. She grudgingly realized that if Letan hadn't come back for her, she would feel even more frustrated and panicked at the suspicion that she was being maneuvered.

"A little east of north," he said.

"Is it just me, or..."

He finished her thought, "we're being forced towards the Crystalline Forest."

She frowned at him. "Crystalline Forest?"

He nodded. "Also a place not many venture into, and none return from. From outside, it looks like a scattered forest of trees made out of crystals. There are even what appear to be leaves of diamond, but the effects of the forest are supposed to be the same as the peaks."

At first she looked at him incredulously, but he gave her a look that made her understand that he was serious. She absently reached into her backpack and pulled out the map that she had bought in Edingard. Sure enough, between the Crystalline Peaks and the ocean shore was the Crystalline Forest. She had been so focused on the peaks and the tales about them that she never even paid attention to what was near them, let alone asked for stories.

"Well," she sighed. "That's just too bad. I am not going to let something or someone force me somewhere I don't want to go." She folded up the map, smiled at him, and walked past him in the direction they had come from.

Letan followed without question, but she noted that he looked even worse. She worried that the power of the Peaks might somehow overpower him, destroy him in some way, burn him out.

She rushed along, until she found that the path they had originally come from was gone. Right where it should have continued stood a crystal, not a tall one, but definitely taller than she was. She looked down at the dirt, and saw their footprints where they had walked only a few minutes ago.

"What in the name of the Six," Letan frowned. "How did that happen?"

She felt a flare of anger in her. "Something doesn't want us going this way," she growled, and turned and stormed past him. As soon as she could, she took another turn that took them in a direction away from the Forest.

That path became a dead end. So she turned back yet again, and came back to the fork, only to find it wasn't a fork in the path anymore, and the way they had come was blocked. She hit the new crystal formation in frustration, but it didn't even so much as shimmer at her.

"I will not be manipulated like this," she muttered. She walked down the only available path, faster, anger fueling her determination. Every turn she found that took her in a direction other than the Forest, she stormed down it, but they always either twisted back towards the Forest or came to dead ends, and any time she tried to turn around, the path was blocked only a few dozen feet later. She couldn't begin to fathom how the crystals rose up from the ground without making any noise.

Finally, she stopped, and shouted, "I will not be manipulated like this!" Her voice echoed throughout the crystal canyons, but there came no response. "I will never be manipulated again! Who are you? What do you want?"

Letan stood next to her as best as he could in the narrow confines, careful not to touch the crystals. He looked around, and she noticed that the barely noticeable pulse beneath the crystals fluctuated a little, but there was no other response.

So she folded her arms, and stood resolute. "I will not go any further! If you want me to keep walking, then tell me who or what you are."

Still no reply, but she was finished. She looked at Letan, who continued to look around in wonder before he turned to her and smiled encouragingly. It was obvious that the effects he felt were becoming worse, and she worried for him. That alone was almost enough for her to break her own resolution and start moving again, but she wouldn't let whatever controlled the crystals force her to do anything.

After several minutes, she sat down cross-legged and stared ahead. Somehow the path had seemingly opened up a little more, as if to make it more enticing to her, but she would not move. Letan sat a moment later, and reached out to take hold of her hand.

She let him, savored the encouragement she felt from it, the warmth it created in her heart. "Are you okay," she asked again.

"I'll be fine," he lied. She ground her teeth in frustration and anger, but looked ahead and remained still.

Several minutes drifted by in complete silence, and she looked up at the sky. She thought she briefly caught movement that looked like a shooting star, but it was day time, so she figured it had been a trick of the light from the crystals.

Then she felt it. It started as a slight vibration in the ground, so she placed her free hand flat on the dirt. It wasn't her imagination. Letan looked around and appeared to feel it too. Then the vibration grew, and before long, it began to shake them both, and the ground rumbled noisily. She stood up, and helped Letan up to ensure he didn't touch a crystal.

In a sudden rush of motion, all of the crystals moved. Immediately around them and towards the Crystalline Forest, the peaks began to part, and the path widened. Some also sank into the ground, but most simply moved aside, as if two giant hands had split them down the middle and parted them.

The path became at least a half mile wide, and ahead, she could just make out the forest far in the distance. The crystals stopped moving, and they looked around in awe. The ground was perfectly flat, and she couldn't figure out how that was possible, as if the crystal peaks had never been there in the first place. There should have been holes or overturned dirt.

She looked at Letan, and he to her. "I don't think they are going to give us a choice," he said.

No sooner had he spoken than did the ground begin to shake again. All of a sudden it lurched beneath them, and they both fell onto their backs. The part of the earth they were on suddenly began to angle up and towards the forest, and then began to move! Within moments, they sped towards the Forest on a slab of moving earth. The ridiculousness of the situation barely registered in her mind, she simply felt the fear of being at the mercy of such a powerful force.

The movement had forced them to lose touch with each other's hands, but as they rode along, both terrified, they looked at each other and began to reach for each other, straining against the force that pushed them against the ground.

They finally reached one another's hands, and held on as tight as they could. By then, however, the speed reduced, and the force that plastered them down decreased. Their speed slowed drastically, until they came to a stop just at the edge of where the Crystalline Peaks had ended, and the dirt that had ferried them flattened into the ground.

On unsteady feet, they helped each other stand, and looked behind them. The distance they had covered was incredible, several miles at least. Then they turned northeast, and stared into the heart of the Crystalline Forest.

Letan's description scarcely did it justice. The trees were at least three or four times as tall as a person, a few were even taller than that, and all were spread out so that there was several dozen feet between them.

It was a mesmerizing sight! They were definitely crystalline looking, but unlike the peaks, they seemed to glow from within. Through their surface, she could see the golden glow inside the center of the trunk and the branches, but that glow faded at the edges.

She had the distinct impression that the trees were alive. She couldn't feel it, but somehow they just looked alive, and she wondered about that, about how crystals could contain life. It must have been her imagination, she decided.

A moment later, she was proven wrong. The trees began to

move, slowly but with definitive purpose. They began to change form with the sound of glass grinding and even breaking accompanying their change. Dozens of them began to move closer to her and Letan, and her heart thundered in her ears. She drew her dagger, while Letan drew his sword, and they stood ready to fight something they knew they could not possibly fight.

Before long, she realized what the trees were changing into. Legs formed, the branches coalesced into arms, and heads began to appear. Within minutes, they were surrounded by crystal giants, all of whom stared down upon them.

Their shapes, though humanoid, were decidedly inorganic, and were very much the product of faceted crystals. Their heads and necks appeared to be single pieces, and where eye sockets formed, points of intense golden light appeared. Mouths took shape, but no noise escaped them yet. Kailar looked over her shoulder, and saw that somehow, silently, a wall of crystal mountains had formed behind them. They were trapped.

She exchanged an incredulous look with Letan, and then looked up at the giant directly ahead of them. The fear in her stomach twisted into a knot, but she forced herself to step forward and looked directly into the giant's eyes.

"Who are you," she shouted.

It spoke, with a deep and surprisingly human sounding voice, though it also had a quality to it that she could only describe as metallic. "We are the Navitas."

It was a word she had never heard before, so she frowned and corrected herself, "*What* are you?"

"Magic." There was little emotion in its voice, yet its speech resonated within her core.

She gave Letan a confused look, and then asked the giant, "What do you mean?"

The giant also exchanged glances with some of its companions, and she found that to be a curious and intriguing act. It looked at her, and nodded, "We are composed of energy, of magic."

Letan stepped up next to her and asked, "How is that even possible?"

The Navitas stood up straighter, taller, but it did not increase her fear. In fact if anything, her fear began to diminish, and she wasn't entirely sure why.

"We came into existence long ago," it spoke. The others nodded in agreement. "Our origin is as much a mystery to us as yours is to you."

She raised her eyebrows. "I see." That left only one other vital question. "Why did you bring us here?"

The Navitas motioned its hands towards the Crystalline Peaks, a very human gesture, as it spoke, "You entered our collectors. They harvest magic from all sources. Primarily your sun, but they can take the power away from any living creature."

At first she wasn't sure what the Navitas referred to. "Collectors?" Then a second later she realized and pointed behind her. "The Peaks?"

"Yes," the Navitas nodded, which since it didn't have a neck meant its entire torso moved back and forth.

"But I felt stronger in there," Letan said. "I could feel more power within myself, not less."

"That was due to your proximity to the collected and focused magic. In time, they would have drained your life energy, and you would have died."

Kailar shuddered at the thought of the life being drained out of him, and she felt a little angry about it. "Is that what happened to everyone else who ever ventured into the Peaks or into this forest?"

"Yes," the Navitas replied simply.

"Why let it happen to them, and not to us?" Letan asked. "Why save us?"

Assuming they have brought us here to save us, Kailar thought inwardly.

"This one is different," the Navitas pointed at Kailar with a long, faceted finger.

"Me?!"

It attempted another nod. "You have no power, no presence." She felt a void open up within at the reminder. "Yet the magic reacts around you as if you were a being of incredible power. There is a prophecy about you."

It felt as if her heart stopped for a moment, and she felt her jaw slowly fall open. "A prophecy? How could there be a prophecy about me?"

"The Powerless One," it continued. "The Powerless One will come forward to find a new source. Then a day will come when she holds the fate of many in her will."

A sudden sense of excitement began to grow within her, and she felt hope rekindled. She would find a new power? Had she truly been right to come to the peaks after all? Afraid to ask, as if doing so would mean her hopes would be dashed, she nevertheless asked, "Are you going to restore my connection to magic?"

There was a long pause, and then the Navitas said, "That is beyond our abilities." Her heart sank, but only for a moment. "Your power must come from a different source. A different kind of power. Not magic as we know it."

She looked up in wonder at the Navitas, and could only begin to form the question in her mind. A different kind of power? What could it possibly mean by that? However, before she could ask, she heard what sounded like a sudden explosion, could even *feel* the explosion as a deafening roar shattered the air around them. She and Letan covered their ears in surprise and pain. They dropped their weapons and looked up to the sky to see a great ball of fire streak from east to west, leaving behind a wide trail of black smoke. When it had passed, so too did the roar.

The Navitas also watched the ball of fire, and then spoke, "Another prophecy us now upon us. We must leave at once."

She looked in fear at the crystal giant. "What prophecy? What was that?"

The Navitas looked at her, and somehow she read in its eyes the fear it felt within its core. "Your skies will burn and a dark one will descend upon this world. Disaster comes to you all. Today." Fear gripped her stomach. "We must leave."

As one, the crystal giants began to walk, at first she thought in their direction, but then she realized that they were headed for the peaks. Other trees further away began to move and reshape into humanoid forms. She realized that they were all moving towards the Crystalline Peaks. They were going to draw power from them.

"Wait!" The one that spoke to them stopped and looked down at her, but the others continued towards the Peaks. "Wait, you can't leave!"

"We must," it replied simply. "We cannot allow the darkness to destroy us. As we have done many times before, we must leave and find another world to call home. We will start again, as we have for tens of thousands of years."

Her mind raced, fear grew within her, and she looked up at the streak of black smoke again. It slowly billowed outward and began to dissipate. Whatever it was, it was unlike anything she had ever seen before, and the only thing she could liken it to was a shooting star, only a thousand times larger!

"So you're just going to run again," she asked. "Abandon another world?"

"This is not our world," it said. She turned and saw that beams of energy suddenly shot out from the collectors and into the Navitas that had approached them. They were siphoning energy. "We must gather as much energy as we can. You must leave at once."

"No!" she shouted. "I won't run, not again, and neither will you!"

"Why would we stay," it asked.

She wasn't sure she had a good answer for him, and she tried to figure out what she could possibly say to make them stay. "Because, you have made this your home. And clearly you are powerful beings! You could help us fight the dark one you spoke of!"

It seemed to pause, as if the idea of fighting was a novel concept. "Why would we do that? Many of us would die."

Without more information, she wasn't sure she could answer him. So she asked, "How powerful is this dark one? Powerful enough to travel to other worlds?"

"Yes," it nodded. "It will one day consume all. We must try to stay ahead of it. We must run, like we never have before."

Its response instilled greater fear within her, so she searched desperately for something to say. "Then what? How long will you run? How long can you run for?"

"As long as we can. As far as we can. We cannot defeat it."

"Not alone," she nodded. "Whatever or whoever it is, you may not be able to defeat it alone, perhaps no one can. But what if you fight together, along with the humans of this world?"

The Navitas attempted to shake its head, which was almost a comical gesture if it weren't for the situation. "The humans will have absolutely no power against it."

Without another word, it resumed its march for the peaks, and she felt as if she had lost. Then one final thought occurred to her. "What about the Sword of Dragons?"

It stopped, and looked down at her. "Dragons?"

"Yes," she nodded, hope kindled within. "A weapon forged by the Dragons and the Vrol three thousand years ago."

She noticed a sudden silence around her, and so looked westward. The other Navitas had stopped drawing power from the collectors, and all turned and faced her and Letan. Even Letan looked at her in surprise. "What are you doing," he asked.

"Whatever I can." She looked up at the Navitas. "I once possessed this weapon, until I abused it, and the dragons stripped me of my connection to magic. That is what you sensed about me." It was a guess, but a good one. "It is now in the possession of a man named Cardin Kataar, and he has been the Keeper of the Sword for seven months. The Sword, and its Keeper, may actually be capable of stopping the dark one you speak of." She paused and looked intently at the giant. "But he can't do it alone."

The Navitas all looked at one another, and she wondered if they somehow silently communicated with one another. After a minute, the one before them looked down at her. "That is the power we have sensed growing upon this world."

"Yes," she said, her confidence building.

"And if the prophecy about you is correct," he paused thoughtfully. "Then he may be the subject of another prophecy."

That gave her a moment of pause. These beings seemed to know many prophecies, and she wondered how. She felt the urge to demand to know more about the prophecies, especially about the one that related to her, but she had the feeling that there were more pressing matters.

"Navitas," she called to them all, "he needs your help. *We* need your help. This world has been your home. Will you run again, to wander aimlessly for the rest of time? Or will you fight for your home?" They remained silent, staring at one another and at her. "Please!"

After another few moments of exchanged looks, the Navitas looked down at her, and she swore it smiled. "We feel the power, and that power has once again begun to grow at an incredible rate. Perhaps we are safer here, if we can help him survive the coming apocalypse."

She smiled. "Then you'll stay?"

The crystal giant attempted to nod, "We shall. But it will take us time to travel to this Keeper. You must leave this place at once."

Letan took a hold of her hand again, and they smiled to one another. "We want to help fight too," he said.

"I am afraid that your destiny lies elsewhere," the Navitas replied. "You must leave at once, all humans must leave the area surrounding our collectors."

She frowned, and asked, "Why?"

Another deafening explosion came from the sky, and she looked up to watch as another streak of flame blasted across the sky. "Meteorites will soon reach the ground," the Navitas pointed at the fire as it passed over. "Many will damage our collectors, and then the collectors will release dangerous energy. Anyone caught by the energy will be destroyed."

She and Letan looked at each other, and he said with fear, "Corlas…"

Chapter 24

THE LOST ELF

Cardin ran, as fast as he could. He lost all track of time, he just knew that the sun had set, the jungle was dark, and he had left behind the only woman he had ever loved. It never occurred to him that he shouldn't have been able to see his surroundings, he just ran.

His head felt like it was spinning, and he started to feel sick to his stomach, so he finally stopped. For several moments, he simply stood there, panting. He could feel the magic around and within him stir and flow rapidly, as if he were an intense focal point of energy creating a magic maelstrom.

He left her behind. She had ordered him to, and he had run, and now she and all of his friends were at the mercy of the undead, while he was miles away, helpless to save them. The anger and frustration began to boil over, ready to explode.

The Sword felt heavy in his right hand, and he brought it up and glowered at it. If it weren't for the Sword, he could have stayed with his friends, surrendered with them, faced whatever fate lay ahead of them. He could have been together, *with* them, not alone.

Without even thinking, he turned to the nearest tree, and punched it with all of his enhanced strength. The tree shook hard and a splintered crater was left in the trunk, while several fruit, branches, and other debris crashed down around him.

At first he didn't feel anything but, but then his senses returned, and pain screamed at him. He cursed and clutched his fist under his other arm.

Suddenly a voice spoke from above, "Why do humans always believe physical violence solves everything?"

Startled, Cardin looked up a nearby tree, where a lone figure dropped down from one of its lowest branches. The man wore what appeared to be normal clothes, a simple tunic and trousers, though it was difficult to see what their colors were in the darkness. What caught his attention were the pair of pointed ears, and the intense golden-orange eyes that glowed a little in the darkness.

"Do not be startled," the elf spoke again, his voice disarmingly soft and soothing. "I realize that my appearance may be strange to you…"

"Baenil," Cardin asked, realizing it could be no one else.

The elf's attempt at keeping Cardin calm was abandoned, and confusion played across his face. A moment later, the confusion turned to fear and suspicion. "You are a member of the Covenant."

Cardin realized he still held the Sword in a defensive stance, so he lowered it and stood up straight. "No," he shook his head, "My name is Cardin Kataar. I came here with Ventelis to find you."

Baenil's head perked up. "Ventelis? He knows not to make contact with cultures that believe themselves alone in the universe."

Realizing there was no threat, and that the undead were nowhere close to them, Cardin raised the Sword up over his head and willed it into its sheath. "Much has changed since you were captured by the Covenant," he said. He shrugged and added, "Although most of Halarite is still coming to terms with the new realities we now face. In any case, seven months ago, it was revealed to us that there were other intelligent species in the universe, chief of which are the Star Dragons. Shortly after, we encountered a Dareann Elf named Elaria."

Baenil's face lit up. "Elaria? Her curiosity often gets her into trouble."

He raised an eyebrow. "You've met her before?"

"Twice," Baenil beamed, "when she brought recovered artifacts from new worlds to our college to study." The smile continued to grow across his face and he looked down at the ground absently.

"She is certainly a unique woman."

Cardin chuckled, which seemed to embarrass the relatively young elf. "You'll be happy to know she's here as well, with Ventelis." And then the dark cloud returned, and his face slackened. "If we're both lucky, all of our friends will be okay."

Baenil stared at him, concern and fear clear in his eyes. "What has happened?"

Cardin turned away and leaned his shoulder against the tree he had punched. "We made land fall this afternoon." He stared into the jungle, searching for something to give him hope, searching for something that would reassure him that he had done the right thing. "We encountered a single undead, and defeated it. Next thing we knew, we were surrounded by an army of them. I had to run, while everyone else surrendered." Baenil walked around to face Cardin. He looked into the elf's eyes and wished he had better news for the man. "I don't know if they were spared or not, but the undead did call for our surrender before the battle began. I'm hopeful that they are ok."

Ventelis nodded, and said, "They never called for our surrender, so that was certainly a new development."

Cardin frowned. "What exactly happened to you?"

Baenil sighed, a haunted stare overcoming his face. "I was a prisoner of the Covenant for years. While I was here, on Trinil, they took me into the jungle to investigate several ancient, ruined structures. They were hoping I could see something in them that they could not. I was excited, actually, the language I found was older than any other human language I've ever found. But that also meant I didn't know how to translate it, and without my books at the college for reference, it became a very long project."

"Why didn't you just create a portal and leave when you were first captured?"

He laughed despairingly, "I tried. They kept a guard on me at all times, specifically a woman named Anila when we were on Edilas. She somehow knew what I was going to do and would hit me on the head every time I tried."

Cardin looked at him curiously. "Interesting. I know she isn't who she seems, but the fact that she was able to predict when you were about to open a portal is...unusual."

Baenil nodded. "Indeed, it did seem like she could sense the power, even though she herself is powerless."

Despite the fact that his suspicions about her had grown tenfold, Cardin did not reveal her secret. Not yet. He had given his word, and until he knew for certain that she was a direct threat, he would not reveal the truth.

"In any case," Baenil continued, "We were exploring a new ruin discovered deep within the jungle when the undead appeared. Actually, even before that, we found what appeared to be several bodies within the ruins, which as you might imagine surprised us – relatively fresh corpses in ruins that had to be well over ten thousand years old. We were even more surprised when, after several hours, those corpses started to move, and dozens more came from the jungle."

Cardin could only imagine what that must have been like, seeing corpses rise and then attack. Even though he had already known he would encounter the living dead when they had arrived, it still unnerved him the first time he'd seen that lone figure in the jungle turn and face him.

"There must have been an actual Necromancer nearby," Baenil continued, "because they didn't hesitate to kill my guards or other members of the expedition, and moments later those who had fallen rose up once again."

"How did you get away?"

He shrugged easily. "I was lucky. In the chaos of the battle, I slipped between the advancing undead and ran, ran as fast as I could." Cardin understood how that felt. "The next day I reached the village, hopeful that I could sneak aboard a ship at some point to get away from here. I had lost the ability to create portals ever since we arrived, so that was my only hope."

Cardin nodded. "The Wizards couldn't create portals to or from here, either. We don't know why, but assume there is someone or something on this continent disrupting portals. What happened to you next?"

"I hid in the jungle just outside of the village, until a ship arrived. I knew my only chance to get aboard undetected would be to swim out to it at night, so I waited. I never had the chance to try. The undead swarmed the village that very night, and they crawled up the ship's hull from the water to attack it. The battle was over very quickly, and nothing living remained. I had managed to avoid the undead by staying up in the trees, they did not think to look up."

Cardin nodded, and realized it had been a smart move on the elf's part. He had survived, and now was perhaps the only person alive on the island who could help him.

"Where are the necromancers? How many of them are there?"

The haunted look once again returned to Baenil's eyes. "Hundreds. An entire civilization. I followed the undead after they left the village, and they led me to an ancient city far inside of the jungle. I could not get an accurate count of necromancers, or undead for that matter, but there are hundreds of necromancers, and perhaps tens of thousands of undead."

Cardin felt his jaw drop. "Tens of thousands?"

"I am afraid so. An overwhelming and unstoppable number."

It was more than he could have imagined or feared, an army of soldiers that were nearly invincible, without conscience, without a trace of humanity. If they ever attacked the four kingdoms, they would overrun them.

Suddenly there was a bright flash of light overhead, visible even through the dense jungle canopy, like a new sun had appeared in the night sky. The light streaked overhead rapidly, and soon was followed by the sound of an incredibly loud explosion, followed by a deep rumbling. Panic washed over Cardin and he grabbed the handle of the Sword, but did not unsheathe it.

His sense of the world around him was still strong, so he knew that the light followed a line from northeast to southwest, and eventually faded, as did the rumbling.

"What in the name of the Six was that," he heard himself ask, scarcely aware of his choice of words.

Baenil looked at him curiously, and then shook his head. "I do not know. However, it could be related to what is happening tomorrow morning."

Cardin looked at him with a frown. "What is happening tomorrow?"

"I have observed the necromancer city for some time, and they seem to be preparing for something. Ships are gathering on the river that runs through their city, and based on what I know of battle tactics, they mean to depart either tonight or tomorrow morning."

Which meant they were already out of time. Cardin would not get any sleep that night. "Alright," he nodded. "If our friends are still alive, we have to rescue them, and we have to find out what is going on. The Wizards are constantly checking to see if they can open a portal here, so we should also try to find out what is disrupting portals, and destroy it."

"Wait," Baenil looked horrified, "I am no soldier, I cannot fight. I have a dagger," he rested his hand on a human-made dagger he had commandeered and strapped to his belt, "but I cannot help you fight."

Cardin placed a reassuring hand on the elf's shoulder. "You don't have to. I can take care of myself. I just need you to lead me into the city, and then help me locate the source of the disruption." He squeezed the man's shoulder reassuringly and added, "I will protect you, I promise."

Baenil seemed hesitant, but he had no choice. He was stuck, and Cardin was the only friendly face he'd seen in years. So the elf nodded. "Very well. Follow me, it will take us several hours to reach the city."

Chapter 25

THE RUINS OF THE DEAD

Reis felt ready to collapse, completely fatigued by an hours-long march through the jungle. After Sira had called out their surrender, several of the Marines continued to fight on, but Commander Devral grudgingly added to Sira's order. Once everyone had thrown down their weapons, they waited for the slaughter, but it never came. Several undead came forward and bound their hands, and after only a few minutes, they were led wordlessly into the jungle.

They had lit torches so that there was light to walk by, but he had the impression that the undead could see in the dark as easily as the daylight. For countless hours they trudged through the jungle, their torturous march broken only by a streak of light above the canopy and the sound of an explosion. Their company had all been startled and unnerved, but the undead marched on unfazed.

It had started to rain, but it wasn't a torrential downpour, just a muggy drizzle that filtered through the jungle canopy. Some of the torches had gone out, and that made it harder for the Marines to walk, but the undead did not attempt to relight them.

Reis marched alongside Anila. She initially had refused to surrender despite the orders, and had fought off countless undead before Reis convinced her to lay down her weapon. He feared the enemy would strike her down out of spite, but they merely captured her along with everyone else.

She was silent the entire march, something he was accustomed to with her. During their voyage aboard the Sea Wisp, when she spoke to him, she did so sparingly. Despite that fact, they had somehow begun to spend a lot of their time together, and he found her presence to be relaxing.

Now he needed all of the help he could get to relax. As the march progressed, he noticed more undead joined their procession on their flanks, and he even noticed new figures in scarlet and black robes. Ahead, Dalin seemed to take an interest in those new figures, but he did not say anything. In fact, the entire company was silent, almost no one spoke, and the few who did had done so in a hushed whisper, as if afraid the undead would kill them merely for speaking.

The first sign he had that they neared their destination was that they stepped onto what appeared to be a half-buried ancient road. Though there was considerable flora overgrowing it, there were no trees upon it, and that created a clear path ahead. He noticed a glow down that road, and as they drew closer, he realized it was from several torches, lamps, and other sources of light lit within what he thought at first was a camp. When the surrounding jungle thinned a little, he realized it wasn't a camp. It was a city.

Reis marched near the head of the column, with only Dalin, Ventelis, Sira, and Commander Devral ahead of him, so he was among the first to see the city clearly. The jungle cleared and they emerged to see an incredible sight.

The towering structures were all made of a pale stone that reflected the torch and lamplight dimly, and their condition suggested they were ancient. Vines and other types of flora grew in cracks around the buildings, and many of them stretched higher than the torchlight could reach. The structures somehow seemed organic in shape, even though they were made from stone, and had smooth curves and tall, thin dome-like structures.

The rain finally stopped, and patches of starlight shone through. It did little to change his mood. When he finished staring up at the buildings, he looked down and found that the city was populated by thousands of undead, all of whom lined the street that they marched along towards the city center.

The tallest building that he could see was directly ahead of them.

Its base was raised up from the rest of the city upon a great square platform. The base was supported by several simple stone pillars. In front of the structure were five chairs that reminded him of thrones, each of them made of stone. He did not know if the chairs had always stood there or if the necromancers had placed them there for some reason, but he hàd the feeling they were reserved for the leaders of the necromancers. He also had a feeling that the thrones were their destination.

Reis looked to the left and saw that a river ran through the city through artificial canals, and upon that river sat countless ships, moored and being boarded by hordes of undead. It was an invasion army.

"Fascinating," he overheard Ventelis state. "I have seen architecture similar to this before, but only in the very oldest of human ruins." No one replied to his statement, and Reis didn't think it really mattered or had been worth mentioning.

They began to ascend the stairs, which didn't help his already aching legs. There were about two stories worth of stairs that they had to climb, and when they finally reached the stone courtyard surrounding the building, he felt ready to collapse. Moments later, the undead brought their company to a stop. Reis and Anila stepped up to join the others, and a moment later, Elaria also joined them, and he felt an increasing sense of worry for her. While he had spent time getting to know Anila during the voyage over, he had also begun to open up to Elaria. He always felt an excited sensation when he saw her now, and he felt embarrassed at those feelings, as well as guilty. He no longer believed she was a demon, but the Covenant still clearly didn't trust her or her kind, and he wasn't sure he should either.

Reis had even confided his attraction to Elaria to Anila, and told her how guilty he felt about it. She simply pointed out to him that Elaria was a person, and his feelings for her shouldn't depend upon her species. He wasn't sure he agreed, but somehow her assurances helped him feel a little better

As they stood before the five thrones, five humans in scarlet and black robes emerged, silent and regal, but clearly very old. Two of them were men, both of whom had grown very long, gray beards, while the other three were women, likely as old as the men but somehow appeared to have aged more gracefully. The lamps in the square turned their faces and gray hair a shade of orange.

The five took their seats, with the center being occupied by one of the elder men. Dalin whispered amongst their group, "I feel an immense power from them, unlike anything I have ever felt from another human before. They are very, very old."

"And very powerful," the center necromancer spoke. His voice did not match his age, it sounded very strong, full of vigor and life. "I have lived longer than you can imagine, Wizard. I have seen entire civilizations rise and fall in my time. As have we all," he motioned to the other four.

"How long have you lived here," Ventelis asked, clearly unable to contain his curiosity.

"We came to this world over five thousand years ago," one of the women spoke, the one right of center. "We fled our world when the dragons destroyed it."

Dalin scoffed, and said in a doubtful voice, "Dragons do not destroy worlds."

The center necromancer suddenly stood up, his face contorted in deep seated anger and hatred. "I was there! I saw it happen, I saw and felt the dragons fight each other high above our skies. Their power tore our home apart!"

Reis didn't have to be a Mage to know that magic stirred in the wake of the necromancer's anger, but he seemed to regain his self control and slowly sat down. Reis looked at Dalin, who managed to hold a resolute face, but he had the feeling that the Wizard was nervous about the necromancer's reaction.

"We knew our world was doomed, especially when our sun began to dim," another woman spoke to them. "Many recalled that several of our kin had come to Halarite to begin a new life thousands of years before, so we fled here, hopeful to find welcoming arms."

"All we found were ruins," the one in the center said. "No sign of civilization on this continent. So we settled in to start a new life of our own."

The only other man added to the story, "Several years later, many of our people began to fall ill. In time we noticed only the strongest of us did not fall ill, but those that did almost always perished. We knew we could not save our civilization if most of us died from disease, so we used our powers to bring them back from death."

"If you call this life," Sira motioned to some of the undead that guarded them.

Anger flared in the leader again. "It was all we had. It was all we could do. Our civilization would have otherwise fallen."

For a moment, no one said anything, but at that point, Reis thought of his own question. "Why have you spared us? Why did you not kill us and raise us as you have the others?"

The lead necromancer smiled, a rather wicked look given his wrinkled face. "It was only recently that we learned a civilization thrived upon other continents. We will conquer that land, but we already have enough undead soldiers to do so. We need living subjects to serve us and to revitalize our civilization."

Sira shook her head. "That won't happen. We will all die before we serve you."

"Is that so?" The leader laughed. "It would not be the first time you surrendered to a powerful adversary. We have learned all about your history. Over three thousand years ago, you allowed yourselves to be ruled by an insane Wizard."

"All while we built up a resistance to fight him," Reis said defiantly. "As we would you. We would eventually overthrow your rule."

"Do not underestimate us," the leader warned. "There are more of us than you realize. For every one of your people that fall, so shall our army be bolstered. You cannot defeat us. You cannot stop us. Today will be the day we conquer your civilization, forever."

Reis and the others exchanged glances, and Sira asked, "Why today? And how? It would take you a month to sail with your ships to Edilas."

"On the contrary," the leader smiled once again, "Our ships will appear off of the coast of your homeland sooner than you might think. Today is the day that prophecy shall be fulfilled."

Reis noticed that Dalin seemed keenly interested in those words. "What prophecy?"

"The one spoken five thousand years ago, when we fled to this world. The time for our civilization to rise again has come. A shattered world shall return to its people, and darkness and fire will descend." The leader leaned forward, a confident smirk upon his face. "We will reclaim our former glory, and you will serve us."

Reis thought that to be a curious prophecy, but he wasn't entirely sure he believed in prophecies either. Then again, he still could not comprehend all of the intricacies of magic, so he realized he could not discount it either.

In either case, he feared for what was to come, feared it so much that his stomach twisted and he felt sick. An army of tens of thousands of undead stood ready to invade their homeland, and he knew countless Warriors and soldiers would die in the coming days.

What made it worse was that there was nothing he or any of his friends could do so long as they stood bound in shackles and were surrounded by their enemies. They were weaponless and hopeless.

The four necromancers on either side of the leader stood, and the central one said, "You will be escorted to one of the ships and will accompany our army. If you resist, you will be killed and become one of our soldiers. You will serve the necromancers, one way or another."

The four walked towards the river, and the undead soldiers began to shove Reis and the others to follow. There was no way their entire company could fit on one enemy ship, so after they descended the stairs down to street level, the undead began to split several contingents of the marines off, though thankfully they left their core group together. Reis did not want to be separated from the rest of his friends. His fear was already close to unmanageable, and he didn't dare face it alone.

As they walked along, he found himself drawn to look over at Elaria, who outwardly showed no fear. However, as they walked along, she looked back at him, and he could see it in her sunset orange eyes, the same fear he felt within himself. He wasn't entirely sure why, but he made his way over to her, and asked what was probably a dumb question, "Are you okay?"

She nodded. "I have faced dangerous situations before." Then he saw a shudder pass over her body. Her effort to hide her fear was admirable.

He smiled as encouragingly as he could, and said, "We'll find a way out of this." It was a bold-faced lie, he knew it. Elaria was trapped with them, as was Ventelis, and they would watch Edilas burn. It was a nightmare that was about to become a reality.

Then he noticed movement off to the side, past Elaria, in one of the abandoned buildings they passed by. He looked as closely as he could into the shadows of the building, and saw a head move forward just enough to catch some of the light from a lamp. It was Cardin!

At first he wanted to shout his friend's name in relief, but then he glanced around and realized that would be a huge mistake. So he looked again at Cardin, who saw that Reis saw him.

It was a bad situation, Reis realized that. If Cardin attacked now, he wouldn't be able to use the full force of his powers, and would be overwhelmed by undead. Sira had ordered him away at the beach, and Reis knew it was for good reason.

So when Cardin made to pull the Sword off of his back, Reis shook his head ever so slightly, hoping no one else saw his movement.

Cardin could still save them, but he couldn't do so if he was dead or captured. It seemed as if, for the time being, there really was nothing they could do except go along for the ride, and hope that they could get out and help fight the undead once they made landfall on Edilas.

They finally reached the docks at the river, and began to ascend a gangway up onto one of the ships. They were not square-rigged ships like the Sea Wisp, but were instead rigged with triangular sails that swiveled on their bases. He wasn't sure how that worked exactly, but he wasn't a sailor either.

As he stepped onto the deck of the ship, his stomach turned a little, not because the ship rocked, but at memories of being at sea. "Not again," he groaned.

Chapter 26

CONSUMED

Cardin had to force his jaw to unclench. Anger and frustration boiled within while he watched his friends and the rest of the company board the necromancer ships. Some of them were being shoved violently, and he wanted nothing more than to come out of hiding and free them.

Reis had warned him off, and despite his frustration, he knew his friend was right. It would be no different than when they were on the beach, he wouldn't be able to use his powers to their fullest extent. It would end either in his having to run or, worse, being captured and the Sword taken from him.

So he had to find some other way. Dalin, Reis, Sira, Elaria, Ventelis, Commander Devral, and Anila all boarded the same ship. That was when he realized that would be their greatest chance. If he could bring down the magical field that prevented the creation of portals, Dalin or one of the elves could get them free and clear of Trinil, and back to Edilas to warn the four kingdoms.

He turned to Baenil, who stood inside of the abandoned building behind him, and whispered, "Do you know what or who is preventing the creation of portals here?"

Baenil, nervous to be in the heart of the necromancer city while legions of undead marched by, glanced around furtively. "I think it has something to do with that head necromancer."

Cardin looked out the window up at the five thrones. "You mean that one?"

Baenil cautiously moved forward and looked at where Cardin pointed. The one that had sat in the center throne remained behind, and simply watched as hordes of undead marched towards the ships. The tail end of the horde passed by, but the necromancer still did not move.

"Yes, he commands them," Baenil nodded.

When Cardin and Baenil had approached the ancient city, he had felt great power, and a massive concentration of energy that felt just as cold and empty as the power he had felt from the undead on the beach. There were tens of thousands, perhaps hundreds of thousands of undead, and still dozens or hundreds of necromancers. Now for the first time he reached out his awareness towards one of those necromancers, to learn what he could from him.

The power felt warped, but Cardin wondered if that was only because he was unused to that particular kind of energy, a power he had never sensed prior to landing on the beaches of Trinil. It was unique, and formed an ice-cold pit in his chest, as if all warmth had been sucked out of him. It was an intense light, but a cold one none-the-less. If he had to assign a color to the necromancer's power, it would be a light, cold blue compared to his or Dalin's warm fire-orange. And it was intense, more intense than Dalin's light, stronger than he could have imagined.

He was, without doubt, the strongest of the necromancers, and just based on that power, Cardin feared he could not defeat him. However, if anyone could prevent the creation of portals, it had to be the leader. That meant that if Cardin wanted to save his friends and warn Edilas of the invasion, he had to face the necromancer alone.

Only a month ago he had rushed into the Fortress of Nasara completely alone to face a unique power within. Although that power was weak compared to what he sensed from the necromancer, he knew that he now faced a similar situation, only this time he wished his friends could fight alongside of him.

It was up to him.

The last of the undead began to board the ships. There were so many moored on either side of the river. The sails of the ships were tall, so they could never fit under a traditional bridge, but the city's few bridges crossed high up between tall buildings on either bank of the river, plus Cardin knew that there were tunnels that crossed beneath the river. The necromancer ships would depart soon enough, and nothing would stand in their way.

Impatiently he waited for the final boarding. The gangways were pulled up or cast off, the mooring lines set free, and the ships began to float gently down the river. The lamps and torches were plentiful both on the ships and on the river bank and he was able to see when they unfurled their sails, triangular shaped rather than square. The sails caught a breeze, pushing them downriver faster. It wouldn't be long before they were out of sight, and that was when he would attack. He looked up at the lead necromancer, and was surprised to see that he still sat alone, and simply watched from his throne as the ships departed.

Cardin turned to Baenil and asked, "Are you able to make portals under normal circumstances?"

Baenil looked at him in surprise, blinked, and then nodded. "Yes. All elves can."

"Good," he nodded. "Get away from the city as fast as you can, there's no telling what kind of damage I'll do fighting that necromancer." Cardin looked up at the tall buildings and knew he could easily bring any one of the ancient structures down without meaning to. He still needed to learn better control and focus. "It won't be safe here. As soon as you can create a portal, go to Archanon. Do you know where that is?"

"Of course," Baenil nodded. "It was where I began my search when I came to Halarite."

"Tell any guards you encounter that you are Baenil and that the Keeper of the Sword sent you, tell them you need to speak to the King. Tell the King what has happened here and what is coming. He must be warned and he must warn the other kingdoms."

Baenil looked absolutely terrified, and Cardin realized that the relatively young elf had probably never been in a life or death situation before coming to Halarite, let alone one of such magnitude. It was a heavy burden to place on the elf's shoulders, but if Dalin and the others couldn't escape, Cardin knew Edilas had to be warned somehow. Cardin still didn't know how to create portals, so it was up to his friends or Baenil.

He placed a reassuring hand on the elf's shoulders and squeezed. "I know you can do this, Baenil. You've survived against all odds, so you can do this."

Baenil took in a big breath, gulped it down, and then nodded. "Very well. I will do so." He looked with intent eyes at Cardin and added, "May your sword swing true, Cardin Kataar."

With that, Cardin released the elf's shoulder, and the elf disappeared into the shadows to sneak out of the city. Cardin looked down river and saw the last ship disappear into the dark. The necromancer would have no reinforcements. It would be between him and Cardin.

Maybe that was best. With Cardin's unfocused, increasingly powerful magic, perhaps having others around him would only hinder him. Memories of the Battle of Archanon flashed through his mind, of the final duel with Kailar, and the destruction they had wrought to the surrounding city. He would have to use his full strength to fight the necromancer.

When he turned back towards the throne, his heart stopped for a moment. The necromancer still sat in his throne, but now he looked directly at Cardin. He knew Cardin was there. He had probably known all along.

There was nothing else left to do. Cardin stepped out of the shadows and walked towards the central building. As he began to ascend the stairs, Cardin drew the Sword and pointed it towards the necromancer.

When he reached the top of the stairs, the necromancer stood up and reached out his hand. From somewhere in the building, a rod flew out, called by its master's will, and planted itself firmly in the necromancer's hand. The rod looked as if it were made out of metal, but it had been painted a near-black color, or that was the natural color of the metal. It had a focusing gem at the top of it, much like a Wizard's staff, but the rod was less than two feet long.

It was something Cardin had never seen before, but he could feel the power that emanated from the weapon, and he knew it would enhance the necromancer's already considerable power. The battle would be even more difficult than Cardin had anticipated.

"I have felt your presence for days," the necromancer spoke. "You are the most unique power I have ever felt."

Cardin took several steps towards the necromancer before he

stopped. He knew he would have to fight the old man eventually, but he also knew not to judge a person's combat capabilities based on apparent age, and he decided he wanted to learn more.

"Who are you," he asked the necromancer plainly.

The old man smiled wickedly, the canyons in his face accented by the torchlight. "My name is Tiresis."

"You spoke of dragons before," Cardin said, having overheard the entire conversation. "It was a battle between Star Dragons and Dark Dragons that destroyed your world, wasn't it?"

It was a bit of insight Cardin hadn't made until just that moment. The Necromancer stared blankly at Cardin for a moment, and then looked specifically at the Sword. "Yes it was," he said quietly. Did he somehow know what the Sword was? "I was the last to leave my world, I held the last portal that brought my people here. The powers of the dragons tore Vestuul asunder, but it was not the final blow that destroyed our world. Moments before I stepped through the portal, I saw our sun explode. I do not know how I know, but that is what truly destroyed our world."

Cardin thought about that for a long moment. One of the things he had learned from Dalin was that their sun, much like Halarite or the other planets around Halarite, was a sphere, but it was thousands of times larger than any planet. To destroy a planet sounded like an impossible task, let alone a sun! Suddenly he realized just how far he had to go before he learned everything there was to learn from the Sword of Dragons.

"We all despaired when we found ruins here, rather than our lost brothers and sisters," Tiresis continued. "However, as the survivors began to fall ill and perish, one of them spoke a prophecy with his final breaths. A prophecy that foretold of our return to our place of power and prestige, and that a new leader would rise up to guide us. That leader would only arrive as cataclysm came to this world." He looked intently at Cardin. "The dark one is coming." Cardin felt a new chill form in the pit of his stomach. "When he arrives, he will lead us to a new age of greatness."

Tiresis raised both of his hands up and looked skyward. "A shattered world shall return to its people," he shouted into the night. "Darkness and fire will descend!"

As he spoke those last words, an explosion ripped through the night, and the sky flared blindingly. A ball of fire streaked across the stars and passed directly over them. Cardin watched in terror as it drew lower. Only moments after it passed over the city, it slammed into the ground in a great flash, and a massive explosion reached into the sky. The ground shook beneath his feet, and he struggled to keep his balance.

Tiresis took advantage of that momentary loss of balance and attacked Cardin. The assault came as a blast of ice-cold energy, and Cardin managed to erect a shield that absorbed most of the energy, but it still threw him backwards. He landed hard on the stairs and tumbled down them end over end. The Sword threatened to be torn from his grip, but he held on with all of his strength.

He landed with a thud on his back just as another streak of fire, smaller than the first, burned overhead. He didn't know if it hit the ground or not, but his mind raced with possibilities of why or how the sky burned. Were they shooting stars, but closer than ever before? Or larger than shooting stars? Or were they some sort of magic that the necromancers called down to rain terror upon the world?

His moment of wonder was over, and he saw the necromancer perch at the top of the stairs, ready to race down and finish Cardin off. Cardin stood quickly, battling pain and breathlessness. He tried to prepare for the next attack, but never expected it to be an elemental. A shard of ice shot out from the necromancer's staff at lightning speed, and in a split second, Cardin raised a shield while he swung the Sword. The shield helped dissipate the energy of the ice, but it was the Sword that deflected it. Another shard shot out, and Cardin also had to use the Sword to deflect it.

Tiresis pushed the advantage, and began to descend the stairs while he continued to release shard after shard at Cardin. At their speeds, if just one got through, it would pierce Cardin's leather armor and impale him. Thankfully the Sword was light, and he had enhanced his strength and agility with magic, so he was able to deflect each one, but as long as Tiresis continued to shoot at him, he would be on the defensive.

At first Cardin backed away, fearful of the necromancer's power, but he realized he had to change strategy if he wanted to defeat the old man. So he stopped, and for a moment stood his ground, and then he began to push towards Tiresis. This tactic surprised the old man, and he hesitated near the bottom of the steps.

That moment of indecision and hesitancy was what Cardin needed. He gathered a miniscule charge of energy in the Sword, as much as he could in the brief moment he had, and he swung the Sword to release it.

It wasn't powerful, and the necromancer easily deflected it with a shield, but Cardin took advantage of it, and gathered even more power into the Sword. The next attack he threw at Tiresis was not much more powerful than the first, but that was only so Cardin could keep some of the power stored within the Sword. He repeated this exercise several times, building a greater and greater surplus within the Sword. The rapid pace in which he shot at the necromancer meant Tiresis could do nothing but defend, just as Cardin had done moments ago.

When he felt like there was sufficient power built up, Cardin drew the Sword back and then jabbed it towards Tiresis and released every bit of energy locked up within it. There was more stored energy than he realized, and as the blast leapt from the tip, it caused a shockwave that tore up the stone stairs. It slammed into the necromancer's magic shield, and threw him back up the stairs.

Cardin didn't hesitate or wait, he climbed up the ruined section of stairs as best as he could, and found that the necromancer had flown as far back as his throne. As Tiresis tried to pull himself to his feet, Cardin once again gathered a large charge, and then swung the Sword to release a wave of deadly energy.

Just as had happened in the Battle of Archanon, the wave was powerful enough to damage the surrounding structures. Tiresis blocked and partly deflected the blast, and it careened into three of the thrones and obliterated them, and even continued into the capitol building behind Tiresis. Several of the stone pillars began to break apart, and the building groaned under new strain. It visibly leaned towards them, but did not fall, yet.

In the heat of the battle, Cardin was scarcely aware that more streaks of fire continued to explode across the sky. The distant or sometimes close impacts blended with the sound of their battle, and the light of the burning streaks cast moving shadows upon their battlefield.

Cardin's moment of distraction when he glanced up allowed the necromancer to fire his own blast of energy, this time a bolt of lightning, but Cardin anticipated the attack, and partly sidestepped it.

The bolt bounced harmlessly off of his shield, but he felt the drain on his own energy and concentration. In practice Dalin had sent elemental attacks at Cardin, but none of them had been as ferocious as Tiresis's attacks.

Another bolt slammed directly into Cardin's shield, some of the charge broke through and danced upon Cardin's chest. He found himself flat on his back again, his chest smoldering, pain wracking his body. He did everything he could to keep his shield up, but another blast lanced out, and this time scorched his left arm. The pain was intense, the smell sickening, and the blast shoved him across the ground several yards. He lost feeling in some of his extremities, and his grip on the Sword waned.

He tried to use the Sword to block the next attack, but he had lost his speed and strength and failed to intercept it. The blast hit his side and sent him rolling several times over. He came to a stop at the top of the ruined stairs, and knew that one more attack would send him sprawling down them.

But the attack never came. He held on to the Sword with all of his strength, tried in vain to push away the pain and move, but for the moment he couldn't. Tiresis had already won. He had failed.

The necromancer slowly walked towards him, clearly shaken by the battle. "You are indeed a worthy opponent. But you are young, and your powers are unfocused." He stood less than a dozen feet from Cardin and pointed the end of the rod at Cardin, the green focusing gem glowing bright. The necromancer began to gather power to finish Cardin off.

"Your weapon has clearly given you power that is not natural to you," Tiresis continued. "So it shall become mine. I will raise you back from death," he grinned, "and just because of the pain you caused me today, I will make you kill those you love most."

A flood of energy coursed through Cardin's body, and he felt a new strength of power gather within him, a power beyond what he was able to summon previously. As a blast of deadly energy shot out from the necromancer's rod, Cardin pushed up to his knees, placed the Sword in front of him, and created a shield stronger than anything he had ever conjured before.

When the necromancer's blast slammed into his shield, Cardin saw something even more terrifying. What had started as an orange and blue glow behind the capitol building grew brighter, until a ball of flame larger than the building itself was a visible halo all around it.

He felt his eyes grow wide, and without even knowing how he did it, he increased the strength of his shield and formed it all around him. In a flash, the fire smashed into the capitol building and obliterated it. Heat exploded all around them as the fire consumed everything, and Tiresis screamed for only a second in pain and misery, until he was silenced, his body consumed. Shards of the building, some larger than Cardin, slammed into his shield, but he held on.

The heat began to push through his shield, and he felt his strength and willpower wane. The fire did not end, the heat did not dissipate, and he knew that his shield would fail at any moment and he would be consumed by the fire as Tiresis had, or pulverized by stone shards.

An image of Sira appeared in his mind's eye, and he felt his heart ache. He would never see her again.

When he came to the end of his strength, for the briefest of moments he felt something else surge in him, a power that felt strange and familiar at the same time.

His last thought before he blacked out was of home...

Chapter 27

RETURN TO EDILAS

Although the ships were now deep within the jungle, the river was wide enough that Dalin and the others had a clear view of the night sky. Normally he would find comfort in such a view, but tonight, streaks of fire arched across the sky, several of which hit the ground not far from their position.

He knew what the streaks of fire actually were, pieces of rock or other debris that slammed into Halarite, called meteorites. He also knew they would destroy anything and everything at their points of impact, and he was afraid one would destroy their ship. To his surprise, the necromancers and undead seemed completely unfazed by the meteorites.

Dalin's group was on the third ship back from the front of the two ship-wide column, and he saw something unexpected ahead, and felt a power he did not expect to feel. There was a large stone half-circle that crossed over the river, perfect in shape and tall enough for the ships to pass through, with several lit lamps or torches all along its outer edge. It felt like the power of a portal, and although he could still feel the magic that blocked his ability to create a portal, two necromancers, one on either side of the river, focused their powers on the half-circle, and he felt the beginnings of a massive portal.

A few moments later, there was a flash in the center of the half-circle, and a wall of blue-white light appeared. It covered the entire mouth of the river, although he suspected it allowed water to pass through the portal's mouth without actually travelling to wherever the portal led to.

"That is how the invasion can begin today," Elaria said quietly.

Sira stepped up next to Dalin and asked, "Is that a portal?"

"Yes," he nodded solemnly. "We will be somewhere off of the coast of Edilas within minutes."

A massive explosion behind them caught everyone's attention, and they looked back towards the ancient city. A great ball of fire expanded out and rose into the sky.

"Cardin!" Reis shouted.

Everyone looked at Reis in surprise, and Sira asked, "What?"

"I saw him in the city as we boarded the ships," he looked at Sira in a near-panic. "He made to rescue us but I shook my head."

Dalin felt as if a knife had hollowed out his stomach. The flames began to darken, and left behind only a dimming column of smoke. If Cardin was in the city when the meteorite hit...

Then he realized something else. As if a veil had been lifted from his eyes, part of his power previously occluded became available to him again.

He looked at Elaria as she looked at him. They both understood what had just happened. Whatever power had blocked portals was gone. At first he had suspected the head necromancer was responsible, but as they boarded the ship, it had finally clicked in his head – the field had to be generated by an enchanted object, that was the only way it could encompass the entire continent.

More than likely, it was within the ancient capitol building. Or perhaps actually *was* the capitol building.

Without his staff, he was unable to focus his abilities as well as he otherwise could have. He was still a relatively young Wizard, and he feared he would not be able to create a stable portal on the moving ship. He could create a stationary portal towards the bow of the ship, and they could pass through it as the ship moved, but that would be difficult at the speed they travelled.

So it was up to the elves. "Elaria," he looked intently at her. "Maradin."

She stared at him for a moment, and then nodded. Dalin looked around at everyone else, who gave him puzzled faces. The necromancers were conversing with one another, and suddenly no one was guarding them. They were worried about their leader, and so now was the moment for them to act.

Dalin looked at Sira, and then the others, and only as loud as he dared say it, he said, "Prepare yourselves."

Sira and the others began to quietly pass the word to their companions, including the couple of marines who had been able to join them aboard the ship. Dalin felt guilty that they wouldn't be able to rescue the marines on the other ships, but no matter what, Edilas had to be warned of the invasion that was minutes away.

Suddenly another meteor streaked across the sky, low and close to the ground. It crossed above them, and he felt a wave of pressure and heat from it. Moments later, it drilled into the jungle not far off to starboard, and sent a shockwave that rocked their ships. The explosion was violent, and probably leveled a mile of trees.

That was closer than Dalin would have liked, and even the necromancers looked frightened now. They congregated at the starboard side of the ship to watch the explosion rise into the air. The jungle was set ablaze.

Now was the perfect moment. He nodded to Elaria, and she quickly and efficiently gathered power around her. Within seconds, at the center of the ship, a blue-white portal had formed, with the main-mast of the ship behind it.

Sira shouted, "Now!"

Every Mage used their power, unfocused without weapons, to shove away undead, and then streamed through the portal. Anila and Reis were the first two since they had no powers or weapons.

Dalin gathered his own power, and released a blast of fire from his hands towards the starboard side of the ship. The necromancers were completely taken off guard, and the flames engulfed them. They screamed in pain and began to jump over the side of the ship into the river.

Sira and Ventelis were the next to pass through the portal, and Dalin and Elaria moved closer to it. Elaria would have to go last, but Dalin would remain with her as long as possible to protect her.

Several undead managed to recover from the surprise attack, and set upon Commander Devral. She struggled with them, and she along with two undead fell through the portal. Dalin hoped there were city guards or Warriors close at hand in Maradin to help dispatch those undead, along with the other three that followed them through moments later. He blasted several more undead with fire before they could follow, but his unfocused power didn't just light them up, it lit up the deck of the ship.

The last of the marines passed through the portal, but the fire quickly spread towards it. Dalin switched to ice magic and pelted the undead with shards of ice, but they were small and slow moving shards, and just barely kept the horde of undead back. Without even thinking about it, he grabbed Elaria and dragged her through the portal with him.

Within moments they were on the other side. One of the undead had tried to follow them through, but the moment Elaria finished passing through, the portal closed, and it cut the undead soldier in half. It fell to the main street of Maradin.

Elaria had created her portal inside of the city walls near the main gates, which was smart since there were city guards at the gates. Sira, the marines, and Reis tried to keep the attention of the five undead that had come through. He saw Commander Devral lying on the ground with a grave-looking stomach wound, but she still lived.

Several city soldiers were already rushing over, but Dalin grimaced when he saw one undead managed to cut Reis's right arm. He cried out in pain, but then rushed the enemy soldier and tackled it to the ground. They wrestled for the undead's sword, but it was stronger, and managed to shove Reis into a storefront.

The soldiers' swords were drawn, and they immediately engaged the undead. One stabbed an enemy soldier, but it simply pushed the city soldier away and then impaled him with its own sword.

"Take their heads off, it's the only way," Sira called out.

Dalin gathered as much power as he could, and fired a blast of arcane energy at one of the undead, but only managed to momentarily stun his target. One of the city soldiers took advantage and took the undead's head off.

Elaria somehow pulled yet another dagger from underneath her cloak, and he wondered at how she had concealed it before now. She attacked one of the undead, but failed to behead it. However her distraction proved enough for another city soldier to take her opponent's head off.

The other three were dispatched relatively quickly, and the only casualty had been that first city soldier. Devral still lived, though she would probably need a nurse to tend to her wounds quickly, and Reis held his arm to try to staunch the flow of blood.

As Dalin expected, meteors also streaked across the sky above Maradin. He looked east out to sea and saw a meteorite slam into the ocean far, far away. However, what really caught his attention was the sight of a massive portal less than a mile offshore.

"The necromancers are coming here," he shouted.

No sooner had he said that than did the first pair of necromancer ships come through the portal. They split their courses and spread out as another pair of ships appeared behind them. The first pair were already in position, and the necromancers aboard released blasts of powerful magic into the city, wreaking havoc on the ships docked there and the buildings on the waterfront. He noted with some satisfaction that the ship they had been aboard emerged completely ablaze. That was one less enemy ship for them to deal with.

"We need to see the Queen immediately," Sira shouted to one of the soldiers. "Those are the first ships of an invasion force!"

The soldiers all looked in fear at the giant portal and the meteors that streaked across the sky. Then one of them came to her senses and said, "Come with me!"

Two of the soldiers helped Commander Devral up, and as a group, they rushed for the city palace as fast as they could. A meteorite crashed right into the northern wall behind them, obliterating that section of the wall and several buildings. Dalin looked back and felt his heart go out to those who had just perished in the fire.

The soldiers were obviously terrified, but Sira had provided them with much needed leadership, and they moved with a purpose. When they reached the gates to the palace, Dalin was pleasantly surprised to find the Queen, General Zilan, Teira, and several more Wizards had just left the palace grounds.

"Sira," the Queen shouted in surprise. Teira saw Dalin and rushed towards him. For a few seconds, their past was forgotten, and he embraced her in a strong hug.

"Queen Leian, those ships are part of an invasion force intent on conquering Edilas," Sira spoke quickly. As Teira and Dalin parted, their past came rushing back. His face felt warm and he intentionally stepped further away from her. She seemed disheartened by that act, but then gave her full attention to the ships and portal as Sira continued to talk. "The force is led by necromancers, the ships crewed with undead soldiers."

"Necromancers?!" Leian said, unbelieving. "Necromancy is a legend, a myth!"

As more ships joined in the attack on the port city, the kingdom's ships that were docked were obliterated, and the docks completely ruined. Fires had started in the city and they rapidly crawled up the hill.

Dalin recognized all of the Wizards present, but couldn't recall all of their names at the moment. They seemed ready to defend the city, and he wondered why so many were there. Clearly something had changed in his absence. He looked at Teira with curiosity and wonder. Had his words to her prior to departing Maradin affected her more than he realized? What had she done to change Master Valkere's mind?

Suddenly a bright flash in the sky caught their attention, and a particularly large meteor streaked from the southeast across the sky. They watched as it drew lower to the horizon, and then far, far in the distance, beyond the horizon, slammed into the ocean.

For the meteor to have appeared that large so far away, Dalin could only guess that it was massive, and the force of it hitting the water had to be enormous. A sense of fear gripped him. Could it generate a giant wave?

"Dalin," Teira spoke in a panic, "we need to get the Queen out of here." More ships had come through the portal, and he counted at least two dozen, with more still streaming through. They were moving fast towards the shores, and before long the undead would disembark to attack the city. He remembered how many had climbed up the shore of Port Hope, and suspected several were already in the water and would rise up from the ocean ahead of the ships.

Although it was still night time, both moons were out and cast their light upon the water. From up the hill, he could see exactly what he feared. A massive wave was already racing towards the shore.

"I do not have my staff," he said and looked at Teira.

Without hesitating, she turned on her heels and pointed her staff away from them. Moments later, a portal formed. He didn't know where it led to, but he hoped that she was smart enough to get them far away from the shore.

"Your majesty," Sira shouted and pointed at the portal. "We have to go now!"

"I won't abandon my city, my kingdom," Queen Leian looked helplessly at the invading ships. She clearly didn't see the incoming wave. Not until the necromancers' portal was consumed by it. "By the gods..."

The wave was moving fast and moments after it covered the portal, it overcame the seawall and crashed into the docks. All buildings in the lower city were covered instantly, dousing the fires but destroying almost everything.

Sira grabbed Queen Leian and dragged her through the portal. Everyone else nearby followed. Dalin stayed next to Teira and watched. The wave hadn't been tall enough to immediately reach the tip of the hill they stood upon, but the waters were rushing up towards them rapidly, and they had moments. The Queen, the General, all of Dalin's friends were through, but more soldiers and Warriors were running towards them to take the portal to safety.

He looked at Teira, and she looked at him. He nodded to her, and she back at him. Both knew that there was no time.

Dalin was only a step ahead of her, and together, they passed through the portal just seconds before the wave consumed the remainder of the city.

Chapter 28

ESCAPE INTO THE CATACOMBS

Baenil had heard stories of fire falling from the sky, sometimes brought down by some of the most powerful practitioners of magic, while at other times it was a natural, if uncommon phenomenon. Never before had he experienced it, and as the skies filled with fire, terror and panic set in.

At first he felt trapped, unable to escape, unable to do anything, but after a few moments of fright, resolve set in. He had been given a mission, and he intended to fulfill it. He had made it outside of the ancient ruins, and ran further away as fast as he could, unsure just how massive the battle between Cardin and the necromancer would become.

Once in the jungle, he could no longer see the sky clearly, but he could still hear the fire raining down, and the sound of explosions in the distance. It did little to assuage his fear, but he knew he had to survive long enough.

Suddenly he heard a jarring boom from behind, and when he turned to look back towards the city, he was knocked over by a powerful shockwave that flung him several feet. With a bone-shaking thud, he landed and tumbled several feet along the jungle floor.

His ears rang, his vision blurred, and for a moment he lost all sense of which way was up. As things began to clear, he noticed that a bright orange light lit up the jungle. He used a vine to pull himself up, and then steadied himself against a tree. He wasn't sure which way was north, so it took him a while to get his bearings. When he finally did, he looked back towards the city, and saw a wall of fire raging towards him.

The jungle burned, the city burned! It was completely destroyed by one of the falling stars, and the jungle was quickly being consumed by the fire.

Then he realized a sensation returned to him that he had not felt for some time. As the fire raced towards him, he knew he had only moments, so he turned on the spot, and gathered the power within him as quickly as he could. He wasn't the most skilled in the arts of magic, his strength lay in research and archeology, so it took him several tense seconds. Finally, the power he needed was ready, and he focused it into the creation of a portal, his mind's eye seeing his destination, just outside the main gate of Archanon.

A burning tree several yards away came crashing down behind him. He yelped and jumped through the portal to the safety of Tal Kingdom.

Or he had hoped it would be safe. Much to his dismay, he instead found chaos.

Fire rained from the skies above Tal, and at that very moment a streak of fire burned across the sky from east to west. He knew it was past midnight in Archanon, but the city gates were opened just enough for people to rush inside to safety. It was not uncommon for people to camp outside of the gates if they didn't reach them before they closed for the night, but the city guards, seeing the destruction outside, let those late-comers in.

Knowing that they would close the gates at any moment, he ran the dozen and a half yards just as the last of the humans entered before him. A guard stepped out and placed a firm hand on his chest, stopping him from entering. "Who are you?" He noticed Baenil's ears and eyes, and frowned. "An elf, but not Ventelis…"

The fact that the human recognized Baenil as an elf gave him hope, because he knew there was no time to argue. "I am Baenil, friend to the Keeper of the Sword."

"Cardin?" The man looked with worried but hopeful eyes. Baenil suddenly had the sinking sensation that this was someone who cared a great deal about Cardin, and it just now dawned on him that he had witnessed Cardin's death only moments before.

"Yes, Cardin Kataar," he nodded. He decided in that moment not to say what he had just witnessed, there was no time. "I have a message from him for King Beredis."

Without another word or thought, the guard grabbed Baenil by his shoulder and pulled him inside. Moments later, the doors closed all the way. "Raise the city shields, now!"

Baenil looked up the wall and saw a blue-white shimmering appear above the top of the battlements. He looked across the city, and saw that a small part of it already burned and must have taken a hit from the raining fire. A small ball of fire streaked out from the sky, and looked as if it were about to hit the city again, but instead it hit an invisible wall that extended above the existing city wall and exploded harmlessly against it.

"Good," the other man sighed in relief. "I wasn't sure the barrier would hold against that."

Finally it snapped in Baenil's memory that he had read how the outer wall was enchanted three thousand years ago to help protect the city against catapults. Today it protected against something much deadlier, but he knew the barrier only reached so high. Some of the falling fire could easily come straight down and still damage the city.

The guard that had let him in turned to Baenil and said, "My name is Draegus Kataar, father to Cardin." Baenil's stomach sank even further. "I know who you are, and I'm glad Cardin and the others were able to rescue you. Come with me, the king was to be evacuated underground for safety."

Once again, Draegus grabbed his shoulder and pulled him along. He shouted orders to city soldiers to get to where the fire was and to help put it out. Several of the city's citizens were outside their doors and stared up at the sky in horror. "Get back inside, it's not safe out here," Draegus shouted at them. Some listened, some ignored him, some were too frightened to even acknowledge he had said anything.

The city's streets were well lit by magically enchanted torches, so their path along the wall and, shortly after, the steep mountain cliff that served as part of the city's borders, was easy and fast. Moments later, they came to the courtyard that led into the Catacombs, where he had been captured so many years ago. To their right, from another entrance into the courtyard, a large group of people entered and rushed towards the mountain wall, where he noticed two of the Covenant's guards still stood, clearly nervous about the ongoing apocalypse around them.

Draegus took Baenil to the two guards, where they waited anxiously for the other group of people. "Your Majesty, please hurry," Draegus pleaded after they saw two more impacts against the city wall. He realized that one of the men that ran towards them must be the King, and as he recalled some of the paintings he'd seen during his first days in Archanon, he knew it was the older dark skinned man, who obviously had been woken up by the emergency and wore only a simple tunic and trousers. Beside him ran a man Baenil knew to be the King's son, Idrill Beredis. Among them were several people he did not recognize, but from two of them he felt an intense power that he'd felt from no other human on Halarite, not even Cardin Kataar.

The group reached them, but when the King saw Baenil, he asked, "Who are you?"

He didn't have time to answer, there was no telling where the next ball of fire would hit, so Draegus insisted, "Your Majesty, please, we must hurry!"

Baenil noticed that the Prince eyed him with extreme suspicion, and Baenil looked at him with a flare of anger. He remembered that the Prince knew of his capture and had interviewed him several times just prior to being taken to Trinil.

The King and the Prince then rushed through the entrance to the catacombs, followed quickly by the rest of their group. Draegus and Baenil were last, as Draegus insisted the guards go in ahead of them for their protection. When they were about to enter, Baenil looked up, and saw what looked like a column of fire coming down directly on top of them.

"Move it," he shouted, shoving Draegus through the entrance. He followed moments later, but the group hadn't kept moving, so they couldn't get any further in. "Further back, now!"

Suddenly there was an explosion outside of the entrance, and the ground shook beneath them with such force that Baenil was knocked into the wall and hit his head hard enough that he saw stars. He went down to his knees, but Draegus wouldn't leave him, and as the roof around the entrance began to cave in, Draegus pulled Baenil along.

The world spun as he did so, and he wanted to stop and let his head stop swimming, but Draegus wouldn't let him.

There was a force of heat from the initial impact, but the fire didn't have a chance to scorch inward as the entrance finally collapsed completely. The shockwave from the impact had blown out many of the torches nearest the entrance, but further along the corridor, Baenil saw the blurry, spinning image of still-burning torches.

Finally the ground stopped rumbling, and the ceiling stopped caving in. Draegus stopped dragging him along, and he fell back to the ground. The world continued to spin, but as time went on, it began to slow, and the sick feeling in his stomach began to fade. Once the world settled, he stayed where he was for a moment, afraid that if he moved, the world would start spinning again.

Someone knelt beside him, and he realized it was the King. "Are you alright," Beredis asked, his voice strong and soothing.

Baenil thought for a moment, and then said, "I will be. I haven't hit my head like that in a long time. The feeling will pass."

"You are Baenil, are you not?"

He turned his head enough to look up at the King, and the world threatened to spin again. "Yes," he said. "I have a message from The Keeper of the Sword."

The King exchanged glances with some of the others in the corridor, and another man who wore white robes with gold trim and embroidery knelt down. He held a staff, and an incredible power resonated from that man. "Please, tell us," that man said.

"There are necromancers who live on the continent you call Trinil," he spoke slowly. "They have an army of tens of thousands of undead, and they intend to invade your kingdoms, to conquer them and make you all their slaves."

The powerful man and Beredis exchanged worried glances, and Beredis asked, "When do they plan to invade?"

He looked at the King with pained eyes. "The necromancers claim they will invade today. I do not know how they intend to cover the distance between Trinil and Edilas in less than a day, but the necromancers are powerful. Very powerful."

Beredis shook his head doubtfully. "I thought necromancy was a myth."

"It is not," the powerful man spoke. Was he a Wizard? "I have heard of such power in my travels beyond Halarite."

The King looked intently at Baenil. "Where is Cardin? Where are Sira and the others?"

Once again, he felt a sinking sensation in his stomach. Slowly he began to sit up, and the King and the Wizard both helped steady him as he did so. He debated what he should and shouldn't say, but then he realized that despite everything that was happening, they all deserved to know the truth.

"The others who came to find me were captured by the necromancers. The last I saw of them, they were taken aboard the necromancers' ships, to be their slaves. Cardin had escaped before they were captured, and he found me in the jungle. He told me he had been ordered to run, that he couldn't be captured because of the weapon he possessed."

The Wizard sighed in relief. "I am glad to hear that he was not captured."

Baenil shook his head slowly. "I am afraid there is more to tell. Cardin asked me to show him into the necromancer city. The enemy soldiers left while we were there, every necromancer and every undead boarded the ships, and the ships departed down river. One necromancer, the leader and the most powerful of them all, stayed behind. We suspected that the leader was the one who prevented the creation of portals in and around Trinil."

"Most likely not the case," the Wizard said. "After further research on the subject, we concluded it would have to have been an enchanted object generating the magic needed to block portals, no living being could hold such a spell continually for weeks or months."

The void in the pit of his stomach grew. "So that is why I was able to create a portal. Cardin sent me away, so that I could come warn you about the invasion. He stayed to fight the necromancer. As I ran, a falling star came down upon the city." He looked to his left, searched the crowd of people in the narrow confines, and found Draegus. "The city was destroyed, with Cardin and the necromancer still in it."

A look of shock crossed Dreagus's face, and his arms dropped limply to his sides. "What are you saying?"

Baenil's throat felt dry, and he spoke quietly, "I am afraid that Cardin most probably perished."

Draegus narrowed his eyes at first, and then closed them. He furrowed his brow in concentration, and then shook his head, "No."

Baenil started to stand up, but had to be helped by the Wizard and the King. "No one could have survived that," he said.

"I would have known it if he died," Draegus opened his eyes and glared at Baenil. "I knew when his mother died even though I was on the other side of Tal when it happened. I would know if he died. Until I see proof that he is gone, I will not accept that."

Baenil didn't know what to say to that, and knew all too well that people could become connected through magic in such a way that they could, indeed, feel when the other was in pain or suffered, or worse, when they died.

"But if he did not die, how did he escape," Baenil asked.

"I don't know," Draegus shook his head. "But I am sure he is alive."

"I hope so," the Wizard spoke. "If he perished, the Sword is once again in danger."

"Trust a father's instincts," Beredis said. "Cardin is alive." He looked at Baenil, and then he looked at the caved-in entrance. "Well, now we're trapped and can do nothing to prepare for the invasion, let alone repair whatever damage has been incurred."

"I fear the storm is not yet over," the Wizard spoke. "There is more to come, and with an invasion of undead and necromancers, Halarite stands upon the brink."

Beredis nodded once, and sighed. "We cannot sit idly by and hope that someone will dig us out soon enough." He looked at Baenil again. "You spent some time in these catacombs?"

"Yes, Your Majesty," he nodded, and was pleased when his head didn't spin.

"Do you know of any other way out of here?"

Baenil looked down the corridor, past Draegus, past the glaring eyes of the Prince, and searched his memory for any clues he had seen regarding another exit. "Not that I found before, but it is unlikely that there is only one entrance, especially for such a vast network of tunnels."

The King looked at him curiously. "Vast network? Is there a chance the catacombs reach outside of the city walls?"

The Wizard looked at the King with realization. "If we can get outside of the walls, I can create a portal to get us out of here."

"The tunnels twist and turn, and it almost seemed as if the city was intentionally built on top of them over the centuries," Baenil said, "However, I have no doubt that we can find somewhere that is outside of the barrier."

"Then please," Beredis motioned further into the catacombs, "Lead the way."

"Father!" Idrill Beredis protested, his voice as young and whiny as Baenil remembered. "We cannot trust this elf."

Baenil realized that the Prince had probably never told his father about his involvement with the Covenant and Baenil's capture, and a part of him felt the urge to tell the King now. However, he realized that now was not the time to fuel family infighting. Too much was at stake.

"We shall trust him because Cardin Kataar trusted him," the King admonished. "He trusted him to deliver information of vital importance to us, and Baenil did so at great peril. We have no reason not to trust him."

The Prince looked as if he wanted to say more, but the glare on the King's face was enough to shut him up. Baenil took pleasure in that fact. "Of course. My apologies, Father."

Baenil still felt a little unsteady on his feet, but he managed to make his way forward. The Prince stood in his way for a moment, but the King shouted his name in warning, after which he let Baenil pass.

It was going to be a very long night.

Chapter 29

EVACUATION

It had taken Kailar and Letan several hours at a near run to get to Corlas from where the Navitas had left them. The crystal beings were at least kind enough to use the same trick they'd used before to move the ground and get them to the edge of the Crystalline Forest, but from there they had to run.

She had managed to eat some of her rations while they ran, but she was exhausted. They didn't have time to rest.

By the time they reached Corlas, the sun had set, and fire began to streak across the sky regularly. In the distance to the southwest, one of the fireballs smashed into the ground and exploded in a bright flash.

As they reached the eastern side of the town, it was in chaos. People ran through the streets in a panic, and many prayed to the Six, but so far none of the falling stars hit the city. She knew that would probably change soon enough.

Worse yet, the warning the Navitas had given them echoed in her thoughts. The Crystalline Peaks would inevitably take a hit, and that meant Corlas and all of its people were in danger.

"We have to get to the Guild Complex," Letan stated. He grabbed her hand and pulled her along through the streets. "Get out of the city, now," he shouted as they went. "Get as far away from the Peaks as you can! You're all in danger!" Most didn't seem to even hear him, as if the burning skies had destroyed their ability to even comprehend the world around them.

The complex was near the center of town, which was unusual compared to the cities of Edilas. In the four kingdoms, because of the frequent Lesser Wars, the Warriors' Guild complexes were all built on the edge of cities nearest where they were most likely to be attacked. Since such a war had never occurred in the colonies, that was not the case in Devor cities.

They rushed through the open portcullis into the small fortress, and were immediately greeted by some of Corlas's Warriors.

"Letan," one of them spoke in surprise, then looked at Kailar. "Is that her?"

"Don't worry about her," Letan ordered. "Where is Gerris?"

"Arrest that woman," another voice called. They looked over to see a man in full armor marching towards them with two non-Mage Warriors flanking. She guessed from the armor that the man was the Guild's Commander, Gerris, and based on the two-handed sword he carried, he was a Mage.

"Stop," Letan physically stopped one of the other Warriors from taking hold of her. She panicked and was tempted to draw her dagger, but a moment later realized that would only make matters worse.

"Do not question my orders, Lieutenant," Gerris scolded. Kailar looked at Letan in shock. He hadn't told her that he was one of the Guild's lieutenants! "Tanneth has told me who she is, and she is lucky we do not strike her down immediately."

"With all due respect, sir, this is not the time to worry about Kailar," Letan stated. He pointed up to the sky, "We have much bigger problems."

"We were warned," she said, "that if one of those hits the Crystalline Peaks, they'll release a deadly energy. Everyone nearby may be killed."

Gerris scoffed and looked at her in doubt. "Really? Do tell, why should I believe you?"

"You don't have to believe or trust her," Letan stepped closer to the Commander. "You just have to trust me."

That statement made Gerris pause, and he looked east towards the peaks. "Why would they pose a danger to us here? How did you learn about this?"

"How we learned about it isn't important at the moment." Letan's words were accentuated by one of the meteorites hitting somewhere in the town, the first to do so. Everyone turned and saw the flash of light and felt the heat from the impact.

Letan looked at Gerris and placed a firm hand on his shoulder. "Please, my friend. We're all in danger. We have to get as far away from the Crystalline Peaks as we can."

Gerris watched in horror as light from the fire that the meteorite had started grew brighter, and even from within the complex, they heard the mass screams of terror from the citizens.

Kailar knew she should have probably left it up to Letan to convince Gerris, but those screams incensed her. "These people need leadership to guide them, to save them." She looked to the Commander with pleading eyes. "They need you to lead them to safety."

Uncertainty played across Gerris's face, but Letan stepped between him and Kailar and forced him to look into his eyes. "She's right, and you know it. The Governor has no power, no leadership qualities, he never has. It's up to you to save the people."

"But the town itself…"

"Corlas is lost!" Letan waved towards where the meteorite had landed. "But the people still live! We have to get them out of here, now!"

That statement seemed to snap Gerris out of his uncertainty, and he nodded. A crowd of Warriors had gathered around them, and anxiously awaited their Commander's orders. So he gave them.

"Sound the evacuation," he ordered. "Every house, every store, everywhere must be evacuated and the people sent away from the Crystalline Peaks. They are to take nothing with them! You five," he pointed to a group of Warriors, "Gather provisions from the Guild stores, we'll provide them to the citizens after we make our escape. Load up all of our carts, but the Warriors will be the last ones out, so make sure there are enough horses to take us," he looked at Kailar, "*all* of us away from here as fast as possible."

"Yes sir," one of the five replied.

"Now move it!"

Kailar realized what had just happened – she had just been

recruited to help the Warriors evacuate Corlas. At first she didn't want to, she wanted to get away from the Peaks now, not later. However, when she looked into Letan's eyes and saw his determination, she knew there was nothing else she wanted to do but help.

He started to move away from her, but she grabbed his hand and looked him in the eyes again. "I'll help, but I'm not leaving your side. We're not going to be separated."

A broad smile crossed his face, and he said, "I hoped you would say that. Come on, we'll go back to the east end and start from there."

Together they ran back the way they came, and were somewhat encouraged that many of those they had told to evacuate were already moving out, but they had burdened themselves with personal belongings. "No, leave those," they told those that they passed by. "There's no time, they'll only weigh you down. The Guild will take care of you, just get out of town and as far away from the peaks as you can!"

Each family they came across, they said the same thing to. Many were hesitant to leave their personal belongings behind, and it was something that Kailar couldn't quite understand. She never had much in the way of personal belongings, at least not beyond what she could carry on her at all times. The cave in Daruun Forest had been somewhat of a home to her, but the only things she kept there were items she thought were essential to her mission.

Never the less, she understood that Corlas was their home, and they were being told to leave it, and everything they had, behind. She could only imagine the terror they felt, the sense that nothing made sense, the truth that everything around them was changing in the blink of an eye.

She knew it was only the beginning. If the Navitas were right, something worse than burning skies was coming. Darkness would fall.

They reached the east end of the town and began going house to house. They split up to take two houses at the same time, and then would meet back up, and go on to the next pair of homes. Only half of the ones she burst into still had residents within them, and they didn't seem particularly inclined to believe her when she ordered them to evacuate. She had to use Gerris and Letan's names to convince them that she represented the Warriors.

Many of the families had horses, but almost none of them had enough horses to carry their entire family away, so they merely led them away. She allowed a few small trinkets to be carried, but one family in particular insisted that they take two large chests with them, and they would simply load up a wagon and have the horse carry it. She told them there was no time, but they wouldn't listen.

Finally Letan came to find out why she hadn't evacuated the house yet, and when he found what they were doing, he used magic to destroy the chests. He said he would do the same to their wagon if they didn't leave now.

They were understandably angry, and perhaps it would have been best to let the families carry their things out, even if it cost them their lives. Perhaps it should have been their choice. However, Letan's sense of duty was strong, and his desire to save as many people as he could was stronger still.

The family left, and Kailar and Letan watched long enough to make sure they didn't double back, before they continued on. Eventually they reached a point where the other Warriors had already evacuated citizens, and there was nothing left for them to do but evacuate themselves.

They made their way back to the Guild complex, and found that all of the Warriors had already left. Two horses remained, so they ran towards them at full speed as another meteorite hit nearby. They reached the horses, who were understandably spooked and strained against their tethers. Knowing that it would be too difficult to try to untie their tethers as they strained, they simply cut them free and leapt up on their backs.

Suddenly a particularly large meteor sailed overhead, and they both watched it in awe. It headed straight for the Crystalline Peaks. Once it hit, she suspected they would be dead. They were too late.

It shattered into the tallest crystal on the eastern edge, and crashed through further into the peaks. There was a bright green flash of light, and the flash expanded. She thought the flash would consume the entire city, with them in it, but then it receded.

They were alive! However, she then realized that it wasn't instant death that came for them, it was something worse. The damaged peaks began to spark bolts of sickly-green lightning, and the glow began to edge outwards again, growing ever larger. The bolts struck further and further away from the damaged crystals, and caused the other peaks to start to glow and flash bolts of their own.

The glow, the bolts of lightning, they were coming towards them, slowly and in spurts, but they were coming.

"We have to move, now!" Letan shouted.

Without another word or thought, they both turned the panicked horses towards the western portcullis and kicked them into a run. She ducked as they passed through into the city, and they immediately found the main road and ran the horses as fast as they could go. She rode low and clung to the horse as tight as possible, worried it might turn suddenly and send her flying.

Within moments, they were out of the city and running at breakneck speed southeast. Even in the low light of night, they saw several Warriors atop horses far ahead of them, and they could even see some of the city's residents running on foot. Would those people make it? Could they do anything to help them?

Her thoughts and desire to help were interrupted when from seemingly nowhere another meteorite gouged into the ground directly in front of them. The shockwave of heat and energy burned, and the ground buckled and heaved beneath their horses. She and Letan were both thrown.

The last thing she remembered was hitting the ground and a feeling of intense cold taking over her core.

Chapter 30

INTO THE FIRE

The first thing Cardin felt was intense pain throughout his entire body. It wasn't what he expected. He should be dead, and he didn't think he'd feel pain in the afterlife. The world around him was dark, but he realized that was because his eyes were still closed. So very slowly, he opened them.

When he realized where he was, he wondered if he was dead or not. Somehow, he was home!

In fact he was in the middle of the living room. The fireplace was cold and empty, exactly as he had left it, and his armor rack still had his steel plate and chainmail armor on it. It was almost peaceful, and he realized that it had been a month since he'd last seen his house.

There was no light inside, but just like in the jungle, he was able to see everything.

He jumped when there was a bright flash from outside. The ground shook and a shockwave shattered his windows inward, showering him in glass. He instinctively raised a shield, but several shards still cut his face before he could block them all.

His pain forgotten, Cardin bolted to his feet and looked outside. Not far from his house, several homes were ablaze. He looked around at his feet, and found the Sword right next to him, so he picked it up, ran to his door, and burst out into the apocalypse.

Another ball of fire streaked overhead, but did not impact near Daruun. The city was in a panic, with several citizens, soldiers, and Warriors running around with pails of water trying to put out fires.

The same rain of fire he'd seen on Trinil was here! How could that be? Did that mean the necromancers had already reached Edilas and were attacking?

He knew it was still the dead of winter in Daruun, but the heat from the fires just a block north of his house made him feel warm. Snow covered the ground, but it had already melted near the fires and was quickly melting further away, turning everything into a muddy, slushy mess.

Suddenly someone who ran by caught his attention, and he grabbed the older man by the shoulder. "Kellis!"

Lieutenant Kellis started to curse, but then saw who had stopped him and his jaw dropped. "Cardin!"

"What's going on? Are we under attack?"

"What?" Kellis frowned at him. "No, the Wizards say these are pieces of rock falling from the sky, they're calling them meteorites."

"Wait, there are Wizards here," Cardin gawked.

"Yeah, well one is right now, an apprentice who is trying to put the fires out with magic." Kellis sighed. "He's not very good, though, and isn't helping much."

Cardin nodded. "I'm afraid I won't be much help in that arena either." He looked at the bucket in Kellis's hands, and said, "But I can contribute." He placed the Sword on his back, willed the scabbard into place, and clasped his hands together. He realized that despite the fires, he was getting cold already. What he planned to do next would change that. "Where do I get one of those?"

Kellis smiled. "Just go to the river, Warriors are looking for every bucket they can find and are leaving excess ones for anyone to use."

Without another word, Cardin ran as fast as he could towards the center of town, hoping that would be the best part of the river to find buckets. He made it to one of the two bridges that crossed the river, and found the area crowded with people getting more water.

He was surprised and impressed with how many people were helping, far more than he had expected. There was panic in all of their eyes, especially when more meteors blazed overhead, but they seemed to be coming less frequently now, and having a purpose helped the people keep their minds off of fear.

Then he heard a voice he wished he hadn't. Idann was nearby barking orders at Warriors, soldiers, and citizens. Cardin looked at the Guild Commander right when he looked back at him. He didn't want to speak to Idann, but he knew he had no choice. So he walked over, and nodded to the Commander.

"What are you doing here," Idann asked in disdain. "You're supposed to be half a world away!"

"Honestly, I have no idea how I got here," Cardin said, realizing for the first time that he really didn't. "Last thing I remember, I was fighting, a meteorite came down on top of me, and then I woke up at home."

Idann yelled at someone to move faster, and then looked at Cardin with a furrowed brow. "Fighting who? Never mind that. Grab a bucket and get moving, or get out of the way."

Cardin wanted to tell him that he needed to get off of his own lazy butt and help too, but he ignored the Commander's attitude and moved towards the river to find a bucket. However, before he could, a panicked woman came running towards Idann, shouting, "Help me, please!" She looked half-crazed with fear and worry, and Cardin felt his heart ache for her.

"We're trying to help, woman," Idann shouted and ignored her. He barked another order at a Warrior. At that very moment, Cardin's blood boiled and he wanted desperately to slug the Commander.

"It's my daughter, she's trapped in our house, it's on fire!"

"A lot of houses are on fire," Idann retorted, "we're trying to put them out." That was about as much as Cardin could take, so he approached the woman. Idann sneered at Cardin. "I said get helping or get out of here."

He ignored the Commander and took hold of the frightened woman's hands. "Show me where!"

"Thank you, thank you so much," she cried, and pulled him into a run towards the burning northern quarter.

It didn't take them long to get close to the blazes, closer than he wanted to be, and she stopped them in front of a house that was almost entirely consumed in flames, including the front door.

"I went out to see what all of the flashes and noise was," she cried, "but I made her stay inside, and then there was an explosion, and the house was on fire, and no one will help me!"

He looked her in the eyes, and said in a soothing voice, "It's ok, I'm here to help now, calm down and tell me what her name is and where she might be inside." The sound of wood cracking under stress and a crash from inside the house made them jump. "Hurry!"

"Her name is Tiana, please hurry! Her bedroom is in the back."

Cardin squeezed her hands reassuringly, and then faced the burning house. Several people came to the house and tried to splash water on it, but it burned too hot and the water did little to abate the flames.

That meant there was only one thing he could think of to do. He wasn't about to abandon the girl, and when he heard a high-pitched scream from inside, he felt his heart race. Without another thought, without even pulling the Sword from its sheath, he shoved his open palm forward and a surge of magic lashed out and blasted the front door in. The floor inside was also on fire, which made his next task even more difficult.

He closed his eyes for a moment, and focused on gathering magic around him. He had created partial shields to deflect magic before, but this would only be the second time he had ever created a shield completely surrounding him.

The shield was up, and he opened his eyes. It was now or never, so he rushed inside. Wherever his shield passed over the burning floor, it put the fires out, but the wood was still super heated, and the inside of the house was likewise blistering. The shield did little to dissipate the heat, and his feet began to burn through his boots.

"Tiana," he shouted. Another crash came from one of the rooms in the back, and another scream accompanied it. He panicked and ran straight for the room the scream came from.

The bedroom door had already fallen off of its hinges, and the house groaned and sounded ready to collapse. When he made it into the bedroom, he saw that the bed was on fire, and an overhead brace had collapsed into the middle of the room. He saw the little girl, she wore a wool nightgown and had found the only place in the house that wasn't on fire, the back corner. However, the brace that had collapsed had sent burning debris her way, and he saw she was trying to kick it off of her legs. She screamed and cried in pain.

Cardin ran as fast as he could to her, hopping over the brace as he went, and then used his bare hands to help her brush the debris off of her legs. "It's ok, you're alright," he said, and extended his shield around her. It wouldn't last much longer, especially as exhausted as he felt from fighting Tiresis.

Her legs were badly burned and blistered, and she cried and whimpered and tried to touch them to soothe them, but that just made her cry harder. He didn't know how he could possibly help with the pain, but then another crash from inside the house made him realize he didn't have time to worry about her burns just now.

So as gently as he could, he gathered her in his arms and stood up straight. She wrapped her arms around his neck and sobbed into his leather tunic. "It's ok," he tried to reassure her. "We'll get out of here."

Suddenly the doorframe he had come through collapsed, and effectively blocked their path. He thought about using magic to blast through it, but that would probably bring the entire house down around them, and he wasn't confident that the shield would last through that. His legs already burned.

There was only one other thing he could think of. "Hold on to me," he said. When she had a good grip around his neck, he let go with his left arm and pointed his palm towards the wall behind them. He hoped no one stood on the other side of that wall.

In an instant, he gathered power into his palm, and then shoved the power out with all of his might. It blew the wall apart outward into the alley, and a second later he leapt through the opening into the street.

Knowing that the house was seconds from collapse, he ran along the alley towards the front, towards the mother.

When he came into view of the mother, she cried out and ran towards them. "Tiana!"

"Mommy," the girl cried and released her death grip on Cardin's neck. He passed Tiana over to her mother, and then pushed them along to get away from the house while it finally collapsed in on itself, sending sparks and ash flurrying into the air.

When they were far enough away, they stopped, and the mother collapsed to her knees, barely holding on to Tiana.

Tiana was crying, but her cries were growing weak, and she said, "Mommy, I'm cold. It hurts, Mommy…"

Kellis suddenly came up beside them and knelt down. He felt the girl's forehead, and said, "She's getting cold, we need to get her warm. This way!"

He helped the woman up, and she and Cardin followed Kellis as he led them far away from the blazing fire. When they were far enough away that Kellis looked convinced that they were no longer in danger, he led them towards one of the houses with a light on inside. They burst in, and the elderly man and woman who lived there cried out in surprise.

"We need help," Kellis said. "Clear your table, now!"

The two looked at the little girl, and without another word went to their kitchen table and brushed everything off. The mother rushed to the table and set Tiana on it. The little girl looked weak, and her eyes were barely open. She whimpered and sniffled.

"We need to get her warm," Kellis said, "fetch some blankets!"

The elderly woman was already ahead of him and began laying a wool blanket over Tiana She cried in surprise when it touched her burned legs, so Cardin, on instinct, reached forward and pulled it up so it didn't touch her legs.

"We need to heal her burns," he said.

"I'll go find the Wizard," Kellis said, "he might know a healing spells. In the mean time, we need to clean those wounds and bandage them!"

Kellis ran out, and the couple who lived in the house began to do whatever they could. The man put a pot of water over the fire to get it boiling while the woman took another blanket and used sheers to start cutting a strip off.

The girl still cried weakly, but he could tell that she was about to pass out, and he worried if she did, she might never wake up again. The mother clutched her hand and caressed her cheeks and hair, trying to comfort her. "Tiana," she sobbed. "It's ok, I'm right here. Don't leave me, please don't go away…"

Cardin felt his insides constrict and he barely held back his own tears. He had to do something, *anything* to help them. His own legs felt burned, his feet were in agony, and he could only guess what Tiana felt. Something began to stir inside of him, a warm, soothing power.

Without another thought, he reached out his hands and touched both of Tiana's burned legs. He felt a warmth flow through him, and saw a soft green glow wash over her blisters and burns. The energy within him surged, and he felt his spine suddenly spasm.

The last thing he remembered was that the world flipped upside down on him, and he crashed to the ground.

Chapter 31

THE ARRIVAL

The stars swam before her eyes. Kailar slowly opened her eyes, and the dots that were the stars streaked as she tried to get her bearings. She also noticed that some of them seemed orange and moved of their own accord, but a few moments later she realized those were sparks from burning fires.

There was a fire nearby. What happened? Why was she on her back? Where was Letan? Where was she?

And then it all came back in a rush, and she jolted up, a move she immediately regretted when her head throbbed and the world spun. She clenched her eyes shut and tried to push away the dizziness and pain. Then she realized it wasn't just her head that hurt. Every muscle she used to sit up ached agonizingly.

After what felt like hours, her head finally stopped swimming, but the pain remained. It was enough, however, that she could open her eyes and get her bearings. The first sight to greet her was a horse, its legs shattered and its body broken. More memories came back, and she recalled that a meteorite had hit directly ahead of them and threw the ground up from beneath them. The horse wasn't moving, and she hoped for its sake it hadn't survived to endure the pain and agony of its broken body.

She turned her head, slowly, and took in the carnage around her. The ground had, indeed, been deformed into a crater, and they were at the edge of where the ground had heaved up. Every other impact she had seen had caused a huge explosion of fire and heat, so she wondered why this one hadn't burned them to death.

Kailar suddenly panicked when she realized that Letan had been ahead of her, so her search became frantic, until she saw the other horse. It was the only other thing near her, and looked worse off than her horse.

She tried to stand, but the world twisted around her again, so she stayed down. Her legs didn't want to work either, so she had to drag herself.

Her heart pounded in her chest, her vision blurred, and she began to feel sick with the worry that Letan was dead. She couldn't lose him! She had just found someone who believed in her, who trusted her even when she gave him every reason not to.

She crawled around the deformed horse and found Letan next to it, but thankfully he was not pinned beneath.

"Letan," she tried to talk, but her voice was hoarse and had no volume. No, it wasn't that it had no volume. That was the first time she realized that she heard roaring fires, and the sound of intense thunder in the distance. She tried to shout louder, "Letan!"

She reached out to touch him, and as she rested her hand on his shoulder, he groaned and stirred a little. He was alive!

Her heart leapt for joy. "Oh, thank the gods." She gently patted his chest and said, "It's ok. We're alive."

There was another clap of thunder, and she looked northwest towards the city, towards the Crystalline Peaks. Her stomach sank when she saw the green glow, larger than ever, coming from the peaks. Worse yet, there were bolts of sickly green lightning lancing out all over the place. She saw at least one bolt hit directly somewhere in Corlas, and even from where they were she saw that the city was ablaze.

They would have to get out of there fast. "Letan, wake up," she shook him. He groaned some more, but did not wake. She continued to shake him, until she heard a rumbling growl from the crater.

Her chest turned to ice and she instinctively drew her dagger. She realized that whatever it was, she probably couldn't defend herself against it, but she had to try. It was better than waiting there for it to come kill them, and maybe she could distract it from Letan.

Finally her legs began to work, and she was able to crawl up towards the rim of the crater, slowly but at a steady pace. When she finally reached the rim, she looked down, prepared for anything.

Even in the light of the moons, she had trouble seeing anything through the haze of smoke. Part of the crater was on fire, but it was a relatively small fire with most burnable material demolished or buried. The crater was enormous, and stretched at least a thousand yards across, probably more since it was difficult to tell in the dark of night. A massive shadow moved in the center of the crater, an uneven mass that had to be whatever fell from the sky.

But as it moved, it began to take shape, as legs stretched out, and a massive, long black tail unwrapped from around a body. Wings, large enough to darken the sky, unfurled as a large, narrow, angular head appeared. It opened its eyes, and she saw a red glow burn with black irises.

It was a dragon, but it was unlike any of the dragons she had seen before. It was far larger than the one that had guarded the Sword or the ones that had taken her powers away, perhaps almost twice the size. All of the other dragons had stars for eyes, but this one's eyes looked almost lizard like, except for the red glow that surrounded the black center, and somehow that blackness felt darker than the night sky. As she looked into one of those eyes, she felt her soul turn cold.

The dragon stood up, and she panicked. She looked at her dagger and realized just how useless it was. She was powerless. It could simply step on her to wipe her from existence.

However, then she realized that it hadn't even noticed her yet. It began to look around, and then it looked up at the sky. It stared at the stars and the moons for a few moments before it started to take tentative steps, as if it hadn't walked in a long, long time.

Slowly, the giant form crawled up the walls of the crater. Fear gripped her when she realized it would come up not far to the left of where she was. Remaining as still as possible, she watched with bated breath.

It took only a few strides before one of its massive, clawed paws reached the rim and it pulled itself up, where it perched and towered high above her. It looked around for a long while, and she tried to remain absolutely still.

And then she felt it, a new sensation within her, a cold darkness that started at the very center of her being, and grew with each passing moment. The dragon's head snapped down to look directly at her. She felt something, a connection between them, unlike any connection she had ever made with magic. She didn't just feel its power, she felt something more, as if she could touch its soul.

It wasn't a pleasant feeling. The creature's soul was twisted, contorted into something so horrendous that it almost drove her mad, so she withdrew from it. It tilted its head when she did that, as if surprised that she was able to do so.

The black dragon began to move one of its clawed paws towards her, but then there was another, louder clap of thunder from the west that shook the ground and set Kailar's teeth chattering. The dragon looked to the peaks, and she followed its gaze. The glow had grown considerably, and the bolts of lightning struck closer and closer to them.

The dragon spread its wings wide, crouched low, and then leapt into the air. It let out an ear-splitting screech of a roar, and pumped its wings furiously. It turned north east and flew away at incredible speed.

She watched until it disappeared into the night, the connection gone. Yet it had left something for her, a new connection to the world around her. She could feel it, the cold darkness remained within her. And there was power. A power far different from anything she thought possible. It didn't feel like the warmth of energy or the flow of a river, in fact if anything it felt like the opposite of everything she had once felt before the Star Dragons had taken her power.

Another clap of thunder brought her out of her reverie and she realized that she had no time to analyze the feeling any further. When she tried to stand, her legs began to give out, but suddenly the new power she felt revitalized her, and she stood straight up.

That was unexpected, but she didn't have time to consider what it meant. She took several steps, tentative at first, down the crater wall towards Letan, and then walked faster, and faster, until she ran. The lightning struck less than a mile away, and she knew they were out of time.

Letan was awake, and he slowly sat up. She knelt next to him and very nearly toppled him over in a hug. "You're ok!"

He cried out in pain. "Yeah, sort of."

She looked and saw one of his legs had a deep gash in its side. That would slow them down. "Come on," she said, "we have to get out of here."

"No argument from me," he nodded. She wrapped her arms under his and helped him stand up. He hobbled in place for a moment, and then looked towards the peaks. "We don't have much time."

She didn't even look, she simply turned them northeast, unable to go directly away from the danger because of the crater, and pushed them into a hobbled jog.

Could they outrun the oncoming storm? She didn't know, but she had to try. She had to save Letan.

More than that, she couldn't lose that which she had just gained. The Navitas were right, and the prophecy had come true.

She had found a new power!

Chapter 32

DARUUN FOREST BURNS

Cardin felt as if there was a warm, comfortable blanket covering his very soul. He slowly returned to the reality of consciousness, but the feeling didn't fade or go away. What was different about it was that it wasn't coming from someone or something outside. It came from within.

He smiled and slowly opened his eyes. When he saw who stood over him, that smile grew wider, and the warmth was joined by a greater sensation of happiness and relief.

"Sira."

She returned his smile and reached out to caress his cheek, which left a tingling sensation in his face. "Hello, Cardin."

"Am I dreaming?"

Her smile grew and her eyes lit up. "No. No you're not dreaming, and you're not dead. Not by a long shot."

"Good," he nodded. He didn't want to look away from her beautiful eyes, but his curiosity got the better of him and he looked around. He was in the Warriors' Guild barracks in Daruun. All of the beds were filled with wounded people. Several more people walked about tending to them. He saw that there weren't enough beds and many lay upon makeshift beds on the floor.

The fact that the barracks still stood meant that the fires were at least under control, but he also realized that he had no idea how long he had slept, or for that matter why he had passed out.

Then he remembered the last time he saw Sira. "What happened," he asked. "How did you get away?"

She reached down, took hold of his hand and squeezed affectionately. "When you brought down whatever blocked portals, Elaria created one just before the necromancer ships passed through a giant portal on the river. No one on the other ships could help those marines," she looked down sullenly, "and after what happened…" She shook her head. "I doubt any of them survived. But we did. Elaria, Dalin, Reis, Ventelis, Anila, and Commander Devral, as well as a couple of the marines. We're all that's left of the expedition."

He felt his spirits sink. "And the portal on the river?"

She hesitated for a moment, and then looked into his eyes. "They appeared off the coast of Maradin and attacked the city." He nodded solemnly. The invasion had begun. "It gets worse, Cardin," she continued, clearly hesitant to tell him the rest. "The burning skies were caused by meteorites, or so the Wizards have explained. Basically large shooting stars, large enough to fall to the ground and destroy everything near them. One hit the ocean not far from Maradin and created a giant wave." She shook her head and squeezed his hand again, this time searching for reassurance from him. "It obliterated Maradin, and destroyed all of the necromancer ships."

The destruction of an entire city was horrible, but he felt even worse when he realized that it was exactly what had happened in his nightmare. He shook his head slowly and tried to come to terms with the staggering number of casualties. Worse still, he realized that those casualties could bolster the enemy forces. Assuming the necromancers somehow survived. He looked at Sira and asked, "The necromancers?"

"They survived," she said with a sigh. "As did most of their undead." She sat back in the chair she had borrowed. Thankfully she didn't release his hand. "The waters receded, and the enemy has occupied Maradin."

He sighed, and then looked towards one of the doors. He could see an orange glow, and asked, "Is the city still burning?"

She also looked, and then smiled and shook her head. "No. That's the rising sun. It's morning. The young apprentice Wizard here was smart enough to seek out more experienced Wizards. They helped put out the city fires." Then she looked at him with hesitant eyes. "Cardin," she paused. "I know how much you love the forest."

A cold emptiness opened up in his stomach. "What happened?"

"The Wizards are still trying to put it out, but Daruun Forest burns. There is a massive cloud of smoke, and ash is falling on Daruun and Falind."

He clenched his eyes shut, and tried to push back anger and sadness. Seven months ago, he knew that his life would be forever changed, but nothing could have prepared him for the kind of death and destruction that befell Halarite today.

"Show me," he said, and sat up. He felt surprisingly well, no disorientation or pain. Sira helped him up, and then released his hand. He could feel that the Sword, in its sheath, was still on his back. He was thankful that no one had removed it. He couldn't risk someone else touching the Sword.

They wove around the wounded and in between the helpers, which prompted Cardin to ask, "Are your parents okay? What about Reis's?"

Sira smiled and nodded, "They are all okay. Although my parents' house is..." She paused and looked down. "Well, there are people a lot worse off than they are." She shook her head as they walked outside.

The sun had just started to rise over the horizon, but it contended with smoke in the air that stung his nostrils and gave the sun more of an orange hue than normal. A black cloud hung over the city, and small pieces of ash gently fell to the ground. Most of the snow around the barracks had melted, and their boots sloshed through ashen mud. Cardin looked to the north and realized that the fires had come very, very close to the barracks.

The Guild fortress was on the western edge of the city, so they were able to leave directly through a gate and out into the open, which gave him an unobstructed view of the carnage. The forest, not a mile away from Daruun, did indeed burn, sending a massive column of smoke high into the sky.

In fact, most of the trees that were close to the city were already ashen cinders, and the fire had spread much further away. In the distance, near the edge of the forest, he saw a line of figures, difficult to fully make out from where they stood, but he could feel their power. Wizards tried desperately to summon moisture into the air to create rain, but the clouds contended with the superhot fire. The rain fell south of the blaze, and slowly made its way north, but he feared not fast enough.

Cardin reached out and held Sira's hand, and she squeezed it reassuringly. She wrapped her other arm around his and held on tight. He could feel the fear and sadness that she felt, but holding on to each other helped them both.

"Cardin," she said, "I heard what you did for that little girl."

He looked at her. "Tiana! Is she ok?"

"You saved her," Sira looked into his eyes and smiled. "The Wizards say you used magic to heal her burns, and at the same time healed your own. Her mother said there was a soft glow, and then you fell over, and you both were healed."

He shook his head and again looked out to the forest. "How?"

"By unlocking new powers," a familiar voice spoke from behind. He turned to see Dalin walking towards him, along with Reis, Elaria, and Ventelis. He suspected Anila was not far away.

Cardin raced towards his friends, and embraced Reis and Dalin in a hug. He looked at Elaria, uncertain what to do given her feelings for him, but she simply smiled and nodded. "I'm glad to see you're all safe," he sighed contentedly. "I feared the worst."

"Hey, we swore an oath, remember," Reis said, jabbing him in the arm. "We stand with you, my friend. You're not alone anymore."

He smiled, looked back at Sira as she came up next to him, and for that moment in time, felt like everything was going to be alright. Then he looked at Dalin. "So I've finally learned new magic," he smiled, and absently reached back to touch the hilt of the Sword. "It finally gave me something new, the ability to heal."

"Yes, but I believe it was before you were ready," Dalin nodded. "That is why you lost consciousness."

"You mean feinted," Reis smirked. Cardin ignored his friend's jibe.

"I believe that is not the only new power you have gained," Dalin narrowed his eyes. "How did you arrive in Daruun?"

Cardin frowned and replied, "I don't know, actually. One minute

I was fighting the head necromancer, Tiresis was his name. Then a meteorite hit the capitol building. My shield held for a moment, but it was too much, and I knew it wouldn't be long before the shield fell. I felt hopeless, and then..." He paused and frowned. "Then I felt something new inside of me, not too much unlike what it felt like when I healed Tiana but still somehow different. That doesn't make sense, does it?"

"Yes and no," Dalin replied with a smile. "It appears as if you learned how to create a portal, and did so without even realizing you did to escape the blast."

He raised his eyebrows in shock, but that quickly turned to excitement. He had finally created a portal! Then another thought occurred to him, and he asked, "Why did I wake up in my house?"

"Your instincts took you somewhere familiar, someplace that you felt was safe," the Wizard replied.

"So," Cardin sighed and thought for a moment. "I've unlocked the ability to heal, create portals," he paused, "and now that I think about it, the ability to see in the dark."

Everyone looked at him curiously, so he explained, "When I ran from the beach, after the sun set, I could still see everything. I didn't think about it at the time, but," and then he paused and looked at Ventelis and Elaria. "Baenil! I found Baenil!"

"What," Elaria asked.

"When, where," Ventelis added.

"In the jungle, after I ran. He showed me where the necromancer city was."

"Where is he now," Elaria asked excitedly.

Cardin hesitated before he replied, "I sent him away after the ships left, with a mission to go to Archanon once he could create portals again, so that he could warn the king of the necromancer invasion. We should go see if he made it."

Reis shook his head. "No go, my friend. The city is sealed, and there's smoke rising from inside. No one is answering our calls to open the gates."

Once again Cardin's spirits sank. "Well, I told him to get as far away from the necromancer city as possible," he nodded. "He should have been safe, and I'm sure he's ok."

"Indeed," Ventelis nodded. "We must hold on to hope."

Cardin resisted the urge to look back at the forest, and simply stared at his friends, not sure what to say or do next.

"What do we do now," Reis asked. He looked to Sira, but when Cardin looked at her too, she looked as lost as Reis. "How do we stop the necromancers?"

"Without an army, we don't," Sira said sullenly.

"They knew this would happen," Cardin nodded, "although I doubt they expected they'd lose all of their ships from the meteors. There was a prophecy that told them of this day, and that they would be able to regain their former glory. They knew this would be the perfect day to invade."

"And while we recover from disaster," Dalin added, "we will be unable to rally our troops and face them with the numbers needed to defeat them."

They all remained silent after that point, knowing it was true. Until Cardin had an idea. "Then we'll do exactly what they don't expect," Cardin looked at Sira confidently. "We'll gather an army and face them, today."

She looked at him incredulously. "How?"

Cardin turned to Dalin. He felt the pang of sadness even before he spoke. "We send Wizards to every city, every town, every village in every kingdom, and to any troops left in the Wastelands. Send them to the colonies if we have to. Gather every able-bodied man and woman able to fight. Use portals to gather everyone somewhere, maybe east of here in the plains and hills, and then we can attack the necromancers all at once. No time for provisions or anything, we attack them fast and we win the war before it has a chance to begin."

"Guild Commanders won't go for it," Reis shook his head. "You know Idann especially won't. They'll want to guard their cities and towns, help the citizens recover from this catastrophe."

"They need to be made to understand," Cardin said. "There's no point in recovering if the necromancers are going to march in and occupy. It's everything or nothing." He looked at Sira. "We make our stand, together, now."

She looked at him, and he saw something in her eyes, something unexpected. Hope and confidence, not in their situation, but in him.

She smiled, and looked at the others. "He's right. We need to attack now, while they are still recovering. Dalin, how many Wizards are in Daruun?"

"Several dozen," he replied, and pointed towards the forest,

"Most of which are out there. If we do this, they won't be able to put out the forest fire."

"I know," Cardin gulped, realizing that the only hope would be that all of the snow would slow down or stop the fire eventually. "We don't have a choice. Not if we want to survive."

Chapter 33

THE IMPOSSIBLE RUINS

Baenil, King Beredis, and the others who had sought refuge in the catacombs searched for hours for another exit, with Baenil in the lead. He started them out by leading them to places he already knew, including the Tomb of the Ascended. They passed through the hidden entrance behind the Tomb and had descended to the map room, the last place he had visited before his capture.

They continued on past that room, deeper into the catacombs than anyone had ever explored. He kept his eye out for additional hidden markers, the same kinds of markers in ancient human languages that had helped him find the map room. But the deeper they went, the harder it was for him to detect them.

The King stayed right behind him, and Baenil believed that was for a few reasons. One was to ensure that the Prince did not get anywhere near him, and he wondered if the King knew just how violent and dangerous his son actually was. Another reason was that the King seemed to have an insatiable curiosity, and he enjoyed exploring with Baenil while asking him countless questions about elven society.

Baenil found it distracting, and always preferred to work alone for that reason. He did not wish to be rude to the King, but he was worried he would miss an important clue if he did not focus on the task at hand. As such, he always gave the King a short answer.

"How many worlds have you travelled to," Beredis asked him another inane question.

With a frown on his face, Baenil touched the catacomb walls. Something seemed off about the rock in the area. The torches planted in the wall had ended a long time ago, and each person in their group had gone back and taken one off of the wall to carry, all except for the Wizards, who produced their own light from their staves. Baenil had learned early on that the Wizard in white robes with gold trim was actually the head of the Wizards' Guild, Valkere, and that explained why Baenil felt a particularly powerful presence from him.

"Only a handful," he replied distractedly. He ran his fingers along the wall, and felt an unusual sensation that piqued his interest. "There's something down here," he said quietly. "Some enchantment." He looked behind Beredis and asked, "Master Wizard, do you feel it as well?"

The tunnel was narrow and it was difficult for them to pass one another, but the Wizard squeezed past the King to investigate. He closed his eyes, frowned, and then looked at Baenil. "Yes, but I do not recognize the sensation."

"I am not sure I do, either," Baenil shook his head, and kept his hand on the wall. It was in the rocks, all around them. "We are getting close to something."

Despite the sensation, there were no glyphs or signs hidden in the wall to give him a clue as to what power was ahead of them. He walked along running his free hand against the wall while clutching the torch with the other. As always, the thought of finding some new power or relic excited him, but in their current situation, it also frightened him. If it was something dangerous, there was nowhere for them to escape to.

"We must be cautious," he said quietly. Just like the rest of the catacombs, the tunnels twisted and turned in under each other, perpetually keeping them within the magical ward around the city. If anything, he hoped the ward only delved so deep before it lost its effectiveness.

The puzzle of the catacombs began to concern him. He had found so many references to ancient human civilizations, especially in the map room, but also in other rooms discovered while under arrest by the Covenant. Inscriptions, artifacts from ancient times, so many exciting discoveries, many of which excited his captors. He thought he knew what the catacombs were.

Now, however, he found himself in the precarious position of admitting that even he was wrong. There was something more to these tunnels than human relics. Something lay ahead, something unexpected, but he did not yet know what.

The King tried to stay on Baenil's heels, but when the elf glanced worriedly at the Master Valkere, the Wizard asked the King to stay further back for his safety. The King grudgingly agreed. Baenil felt more than saw Valkere reach out his right hand to also touch the wall and trace the source of power.

Suddenly the magic shifted beneath his hand, not because anyone had done anything, but because they had reached a place where the enchantment came to a head. He stopped and stared at the tunnel wall. It seemed like ordinary dirt and rock, but it felt like a wall of energy. The more he examined it, the more he realized that it was actually a simple spell, even if unexpected.

"Here," Valkere also felt the same place in the wall. "What is this?"

"A hidden passage," Baenil closed his eyes. He wasn't the most powerful elf, but he still felt a deep connection to magic, the kind of connection that always served him well when examining enchanted ruins.

Suddenly, with his eyes still closed, he could see the power in front of him, and he realized it was an archway, perfectly carved, with a core of magic where the empty space should have been. Where the empty space still existed.

"This is a magical barrier," he spoke more to himself than to anyone else. "There's something behind here."

"We're near the southern edge of the city and the barrier," Valkere commented, "but whatever is behind there takes us further in."

"Then that takes us in the opposite direction of where we need to go," the Prince commented, his voice full of spite, his youth betrayed in his impatience.

"Yes, but beyond it could be a clue," Baenil commented. "And I am sorry to say that even under dire circumstances, my curiosity gets the best of me."

"As it does me," Valkere said. "What can we do to get past this barrier?"

Normally Baenil would have had to press his hand against the barrier and focused on unlocking the inner magic, a process that could take hours or, in rare instances, days. The magic he felt in the wall was not that sophisticated, so he knew an hour or two was all he would need. However, for once he was glad there were others with him.

"Simple," he looked at Valkere. "Your staff can focus your powers. Press your staff against the center of the barrier, and absorb the magic."

The Guild Master frowned at him. "Is that wise?"

"If it were a more powerful barrier, no," Baenil replied, "it would more than likely kill you. However, this barrier feels old, perhaps thousands of years old, and much of its original power has dispelled. I believe it will weaken you." Valkere raised a concerned eyebrow at him, but he raised his hands and assured him, "but nothing more. You will be okay."

The Master Wizard hesitated and looked back at the other Wizard that accompanied him. That one raised a curious eyebrow, but did not say anything else. Finally, Valkere nodded. "Very well. Step aside." As Baenil did so, Valkere added, "I've never done anything like this before…"

The Grand Master slowly lowered his staff and tentatively placed the white focusing gem against the wall. Baenil closed his eyes and saw the core of power in the wall, as well as the core of power that was Valkere. The Wizard did not do anything at first, but then it began, a flow of energy streamed from the wall and into the staff, and then into the Wizard. The Wizard's core of power fluctuated and grew intense, and a breeze suddenly kicked up within the tunnel, a result of the transfer of energy.

The core glow in the wall began to fade, and Baenil opened his eyes. In the shape of the arch he had seen in his mind's eye, the wall began to fade. The others, at least those who could squeeze in enough to see, watched in wonder.

When the wall completely disappeared, Baenil discovered that what he had seen wasn't just a magical archway, but a perfectly formed tunnel that led into darkness beyond. Valkere lowered his staff, and slowly stepped back until he could lean against the opposite wall. He looked exhausted.

There were words on the top of the archway, so Baenil brought his torch closer. "This is the same ancient language I saw in the map room," he commented. "The arch is a human construct." At first that discovery startled him, as he had felt certain that the tunnels were not originally human constructs. However, he became excited when he realized something else. "I know now that this is not the origin world of humans, but perhaps there is something beyond that could lead the way to it!"

He looked at Valkere with excitement, but the Wizard simply raised an exhausted eyebrow and took in a deep breath. "You found this secret, the honor to enter first is yours."

"I agree," King Beredis smiled at him. "However, I should like to follow directly behind you."

"As you wish, Your Majesty," Baenil nodded.

With his everlasting torch in hand, Baenil drew in a deep breath, and then stepped through the archway. His torch lit up only the area immediately around him, but as he walked out the other side of the short tunnel, the flickering light illuminated a few pillars several yards away. He looked down, and suddenly stopped, and shot out his hand to stop the King from walking past him. They had both almost walked off of a precipice.

They were in a cavern much larger than he anticipated, and the entrance led out onto an artificial cliff side. He could not see into the shadows below, so he had the impression that they had just stepped into a large, massive chamber with supporting pillars. He looked right, saw a wall, looked left, and saw that the platform they stood upon had stairs carved into the stone that led downwards.

"Watch your step," he said. Valkere followed the King in, but there was not much room on the platform, so they would have to move before the crowd pushed them over the edge.

As he started past the King, Valkere stopped him. "Wait a moment." The Wizard pointed his staff out past them, and a moment later Baenil felt a soft pulse of magic. The light at the tip of the Wizard's staff flared and shot out into the room, increasing in brightness as it went.

Just as Baenil had suspected, it was a large cavern that stretched seemingly endlessly away from them, deeper into the area under the city.

And that was when he realized it was actually an underground city! As the Wizard's light grew brighter, it illuminated the base of the pillars, revealing countless buildings surrounding them. The further the light traveled, the easier it was to see that the buildings were laid out in a grid pattern, creating obvious roads crisscrossing along the artificially-leveled cavern floor.

Baenil felt his jaw drop when he recognized the architecture. "Impossible," he said quietly.

"What is?" the King asked.

He looked at Beredis, hesitated, and then looked back down. "I do not wish to say yet. I must inspect these buildings closer. Come, follow me. Master Wizard, if you can, please generate additional lights."

The Wizard complied, and while his original one continued to float several hundred feet away, a few more were sent out to various parts of the underground city, including above the stairs. The stairs were long and ran along the wall, which Baenil just now realized was a curved, cylindrical shape rather than a rectangle. This further fueled his suspicions about who built the city.

He began to descend the stairs, wary of the fact that there was no railing, with the King and Valkere right behind him. The others took their turn to stare out into the city in awe, and then followed them.

If Baenil was right about who built the city, this entrance looked like an auxiliary entrance to the surface. That meant there could be another, larger entrance somewhere else, and could be their way out. However, he also realized that it may have caved in millennia ago, otherwise how could the city have gone undiscovered for so long?

The descent was long, but the stairs were in surprisingly good condition considering he believed them to be older than human civilization. The Wizard's glowing spheres helped him see, and the further he descended, the more certain he was that he recognized the architecture.

When they finally made their way to the bottom, he slowly walked away from the stairs and into the edge of the city. The buildings were made of various kinds of stone dug up from who knew where. The ones on the edge looked simple and poor. The large ones on the edge he knew were not actually homes, but complexes of homes connected to each other and on top of each other, apartment homes. Further along the avenue towards the center, the apartments became scarce, and the homes appeared to be much more elaborate and rich, some of which were made of various types of marble rather than stone or mud-bricks.

There were cobwebs everywhere, and that made him nervous. Spiders and spider-like creatures were common across many worlds, and he absolutely detested them. But worse still was that he knew there were other far more dangerous web-building species. He hoped none of them had taken up residence.

"What is this place," Prince Beredis asked, his own disdain for the elf forgotten in the amazement of what lay before them. Everyone had made it to the bottom of the stairs and had spread out around Baenil to inspect the homes.

"I've never heard of anything like it," the King added.

"Nor I," Valkere added. "Even on the other worlds I have visited."

Baenil shook his head slowly. "But this city actually is of another world." He looked at Valkere, whose brow was furrowed in confusion. "Though why a human-built archway would lead to this is beyond me. These are dwarven ruins."

"Dwarves," Valkere asked, shock in his voice. Although no one else recognized the name, as Baenil had expected, he was surprised that the Wizard knew enough to be shocked.

"You know of them," he asked Valkere.

"In passing, yes, but I have never seen one," he looked out into the city. "They are said to be excellent metal workers."

"A common misconception," Baenil nodded. "That is not the only skill they excel at, but it is one of them. They are like humans or elves, they are a diverse species with many talents, and they have many subspecies and can be found throughout the universe. There are dwarves on Dareann, in fact."

Everyone looked at him in surprise. "There is no time to get into our history with the dwarves, that will have to be a story for another day." He shook his head, looked up the stairs towards their entrance, and then began to look around.

"I have explored only one other ancient dwarven city, but I spent a lot of time there. If I am right," he pointed in a direction left of the center of the city, "there should be a main entrance somewhere in that direction. The avenues are laid out in a grid, so we will need to cut over to make our way in that direction."

"Then let us hurry," the King said. "I do not know what the time is, I have lost all sense of it down here, but it would not surprise me if it is morning by now."

Valkere closed his eyes, and Baenil knew he did so to get a sense of the magic around them. "I cannot tell down here either, the magic is so different in this place."

"Follow me," Baenil led the way, and the others fell in next to or behind him. "Legends say that the dwarves of ancient times had magical powers themselves, but somehow they lost it thousands of years ago. No one knows how an entire species, spread across countless worlds, could lose their connection to magic." Even though his own studies had focused on human history, that was a mystery that had caught his attention a long time ago. "History reads that the dwarves were able to change magic to fit their needs, a power very much unique to them. Using existing magic is one thing, but to actually change the nature of the power? That is a terrifying prospect."

"Change its nature how," Valkere asked, doubt and bewilderment in his voice.

Baenil shrugged, "I do not actually know. It was only a legend, and incomplete."

"Perhaps the legends were true," the King said. He looked at Valkere, "How does the magic feel different to you?"

"It is difficult to explain," Valkere replied. "I have felt various types of magic, and learned in my travels that each feels different. The magic found on Halarite is usually warm and comforting. Magic of the elves also feels warm, but is more intense. To use an analogy, our magic feels like the warmth from a fireplace, while elven magic feels focused and intense like a beam of light focused through a crystal."

"I can feel the difference too," Draegus Kataar spoke up for the first time since they had entered the catacombs. "Which is saying something. Mages usually aren't that attuned to magic."

"The current is different here," the other Wizard, who's name Baenil still couldn't remember, added. "More rapid."

"Like the river after a rainstorm in the mountains," Draegus nodded.

It didn't take them long to leave the poor, outer fringes and enter the richer, more elaborate inner city. They passed by a particularly grand structure that Baenil knew to be the seat of government for the dwarven city. It was not a castle, but it was a grand marble structure that reached towards the ceiling of the cavern, with structures that could have been mistaken for turrets but were in fact places for the dwarves of ancient time to look out upon their city in pride.

Shortly after finding that structure, they found the main road. It was as wide as the area between pillars, and remnants of ancient carts and stalls lined it, everything covered in webbing.

In fact in some places, the webbing seemed particularly thick, beyond what spiders could possibly build. He looked up, and saw webbing between pillars, but no movement was visible in the Wizard's lights.

"Keep an eye out for any movement," he spoke, catching the rest of their group off guard. "Hopefully whatever built these webs is long gone…"

Without another word, Draegus drew his sword, as did the two guards. "Why does that statement make me nervous," Draegus asked.

"It should," Baenil warned. "I don't think spiders built them."

King Beredis glanced warily at him. "Dare I ask what else could have built them."

"Any number of species," Baenil replied. "Although there are only a few who build underground like this. I would not expect them to have found their way to your world, as isolated as it is, but then I never expected to find dwarven ruins here either."

"Great," one of the catacomb guards grumbled.

As they continued on down the main avenue, Baenil start to feel as if something or someone watched them, and his fear doubled.

They should have been able to see the wall ahead at the end of the main avenue, but the Wizard's sphere of lights hadn't travelled that far. So Valkere and the other Wizard simultaneously thrust their staves forward, and two spheres of light shot out at ground level ahead of them.

The shadows around them moved rapidly, and his eyes darted back and forth. Some of the movement didn't seem to match up with the movement of the light spheres. However, whenever he caught something out of the corner of his eye and looked, the movement was gone. Was it a trick of the light and shadows?

"I'm starting to get a bad feeling about this place," Draegus said quietly.

"As am I," the King spoke. "Perhaps we should hurry."

"Agreed," Baenil said, leading them into a hurried walk.

Suddenly there was the sound of falling stones nearby, and stone grinding on stone. It startled everyone, but they didn't know where the source was.

That was when they broke into a run.

The light finally reached the end of the avenue, and his heart sank - the entrance had collapsed. However, they had travelled a considerable distance, and he wondered how close they were to the edge of Archanon and its barrier.

"Now what," the Prince asked, panicked.

"Keep going, we might be able to get far enough through," Baenil shouted.

That's when it happened. The shadows shifted of their own accord, and black shapes emerged. The webs shook as something heavy moved upon them. And the one species he feared more than any other appeared in the webs above and around them.

They were arachnids, but they were not spiders, and they were massive, larger than elves. They walked mostly on their back six legs while their bodies curved upward, allowing their forward legs to act as arms, with pincers that formed into three appendages, essentially turning them into hands. Their heads were triangular shaped, and they had three sets of black, spherical eyes.

In a voice belying any fear, Valkere asked, "What are they?"

Several of the monsters screeched, an ear-splitting noise that echoed throughout the cavern. "They are called kiklar," Baenil shouted. "Hurry!"

He tried to run faster, tried to make his weary legs work harder, but he knew that the kiklar were faster. Their species was wide-spread, some more sophisticated than others, but they were deadly all the same.

For them to have set up their home down in the dwarven city, there had to be another way in and out, otherwise they would have starved a long, long time ago.

When he saw two of them on webs between pillars ahead, he knew that they would have to fight, so he shouted, "They are sensitive to magic!"

The two dropped down right as Baenil passed beneath, but

Valkere and the other Wizard saw them, and blasted them with bolts of lightning. The horrifying monsters reacted violently, flying away from the impact before they exploded in a mess of blue-black blood.

Draegus and the catacomb guards used their swords to focus their magic as well, and sent out waves of energy that stunned or destroyed some of the Kiklar that approached on the ground.

"Faster," he shouted, the end of the avenue only a thousand feet away. Magic flew everywhere as everyone tried to keep the swarm at bay, but then he noticed several drop down directly between them and the entrance. "Destroy the ones ahead!"

The Wizards shifted their attention to the road ahead and used lightning to obliterate those in the way. More seemed to come out of nowhere to replace them, but the Wizards were fast and powerful. The Mages tried to keep the rest at bay, but the Kiklar were slowly closing in, their shrieks growing louder and louder.

By the time they reached the end of the road, at least two dozen Kiklar had been destroyed, leaving the ground a slippery, disgusting mess. They reached the ruins of what had once been the main gate, giant stone doors that had crumbled and the rock above them had collapsed in, but much to Baenil's disappointment, there was no way through.

"That's it," he cried, "we're dead!" He came up against the collapsed rock and smacked it with his open palm in frustration.

However, that was also when he felt a distinct change, and as Valkere turned to face the incoming Kiklar, he must have felt it too, since he turned back to face the rock wall. "We're at the edge, we can create portals!"

"Then do it," King Beredis shouted as the Mages and the other Wizard fended off the advancing Kiklar.

"But where to," Baenil asked. "Anywhere we create a portal to could be on fire and we'd never know it until we stepped through."

"We have to believe that the whole world isn't set afire," Valkere replied, having to shout louder above the shrieks. "An open, grassy area, the fields west of Archanon."

"What if it isn't safe," the Prince asked. "What if we perish the moment we step through?"

"We do not have a choice," the King snapped. "We cannot stay here."

Without waiting for further debate, Valkere focused his magic, and in an instant, a portal appeared right up against the collapsed entrance. "Go, now!"

The King didn't even hesitate, and knew that those without magic had to leave first, so he stepped through, followed by the Prince and a few of the other politicians that had fled with them. That left Baenil, the Wizards, Draegus, and the two guards.

Baenil had no combat ability, so he knew he was next. He stepped up to the portal, and then looked at the Master Wizard, who blasted a Kiklar crawling down the wall towards them. "Thank you," he said.

"Go," the Wizard shouted.

Baenil clenched his eyes shut, and stepped through. He half-expected searing heat to burn him, but was pleasantly surprised by intense cold. Once he was through, he opened his eyes, and was glad to find himself on an open, snow-covered field. The sun was just above the mountain peaks to the east, but did little to fight the cold of winter.

He moved aside immediately, and watched the portal impatiently. The Master Wizard was the only real choice to create a portal, since he would have to follow last, and he was probably the only one who could fend off the Kiklar once he was alone, or at least long enough to escape through his own portal.

One of the catacomb guards came through next, followed by the other. Next came Draegus, and he sighed in relief. If Cardin was indeed alive, he didn't want to bear him the unhappy news of his father's death at the hands of giant arachnids.

The less experienced Wizard was next, and he backed through, as if he had been fighting right up until the last possible moment. He stumbled backwards and nearly fell over, but the King caught him and helped him get out of the way of the portal.

Everyone waited, their breath held while the seconds passed. Finally, the Wizard dove through. One of the Kiklar tried to follow, and succeeded, but the portal closed on its back legs and abdomen, and it shrieked in pain.

Without a second thought, Draegus infused his weapon with magic and jabbed it into the monster's head. It fell over, instantly dead.

"We made it," King Beredis sighed in relief. "We made it..."

That was the first time they took in their surroundings completely.

They were just outside of the valley that led to Archanon's western gate. The stone road was just south of them. They looked in at the city to see that smoke rose from within, and the gates were still closed. Baenil looked around to find a few more impact sites in the fields and forests. Meteorites had rained down everywhere, and if the whole world looked like this, he feared that casualties would be in the tens of thousands.

They were all startled when another portal opened right next to them. Baenil backed away from it, while the Mages and Wizards prepared to fight whatever came through. A moment later, they were relieved when a figure clad in silver Wizard's robes stepped through.

She paused in surprise as the portal closed behind her, and looked around in curiosity. Then she saw her Guild Master. "Grand Master Valkere," she said excitedly, and bowed deeply. "I am relieved to see you. I was waiting near the city gates, hoping someone would eventually open them from within, when I saw your portal."

Everyone relaxed and crowded around the newcomer. "Eril," Valkere clasped her on the shoulder. "I am relieved to see you as well."

She nodded, then looked at the King, and finally at Baenil. "Ah, you must be the elf that Cardin Kataar spoke of."

Everyone exchanged surprised and hopeful looks, and Draegus stepped forward. "Cardin is alive?"

"Yes," she smiled, "he is. He is attempting to rally support to attack the undead."

Valkere exchanged glances with King Beredis, and then nodded to Eril, "Take us to him immediately."

Chapter 34

DARKNESS DESCENDS

King Lorath scowled as he emerged from the safety of the siege tunnels of his capitol city, Sharenth. It had been a long, long time since anyone had used those tunnels, but when the skies burned and stars fell to Halarite, he knew of nowhere else to go.

Sharenth was one of the most unique cities on Halarite, built on a coast nestled up against tall mesas. The only access to the city other than the sea was through several narrow chasms carved through the mesas by rivers. This made it an extremely defensible city in that sense, but they were also vulnerable from above, as armies could march along the tops of the mesas and launch attacks.

The siege tunnels were set into the mesas, and were usually meant for children, elderly and anyone else incapable of fighting. Since there had been no one to fight this time, and the fire came without warning, few had been able to make it into the siege tunnels other than the King and his court.

Now that they emerged, he was pleased to find that his city was mostly intact. From where he stood, he saw several columns of smoke that rose into the morning sky. The governor, a long-time friend named Ebil Dressik, stood beside him and stared in awe. "By the gods…"

They wandered into the city, towards the castle in the center, which stood upon a rise. Several rivers that converged on the city divided it into islands, and the castle stood upon its own island. Unfortunately, the bridge they would have normally taken was destroyed, and the river had partially diverted and flooded into the city from a small impact crater. Lorath grimaced when he noticed that one part of the castle was damaged and burning.

Wanting to know more about the fate of his city, Lorath was pleased when he saw the guard captain, Lara, run up to them. "Your Majesty," she bowed low, out of breath. "I'd heard you made it safely to the tunnels. I am relieved to see you."

"As I am you," he said dismissively. He found it was always a good idea to at least feign concern, but he mostly just wanted a report from her. "What damage have we suffered?"

She looked up at the castle across the river, and then sighed. "We haven't been able to get most of the fires completely out, but they are under control and the city is no longer in danger of burning down. The docks were obliterated by large waves, but the tidal walls helped protect us. Some parts of the city are still flooded, but the water is beginning to recede."

Lara looked towards the docks. "There's also another Wizard here, named Danika. Says she was sent to rally troops for an attack against an invading force."

It took Lorath a moment to truly comprehend what she had just said. He asked, "What invading force?"

"Supposedly undead and necromancers," Lara replied. She frowned and added, "I thought necromancy wasn't real."

Lorath's court Wizard, a young man named Wilick, stepped forward to say, "If Danika says they are real, they are."

"She says that the undead have established a beach head in Maradin," Lara continued, "and they intend to invade the rest of Edilas from there. Someone in Tal wants to assemble our armies and stop them now, but I told the Wizard that we can't commit any troops until we finish damage control in our city. In any case, I told her we would have to wait until we found you, Your Majesty."

"Good," he nodded, pleased that she knew better than to deploy troops without his orders. "Let us go meet this Danika, and I will judge for myself if she speaks the truth."

Wilick obviously wasn't pleased to have been ignored or

discounted, but as always, he grudgingly accepted that the King's word was the law of the land. His relationship with the Wizard was strained from day one. Wilick was a full-fledged Wizard, and had been for a century, but he held no real influence with the Wizards' Guild. Therefore, Lorath had little use for him except to learn how Wizards in general thought and acted. This barely gave him an advantage in Alliance Council sessions.

Lorath and Lara led the way towards the docks. The city was surprisingly still and quiet, the panic from last night having passed. His people were picking up the pieces, in some cases literally. They walked near another small impact site and he caught a glimpse of the destruction it had caused. A crater was gouged into the ground and fires still burned as people worked fervently to put them out.

"What magic could have done this," he asked absently.

"I did not sense any magic behind it," Wilick replied, but Lorath ignored him.

When they reached the docks, Lorath was shocked - the destruction was absolute, the waves had destroyed the piers and some of the buildings, and the group stepped into water an inch deep. Lorath scowled, and realized he should have had Danika come to them.

However, before he could even think about telling them all to turn back to drier ground, an ear-splitting roar echoed across the sky. Everyone stopped, the city became eerily still. He searched the skies for the source of the roar, not sure of the direction. Someone pointed to the Southwest, and he saw it, between buildings, a black shadow moving across the sky. The roar came again, closer and more terrifying.

The shadow had wings, he realized, and he could see it pumping them furiously, moving closer at impossible speeds. At first he thought it was just a bird, but no bird could have created such a roar. As it drew closer, he realized just how large it was, and monstrous was the only word he could think of to describe it.

The shape was familiar, based on legends and the stories he'd heard from the Battle of Archanon. "A dragon," Wilick echoed Lorath's thoughts.

It was impossibly large, and he began to wonder if reports from Archanon had been woefully inaccurate.

But there was something wrong. Even from a distance, the

dragon did not fill him with the sense of wonder and hope that he'd read about. This beast filled him with dread.

It was very high in the sky, but once it was practically on top of them, it suddenly folded its wings and dove at an insane speed. In fact, it dove right for the port!

Lorath and the others scrambled to get away from where they thought it would land, but it hit within seconds, right on top of an already damaged building that collapsed under its weight, and the world trembled.

It roared again, the sound almost driving him mad as he clutched at his ears, and the black dragon glared at everyone with piercing red eyes. Something caught its attention, and it looked down near its feet. *"Who are you,"* Lorath heard the beast's words in his mind. Its speech was not directed at him, but it was low and menacing and raised the hairs on the back of his neck.

From where they stood, Lorath could barely see a Wizard near the dragon. It spoke up to the great best, but the dragon did not say anything else. The Wizard, most likely Danika, gestured and spoke, but Lorath could not hear her words from where he stood.

This would not do, someone wouldn't negotiate with a dragon in his city without him. He marched towards them, but Wilick caught his shoulder. "Your Majesty, no!"

"Do not touch me," he shouted and batted the Wizard's hand away. But when he looked back, the dragon reached a paw out and, with a single giant talon, flicked Danika away violently. She crashed into another half-destroyed building with a thud even he heard, and then fell to the ground, dead.

"No," Wilick shouted. He took off at a run towards the woman's body. The dragon heard his shout and looked in their direction.

Suddenly a blood-red glow formed in its mouth, and a moment later, a blast of energy lanced out and engulfed Wilick. He screamed for a moment, but soon there was nothing left of him, and the building behind him was obliterated.

"Wait!" Lorath threw his hands up, feeling panicked. "Stop! I mean you no harm!"

The dragon looked at him, and then laughed, which would have been a comical sight under less terrifying circumstances. *"As if you could harm me, little one."*

Lorath felt his cheeks flush at being called 'little one' but he realized he was not in a position to correct the monster. This wasn't a kind, sympathetic Star Dragon, and he realized it had to be the other type he had been warned about, a Dark Dragon. But how? The Wizards said they had all been destroyed by the Sword of Dragons three thousand years ago!

He walked towards the dragon, the inch-deep water forgotten. "Please, do not harm anyone else. Tell me what I can do for you."

The dragon looked ready to reach out and flick him as it had Danika, but then it stopped and rested its paws on the rubble. It regarded him with its red eyes, which seemed to dig into his very soul and stole the warmth from his body.

"There is only one thing you could possibly give me that is of value. Information."

Lorath drew closer to it, and had to crane his neck to look up into its eyes. "Anything, as long as you promise to spare my city."

The dragon seemed to chuckle at this, but then it slowly bowed its head in an attempt at a nod. *"I have not a care for what happens to you or your city. If you tell me what I need to know, I shall spare you."* Lorath thought that it gave him a wicked smile. *"Ever since I landed on this world, I have sensed a power unlike anything I have sensed before. And it grows stronger."*

Lorath felt his blood turn ice cold. He shouldn't have been surprised that it would sense the presence of the Sword of Dragons and would want to know what it was and where it was. However, at the same time he wondered how it could possibly not have known about the Sword. If it had survived the destruction of the other Dark Dragons, it should have known exactly what that power was.

The dragon regarded him with an even stare. *"What is this power? Who is this human that grows more powerful than any previous human? Where can I find this one?"*

Perhaps it was a blessing in disguise. He was unhappy with the fact that a Tal citizen was named Keeper of the Sword. Perhaps this monster could destroy Cardin. It could hardly use the Sword of Dragons itself, it was not human or even human-like.

Lorath smiled. "I am only too happy to tell you. A weapon that the Star Dragons helped build resides on this world in the care of one named Cardin Kataar. It is called the Sword of Dragons, and was constructed to destroy Dark Dragons."

The dragon raised its head in surprise. *"When was this forged?"*

"Three thousand years ago," Lorath replied, his chin raised. "When it was subsequently used to wipe out all of your kind. How do you not know this?"

"That is not your concern. Where is this Cardin Kataar?"

Lorath again smiled, and pointed east by north east. "The continent far to the east of here. He was sent there on a mission, and he should have reached it by now."

The dragon looked where Lorath pointed, and then snorted. *"I shall find this one and take the Sword from him."* He looked at Lorath, and again he felt the warmth of his body stolen from him. *"You have served me well."*

"And I would love to serve you again," Lorath said quickly, seeing a very valuable opportunity before him. "I am your humble servant."

"As you should be," the dragon crouched low and partly unfolded its wings. Without another word, it leapt up into the sky, spread its wings and pumped them hard, taking to the air towards the east.

Lorath sighed in relief and looked back. The others of the royal court had not joined him, only the city guard captain had stayed nearby. He applauded her restraint since she had never drawn her sword.

"I believe we narrowly avoided further disaster," he told her, but her eyes were fixed on the departing dragon. Lorath shook his head and also looked to watch its departure.

Then it banked in a wide half-circle, and let loose a terrifying roar. Lorath felt his stomach sink as the dragon flew towards them. What was it doing?

"Oh gods," Lara grimaced.

Lorath never had a chance to say anything else. A red glow grew within the dragon's mouth, but this time much stronger, much larger, much brighter than before. An instant later, it shot out the blood-red beam of energy right at Lorath.

Chapter 35

A NEW POWER

Kailar and Letan hadn't stopped running, not since the crater, not since the black dragon had crawled out and connected its icy soul to hers. She didn't know how long ago that was, but she was certain that the sun wasn't long from rising.

Her heart thundered in her ears. Letan had gradually placed more of his weight on her throughout the night. Her new power gave her renewed strength, but even that was beginning to wane. Whatever she felt, her connection to it was still tenuous and she worried that it was beginning to fade.

The beating of her heart blocked out most other sounds, but she could still hear Letan's labored breathing and occasional grunts of pain when he stepped on his left leg wrong. He began to feel like dead weight, and she realized he couldn't go any further.

She stopped and looked at him. His head hung low, and with both moons at their backs, she couldn't see his face very well, but he looked ghostly white. They hadn't run into any other refugees since they left the crater, so there was no one else to help care for him, no one else who knew how to help him.

With greatest care, she lowered him to the ground, and he heaved a sigh of relief. He sat with his left leg straight and his right leg bent under him as if he had meant to sit cross-legged, but he still held onto her right hand. She didn't withdraw, and instead sat next to him and held his hand firmly.

He looked at her wearily, but managed a weak smile. "We're safe."

She looked west and could see the pale, sickly green glow from the damaged Crystalline Peaks in the distance, bright enough to occlude the Peaks themselves, but she could no longer see any lightning, nor could she hear any thunder. "I think so."

His grip on her hand weakened a little, and she tried to look into his eyes. "How are you faring?"

"I'm not," he laughed a little. "But you've kept me going. We need to dress my wound."

She looked around, and asked, "With what? We left the packs behind, the supplies were on the horses and I didn't think to grab them." It had been a lapse in judgment fueled by fear and the excitement of the new power she felt connected to.

"Any cloth will do," he smiled. "A shirt sleeve, anything. The bleeding has mostly stopped on its own, but we have to stop it completely. We need a fire, too."

She looked around, but they were in the middle of a grassy field. "I'm afraid a fire is probably out of the question until we can travel further."

She thankfully still had one of her water flasks strapped to her belt, so she let go of Letan's hand, pulled the flask off, opened it, and helped Letan drink some of it. Then she closed it, set it down, and pulled out her dagger. She cut a long piece out of her cloak, from up near her shoulder where it was clean rather than further down where it was dirt-encrusted.

There was no way that she could be gentle about it, so she looked at Letan and said, "This is going to hurt. A lot."

"I know," he clenched his jaw. "Get it over with."

She set to work, and winced every time he groaned in pain. She hated hurting him, but he had lost a lot of blood and she worried that he couldn't afford to lose anymore. The wound wasn't clean, and that was why they needed a fire, to boil water to use to clean the cloth and the wound, but this would have to do until she could get him somewhere safe.

When she was close to running out of the strip of cloth, she tied it up as tightly as she could. His hand shot up and clenched her shoulder, but the moment passed, and his face eased.

"It's ok, it's over," she raised her hand, covered in his blood, and took a hold of his. "Relax, and breathe."

His eyes were clenched shut, but he nodded twice in understanding. "Yeah," he spoke through gritted teeth. "We need to figure out a way out of here, we need to get somewhere where a doctor can look at my leg. I don't want to lose it." He opened his eyes and looked intently at her. "I can't afford to. I am a Warrior."

"We'll figure something out," she tried to sound reassuring. "Just relax, and let me worry about it."

He nodded, laughed, and said, "Easier said than done."

She laughed too, and patted his hand. Then she remembered the blood and began to wipe it off on her cloak. They had precious little water left, so she didn't dare use it to wash her hands.

Letan released his iron grip on her shoulder and wiped his bloodied hands on his tunic. "Kailar," he looked at her with haunted eyes. "I swear I saw something crawl out of that crater. It looked like a giant shadow." She looked at him with haunted eyes. "What was it?"

She hesitated, and realized she hadn't spent much time thinking about it. Despite how long they had run, she had focused mostly on the task of getting away. Now that they had stopped, she thought back to what she saw and felt. To what she felt now.

"It was a dragon." His eyes grew wide. "But not like the other dragons I saw, not like the ones who took my powers away."

"How was it different?" He shifted his weight a little, winced and took in a sharp breath, but then slowly let it out.

"I don't know exactly. It didn't have stars for eyes, and it was larger than the other dragons I've seen." She looked at him, and waited for him to meet her gaze. When he did, she looked as intently at him as she could, so that he fully understood the magnitude of what she said next. "I connected with it. Through magic."

His eyes grew wide. "What?!"

"But not normal magic." She shook her head. "I don't know what it was. What it is." She reached out a hand to take hold of his, and said, "I can still feel it, Letan. It unlocked something inside of me. A new power."

His eyes grew distant for a moment when he said, "Like what the

Navitas said."

"Exactly. I think this is what the prophecy is about. His magic isn't normal magic. The Star Dragons took my powers away." She hesitated, as the connection was made in her head moments before she said it, "I think it was a Dark Dragon."

He frowned and shook his head, "What's the difference?"

She shook her head, "I don't know exactly. But when I first learned about the Sword of Dragons and searched for it, I found out that there was a civil war between Star Dragons and Dark Dragons long ago, and the Sword was forged specifically to end it."

"So maybe this Dark Dragon undid what the Star Dragons did to you."

"No I don't think that's it, this feels too different." She raised her hand up, and realized she hadn't done anything with the power except unconsciously revitalize her body and keep herself running. She had learned to do that with normal magic when she had the Sword.

Did that mean she could do everything that she could before, just with a new kind of power? She used to have to draw energy into her, so maybe she could do that again. She focused on the power she felt within her, and tried to draw more into her.

Nothing happened. She felt no increase in power, no potential energy. She still felt the connection, still felt the power, but her attempts to draw it into herself seemed to have no effect, or even felt like it had the opposite effect.

"What was that," Letan asked. "I felt something shift around us, but I still get nothing when I focus on you."

"A failure," she hung her head. Then another thought occurred to her. "Wait... The civil war was between Dark Dragons and Star Dragons." She looked at him with a furrowed brow. "Stars are points of light. Light and dark." She again looked at her hand. "Opposites."

Once again, she concentrated, but this time on doing the opposite. She began to push what she felt inside of her out, which in a sense created an absence of magic within her. Suddenly the world around her came alive, and there was the potential of movement and power.

It made absolutely no sense to her, but by creating that absence within her, suddenly she had the power. She turned her hand and thrust her palm outwards, and an invisible blast of energy pulsed out and gouged into the ground a few feet away. A clap of thunder followed, and startled her.

Letan nearly fell over in surprise. "What was that?!"

She turned her hand back towards her, stared at her palm, and smiled. "That is the secret, the answer." She looked at him and her smile grew. "I don't know how or why, but somehow I have powers that oppose normal magic. Whatever that Dark Dragon unlocked in me, it is the opposite of normal magic."

Standing up, she looked to a point in the air several feet away. "And if that's the case, I should be able to figure out how to recreate the same abilities I had before." She sighed, and once again raised her palm up and outward. "In time, hopefully a very, very short amount of time, I'll be able to create a portal." She looked down at him, feeling absolutely determined to save his life at any cost. "And then I can get you the help you need."

Chapter 36

SETTING THE BOARD

It was past mid-morning, and Cardin felt extraordinarily nervous. The leaders of the Alliance, the Warriors' Guild Commanders, and their Generals continued to gather in Daruun, all at his request. All because he believed they needed to leave their cities, in the wake of an apocalypse, to attack one of the most powerful armies ever assembled on Halarite. In a short time, it would be his job to convince them all that his plan was their best course of action.

Sira supported him. All of his companions did. But she had pointed out to him that because it was his idea, he had to be the one to convince everyone. She also pointed out that he could be quite the motivational speaker when he wanted to be, and he was far braver at saying what needed to be said than she was.

They waited impatiently within the Daruun Warriors' Guild training grounds. Most of the Wizards they had sent to gather the leaders across Edilas had returned with their charges, but not all had returned yet. Queen Leian was already present, as was Sal'fe, and several Guild Commanders from countless towns throughout Edilas. They still waited for some leadership from Archanon or the Wastelands, either General Artula or King Beredis, preferably both. If they started without either of them, Idann would be the highest ranking military member of Tal, and that wouldn't bode well for Cardin's plan. They also hadn't heard from the Wizard they had dispatched to Sharenth to find King Lorath or his Guild General.

Cardin stood idly by the main gate into the fortress with Sira and Reis. They hadn't said much, but he was glad they were alive and just wanted to be near both of them.

"Who would have thought," Reis spoke idly, his gaze looking back into the training grounds. "More than a decade ago, we were here, training to defend Tal from Falind and bandits. Now we're preparing to defend the world from an invasion of the undead."

Sira and Cardin both chuckled. She smirked and said, "And yet I get the feeling that this is still just the beginning of the strangeness that has become our lives."

Cardin nodded, but said nothing. His nightmare, at least in part, had come true. The skies had burned, fire had fallen to the ground, Maradin was engulfed by a giant wave, and for all he knew, the necromancers were the darkness that would engulf the world.

Was he able to see the future now? Or was this a unique situation? He wasn't even sure they would all survive the coming days, so he feared that he would never find out.

He didn't realized he'd been staring at Sira, but when she looked at him and raised a curious eyebrow, he blushed and looked down. More than anything else, he didn't want to lose her, but he was afraid that was precisely what was coming. The end of all things.

Sira reached out and took hold of both of his hands. He looked at her, and she searched his eyes. "Are you okay?"

The smile he gave her was weak, but it was the best he could do. "I think so. I'm just not sure what's going to happen next."

She shrugged and replied, "No one ever does. That's life, Cardin."

"I know," he nodded. "But Reis is right, our world has turned upside down, more so than ever before. The future of everyone on Halarite rides on our shoulders."

She shook her head. "Stop that. Stop thinking about it like that. You aren't responsible for our entire world!"

He laughed and motioned towards the Sword strapped to his back. "I'm not so sure about that."

She rolled her eyes and squeezed his hands. "Just focus on the moment, Cardin. Focus on what is directly in front of you."

For a moment, neither of them spoke, they just gazed into one another's eyes. In that moment, he reached out with his senses, reached out to touch the magic that existed within her, and he felt his face warm and his pulse quicken. "I am," he said.

She blushed and smiled. "Good."

Reis sighed impatiently. "Would you two stop dancing around each other and just kiss already? This is embarrassing!"

Cardin's face grew hotter, and he looked at his friend apologetically. "Sorry."

Reis chuckled and clasped both of them on the shoulder. "You two never stopped loving each other, but if you had, I'd say you've fallen in love all over again. Stop pretending there's something keeping you apart."

When he looked back at Sira, she had a broad smile on her face. Reis was right. The time they had spent together since the Battle of Archanon, time spent on the Sea Wisp, fighting side by side on the beach... They had fallen in love with each other again. The look that she had in her eyes at that moment, the smile, the sense he felt from her when they connected, and the fact that she didn't push him out like she used to, all of the signs were there. She loved him.

Reis patted their shoulders, and said, "And on that note, I should leave you two alone to talk." He turned to leave, but before he could take even one step, a sudden wind stirred, and Cardin felt the surge of a portal.

Everyone turned to look at the source, and as expected, a silver light suddenly flashed outside the portcullis, and a moment later a portal appeared. Sira let go of Cardin's hands and everyone in the training grounds turned to see who the new arrivals would be.

To Cardin's surprise and relief, the first face to pass through was King Beredis's. "Your Majesty," someone shouted excitedly.

Cardin, Sira and Reis all hurried to greet him, and bowed before him as he cleared the portal. "King Beredis," Sira smiled, "Welcome to Daruun."

The King nodded his head and smiled. "Thank you, Sira. It has been too long since I visited."

Then to Cardin's chagrin, the Prince followed him. He still didn't like the kid, but he had learned to tolerate him and to show him the respect that protocol demanded. Cardin and the others bowed to the Prince, but he barely looked at them as he stalked past into the fortress.

Valkere stepped through next, which was also a relief to Cardin. That meant most of the leadership of the Alliance had survived the cataclysmic events. Although Sal'fe was still a bit of a wild card, the others present would most likely support him. Lorath was the only one left.

In the next moment, Cardin's heart leapt into his throat when another figure stepped through the portal. "Dad!"

His father, clad in a simple tunic and trousers with a sword strapped to his belt, saw Cardin, crossed the distance between them in a short bound, and pulled him into a tight hug. "Cardin!"

"No one's been able to get into Archanon," he spoke as he squeezed his father as hard as he could, afraid that if he let go, his father would vanish. "There's still smoke coming from inside."

"I know, I know," his father replied, and released his grip on Cardin. They both stepped away, but his father kept his hands on Cardin's arms. "We escaped into the catacombs just before the entrance was destroyed. We've been trying to find a way out ever since, and only a few minutes ago got out."

Yet another unexpected face appeared through the portal, but this time it was Elaria's voice who shouted in surprise, "Baenil!"

Baenil smiled and rushed past them all to greet Elaria and Ventelis.

"He did exactly what you asked him to," Draegus beamed. "He told the King about the impending invasion, but then he also saved our lives. He helped us navigate the catacombs, find an ancient underground city, and find a place where Master Valkere could create a portal and get us out safely."

Cardin smiled. "I'm glad he's been so willing to help, especially considering what he's been through."

Draegus smirked. "Careful who you say that to."

He frowned at his Father, but then glanced back towards where the Prince had stalked in. Draegus nodded and said, "Yeah. He has been less than pleasant towards Baenil."

Cardin rolled his eyes. Another Wizard had just passed through the portal, one Cardin didn't recognize. Then Eril, the Wizard they had asked to keep an eye on Archanon, followed through and the portal closed.

"Where is General Artula," Cardin asked.

"We don't know," Draegus said. "He was still commanding the army in the Wastelands before the meteorites fell."

Cardin sighed. "I was afraid you'd say that. His troops reported that he disappeared during the night. I had hoped he had reported back to Archanon."

His Father frowned at him. "I do not believe he would have left his command during such a dire situation. This is not good."

"No kidding," Cardin grimaced. "We need his leadership, and I was hoping for his support."

His father frowned at him, but then grinned. "Eril told us you wanted to gather all of the surviving Warriors and soldiers to fight the invading army."

"Yeah," Cardin felt his face turn warm.

Draegus clapped Cardin's arm and laughed. "You never cease to amaze me, Son."

"Thanks, I think."

Everyone filed back into the training grounds, but it was spacious and there was still plenty of room all around. Cardin, Sira, and Reis stayed near King Beredis, and when everyone settled down, they began to converse. The King filled them in on the ancient dwarven ruins and the kiklar, and Cardin listened in awe and amazement. It sounded like a great adventure, and he was sorry to have missed it. He hoped someday he could go down into the ancient city and explore, as well as help drive out the kiklar.

Then the King asked him and Sira what had happened on Trinil, so they filled him in. When they finished their story, Cardin felt like everyone was growing impatient. It had been a couple of hours since Danika had left for Sharenth.

Finally Valkere decided too much time had passed, and he suggested they send another Wizard to scout out Sharenth and find out what happened. Eril volunteered and left immediately. Cardin settled in for another long wait, but she returned only a few minutes later. When she stepped through the portal, her face was pale and she looked horrified.

The grounds grew deathly quiet, and waited for her report. She walked into the center, looked around, and then looked down at the ground. "Sharenth has been destroyed."

No one said anything. Everyone looked around at each other, confused, finding her statement difficult to comprehend.

Master Valkere was the first to break the chilling silence. "What exactly did you see?"

"There is nothing left. The city was leveled. The castle, the port, everything." She shuddered. "However, I do not believe it was a meteorite or a tidal wave. There are a few impact craters, but they are small."

"What else could demolish an entire city," King Beredis asked.

"I do not know," she replied. "But the magic in the area felt strange, warped." The haunted look in her eyes did not fade, and she simply stared at Valkere. "I have never felt anything like it before."

The implications were staggering, not just about the magic in the area feeling warped, but also that the capitol city of Sharenth was gone, and every single citizen, including the Saran King, were dead. It made Cardin feel weak, and his chest felt like a void ready to collapse in on itself.

"Could it have been from the undead," someone asked, Cardin did not know who.

He shook his head, "Not likely." All eyes turned on him, and he felt his stomach twist even more. However, this wasn't the first time he'd been in the spotlight, so he pushed past the feeling and stepped into the center. "Even if they have the power, their interest is in conquering Edilas, conquering all of Halarite, not destroying it, so that they may reclaim their place of power."

"Reclaim it from what," Queen Leian asked.

"Their world was destroyed during the dragons' civil war, some five thousand years ago." He met the gaze of every leader present, a habit he had picked up in the many times he had spoken at the Allied Council. "They want to rule over us, have servants to do their bidding. Destroying an entire city and all of its citizens would be counterproductive."

"He is right," Baenil spoke up. "Necromancers would have also left no corpses."

"There were corpses," Eril said quietly. "Not as many as there should have been, but they were charred beyond recognition, every single one of them."

"And necromancers are able to raise even skeletons, let alone charred corpses," Ventelis added.

King Beredis looked at the elf with a raised eyebrow. "You know of necromancy?"

"Yes," he nodded. "It has been practiced by many cultures across the universe, but it is difficult to learn. Its original intent was prophetic, the dead would be raised to tell the future." The elf looked sickened by the thought of it. "Some cultures believed this to be atrocious, while others thought it to be a legitimate use of the dead. In either case, over the millennia, it was perverted, and used to raise armies."

"Which is what we face now," Cardin said. "What destroyed Sharenth is a puzzle that we will need to solve, but the original reason for this meeting today must still be addressed."

"I have been told," Sal'fe said, "that you wish to gather an army to march upon Maradin, to attempt to defeat the necromancers today."

"That's right," Cardin nodded confidently. He didn't feel entirely confident in what he said, but he knew he could show no hesitation. They had to believe that he knew what he was doing.

"What of our cities, towns, and villages," Prince Beredis asked. "Have they not suffered enough without sending their loved ones to war?"

"War has come to Edilas," Cardin replied evenly. "We can't avoid that truth." He looked the Prince squarely in the eye, in a manner he hoped would tell the Prince that he would not back down today. "The enemy is on our shores, now. They have established a beachhead and will begin their invasion as soon as they have recovered."

"The necromancers have suffered losses as we have," Idann spoke up. Cardin clenched his jaw and ground his teeth when he heard the Daruun Guild Commander's voice. "They will take time to recover. We must look to our own cities and towns, our own people. Many were wounded in this cataclysm, and must be cared for. Our cities must be repaired or rebuilt. Plus without King Lorath or his General, organizing the Saran army will be all but impossible."

One of the Saran Guild Commanders, the one from the city of Alioth, spoke up, "I can help organize our Warriors and soldiers. They will listen to me in General Premin's name."

"That does not change the facts before us," Idann glared at the Alioth Commander. "It is an invading force and we are in a weakened state. We must close our cities up, repair defenses, and make a stand through traditional warfare."

"And what, let them lay siege to all of our cities," Cardin asked.

"We will be cut off from supplies, from farms beyond city walls. They can dam our rivers, destroy our fields, slaughter our animals. The undead do not eat or drink, they do not sleep, they do not get tired, they do not hesitate in their master's commands. Only the necromancers need to eat and drink. They will outlast us! Scouts have regularly reported back from Maradin, most of the necromancer army appears to have survived, and they are recovering weapons from their wrecked ships and the sea floor as we speak. For now they are contained to Maradin, but once they are ready, they will spread out.

"This is our chance!" He spoke passionately, and didn't even realize that he paced around the center, looking from one person to the next. "Our one and only chance to attack them while they are still in one place. We can surround Maradin, prevent them from leaving, and destroy them before they can harm another innocent again."

There was chatter amongst the gathered groups, but he could not tell how many were in favor of his plan and how many thought he was crazy. But as he spoke, he knew more than ever that he was right. "I'm asking you all to stand together again, to take the fight to the enemy on our terms, not theirs. I'm asking you all to trust me."

The first person he looked at after that was King Beredis, who smiled at Cardin and nodded. "I agree with the Keeper of the Sword." He knew the King's use of his title was intentional. "Tal will take the fight to the necromancers."

"The Wizards will stand with the Keeper," Valkere planted his staff firmly before him for dramatic effect. "We can prevent the necromancers from creating portals and escaping. We must take advantage of this opportunity."

To Cardin's surprise, Sal'fe was next to voice his support. "I agree. Falind will join battle with our neighbors to fight the undead before they can take one more step onto Edilas."

"Erien stands with the keeper," Queen Leian stated. "We will fight with the Alliance. With the Keeper of the Sword."

All eyes fell upon the Guild Commander from Alioth, the man's name coming to him only moments before he asked, "Commander Asil?"

The Alioth Commander nodded, "We will also stand with you. Our losses from Sharenth are," he hesitated, "staggering. But Alioth has the second largest regiment of Warriors in Saran, and we have many scattered throughout the smaller towns and villages. With the help of the Wizards, we could bring a formidable army to this battle in short order."

"And it must be in short order," Cardin nodded, and then addressed everyone. "We do not have much time left before the undead march. Our combined forces will need to move out quickly, and I do not anticipate this to be a long, drawn out battle. Sira told me the walls of Maradin were breached by meteorites, and the Wizards could easily create new breaches, so this will not become a siege."

"Which means we must not tarry upon gathering supplies," General Zilan spoke up for the first time in the meeting. He looked at Queen Leian for permission to continue, and she nodded. "I recommend we leave soldiers in the cities to defend against looters, or other unforeseen dangers, while the Warriors in every city, town, and village should take up arms and armor at once, without hesitation."

Cardin nodded his thanks to the General for his support, and said, "We should gather in the fields east of Daruun, there is plenty of open space for the army to assemble. Once we are ready, we can coordinate our departure for Maradin."

"I have a map of the area," Lieutenant Kellis spoke up and pushed his way into the center.

"We can use it to designate areas for each group to gather," Zilan met Kellis in the center. Cardin noticed that Idann looked less than pleased with Kellis, and he knew the Lieutenant would likely take a severe dressing down for supporting Cardin.

Cardin looked at Valkere and asked, "Are the Wizards willing to help us gather this army?"

"Of course," Valkere nodded. "We will do whatever we can to assist."

He smiled at the Grand Master. He had not expected the full support of each and every leader, certainly not from Sal'fe.

Now he just had to make sure that their trust wasn't misplaced.

Chapter 37

THE BATTLE FOR MARADIN

It was a sight that Reis never would have thought to see in all of his life. East of Daruun, the rolling hills were brimming with armed Warriors and Wizards ready to go to war. Mere hours had passed since Cardin had rallied the leaders of the Alliance, and now he stood in the assembly area closest to Daruun, along with every Warrior from his home town.

Anila stood next to him, as quiet as ever. She wasn't a Warrior, but she had decided that she wanted to fight alongside all of them. He had come to rely on her presence, as strange as that sounded even to himself. She was his friend, and he was grateful for her presence.

He realized that part of that was because she was like him, she had no powers. He had been friends with Sira and Cardin since childhood, but he always felt like an outcast, the only one without magic. That feeling intensified when Cardin and Sira fell in love with each other, and now that they were falling in love again, his feelings of exclusion returned.

He would never admit that to them, he felt guilty for even thinking it. That was probably why he felt drawn to Anila. She was at least as skilled as he was, and he could relate to her. Furthermore, she was one of the most trusted guardians of the Covenant of the

Order of the Ages. Neither Cardin nor Sira believed much in the core beliefs of the Order, but he still did.

Reis looked at Anila, but she didn't seem to notice and simply stared out across the field of troops. She seemed to study the armies, to study the Warriors and Wizards and how they interacted and how they prepared for battle.

"I never thought to see an army like this," he spoke to her.

She opened her mouth to say something, then seemed to think better of it and closed her mouth. Her eyes narrowed and she looked at him. "No, I suppose not."

His curiosity got the better of him, and he asked, "Why did you insist on joining us?" Reis then hastily said, "Not that I don't want you here, but I mean, you don't have to be. You're a guardian of the Covenant."

"And this is a threat to the Covenant as much as anyone else," she said simply. It wasn't the answer he had hoped for, and he wondered at that thought. He realized he had hoped she would say she stayed for him.

Unsure what to say next, he stumbled with his words a little. "I see. Well, your skills in battle will certainly be welcome. I mean, I've seen you fight briefly a couple of times now, you can certainly handle yourself, and the more people we have to fight against the undead, the better. That sword of yours is something else, too," he wasn't sure where she had obtained a new sword from, but it was almost identical to the one that was taken from her on Trinil. "You're able to easily cut their heads off. And arms. And legs. And, well, anything else, I suppose."

Her face slowly turned to a frown as he continued to talk, and she seemed almost uncomfortable by his sudden rambling. "Is something wrong," she interrupted him.

"Uh, no," he shook his head. "Nothing at all."

She tilted her head to one side, and then shook her head. "No, something is going on. What is it?"

He felt his face grow warm, so he shook his head and looked away. "Seriously, it's nothing."

For a moment he stood still in uncomfortable silence. Then he was surprised when he felt her lightly touch his arm. Light being relative, considering he felt it through leather and chainmail armor.

"I think I know what is going on," she said. He looked at her, hoping for a smile, but was greeted by that same stoic face. "I am afraid I am not very good at this sort of thing."

"What sort of thing?" he asked nervously.

"People in general," she looked down. "But also interpersonal interaction on a more," she hesitated, "well, personal level."

He nodded, "Which would explain why you often hang back in the shadows, and don't talk to people."

"Exactly," she nodded, her eyes still averted from his.

He debated whether or not to ask her what was on her mind, until he glanced out at the assembled army and decided there was nothing to lose. "So why did you talk to me during the voyage? Why aren't you hidden in the crowd? Why are you here, ready to fight side by side with me?"

He swore her face turned a little pink, but that could have been due to the cold winter breeze that swept across the field. "You're not like the others," she said. Then she looked at him, and said, "I don't know how else to say it, or to tell you how exactly you are different. You just are."

"Thanks," he said with a frown. "I think."

She smiled, one of the few times he'd ever seen her smile. "It was meant as a compliment." But then her smile vanished. "I don't deserve the friendship, the companionship you've given me over the last few days."

A frown crossed Ries's face. "Why do you say that?"

She averted her eyes again. "Because." He impatiently waited for her to say more. "Reis, I am not who you think I am."

He raised a curious eyebrow. "In what way?"

"In every way. Or at least, in one way that counts more than any other."

He grew frustrated by her cryptic response. "Could you be more specific?"

Before she could answer, Lieutenant Kellis blew into the horn of Daruun, signaling everyone to form up. The Lieutenant stood before the assembled Daruun army along with Idann and Cardin. Idann still commanded the Tal Warriors' Guild, but Cardin essentially would be the one out front, and it would be the Daruun Warriors that would lead the charge.

"Just, I am," she struggled with her words, and then started to walk away to form up. He jogged to catch up, but she shook her head. "There's no time to talk about this anymore. We'll talk after the battle."

At least she believes we're both going to make it out of this alive, he thought with a half-smile. "Alright," he assented. "But I'm going to hold you to that."

She didn't acknowledge him, and simply took up a position in the front row of the battle formation. He stood next to her, and then noticed that Sira came up on the other side of him. He smiled at her, but her eyes were fixed on Cardin.

Yep, he thought. *They definitely are in love again.*

It looked strange, seeing Cardin standing next to Idann, and he could tell that Idann didn't enjoy the situation. Reis inwardly smiled, and then waited.

"The hour is at hand," Kellis shouted as he came up next to Cardin. "Draw swords!"

As Reis and all other Warriors drew their weapons, several Wizards came around from the peripheral and formed a line in front of them. Reis remembered the tactic, it had been used seven months ago to attack the Falind Warriors on the Great Road, and then had been used again several times during the campaign against the orcs. Every other Wizard in the line would create a portal in front of them, and then the Wizards in between them would rush through the portal to fend off anything in front of the portals on the other side. The assembled Warriors would rush through behind them, and then the creators of the portals would follow last.

Queen Leian hadn't been too pleased with what was going to happen after they passed through into the desert outside of Maradin. Scouts had reported that there were only a couple of holes in Maradin's walls, which meant that for the army to effectively breach the city, more holes needed to be punched through. They would not have time to form up once they were through the portals. The Wizards would do their job, and then all would rush into the city to attack the necromancers and the undead army, hopefully unprepared.

"I know you're all afraid," Cardin shouted. Idann scowled and rolled his eyes. "Remember that the undead will show no mercy, no fear, no regret, so do not hesitate! Their heads must be severed or destroyed, that is the only way to kill them. If you see a necromancer, be cautious, for they are powerful. But if they can be killed, we will severely weaken their ability to fight."

That was a topic of discussion during the planning phase of the battle ahead. The Wizards and the elves did not know exactly what would happen to the undead when the necromancers were killed. They would either lose their unnatural life and fall to the ground, or they would simply become distracted and aimless, still a threat, but uncoordinated and disorganized. Either way, necromancers were the key targets.

Reis wondered about Elaria, and realized he hadn't seen much of her since they had returned to Edilas. Was she avoiding him? He looked around, but then was surprised to notice that she had taken up position next to Anila. She also had no obligation to fight, but she was drawn to Cardin, as she always had been. Both of her daggers were drawn, her cloak was left somewhere in Daruun, and her leather scale armor matched the color of the pale sand in and around Maradin.

"Remember what we fight for," Cardin continued. "Remember that if we fail here today, we will have paved the way for them to invade our homes! Fight today not just for yourselves, but for your families, your homes, your kingdoms!"

He looked to Dalin, who was one of the Wizards that had assembled in front of them, and nodded. He held an ash wood staff, a temporary one obtained from the Wizards' Guild until he could either recover his own or, more likely, craft a new one in haste. The Wizard raised his staff into the air, and a magical, extraordinarily bright flare shot up into the sky. That was the sign to begin.

Reis's pulse raced, and he held firmly to his sword. His bronze-dyed sword was taken by the necromancers, so the one he brandished now was a borrowed two-handed weapon. It was one of Veral Adas's latest forged weapons, and he couldn't ask for better craftsmanship, but he still missed his own weapon.

As planned, half of the Wizards turned on the spot, and planted their staves firmly in the grass. There was a sudden rushing wind when several portals flashed into existence, which likewise happened all across the field in front of every single Warrior contingent assembled. Hundreds of portals formed by hundreds of Wizards, all to pre-coordinated locations surrounding Maradin.

Never having known what magic felt like, Reis could only begin to imagine what that kind of sudden power surge must have felt like to the necromancers. Hopefully they would fear it.

"Now!" Cardin shouted, and then he turned and ran with the front line of Wizards towards the portals.

"Warriors, charge!" Idann ordered.

With his heart pounding in his chest, Reis rushed towards the portal in front of him. Cardin and the lead Wizards all vanished into the portals just as Reis passed through the back line of Wizards. Idann ran just ahead of him, Kellis ahead of Sira. Within seconds their leaders were through the portal, and seconds later, he followed without hesitation.

They had timed their attack well, and it was well past midday in Maradin, putting the sun at their backs. That would give them another advantage against the undead, he hoped.

The city wall lay ahead only a thousand feet, and was mostly intact, but he could see at least one breach from a grazing meteorite ahead of them. No smoke rose from the city, and that was probably due to the wave having put out any fires the meteorites had caused.

Cardin and the front line of Wizards continued to run ahead of them, and he felt some amount of surprise that Cardin didn't use his powers to rush ahead of the Wizards. His friend finally understood the need to work together!

They did not stop their charge, and he felt encouraged by the fact that they were still unchallenged. There were no undead on the city wall to watch for an attack, the necromancers probably never even considered the possibility. Despite the fact that the allied army had been scattered in the fields of Daruun, their assault was well coordinated, and as he glanced to his left and right, he saw that their army now surrounded the city and closed in quickly from all sides except from the sea.

Suddenly Cardin and the Wizards all stopped at once. Cardin was slightly ahead of them, and while the Wizards worked together to build up charges at distinct intervals, Cardin simply leapt forward and jabbed the Sword towards the main gates. A bright blast of blue-white energy shot out of the Sword and slammed into the doors. In an explosion as loud as a meteorite, the door shattered inward.

The Wizards finished concentrating their power and released their own attacks. It was as if a thunderstorm had released two dozen bolts of lightning, the claps of thunder were deafening and set Reis's teeth chattering. The walls exploded at regular intervals into the city, and he knew that several of the undead would be smashed by the debris. He hoped some of the necromancers also met their demise.

He could only imagine what it looked like from within, as if the city walls had betrayed them and everything came crashing down on them. He found himself laughing at the thought, but either no one heard his laugh, or no one paid him any attention.

They had caught up to the line of Wizards, but the caster's first task was done, so they and Cardin took up the charge again. Reis was just behind his friend by no more than a few yards. Sira let out a battle cry that spurred the entire army to follow suit, and Reis joined in. They reached the holes in the wall and clambered over the rubble and into the ruined city.

From the main entrance, he could see the entire city, and he was surprised that many of the buildings remained intact, even if greatly damaged.

What surprised him even more, however, was the number of undead that stood, armed, filling the streets, standing atop some of the buildings, elbow to elbow. They hadn't caught the enemy off guard after all.

That didn't stop them. Cardin raced forward, and the Sword flared. He swung it, releasing a wave of destructive energy. Buildings exploded, undead were completely pulverized, but only those in the front rows.

The necromancers had raised shields, strong enough to absorb or deflect most of Cardin's attack, and in the end, only the closest row of buildings were toppled and the first few lines of undead destroyed. The necromancers were prepared.

The Wizards unleashed their own volley of magic. Fire, ice, arcane blasts, bolts of lightning, they picked off the undead in waves, but the necromancer shields saved their own skins.

The Wizards and the Warriors continued their charges undaunted, and the Wizards continued to attack, hopeful that they could weaken the shields or bring down some of the necromancers. Then, as was the plan, several yards before the Wizards reached the line of undead, they stopped and allowed the Warriors to pass by. Wizards could hold their own in a pitched battle, but they were not experienced in close-quarters combat and certainly not in melee, so they left that to the experienced Warriors.

Cardin did not stop, which Reis expected, and almost literally threw himself into the line of undead.

Then the allied army overtook the enemy front line like a wave crashing into the shore, and Reis let out another battle cry as he swung his sword. It was parried by one of the undead, but he let his momentum carry him into the decaying soldier and toppled it over. If he hadn't worn his chainmail armor, the undead's sword would have cut his arm, but he was uninjured.

He left that enemy soldier for someone behind him and continued his charge into the enemy, swinging his sword, blocking attempts to strike him and managing to get in a few blows of his own.

Before long, his momentum was stopped, the mass of undead was too much. He shoved one of the enemy soldiers away from him, and then swung his sword at another, successfully disarming it.

He didn't know where Cardin was, and he couldn't see Sira, but several other Warriors were around him, and the battle quickly turned into chaos. He searched for a necromancer to face, but every time he saw one and moved towards it, more undead would stand in his way and he would have to face off against them.

Reis moved with the battle, found that as he worked his way through the enemy soldiers, he had little control over where he went. Before he could do anything about it, he was suddenly deep within the city, and surrounded by the undead.

One of the Warriors nearest him was suddenly cut down by two enemies, and that incensed him. He charged at the enemies and swung his sword, decapitating one. The other was fast and managed to block his swing, but he didn't relent, he kept at it, kept pushing the undead back, until he was able to cut off its arm, and then its head. He turned towards the fallen Warrior, only to find that the Warrior stood again, but with glowing blue eyes. He was a servant of the enemy now.

Unfortunately the fallen Warrior was a Mage, and he used his powers to slam Reis into the ground from afar. It's attack wasn't as strong as it could have been, but it was enough to knock the wind out of him. The soldier was on top of him in seconds, but as it raised its sword to strike down on him, its hands were severed by a slender, curved blade. Anila then swung again, and neatly cut the former Mage's head off.

"Come on, get up," she shouted. He took her offered hand, and then they stood back to back and found that they were surrounded, without a single ally in sight. He smirked at the undead soldiers, and then he and Anila attacked.

There were several close calls, but he managed to fend off several of them. More than once, he and Anila came to each other's rescue.

Before they knew what was happening, they found themselves facing off against one of the necromancers. There were still no other Warriors or Wizards nearby, so it was just them against the one necromancer. He looked almost as old as the five that had sat in the thrones in the ruined necromancer city, and as he smiled at them, the creases and wrinkles in his face grew deeper.

Anila suddenly shoved Reis out of the way as a blast of magic shot out at them. He rolled with his momentum, was on his feet in moments and charged at the necromancer. The old man raised his rod and deflected Reis's attack with a magic shield, and then, moving faster than Reis thought possible for his age, he spun around and physically blocked Anila's attack.

They worked together to fight the necromancer, pushing him further and further back with each blow. Recognizing that he couldn't possibly contend with them alone and that they would eventually wear him down, the necromancer must have silently commanded necromancers to his aid. Several came barreling around a corner and charged right at them.

Reis exchanged looks with Anila, and then he broke off to fight the reinforcements while Anila continued to attack the necromancer. Three of them attacked him at once, but he ducked and maneuvered between them, relying on his speed and agility as he always did against Mages.

He cut into the side of one, disarmed another, and then took out the leg of the third. The one he had cut into the side was undaunted by his attack, and swung at Reis, but he deflected the swing and jabbed into the enemy's abdomen. He knew it wouldn't stop the soldier, but it temporarily immobilized it, which gave Reis a moment to consider his next move.

Anila didn't give him time. Even while fighting the necromancer, she spun around and swung her curved blade, neatly cutting off his opponent's head. He pulled his sword out of the slain enemy as it fell, but the necromancer took advantage of Anila's distraction and used magic to send her flying against one of the half-destroyed buildings.

Reis used the necromancer's distraction to his own advantage, and sliced his sword from his lower left to upper right and cut deep into the necromancer's chest. He staggered back, looked down at his own blood, and fell back.

Satisfied that they were safe for the moment, Reis hurried to Anila's side as she groaned and picked herself up. Reis was surprised that she was still conscious, he hadn't thought anyone could have stayed awake after that kind of blow!

"You ok?"

"Yeah," she grimaced. "I'm going to be feeling that one later." Her eyes grew wide and she shoved him down and followed him. A powerful blast of magic flew over them and demolished the wall she was thrown into moments ago. Tiny pieces of stone pelted them, and then the wall began to collapse. Reis rolled with Anila out of the way as dust billowed out and the wall collapsed right where they had been.

They sprang to their feet, weapons ready, and searched for their assailant. It was the necromancer they had just slain, now risen back from the dead.

"Oh that's just not fair," he groaned.

The necromancer shoved its casting rod towards them again, but this time they both saw it coming and dodged the blast of magic. Behind them, another section of a building exploded. "Careful, it looks like he's even more powerful now," Anila warned.

The man's eyes glowed eerily, brighter than most of the undead they'd faced, and he smirked. Did he retain some of his personality?

The necromancer drew back, and the casting rod glowed a bright blue. Anila's eyes grew wide, and Reis knew that a wave was coming, a wave that he doubted he could dodge if it was as powerful as he feared.

Anila stepped in front of him and raised her hand up. The undead unleashed the blast of magic, but the blast was absorbed by a shield cast in front of Anila. Reis felt his heart skip a beat, and the world stopped for a second. She had cast magic?!

The blast from the necromancer dissipated, and the shield disappeared, but there was no mistaking what she had done. She turned her head towards Reis, and they locked eyes for a moment. She was a Mage!

Or so he initially thought. When she turned back towards the undead, she didn't raise her sword, and instead simply kept her hand towards the undead. The necromancer tilted its head in unthinking confusion, and before it could consider another move, a blast of violet energy shot out from her palm and slammed into the undead square in the forehead. It flew back, or rather its head did, and its body simply fell back lifelessly.

The battle raged around them, but for that moment in time, no other necromancers or undead approached them. Sullenly, she turned back to him and looked into his eyes. He felt his stomach twist, and his head swam.

She had lied to him. She wasn't just a skilled combatant, she was a Mage. No, not just a Mage, no Mage could have done what she had just done. Only moments passed, but the look they exchanged felt like it lasted an eternity.

A look of guilt crossed her face, and she averted her eyes for a moment. He didn't know what to say, what to think, or what to do. She had kept it a secret from him. From everyone.

Finally, she looked into his eyes, and said, "I'm sorry. Please don't tell anyone." She glanced at an undead that charged at her silently. She easily side-stepped it and sliced its head off as it stumbled past her. "I will explain later, I promise."

She then left him there, walked away with her sword held low. Her leather, form-fitting armor was splashed with the blood of the living and the dead, her short hair had dried mud in it, and somehow the whole scene seemed surreal to him.

Moments later, he was snapped out of his thoughts when two more undead attacked him. He wasn't sure where the anger came from, but for the rest of the battle, he fought with a fury he had never known before.

Chapter 38

AVATAR

As the battle raged on, Cardin realized that he had lost track of Sira, Reis and Dalin. At first he panicked, but he drew in a deep breath and reminded himself that they were battle-seasoned veterans.

A grin stretched across his face when he realized that this gave him an advantage. With no other Warriors or Wizards near him, he used his powers with only mild restraint. It made fighting the undead easier. He usually didn't kill them, except for the occasional one he was able to behead, but otherwise they were blown away, parts of their bodies mutilated or mangled, rendering them less of a threat to him and the Allies.

The challenge came from the necromancers. None of them were as powerful as Tiresis, but he felt the incredible power behind each of their attacks. He didn't recognize any of them as the four remaining leaders, but he knew that they were the greatest threat, and he wanted to find them and end the battle quickly.

Cardin lost track of time has he engaged one enemy after another. The hardest part was when he came across undead bearing Tal, Falind, Saran, or Erien tabards. His allies were falling, and the necromancers raised them up to replace their own fallen ranks. They were the threat, not the undead!

So it was then that he decided to stop fighting the undead in general, and he focused entirely on finding necromancers. He crouched low, gathered energy into his legs, and leapt up onto one of the half-destroyed buildings. There he found undead archers, but he casually swept them off of the roof with magic, beheaded the one closest to him, and sought out his next target.

He immediately saw another necromancer a half block away. He gathered energy into the Sword and jabbed it towards his opponent. The necromancer anticipated his attack and deflected his magic without looking. The building next to the target took the brunt of the damage and one of its walls exploded into pieces, some of which smacked into the unassuming necromancer and knocked him onto his stomach.

Cardin took advantage of his opponent's disorientation and leapt as close to his opponent as he could. He dispatched a few hapless undead as he stalked towards the necromancer, but his opponent was fast and used his casting rod to fire a blast of green magic at Cardin.

He instinctively raised a shield and deflected the blast into one of the undead, tearing the enemy soldier apart. The necromancer was on his feet and used the rod to block Cardin's physical attack, but when the Sword met the rod, it cut through cleanly and embedded deep into the necromancer's shoulder. His opponent looked at the Sword in surprise, and then fell down, dead.

He knew the necromancer could rise again, so Cardin quickly severed his opponent's head. It should have bothered him, cutting an already-defeated opponent's head off, but he knew it was the only way to keep the enemy down.

Knowing there was nothing he could do but fight on, he looked for another necromancer, but never got a chance to find one. An impossibly loud, teeth-chattering roar pierced the air. He nearly dropped the Sword when he tried to cover his ears. The roar was long and drawn out, and he felt incredibly relieved when it stopped.

The sounds of clashing weapons and exploding magic ceased, and he realized that everyone on both sides stopped fighting. All eyes looked to the east, where the roar had come from. A shadow descended through a tuft of cloud, the sight instantly chilling Cardin's stomach. Its size was impossible to judge at distance, but as it drew closer, it realized that it was enormous.

Something in the back of his mind stirred, a sensation he had not felt before, one which immediately twisted his stomach. He felt the presence of the approaching creature. A cold darkness grew inside of him, one that threatened to consume him, but it didn't just come from the monster. Whatever it was, it came from within himself.

The monster drew close enough that he was able to identify its shape, and he felt his jaw drop. It was a dragon! And based on its color and what he sensed from it, he feared that it was not a Star Dragon coming to save the day and end their war, as they had done seven months ago.

The dragon reached the shoreline and turned sharply to circle the city, its shadow passing over them all. It slowed considerably, but remained aloft as it circled Maradin and looked down at them. The battle seemed forgotten for a moment as all stared in unison. Somewhere nearby, Cardin heard a necromancer shout, "It is the prophesied one!"

After its second orbit around the city, the dragon pumped its wings and flew higher, and then it folded its wings and came crashing down upon the main gate, crushing the frame to the foundation and shaking the ground beneath the entire city. The dragon was taller than the palace!

Whatever or whoever the dragon was, Cardin knew it was there for him. Or more likely the Sword of Dragons. So he leapt off of the roof and marched towards it.

The undead did not move out of his way, but he dared not start the battle again, so he weaved in between them. The dragon looked down upon them all, regarded them with soulless red eyes. Its eyes were not starlight, and that was another clue to him that it was not a Star Dragon.

It was a Dark Dragon. He didn't know how it was possible, but he knew it was the truth

One thing the dragon had in common with the Star Dragons was that it did not speak with its mouth. It spoke through its mind with a dreadful, terrible voice that sent pins and needles up and down his back. *"Where is the one who keeps the Sword of Dragons?"*

Cardin continued unfazed. He took in a deep breath, knew that he probably wasn't ready for what was about to come, but also knew that he had no choice. "I am the Keeper of the Sword," he shouted.

The undead and a couple of the nearby necromancers looked to him, startled.

The Dark Dragon's eyes focused on him, and he felt them penetrate his soul. He felt the monster connect to him, and the feeling he had sensed moments before suddenly exploded. The Dark Dragon linked with him, and he felt its soul probe his.

In a panicked moment, he pushed it out of his head, out of his very being, violently. The dragon recoiled as if shocked and in pain. It eyed him curiously. *"You are the second one I have met today who could do that to me. Very curious."*

Cardin hesitated at the Dark Dragon's words. A second one?

He continued to approach the creature and passed the front line, surrounded by allies who parted for him. Sira was suddenly beside him, walking as if she had always been there. He looked at her, ready to give her a signal to leave his side so that the Dark Dragon wouldn't hurt her, but she simply stared resolutely up at the shadowed monster. If she felt fear, she did not show it. She wasn't going to leave him, not for anything.

The dark cold that had formed in his chest lessened, enough to make him smile. He looked back up at the dragon and asked, "Who are you?"

The dragon considered him for a moment, and then spoke, *"I am Nuuldan. I am the first Dark Dragon."*

Cardin felt a cold pit form in his stomach. "But you were all destroyed," he raised the Sword up, "by this. Three thousand years ago."

They reached the edge of the troops, and they were suddenly alone, standing a few hundred feet in front of Nuuldan.

That is, they were alone until Reis stepped out from the crowd and stood on the other side of Cardin. He looked at Reis, who seemed distant and angry, but resolute. A moment later, Dalin emerged from the crowd as well and stepped up next to Sira.

He was not alone.

"I was defeated by the Star Dragons long before that," Nuuldan spoke. Its mental voice sounded amused, as if the four that now stood before him was a jester's act. *"The star we battled over exploded, and destroyed the world we flew above. Pieces of which crashed to your world today, pieces that I floated beside in the void between worlds. Pieces of their world,"* it motioned its snout further into the city.

Cardin looked back, and saw beyond the Warriors and Wizards only undead and necromancers. That's when he realized what it meant, the prophecy that Tiresis spoke of. He turned back to Nuuldan, as part of the prophecy played through his memory again. *A shattered world shall return to its people; darkness and fire will descend.* One of the necromancers, a leader, had followed him and stood at the edge of the crowd, but did not dare cross into the open. "The meteorites that fell to Halarite last night," Cardin said to the necromancer. "They were pieces of your world."

"Of course," she replied with a smile. "The prophecy has come true, but in an unexpected way." She suddenly fell to her knees before Nuuldan. "Great one, a prophecy told us that on this day, one would come to lead our people. That one is you, it must be!"

Nuuldan huffed, and laughed down at the necromancer. *"Lead your people? I have no time for humans. Your world was to be conquered and ruled by the Dark Dragons."*

The necromancer looked up in shock, eliciting further laughter. "But the prophecy," she started.

"I know nothing of your prophecy," it growled. *"I have remained on this world for one reason only. The Sword of Dragons,"* he looked directly at Cardin, his eyes glowing brighter. *"Give it to me, or I shall destroy your world."*

Cardin frowned and looked at Dalin, who gave him a cautious look. He sensed that Dalin felt as powerless as Cardin. He looked back into the dragon's eyes and asked, "What good would it do you? You can't physically wield it."

"My reasons are my own," Nuuldan replied. He took a menacing step closer to Cardin, his giant, clawed paw only a dozen yards away. *"Give me the Sword, now."*

Cardin knew very little about the Civil War, about the Dark Dragons, and most of it was second hand knowledge from Dalin. However, it was enough for him to know that he could not, under any circumstances, let Nuuldan or any other Dark Dragon have the Sword.

So he stepped ahead of his companions defiantly. His hands shook, but he knew that it would be up to him, and him alone, to protect everyone. "No. Leave this world now. It is under my protection."

Once again Nuuldan laughed, throwing his head back in a surprisingly human-like gesture. *"You think I fear you?"*

"Yes," Cardin said with more courage than he felt. The dragon looked at him in surprise. "The Sword of Dragons was constructed specifically to destroy Dark Dragons and end your war with the Star Dragons, and it succeeded. Now, three thousand years later, it can do it again."

Nuuldan snorted defiantly. *"I sense no more power within you than any others present. You are nothing to me!"*

Cardin took a few more steps forward. He stared resolutely at the dragon. "I will not give you the Sword."

The dragon stared back at Cardin, and he felt it try to probe his thoughts and soul again, but he was able to resist. *"Then you will die."*

Cardin felt the strange sensation at the back of his head again, but it did not come from the Dark Dragon. It came from within him, as if the same power that the Dark Dragon wielded was within him. This allowed him to sense the sudden shift of power as the dragon drew his head back and a red glow appeared within his half-open mouth.

Suddenly Nuuldan thrust his head towards him and a wide beam of red energy lanced out at Cardin. In an instant, he raised a shield not just big enough to protect himself, but large enough to keep everyone behind him, both armies, safe.

The blast slammed into him like a war hammer! He had never dreamt such force and power could be brought to bear, and it ate away at his powers like they were kindling in a fire, as if the Dark Dragon's powers cancelled his. He drew in more magic, fought to keep his shield up, used every bit of mental strength he had to keep it going, but the dragon had a seemingly inexhaustible amount of energy, and the beam did not cease.

Moments later, he couldn't keep the shield up any longer, and he knew he was dead. The shield faded, but so too did the beam of energy. When the last of his energy was spent, the dragon ceased his attack. Seconds passed in silence, and Cardin fell to his knees as the Dark Dragon stared him down. Sira came to his side and held onto his shoulders. At the edge of where Cardin's shield extended to, deep gouges were burned into the ground, and smoke stung his nostrils.

Sira held on to him with both hands, "Are you okay? Cardin!"

He shook his head, and then looked at her. "I don't know what just happened..."

"You wield only the power of the stars, human," Nuuldan laughed. *"I*

wield something greater, something far more terrible." Cardin looked up at it as it stared down at him in glee. *"I have no desire to search for the Sword in what is left of this city after I destroy it. Give it to me now, and I will spare your people."*

Cardin shook his head and, with Sira's help, stood up. "Like you did Sharenth? You were the one who destroyed it, weren't you?"

"You cannot protect everyone. I will destroy this entire city, this entire world if you do not give me the Sword!"

He shook his head defiantly and gently pushed Sira back. "I can protect them. And I will."

The feeling in the back of his mind flared again, and this time grew stronger, and stronger. Something stirred within him, and for a moment he felt as if his thoughts and feelings suddenly went to war with one another, as if two powers within him twisted and fought one another. It was overwhelming, and he almost collapsed to his knees again, trying desperately to push the new power out of himself.

He didn't have time to. Nuuldan accepted his defiance, and decided to end the conversation. The dragon drew its head back again, charged up its dark magic, and let loose another blast, much larger and more powerful than the previous one.

Cardin didn't know how, but he raised a shield. Only this wasn't a shield of normal magic. He didn't know where the power came from, or how it worked, but it met the beam of energy from the Dark Dragon and did not waver. The shield was not white or blue like all previous ones he had summoned, but was blackened, and seemed to absorb all of the light around it. Bolts of black lightning lanced out from the point of impact. Pieces of the city wall and nearby buildings exploded from a shockwave.

There was still pressure on his mind, but the energy he felt within seemed empowered by something new, not an addition of energy, but an absence. Absence and presence, working together somehow within him. If he had had time to think about it, it would have confused him, but all he knew was that thousands of Warriors and Wizards stood behind him, and if his shield failed, not only would he die, but so would they.

He pushed with all of his strength, pushed harder and harder, focused, thought about nothing else. He could win, he knew he could. He had to.

The onslaught continued, the dragon's energy seemed

inexhaustible. The shield held, but Cardin began to feel himself waver. *No,* he thought. *I won't give in! I can't!*

The effort became increasingly difficult, and fatigue clawed at him. The new power wasn't enough to contend with such an ancient and powerful monster. His determination did not fade, but it couldn't summon more strength.

"No," he said to himself. "No…" He closed his eyes, and an image of Sira appeared in his mind. An image from his dreams, when the darkness engulfed the world, and took her away from him. "NO!"

And just when his powers were about to fail, and all was to end, his soul exploded in power, and the shield he had put up condensed and shot through Nuuldan's attack to smash full-force into him. A bright white light flared, and Nuuldan sprawled backwards out of the city limits into the sands to the west. He landed on his back, but the white flash had not faded.

It moved. It floated out over the wall, and then stopped between Maradin and Nuuldan. A moment later, the flash coalesced into a new shape. The shape of a dragon.

Before everyone's eyes, a dragon of white and black appeared, and stood between those whom Cardin loved and the one who threatened them all.

It was the dragon from Cardin's dreams! Its scales were mostly white, but the harder scales on its underside were black, as were its spikes and other areas of accent on its body. It was slender and muscular, its snout long and ferocious, and it looked ready for battle.

More than that, Cardin could feel its presence. Not like he could sense Endri or the other Star Dragons, but as if the dragon was a part of him, and he a part of it. This wasn't a Star Dragon. And given the power he felt within himself, and within the new dragon, it did not just wield the same magic that Star Dragons wielded. It commanded dark magic. Absence and presence realized within a single entity.

Nuuldan slowly rose to his feet, and that was when Cardin realized that he didn't just look at the Dark Dragon through his own eyes, but also through the eyes of the black and white dragon. He watched Nuuldan tilt his head and stare in wonder at the newcomer.

"What are you," Nuuldan asked, a slight tremor of fear in his words.

Without a word, the dragon leapt at Nuuldan and reached out white paws with black claws to strike, but Nuuldan was surprisingly quick for his size and backed out of range. The new dragon was smaller than Nuuldan, but not by much, and was just as quick.

Nuuldan swiped back at it, but missed, and the newcomer thrust forward and sunk its teeth into Nuuldan's leg. The Dark Dragon roared in pain and surprise, but with the new dragon attached to his leg, he was able to swing it around and send the newcomer flying. It sprawled to the sandy ground, crushing several cacti that was harmless against its thick scales, and was back on its feet in moments. All of this Cardin saw from its perspective, and he realized that although it had a mind of its own, it did what Cardin wanted it to. It finally dawned on him what had happened – he had summoned the black and white dragon!

Nuuldan took to flight, his black wings spread out in a terrible shadow, and he launched another attacked from his mouth. Cardin's dragon blocked it with a shield, and then leapt into the air as well. It spread its wings, and Cardin felt his wings catch the air and lift him up! It exhilarated him, his heart pounding in unison with the wings.

Now it was his turn. Cardin charged up pure white magic, a white glow grew within the newcomer's mouth, and he unleashed a beam of energy at his enemy. Nuuldan erected a black shield, but just as he had initially done to Cardin, the white light cancelled out Nuuldan's shield, and it pushed through and slammed into the Dark Dragon's chest. He somersaulted backwards once, but then caught the wind again and pumped his wings hard to pick up speed and dodge another blast of magic.

Cardin flew up to meet his opponent mid-air, but missed as it flew past him, so he banked around and pumped his wings as hard as he could to follow Nuuldan. The Dark Dragon was agile in the air, exceedingly so, and managed to double back before Cardin knew what was going on. Another attack lanced out, but Cardin knew it was coming and was able to twist his wings and dodge the blast. The red beam strayed into the heart of Maradin and destroyed an entire block in a roaring explosion.

The two battled above the city, rising higher and higher as they pumped their wings to try to gain the high ground over one another. Stray blasts lanced out from both of them, some went harmlessly into the sky, while others hit the ocean or the ground not far from Maradin. Higher they rose, and their attacks became more vicious as they tried to outdo each other, tried to just hit one another at least once.

Another stray blast, this time from Cardin, hit no more than a hundred yards from Maradin, gouging a large crater into the desert and sending a cloud of sand and dirt into the air. He realized that if the battle continued for much longer, they might kill some of the Allies.

So he lunged forward and caught Nuuldan in the shoulder with his teeth, grappling with the Dark Dragon's wings with all of his legs. With neither of them focused on flying, their ascent ended and they plummeted towards Halarite.

Nuuldan struggled with him, sunk his teeth into Cardin's left wing joint, nearly breaking the bone and sending jolts of pain through Cardin. He noticed that they would land directly on top of a crowd of people, so in a panic, he threw out his one free wing and pumped as hard as he could, and managed to divert their crash into the bay. They hit the water and slammed through to the seabed. Nuuldan was beneath him and took the brunt of the impact, and a huge wave spread out away from them and crashed into the already ruined docks.

Nuuldan didn't waste time and didn't seem to be disoriented. He jerked his head, his teeth still sunk into the wing joint. Cardin screamed, and Sira once again was beside him, holding him and asking him what was wrong. He ignored her and focused on the battle.

He charged up another blast, and pointed his mouth right at Nuuldan's face. The Dark Dragon knew what was coming and released his grip before pushing Cardin off of him. Cardin crashed into the water as Nuuldan stood and lunged at Cardin to grapple with him. They rolled in the shallows, and then Nuuldan spun around, with Cardin in the grip of his front claws, and threw Cardin ashore, where he smashed into the waterlogged city.

Nuuldan leapt into the air and covered the distance between them in an instant. Before Cardin had recovered, the Dark Dragon landed on top of him. Cardin used that momentum and threw Nuuldan as hard has he could into the air. His opponent was thrown over the city wall and crashed just outside. Cardin recovered, leapt into the air, gritting his fangs against the pain in his fractured wing joint, and glided the distance to land next to Nuuldan.

When he landed, he did so at a run, and he bashed head-first into the Dark Dragon. They grappled with each other and rolled across the sands, until Nuuldan stopped them with Cardin pinned beneath. He looked down at Cardin with a murderous leer on his face, and then fired a quick, unfocused blast straight into Cardin's face. He felt searing pain explode across his entire head, and he screamed in agony.

The blast ended, but Nuuldan prepared another. Cardin managed to twist his body just enough to throw the dragon off, and then he staggered back onto his feet. Another blast caught Cardin in the left side, and sent him sprawling to the ground.

Nuuldan laughed, and slowly circled towards the north. *"Your avatar cannot defeat me, human. Your powers are still untrained, un-tempered."* Cardin tried to stand again, but the Dark Dragon released another blast and forced him down. He continued to circle around to bring himself closer to the city, and Cardin knew that he intended to kill everyone in it.

Every time he tried to stand, Nuuldan knocked him down again. *"I will destroy everyone and everything you love, human."* Another blast. *"You have annoyed me, so I will take not just your city, but your entire world."* Another. *"I shall destroy it as I have so many others!"*

Suddenly a golden blast of energy slammed into Nuuldan from the north, sending the monster sprawling in a cloud of sand. The blast was massive and powerful, but Cardin hadn't sensed it until it hit the Dark Dragon.

He finally managed to stand up and looked north to see something he could scarcely believe. Several large, tall crystalline creatures rose up from the sand. The lead one had its hand outstretched, and he realized that the blast of magic had come from it.

Hundred more emerged from the sand, almost all at once, and Cardin realized that they surrounded the Dark Dragon. Nuuldan stood up and fired a blast at one, shattering it into thousands of tiny pieces, but this only angered the rest. Every single one of them raised their hands up and released blasts of golden energy at Nuuldan.

Every single one found their target. The Dark Dragon roared in agony and tried to leap into the air, but was knocked down by the blasts. A hole at least three feet wide ripped through one of his wings, so he drew them in protectively. He surrounded himself with a shield, but the blasts did not cease, and they ate away at his magic shell.

Several more crystal beings rose up from behind Cardin to completely surround Nuuldan, so Cardin leapt into the air and spread his wings, trying to ignore the pain he felt in his left wing joint, and did his best to stay aloft above the constant stream of rapid firing energy.

Nuuldan managed to fire off several more blasts of red energy, and destroyed a half dozen of the crystalline creatures, but more rose up from the sand to take their place, and they continued their assault undaunted.

Just when Nuuldan's shields began to fail, and blasts began to sizzle against his scales, he roared in anger. Cardin felt a dark well of nothingness grow. Suddenly the Dark Dragon's shield expanded out in a destructive wave of energy, absorbing blasts as it went, until it crashed into the ring of crystal people. The blast did not destroy them, but they were all thrown back, away from Nuuldan. The blast hit Cardin's dragon as well, but by the time it reached him, it barely pushed against him.

With a lull in the attack, the Dark Dragon released more blasts of deadly energy, shattering one crystal giant after another. With the destruction of each of the strange, giant creatures, Cardin felt a surge of energy that escaped into the world. Whomever they were, they were powerful, and their deaths left a scar in the magic around them.

He had to do something, anything to save them! Several of the crystal beings recovered and counter attacked, but they had lost their momentum. It was up to Cardin, momentarily forgotten by the Dark Dragon.

That's when the thought occurred to him. There was no defeating the Dark Dragon, but perhaps he could weaken Nuuldan enough to scare him away. Since Nuuldan seemed to be a creature solely of Dark Magic, perhaps that was his answer. It had worked before, when Cardin's dragon had pierced Nuuldan's shield.

But it would take far more power than he had used before. Since he wasn't in the midst of combat, he could take time to charge up the most powerful blast his dragon could conjure. So he began channeling the surrounding magic in the universe into his avatar. The scars that the destroyed crystal beings had left behind hampered his efforts, but it did not deter him.

Coming as a great surprise to him, as he charged up the energy, the crystal beings looked up to him, and redirected their energies. They sent blasts of magic at him, but rather than harm them, they infused him with more power.

Nuuldan followed their energy with his eyes, saw what was happening, and looked in terror.

When Cardin felt ready to burst, he looked at Nuuldan, opened his mouth, and let loose a beam of gold-white energy. In the blink of an eye, it crashed into the Dark Dragon, a concentration of magic that no being in the universe was meant to be able to withstand.

But he survived. His beaten body lay at the bottom of a new crater in the sand, but he had survived. He groaned and started to pull himself up, but the effort it took just to do that was great. The absence of magic that surrounded him was filled with light, and Cardin somehow knew that meant he was nearly powerless.

It had taken its toll on Cardin. He could not remain aloft, and so he swooped down and landed almost uncontrollably. Slowly Nuuldan climbed out of the crater, and then stared around at the Crystal beings, and at Cardin.

Within the wall, Cardin saw himself surrounded by his friends. He opened his eyes, looked around, and saw Sira's worried face greet him.

"I'm ok," he managed to say. He clasped her hand in his, squeezed reassuringly, and stood up. Gingerly he touched his own face, and then his left shoulder. There was no actual physical damage to him. It was the black and white dragon that had taken the punishment, and his pain had become Cardin's.

"What happened," she asked.

He looked at Dalin, Reis, and then found that Elaria, Anila, his father, and several others surrounded him as well, concern on all of their faces.

"I'm not sure, exactly," he replied, shaking his head. He looked at the Sword, and then secured it in the magic sheath upon his back. "Come on."

He felt unsteady on his feet, so he welcomed Sira's assistance as they followed the crowd out of the city walls and into the desert.

Even behind the crowd of enemy and Alliance soldiers, the tall crystalline creatures were easy to see, towering over the battlefield. Cardin still felt his connection to the black and white dragon, still felt that he controlled it.

From its eyes, Cardin saw that Nuuldan still gawked at him, and a low growl emanated from his throat. *"You will have to do much more to destroy me."*

One of the crystalline beings stepped ahead of the others and faced Nuuldan alone. "We know this," it spoke with a surprisingly human sounding voice. "However, with the help of the Keeper of the Sword and all of his allies, we can defeat you."

"Not without casualties," Nuuldan said defiantly.

"You would still lose," Cardin spoke through the black and white dragon.

Nuuldan glared at him and looked ready to attack, so Cardin prepared, despite his avatar's fatigue, despite *his* fatigue. But the crystal entities intervened again, "No! No more fighting. This world is protected, Dark One. If you wish to live, you will leave while you still can. You cannot win alone."

The Dark Dragon looked at the crystalline being and seemed to consider that claim. *"Perhaps you are right. Not alone. I will return, and I will take the Sword of Dragons. On that day, I will destroy everything!"*

Without another word, Nuuldan crouched low and then leapt into the air. A black portal appeared directly above him and he shot through it like an arrow. Moments later, the portal closed, and he was gone.

It ended so suddenly that Cardin felt stunned. He wasn't sure what to do or how to react, but he was glad that it was over, glad that the Dark Dragon was gone. He turned to the crystalline being that had spoken, and then was surprised when it fell to one knee and bowed before him. The others followed suit.

"Who are you," Cardin asked, puzzled.

The leader looked at Cardin, its eyes glowing gold under the blue crystal. "We are the Navitas. You know us as the trees of the Crystalline Forest."

Shock washed over Cardin. *"The Crystalline Forest? From Devor?"*

The Navitas nodded. "That is your name for the land that we came from."

Cardin tilted his head to one side curiously. *"I feel a kind of magic from you that pulses with energy and complexity. You are actually composed of magic, aren't you?"*

He wasn't entirely sure how he knew that, but the Navitas

confirmed it. "Yes. These crystalline forms are merely our vessels. We grow and manipulate them. We were prepared to leave this world before the cataclysm began, but another human who was once like you convinced us to stay and fight."

Cardin felt curious as to who it was the Navitas spoke of. That was the second time a 'second one' was mentioned. Then he felt himself smile, which must have looked amusing on his dragon. *"Thank you for intervening. I'm not sure I could have defeated Nuuldan without your help."* Then he frowned. *"Why do you bow before me?"*

"You are the first and only being in the universe to wield the magic of stars and the magic of darkness. This was thought to be impossible, and yet there was a prophecy that spoke of such a being."

"Another prophecy," he muttered. *"Fantastic."*

"You are the only one worthy of our reverence," the lead Navitas said, and then stood up. The others followed suit. "Now that we have intervened, your future may be different from what the prophecy spoke of. Tread carefully, Keeper of the Sword."

It started to sink into the ground, as did all of the other Navitas. *"Wait, where are you going?"*

"To return to our home, to repair the damage that was done. Goodbye, Keeper. Good luck."

A moment later, they were gone, sunk into the ground as if they had never existed. Only the shattered remains of their dead gave physical proof of their intervention. An instant later, Cardin felt his connection to the dragon waver, and he was back next to Sira. They had made their way past the armies and now stood together in front of the city walls.

The dragon turned to face the army and casually stalked over to them, covering the distance quickly with long strides. It stopped and lowered its snout to be level with Cardin and the others, and stared into him. He noticed that its eye sockets were pitch black with white points of starlight within.

"And...what are you," he asked hesitantly. "How did I summon you?"

"I am you," it replied, his own voice speaking in his head. *"A projection of your soul and spirit, of your power."*

He frowned. "But if I controlled you, how can you have a mind of your own?"

He heard himself chuckle in his thoughts, *"The same way that the drakes Kailar summoned could act and think of their own accord, the same way her orcs could, or any humans she controlled. You control me, but when I am summoned, I am still my own person, a reflection of the inner you."*

That caused ice to form in the pit of his stomach. "So then there is darkness within me?"

The dragon nodded its massive head once. *"Yes. Do not be frightened by this. You have found a near-balance. Your future will depend upon you stabilizing that balance of two powers."* It rose up tall and seemed to smile. *"Your adventure has just begun, Cardin Kataar. You still have much to learn."*

Its features blurred, and Cardin realized that it was fading from the world. It had accomplished its mission, and now it would return to the nothingness it had come from.

As the last of its image faded, it spoke only for Cardin to hear, *"No, not nothingness. I am returning to you. I am you, as you are me."*

Once the avatar was gone, Cardin stared after it. His head swam, the events that had just transpired still unraveling in his head. He turned to look at Sira, who still held onto him tight, and then looked at Dalin and Reis. They both stared back at him in awe.

Then they heard a commotion from behind, the sound of weapons being dropped. They all turned to look. Sira released her grip on Cardin and he managed to stand on his own, but she stayed by his side.

Every single undead and necromancer, including the woman who had groveled before Nuuldan, dropped their weapons. She stepped towards him, but was stopped by Reis's sword tip.

"I mean you no harm," she said. "We were wrong." She looked down at the ground in shame, a slight tremble in her voice. "He was not the one. That monster destroyed our home, our world, our empire!" She clenched her jaw in anger, and a single tear wove its way down her wrinkled face. But then the anger subsided, and she again looked at Cardin with calm, cool eyes. "You are the dark one the prophecy spoke of, Cardin Kataar."

Then without warning, she fell to her knees before him, and lowered her face to the ground. "We surrender to you, Keeper of the Sword."

Chapter 39

SECOND CHANCES

The first thing Letan felt when he woke was the dull ache in his left leg. He realized that he must have passed out, but he had no idea when that happened, or how long he had tried to stay awake watching Kailar figure out her new powers.

He swore it had felt like a void had grown in and around Kailar, but it was a very vague sense, and she became frustrated often during her attempts to open a portal.

Now, when he opened his eyes, he realized that she must have succeeded. He recognized the Warriors' Guild barracks in Tieran, but it had been converted into a triage center for the wounded. Cots were laid out, and in some places the wounded sat on bare floor.

Through the windows and the open doors at either end of the barracks, he saw daylight. He pushed himself onto his elbows and looked around, and then smiled when he saw Kailar approaching from his left. She weaved around the wounded and some of the nurses, but stopped for a moment when she saw that he was awake. The two Warriors that flanked her also stopped, and she glanced nervously at them.

He noticed then that she was no longer armed with her dagger, nor did she wear her cloak. Then he noticed the shackles around her wrists. She smiled weakly, but his smile faded into a frown. "What's going on," he asked. She covered the rest of the distance and stopped beside him. He looked pointedly at the shackles, and then at the two Warriors, both of them Mages.

"It's ok," she took hold of his hand. "I surrendered to them after I brought you here."

Letan recalled the bounty on her head, five hundred gold pieces for her capture and return to Falind. They would likely ship her back to Edilas for trial and execution.

"No," he shook his head. "Why would you do that? You know what they'll do!"

She squeezed his hand and smiled reassuringly. "It's ok. I realized something this morning after I brought you here. I failed Halarite seven months ago, and now it is time for me to atone."

"Not with your life," he shook his head. "You can atone in other ways!"

"Letan, I have to do this," she started.

He ignored her and looked at one of the Warriors, "You. As a Lieutenant in the Corlas Warriors' Guild, I order you to fetch your Commander and the Mayor of the city immediately."

"My orders are to guard the prisoner," he looked down at Letan with contempt.

"Letan," Kailar tried to stop him.

"Then send someone to get them, now!"

The Warrior sighed, but was willing to recognize Letan's rank and grabbed one of the nurses to whisper something in her ear. She looked at Letan for a moment, looked at his leg, and then hurried off. Letan also looked at his leg, and saw that it was heavily bandaged, but there was no blood seeping through. He was just glad that they hadn't cut it off.

"Letan, I don't want to run or hide anymore," she shook her head.

"Why not," he looked at her in desperation. "I don't want to lose you!"

"You would lose me anyway if I kept running," she looked down and took in a deep breath, as if to give herself strength for what she was about to say. "You're a Warrior, Letan." She looked up at him intently. "And I'm a wanted criminal. What kind of life could we have together? I won't let you compromise your position in the Guild over me."

"To hell with the Guild," he raised his voice, more than he meant to. The two Warriors looked at him in surprise. "You've seen how it is out here, people bend the rules all the time."

"It isn't about that." Frustration gave her voice an edge. "It's about losing you, who you are, the good man that you are. I've done horrible things, but the only reason that bothers me now is because of you. I look at you, and I remember everything I've ever done, and it tears me apart, because I used to be a good person, too. My intentions never changed, I just..." She clenched her jaw and squeezed his hand. "I lost my way. And I don't want to lead you down that same path."

She started to pull her hand away, but he held on tight and wouldn't let her go. "No," he shook his head. "If you want to make up for the things you've done, do so another way."

"Letan, please," she tried to pull away again.

"Just wait here until the Commander and Mayor arrive," he looked at her pleadingly, desperately. "Let me talk to them."

She closed her eyes and clenched her teeth, but then stopped pulling away. "Fine." She looked at him, clearly annoyed. "Fine, I'll wait."

The cold feeling he sensed from her hand told him he needed to let go, so he did. She turned and walked to the foot of his bed, where she stood and waited impatiently. The Warriors kept a close eye on her.

After a couple of minutes, the local Commander, Kent Querlin, arrived with the city's mayor, Warreck Evern. For them to have arrived at the same time, he assumed that the Mayor was at the Guild Barracks already, probably to discuss disaster relief with the Commander.

They both obviously knew who Kailar was, as they looked at her with disdain before they came to Letan's side.

"I am not accustomed to being summoned by a Lieutenant," Kent glared at Letan. "However I am well aware of who you are and your trusted status in Corlas. So speak quickly, Warrior."

"Commander," he sat upright, despite how much it hurt, and nodded. "Mayor Evern. I called you here to ask what was to be done with Kailar."

"She is to be shipped to Falind," the Mayor replied, his voice and language proper and precise, a true politician. "She will be delivered to the King, and the bounty will be used for our relief efforts."

"*Our* relief efforts," Letan emphasized. "You know that they will never send supplies or relief from Edilas. The kingdoms don't care about us, they never have. This disaster is probably world-wide," he waved his hands around for emphasis, and looked at all of the wounded. "Do you really think they'll spare five hundred gold pieces to give to us if they have suffered as we have? They'll need that gold for their own relief efforts!"

The Commander and Mayor both looked at each other knowingly, and likely realized he was right. "Then what do you propose," the Commander asked. "Let her go? She is a criminal!"

"No," he shook his head, "don't let her go." She looked over her shoulder in surprise. "She wishes to atone for her failures and crimes, so I suggest we let her. She has regained her powers," he lied, but only partly. He knew the powers she had now were not the same. The Mayor and Commander exchanged surprised looks. "Let us conscript her into our own Warriors' Guild."

"To what end," the Commander asked.

"Things are only going to get worse," he looked at them intently. "This disaster will allow the criminals to get an even greater upper hand in the days to come." He looked directly at the Commander. "I know that you, like me, despise the deals we've had to make with the criminals here. And I happen to know that Kailar has already enraged some of them." She smirked.

"Careful," the Mayor raised a finger. "You sound like you want to declare war."

"It's either that or let them rule over us in fear," he threw his hands up. "Like I said, Edilas will never send us the help we need to get them under control, they never have before and they certainly won't now. Kailar is more powerful than any Mage, she could give us the edge we need to turn this continent into a lawful place."

The Mayor scoffed. "You're suggesting using a criminal to fight other criminals!"

Letan clenched his jaw, knowing all about the rumors that the Mayor of Tieran was corrupt and supported at least one of the criminal rings on Devor. That was why he focused his attention on the Commander. He was a good man, and he was the one he needed to convince.

"Sir," Letan looked directly into his eyes, "she has made mistakes, done horrible things, that's all true. But now she wants to make up for them."

"How do you propose we keep her on our side," the Commander asked. "How do we keep her from escaping?"

Letan looked at Kailar, and she stared right back at him. She understood now what he was doing, and she looked ready to accept his proposed atonement. "If she wanted to escape, she could do so now, and there wouldn't be a thing you or anyone else could do to stop her." He looked again at the Commander. "She is that powerful, sir. I've seen that much. It was her decision to surrender, and her decision to keep the shackles on. She wants to make up for her crimes."

The Commander looked at Kailar, and she met his gaze with determined eyes. "What do you have to say for yourself?"

Before she could say anything, the Mayor scoffed and backed away. "You're not seriously considering his proposal?!"

The look that the Commander gave the Mayor said a thousand words. "Do you have something to fear? Please don't tell me that the rumors of your corruption are actually true, Mayor Evern. I don't want to have to arrest you in the wake of this disaster."

He glared at Kent, and then looked down silently. "No." Letan swore he caught a spark of rebellion in his eye. They were going to pay for today somewhere in the future.

"Good," the Commander nodded. "Well, Kailar? What say you to Letan's proposed course of action?"

She glanced at Letan, and then back at Kent. "With all due respect, Commander, there is nothing that I could ever do that would make up for the sins of my past." She stood up straight and looked at him evenly. "However, everything I did was with the intention of making this world a better place, and I failed. What Letan has suggested would give me a chance to work towards that goal again. Maybe that's a good start."

"How am I assured of your loyalty to Devor," the Commander asked. "If you are to represent our Warriors, you would need to act in our best interest. As Letan has pointed out, we have no support from Edilas."

She smiled and said, "As I'm sure you know from my past, I hold no loyalty to my home kingdom. It is here, on Devor, that I have regained both my power and my sense of purpose in life. More than that," she smiled at Letan, "I have a particular fondness for one of Devor's citizens." She nodded to Kent, "If you will have me, Commander, I would swear an oath to serve the Warriors of Devor."

The Commander looked at Mayor Evern, who still stared at the ground. When he did not object, Kent nodded. "Very well. We'll handle the formalities later. Barlic, Ogrin, I am releasing her from incarceration, please remove her shackles."

Neither of them looked happy to do so, but they nodded, and the one Letan had spoken to before produced keys and removed Kailar's shackles. She rubbed her wrists and winced.

The Commander looked at Letan, and then nodded. "I have heard that Corlas was completely destroyed in this catastrophe." Letan nodded. "Consider your service officially transferred under my command. This was your idea," he motioned towards Kailar, "so once you're on your feet, she'll be your responsibility. Her failures will be yours, and you will accompany her anywhere she goes. Is that understood?"

Letan couldn't help but smile, and felt his heart nearly burst in happiness. "Understood, sir. It would be my honor."

Chapter 40

SHARED SECRETS

The sun crept over the mountains to shine down upon the capitol city of Tal. Reis, Sira, Cardin, and Dalin climbed up the shallow hill through the inner gates into the castle district. Thankfully the castle was undamaged, and several hours after the Battle for Maradin, someone inside of the city finally opened the gate.

Although the inner city, where the wealthiest and most influential resided, was intact, the outer city was gravely damaged by fire, and it had taken the city soldiers two days to put a stop to the roving gangs of looters.

Never-the-less, Reis smiled at the familiar sight of the castle. It continued to stand as a beacon of hope even amongst such devastation.

However, his smile did not last. The casualties over the past two days were staggering, and many were still missing. Among them was General Geildein Artula. If he could not be found, if he was presumed dead, the leadership of the Tal Warriors would be vacant, and the Commanders would vote on a replacement.

Reis had felt troubled ever since the Battle for Maradin, now four days past. He and the others had helped with relief efforts all over Edilas, and while the tasks of rebuilding or running supplies helped keep him busy, his mind kept going back to Anila and her powers.

Shortly after the conclusion of the battle, he saw her once, but it was amongst countless Warriors and Wizards, so there had been no time to talk. He wasn't sure he wanted to talk to her. Therefore when he saw her near the main entrance to the castle, he cringed.

"Anila," Cardin nodded as they approached. "I figured they would ask you to be here today."

They had come back to the First City for the necromancers' hearing, to determine their fate. Reis and Sira wore their ceremonial armor, complete with black tabards with their kingdom's symbol, a mountain guarded by two crossed claymores with their hilts in the air, inlaid in silver. Cardin was not a part of the Guild, so he simply wore a nice blue tunic and black trousers, as well as his black cloak to help stave off the cold winter air. Dalin still wore his normal robes, and Reis wondered if he ever changed his wardrobe.

Anila, as unfashionable as ever, wore her leather armor, her unusual sword strapped to her left hip. She gave a half-bow to the approaching group. "Indeed. The Allied Council wishes to take depositions from everyone who survived on Trinil."

Cardin nodded, then motioned for her to follow, but she did not move. "If it is alright with all of you, I wish to speak with Reis, alone."

Everyone stopped and looked curiously at her or Reis. He felt himself blush, but also felt uneasiness at her request. "Well, we still have some time before the hearing begins," Cardin replied, "so I don't see why not."

As the others made their way in, Sira looked back at Reis and said, "Don't be late."

Reis smirked, but it faded fast when looked at Anila. She met his gaze and stared into his eyes, and that made him feel uncomfortable. Was she somehow using her powers to look into his soul? He looked away and asked, "What do you want?"

Another group of people walked out of the castle and past them, and she watched them uneasily. "Walk with me, please."

She did not wait for him, turning and walking away. He looked after her with hesitation, but then his curiosity got the better of him. He quickly caught up to her and fell into step beside her.

For a short time, they simply continued to walk, until there was no one around. She finally glanced at him, and then said, "I am sorry that I lied to you. I am, however, thankful that you have not told anyone the truth."

When he thought about it, he wasn't entirely sure why he didn't tell anyone. There was no mistaking that she was more powerful than any Mage, which meant she was definitely not a normal human. For all he knew, she was a threat, so the prudent thing would have been to tell someone what he saw her do. But when he thought about doing so, he felt his stomach twist. Even though he felt betrayed, he wasn't ready to do the same to her.

Reis didn't know what to say or do, except to keep walking. Before he knew what he was doing, he asked, "What are you?"

She didn't react to his question, and that didn't surprise him. She was always very stoic, and seemed unfazed by everything that happened around her. All she ever seemed to be was determined and focused, and only on two occasions had he seen her smile.

"I am complicated," she replied at length. She stopped, looked around to make sure they were alone, and then looked at him. "I am the child of a Wizard."

He felt shocked, but only partly so. That explained her powers, but not her physical combat prowess. "So why aren't you with the Wizards' Guild?"

She shook her head and replied, "You do not understand. My parents weren't both Wizards, only one was. An exile named Zenil."

Reis felt his jaw drop, more surprised than ever. "Are you saying that an exiled Wizard and a…"

"Yes," she nodded. Did she just blush a little? "He fell in love with a Mage here on Halarite. They had a single child, me, but my mother died giving birth to me. That left my father, an exiled Wizard who hid who he was from everyone, alone to care for me."

He felt impatient and asked, "So why lie? Why have you not told anyone about who you are and where you come from?" As he spoke, he grew angrier. His voice trembled when he asked, "Why did you lie to me?"

"Because society would never accept a half-breed like me," she looked down. "That was made obvious when I was very young."

"That still doesn't explain why you lied to me."

Suddenly her own emotions burst out and she nearly shouted at him, "Because of how you looked at me, what you thought about me!" She stared at him with a mixture of anger and frustration, but also surprisingly with fear. "You were the first person since my father died that I let in, but I realized very early on that part of why you liked me was because you thought I had no power." She placed her hands on her hips and gave him a hard stare. "If you had found out who I really was, even in the beginning, would you have grown so close to me?"

"Yes!" He realized it was a lie as soon as he said it.

The disappointment in her eyes told him she knew it too. "Now who's being dishonest?"

He looked away and clenched his jaw. She was silent for a while, but finally continued, "Reis, I have to hide who I am from everyone. My father taught me how to hide my powers so that no Wizard or Mage could tell what I was. The Sword of Dragons allowed Cardin to figure out I had power and he confronted me about it, but he's the first person to ever..."

He interrupted her, "Cardin knows?!"

"Yes," she replied, sudden regret on her face.

His stomach sank and he felt a void grow within him. "How long?"

"He confronted me in Maradin during the banquet."

He had known, for over a month he had known. During their entire voyage from Edilas to Trinil, he had watched as Reis grew closer to Anila, watched as he trusted her even though he knew she couldn't be trusted.

His best friend had betrayed him. All to hide magic.

"Reis, I am truly sorry," she looked at him pleadingly. "Please don't hate me. Please don't reaffirm why I have to hide who I am."

Her words barely registered in his mind, he felt too much anger. Not just at her, either, but at his friend, at magic, at everything. After several moments of considering his next words, he glared at her and said, "Have you ever considered that hiding who you are is why people hate you?"

She took a step back, but then spoke in a shaky voice. "If you had any idea what I went through as a child, the way people who knew about me treated me, you would know why." She frowned at him, "But you don't even care to find out, do you?"

"Not really," he shook his head. "It doesn't change the fact that you lied to me."

She shook her head. "I'm not the first person to have ever lied to you, I know that, you've told me as much."

"Your point?"

"Consider that you're angrier with me because of how you feel about me." He frowned, but did not reply, so she continued, "Because you didn't just consider me a friend. You started to fall in love with me."

He scoffed at her suggestion, but then stopped and considered it for a moment. "Yeah, you know what, maybe I did. Or rather, I started to fall in love with the woman I thought you were."

She looked down and nodded. "And now you feel like you have no idea who I really am."

"I don't," he replied evenly. "If you lied about something that big, how do I know you haven't lied to me about everything else?"

For moment, she remained silent. Then she looked at him with solemn eyes. "You don't."

He nodded and felt like what he was about to say was justified. "Then this shouldn't surprise you. Do not ever speak to me again."

With that, he turned and walked towards the castle. He barely overheard her reply, "I won't."

EPILOGUE

Cardin shifted uncomfortably in his seat at the Tal table in the Council chamber. The hearing went on longer than he expected. Several hours had passed and he realized that it was well past lunch time. However, the final depositions were over, and the four surviving leaders of the necromancers stood in the center.

King Beredis stood up and waited patiently as everyone at the other tables finished their conversations. The Saran table was empty. Commander Asil may have been willing to organize the Saran army to battle the necromancers, but he did not feel comfortable representing his kingdom.

In fact, no one knew what to do with Saran. King Lorath and his entire family were gone, so there was no heir. With the General and the capitol city's governor also dead, there was no clear method for establishing a successor.

For all intents and purposes, there no longer was a Saran Kingdom. That left a power vacuum, and Cardin worried how the Alliance would deal with that in the coming months. Hard times were still ahead.

When the other tables finally quieted down, all eyes fell to King Beredis. "You have all heard the details of what has transpired at the hands of the necromancers, and they have admitted to their guilt. The time has now come to propose punishment for their crimes."

The other tables nodded their agreement.

"In light of all that has transpired," Beredis continued, "I would like to suggest that we do not sentence them to death."

It was Queen Leian who reacted vocally to this request. "You must be joking, Eirdin!"

The use of the King's first name was a familiarity that seemed to have become common place in the Council ever since the meteor shower. "I am not," Beredis replied. "There has already been so much death and destruction."

"Precisely," the Queen replied. "Tens of thousands lay dead today, and this time, Sal'fe was unable to bring them back with his staff. They must have justice!"

"Please," Beredis raised a hand to calm her and keep her from continuing, "You know as well as everyone else that most of the deaths that have occurred were not at the hands of the necromancers. They did not call down the meteor shower, nor did they bring the Dark Dragon back."

"Never-the-less," the Covenant leader, Alaia, spoke up, "they are still responsible for several thousand deaths, including every colonist of Port Hope, the crews of several ships, and every Warrior killed in the Battle for Maradin." Much to everyone's dismay, the Staff of Aliz could not bring the undead back to full life. To attempt to do so would leave a soulless shell of a human. That meant every person the necromancers had turned could not be resurrected.

"Yes," Beredis nodded, "they are guilty. But as the Keeper of the Sword reminded us all earlier today, they are the last survivors of an entire world. To sentence them all to death would be akin to committing genocide."

That fact silenced Alaia, but the Queen was not quite so satiated. "Then what do you propose for punishment?"

Cardin felt his cheeks grow warm as his King looked to him. He had known this was coming. "The Keeper has suggested what I consider to be a very wise course of action. I would like to let him propose it to you all."

Cardin stood up and walked around to stand in front of the table. The King's choice to have Cardin make the proposal was understandable. In the past, Cardin was able to sway the Council through words alone, so Beredis hoped he could do so now.

The necromancers looked at him expectantly and with hope. He felt uncomfortable by how they looked at him, they way they spoke to him. They saw him as their prophesied savior, but that was more than he was prepared to deal with.

That didn't change the fact that they had specifically surrendered to him after Nuuldan left Halarite. For that reason alone, he felt responsible for their fate. However, there was one fortunate fact about their reverence – they would do whatever he asked of them.

"First, as we have already discussed, they should be made to return all of their undead back to death." The tables all nodded their agreement. The necromancers were not surprised, but he could tell that they weren't happy. He also knew they would not like his next suggestion. "Second, necromancy should be banned on Halarite from this day forward." Again, all of the tables nodded in agreement. The necromancers, on the other hand, looked horrified and betrayed.

"As for the hundreds of necromancers left," he hesitated and looked at each of the four necromancer leaders. "The first part of their punishment should be to help us rebuild. I recognize that at least half of the necromancers are physically very old, but even the oldest of you, Tiresis, showed great physical prowess when we fought. Am I correct in assuming that all of your people would be able to perform manual labor?"

The four necromancers looked to one another, and then nodded in unison. "We are," one of them spoke.

"Good. Finally, once all is said and done, I recommend we return the necromancers to Trinil."

"Returned to their home," Leian asked, aghast. "That is not punishment!"

He looked directly at her, and said, "Their city was destroyed by a meteorite. They have no home to return to. They will instead build a penal colony for themselves, to be administered by representatives of the Alliance."

That seemed to allay the Queen's objections, and she sat back in her chair with a thoughtful look on her face. "I see."

"And then what," one of the necromancers asked. "We have placed ourselves under your care, Keeper. The prophecy said you would lead us to our former glory."

He really started to hate prophecy. However, today it would work to his advantage. "Then trust in that prophecy," he said. "I do not know what role I am to play in your future, but if you truly believe me to be the one that your prophecy spoke of, trust that this is the right course of action. The alternative is to let them sentence you to death." That fact silenced the necromancers' objections.

King Beredis stood and looked around the room. "All those in favor of the Keeper's proposal?"

Much to Cardin's surprise, every single group agreed that it was a valid course of action. Even Queen Leian was satisfied with the punishment.

"Very well," the King spoke. "Guards, please escort the prisoners back to the dungeon."

City soldiers, led by Cardin's father, stepped forward. Without argument or fight, the necromancers left.

Cardin moved to sit back down, however Beredis raised a hand to stop him. "I know we are all very hungry at this point, but before we recess, I would like to attend to one last item of business." When no one objected, at least not vocally, Beredis nodded. "Cardin Kataar, Sira Reinar, Reis Kalind, Anila Kovin, Dalin, Elaria, Ventelis, and Baenil. Please step forward."

Unsure what to expect, Cardin stepped into the center circle. The others joined him, each appearing as uncertain as he was. Reis seemed particularly distant and he noticed that his friend would not look him in the eye.

It felt crowded with so many people in the center circle, but Cardin realized that he considered each one of those that stood with him his friend.

"The eight of you have gone above and beyond what would ever have been required of you," Beredis said. "Elaria and Ventelis in particular, and especially Baenil, who was mistreated by the Covenant. You risked your life to travel to Archanon to find me and warn me about the invasion, despite holding no obligation to do so. Each of you deserve recognition for your acts of courage and valor in recent days."

While the King spoke, a sudden sensation sparked in the back of Cardin's head. At first he ignored it, but it grew stronger.

Beredis looked around at each occupied table and continued. "This Alliance is still very new, and we have no medals or honors that we may bestow upon you. Yet even if we did, I feel like they would fall short of what you truly deserve. Know that you have earned the respect and admiration of everyone here, and we will try to honor you as best as we can."

The feeling had grown such that Cardin could no longer ignore it, and as he finally gave it his attention, he realized it felt familiar. The King drew in a breath to continue his speech, but was interrupted when a soldier burst into the chambers. "Your Majesty," the soldier shouted, out of breath and hysterical.

All eyes fell upon the interloper, and when he realized this, he gulped and stood up straight. "I apologize," he suddenly found his etiquette, and bowed.

Beredis narrowed his eyes and said, "What is the meaning of this intrusion?"

"A dragon," he replied. "A green dragon has appeared in the city. He is just outside of the inner gates, and asked to speak to the Keeper of the Sword!"

Everyone turned to Cardin, but he simply felt excited. He looked to the King, who nodded. Without another word, Cardin ran out of the chambers, everyone following behind him.

He flew through the corridors of the castle, faster than any other human could. When he reached the foyer at the castle entrance, the attending guards had already opened the doors and were gawking outside. Cardin caught a glimpse of the massive, verdant creature standing beyond the inner city. He was as big as Cardin remembered, and the sense of warmth and power emanating from him was familiar and comforting. It was the same green dragon that had spoken to him seven months ago.

A crowd had already gathered around the dragon, and it seemed to be amused by this. Cardin covered the distance between the castle and the inner gate quickly, and the dragon took note of his approach. It spoke, as all dragons did, through thought, *"Greetings, Keeper."*

Cardin had never forgotten the name of the dragon, the memory of their first encounter etched into his mind. "Endri!" He smiled as he pushed his way through the crowd.

"I apologize, the Wizards attempted to call for me some time ago, but I could not come back until now."

As Cardin passed through the inner gates and walked down the shallow hill into the main city, Endri lowered his head to be closer to Cardin. "I'm glad you came." His smile and sense of jubilation faded. "I'm afraid I have some disturbing news."

"I know," Endri replied. The green star points of his eyes glowed

brilliantly, helping soothe Cardin's troubled soul. *"Master Syrn told me about Nuuldan's return. I have also learned about your ability to wield both the power of the stars and of darkness. This is unexpected."*

He looked at the dragon in surprise. Before that moment, he assumed that the Star Dragons knew everything there was to know about the Sword.

"That is why I am here," Endri looked at him reassuringly. *"Nuuldan was once one of the oldest Star Dragons, more powerful than any surviving dragon today. We cannot hope to defeat him ourselves. I have only found a few more of my kind, while the rest are still scattered throughout the universe. Our numbers are too small. You, Keeper, are the only one who may stand against Nuuldan."*

Quite unexpectedly, Cardin felt someone take his hand. He looked to find Sira next to him. She looked at him and smiled reassuringly, but he could tell that what Endri had just said frightened her.

When he looked back to the emerald dragon, it nodded once. *"I have come to help train you, to help you learn from the Sword of Dragons, and to hopefully discover how you are able to wield both powers when no other creature in the universe has ever been able to do so."*

He took one giant step forward, which brought his snout mere feet from Cardin's face. *"You, Cardin Kataar, may be our only hope."*

ABOUT THE AUTHOR

Jon Wasik has been telling stories since he was a little boy, usually with a cookie and milk at his Great Grandma's kitchen table. It wasn't until 5th grade that he finally put pen to paper, and from that moment on, writing has been his greatest passion.

When he isn't writing, Jon likes to read, play video games, and watch insanely geeky movies with his wife. His Gollum voice impressions are eerie, he quotes Doctor Who like others quote the bible, and he can leap terabytes of data in a single bound!

You can find out more about him by visiting his blog,
http://kataar.wordpress.com/

Want to keep up on the latest news about Jon's books? Subscribe to his mailing list! Just go to the Sword of Dragons website and click "Join Mailing List" at the top!
http://www.theswordofdragons.com/

Made in the USA
Monee, IL
05 December 2020